WH

mystery +

near fine in near fine dj;

"force of reality and appeal of romance"

Beulah Amr Buchanan

From A. M. v. d Linden

Washington

DC

July 4 1936

The Doctor

Books by MARY ROBERTS RINEHART

A POOR WISE MAN
AFFINITIES AND OTHER STORIES
BAB: A SUB-DEB
DANGEROUS DAYS
K
KINGS, QUEENS AND PAWNS
LONG LIVE THE KING
LOST ECSTASY
LOVE STORIES
MARY ROBERTS RINEHART'S CRIME BOOK
MARY ROBERTS RINEHART'S MYSTERY BOOK
MARY ROBERTS RINEHART'S ROMANCE BOOK
MISS PINKERTON
MR. COHEN TAKES A WALK
MORE TISH
MY STORY
NOMAD'S LAND
SIGHT UNSEEN AND THE CONFESSION
TEMPERAMENTAL PEOPLE
TENTING TONIGHT
THE AFTER HOUSE
THE ALBUM
THE ALTAR OF FREEDOM
THE AMAZING ADVENTURES OF LETITIA CARBERRY
THE AMAZING INTERLUDE
THE BOOK OF TISH
THE BREAKING POINT
THE CASE OF JENNIE BRICE
THE CIRCULAR STAIRCASE
THE DOCTOR
THE DOOR
THE MAN IN LOWER TEN
THE OUT TRAIL
THE RED LAMP
THE ROMANTICS
THE STATE VERSUS ELINOR NORTON
THE STREET OF SEVEN STARS
THE TRUCE OF GOD
THE WINDOW AT THE WHITE CAT
THIS STRANGE ADVENTURE
THROUGH GLACIER PARK
TISH
TISH PLAYS THE GAME
TWENTY-THREE AND A HALF HOURS' LEAVE
TWO FLIGHTS UP
WHEN A MAN MARRIES
WHERE THERE'S A WILL

In Collaboration

THE BAT
ISN'T THAT JUST LIKE A MAN?
OH! WELL! YOU KNOW HOW WOMEN ARE

The Doctor

By

Mary Roberts Rinehart

Farrar & Rinehart, Inc.

New York Toronto

PRINTED IN THE UNITED STATES OF AMERICA
BY THE FERRIS PRINTING COMPANY, BOUND
BY THE HARRIS WOLFF ESTATE, NEW YORK

Part I

THE YOUNG DOCTOR

CHAPTER I

YOUNG Doctor Arden was going through the process of reorienting himself after a night's sleep. He had been doing that now for two weeks. He would open his eyes, gaze for a second or two at his strange surroundings and then close them again. For that brief instant the room had the unreality of a dream carried over into waking, and as he drowsed it disappeared from his consciousness. The wide brass bed with the sagging springs became the narrow one of his hospital bedroom; the gaudy wall-paper with its trailing morning glories, not too clean and bearing the outlines of long-departed pictures, was the dun-colored hospital wall; and the telephone beside the bed would ring at any moment, and he would have to hurry into his clothes or his dressing gown, and go, half awake, to the slow old elevator, with the ancient colored Joe inside.

"Let me off at the corner of the park, Joe. Got to meet a lady."

"Yessir," Joe would say, grinning.

It was an old joke between them, but for Joe it had never lost its humor.

The elevator would rise with deliberation. It was an open cage, and there would be vistas of long bare halls, poorly lighted, and of tired night nurses waiting hopefully for the dawn, or of convalescents from the wards, in hospital trousers or loose wrappers, shuffling along in carpet slippers for this purpose or that.

Then somewhere the elevator would stop and he would step out, a tall disreputable figure, to find an anxious nurse waiting for him.

"It's Baird in D ward, doctor. Her temperature's been dropping since three o'clock."

For a little time then he would be king. More, he would be a god of sorts; nurses hurrying to obey his orders, the ward around and watching him with interest, and perhaps some feeble life hanging on his quickness, his skill.

"Tray here?"

"Yes, doctor."

"All right, Baird. This will make you feel better."

He would stand or sit by the bed, holding to a wrist, watching the rise and fall of a chest. His world always sharply contracted at such times. It consisted only of the patient on the bed and himself, with a nurse hovering by. But sometimes, especially if the call came early in his sleep, he acted by a sort of automatism. He would go through the proper motions, but in the morning he would hardly remember. There might be an empty bed in a ward, the patient gone and the mattress rolled up on the wire springs, ready for sterilizing. It would come to him then with a shock that he had seen a human soul pass on the night before, and had gone back to bed and forgotten it.

"Well, you did all you could, doctor."

"I wonder!" he would say, and feel the eyes of the ward on him. All day he would have a sense of guilt. Then it would pass. By evening in the interns' room he would be drinking a surreptitious glass of beer and saying: "Nothing to do with that fellow in A. Came in too late. Who wants some poker?"

But it was not quite so easy as that. He had a bad habit of going back over his cases. The poker game would start, some of the interns, Scott, the X-ray man, then perhaps Dickinson from the laboratory.

"I'm playing these."

"Holy cats! And I raised it to come in!"

The game would go on. It was never static. Sometimes six were playing, sometimes only two were left to mark time. The ambulance would roll out, one of the players on the seat beside the driver, to return in due time with some bit of human misery; or there would be the furious clanging of a police patrol, and one or two of the men would quietly put down their cards and disappear. There was constant movement, talk, more or less remote sound. Under the light over the poker table the faces of all the men showed strain and loss of sleep; he could look around and see that. But there would be times when his mind wandered, back to some empty bed in the silent hospital overhead.

"Wake up, Chris! What are you so glum about?" His name, which was Noel, had been altered by some wag to Christmas, and from that to Chris.

"Sorry. I'll check the bet."

It would pass, he knew. In a few hours or a day he would have forgotten. His big heavy-shouldered figure would once more move with assurance into the wards, and once more at times he would be king or even God to his small domain. He would whistle in the corridors and make his little jokes in the wards.

"Hold still now. This is going to hurt you more than it hurts me!" Or: "Kick with that leg? Sure you will. You've been kicking ever since you came in here!"

The dressing table would move from bed to bed on its rubber wheels, and in his white coat he would move with it. It was a bad hour, the dressing hour. Now and then a man yelped, and the ward would comment cheerfully. "Louder and clearer, Bill!" But when the table drew up beside their own beds they were silent, apprehensive. "Go a little easy, doc. It hurts like the devil."

Sometimes, straightening from some bed or other, he would glance over the ward, now sharply divided into two parts, the dressings done and those remaining. The first was quiet, relaxed, the second boisterous and anxious, awaiting its hour. Probably life was like that. Nothing was so bad as one expected it to be, and once it was over—

"Hold still, Smith. Do you want me to cut you?"

There would be a triumphant swing to his shoulders under the white coat when at last the dressings were done and the wards quiet. He would change his soiled coat for a fresh one, light a cigarette, stop to chat with a pretty nurse.

"Well, I suppose you were out dancing last night?"

"Dancing! I've got other uses for my feet."

"Well, they're very nice feet," he would say and wander on cheerfully.

But there were many times when he felt that he had failed. He would sleep through the ringing of the telephone, be wakened by a night watchman shaking him, to put on his shabby dressing gown and slippers over his pajamas and, with his heavy shock of dark hair standing out like a mop, would find himself once more by a bed.

"How long since it started?"

"About an hour, doctor."

He would stand by the bed, his hand on a flagging pulse, his eyes on a gray-white face, his mind darting from this expedient to that. Sometimes when the screens were up around the bed he would be alone with the patient; just the two of them, and it would seem strange to him that one of them was going on into death and the other back to a warm room and to sleep. It seemed unfair. He felt ashamed then of his vitality, and of the fact that when it was over he meant to see if there was anything left from the night nurse's supper.

"He's gone, poor devil."

"I'll get the orderly, doctor."

"What's the hurry? Give him an hour or two of peace, can't you?"

But he knew that the business of the hospital must go on. There was no time for sentiment. The bed would be needed, and in five minutes, or ten, it would be empty once more. He would leave the ward and wander into the nurses' dining room.

"What have you got tonight, Sarah? Not canned salmon!"

"No, doctor. I've a nice piece of beefsteak for you." And he would eat heartily, drink a cup of coffee and go back to bed and to sleep. None of them ever had enough sleep. Not until the next morning, shaving and bathing, would he begin once more to have the sense of failure which death was to bring him all his life.

He grunted and turned over. He was slowly waking now, beginning to remember. That last night in the hospital, for instance. He had made his final rounds at midnight, saying a sort of mute farewell to all familiar things. Shabby and old as it was he had loved every corner of it. Here and there in the wards a patient had been awake, and he had stood by the bed in the semidarkness.

"Sorry you're going, doctor. We'll miss you."

"Sorry to go, old man."

It was in the children's ward that he had remained the longest. A small girl there was crying, and he had gone in and picked her up.

"What's the matter, sweetheart? Can't you sleep?"

"I want my mother."

He wrapped a blanket around her, and she had stopped crying. Always in that ward he felt helpless and filled with pity. These little waifs and strays—the hospital gave them care, but it could not give them love. He held her closer in his arms.

"If I sit down with you, will you go to sleep?"

"I'll try."

So he had sat down with her on one of the hard ward chairs, and after a time she had fallen asleep. He did not put her down at once, however. He sat there for some time, listening to the night sounds of the hospital, the slow movement of the elevator, the brisk steps of the nurses. Now that he was leaving it he felt that it was a part of him, familiar and infinitely dear.

The child stirred and he tightened his hold on her. Somewhere ahead of him lay the future, unknown and mysterious; but somewhere and some day, God willing, there would be in it some quiet room, and he would be in it, like this, holding a child of his own.

That had been his real farewell to the hospital, although he made a formal one the next day, going about cheerfully, shaking hands, laughing, promising to come back often. Then at last he heard the big front doors close behind him and knew that he was through with that phase of his life and that he was at last alone in a not too friendly world. . . .

He was fully awake now. He opened his eyes, yawned and stretched, and as he did so a brass ball from the top of the bed fell down and struck him sharply on the head. His reaction was instant and indignant. He caught it up and flung it across the room, and the resultant clamor broke the Sunday morning calm like an explosion. When it had subsided he heard slow footsteps climbing the stairs, and a drawling voice outside which he recognized as belonging to Henry Walters, with whom and whose family he shared the house.

"Anything wrong, doc?"

"That ball fell off the bed again and hit me. And don't call me doc!"

"I fixed it yesterday, doctor."

"Well, it didn't stay fixed. Can I get through to the bathroom?"

Henry outside cleared his throat.

"I'll tell you, doctor. Dick got home kinda late last night, and his mother thought he'd better sleep this morning. He ain't so well. If you wouldn't mind using the back stairs—"

"It won't kill him if I go through, will it?"

Access to the bathroom was through the room occupied by Dick, and a part of the arrangement had been that Dick should be up and out early for that reason. But the last thing in Dick Walters' mind at any time was to be up and out early, and now Chris heard Henry's apologetic cough again.

"I'm sorry, doctor. He's locked the doors."

Chris sat up on the side of the bed. Already he knew that he had made a mistake in adopting the Walters family. He felt, however, a vague sympathy for the mild inefficient man outside, and a sort of pity for the drab and listless woman who was his wife. This sympathy at that moment was not lessened by a voice, young, feminine and sharp, from the hall bedroom next to his.

"For heaven's sake, father, what's the idea? And on Sunday morning at that!"

"It's all right, Katie. You go to sleep again."

"I've got a fine chance of going to sleep again."

Chris smiled grimly to himself. After two weeks he knew Katie Walters, and that she would not appear downstairs until she was certain that the morning work was done.

"All right, Mr. Walters. I'll use the back stairs," he called, and listened to that gentleman's apologetic retreat with something very close to compassion. Then he got out of bed, put on his old dressing gown, gathered up his towel—he had already learned not to leave it in the bathroom—and with a cautious glance at Katie's closed door went down the front stairs and through the dining room to where a narrow flight of steps led up to the bathroom. Quietly as he had moved, however, Mrs. Walters in the kitchen had heard him, and now she confronted him with a worried frown. She was a small woman, with untidy faded blonde hair and an air of having known better days. Now she looked frightened, as though this new security for her and hers was threatened.

"I'm terribly sorry, doctor. I've tried to get Dick out, but—well, I guess you know how it is."

"Don't you worry about it," he told her cheerfully. "A little exercise in the morning is good for me. Later on when the waiting line of patients extends out into the hall it might be awkward. But not yet."

She was very near to tears, he saw, and he got himself away and up the steps in a hurry. After all, it was not entirely her fault that her children were what they were. Nor, he considered, as he ruefully surveyed the bathroom when he reached it, was it her fault that the tub had not been cleaned by its last user the night before. That would have been Katie, he knew. The scent of cheap bath salts filled the air, and her towel lay in a damp heap on the floor.

He cleaned the tub absently, his mind still on the Walters family and his own situation. The Walters', he realized, had been an error, but what was a man to do? Medicine as a profession made no allowances for poverty. It exacted years of preparation and study, it cared for him during his internship in some hospital or other, and then it shot him out into the world to sink or swim. It gave him ethics and even ideals, but it made it damned hard to live up to them, or even to live at all. And now he had the Walters', and the Walters' had been a mistake.

He bathed and shaved carefully and with deliberation. Once somebody impatiently tried the door, and he grinned into the mirror. That also would be Katie, he thought. Well, let her wait. He had had plenty of Katie, and he was likely to have more; for he knew now that without his help the Walters family had reached the end of the road. His mind harked back, to a sulky girl in a ward bed after an operation for appendicitis, and Henry Walters beside it, shabby but with the voice and manner of better times.

"I hear you're leaving the hospital, doctor. Is that so?"

"Yes. My time's up pretty soon."

"I was going to say that we have two parlors that would make good offices if you care to look at them. They've been rented, but they're empty just now."

The girl had said nothing. She was very young and rather pretty, with two long braids of blonde hair and a sullen mouth, and Chris had smiled down at her.

"How about it, Katie? Want a doctor in the house?"

"I never want to see a doctor again."

Nevertheless he had taken the offices. The location was good, and Henry Walters was a salesman, if he was not much of anything else.

"Look at them, doctor! Blaze of sunshine in them both. And the street cars stop right at the door. That's an advantage too."

"Very good sunshine," said Chris, giving praise where

praise was due. But there was an urgency in Henry Walters' voice which was not far from desperation, and so in the end Chris had taken the rooms. For the payment of the modest house rent and the light and heat he was to have his offices and a furnished bedroom, and the service for all three. "And if you'd like a bit of breakfast," Henry added largely, "well, I don't suppose we'll quarrel over that."

They might well have quarreled over the breakfasts, as Chris had soon discovered; two scraps of dried bacon, a plate of scorched toast and something which Lily Walters called coffee, but which by any other name would have smelled as weak. However, he had taken the Walters' for better or for worse, and already Chris knew that he could not turn them back to despair.

Katie's voice came up to him from the kitchen below, shrill with resentment.

"Well, I don't care, mother. First he wakes me up, and then he spends an hour in the bathroom. I've got as much right there as he has."

Something of Chris's morning cheerfulness left him. He picked up his towel and razor, put on his dressing gown and returned by the way he had come. Dick, it appeared, was still sleeping.

CHAPTER II

WHEN young Doctor Arden, in the better of his two suits, descended the stairs at nine o'clock that Sunday, there was nothing to distinguish the morning from the two which had preceded it or the many which were to follow it. There was perhaps a trifle more of jauntiness in that descent of his, such as belongs to a young medical man on his way down to his office on a bright spring day, wearing a new necktie of joyous rather than gaudy colors. Otherwise there was nothing to show that it was not just another Sunday morning, with a comic section to the newspaper and an entire city seemingly unaware that here was a new doctor ready to serve it. But years later he remembered it in every detail, his slow descent of the stairs, still thrilling although the bright morning sun showed only the frayed stair and hall carpets and the battered table with a crooked mirror over it; his apparently casual glance out the front door to see if Lily had polished the new brass plate with his name on it; and the final firm and professional steps with which he entered his waiting room that morning.

He stopped there and glanced about him. It had a certain dignity, he considered, with its line of chairs around the walls and its center table covered with new magazines. That it was also empty of patients seemed comparatively unimportant at the moment. What was important was that it had not been dusted that morning. There was a considerable film of dust on the imitation mahogany of the table and on the black marble mantel, and after some hesitation he took his best Sunday handkerchief out of his pocket and wiped them off.

Some of his morning enthusiasm faded with that, and was not restored by the discovery as he went through the double doors that the back office was in the same condition. Casually inspected, however, it revealed itself as everything that a consulting room should be, and ready for any emergency from babies to major surgery. There between the windows, for it was a corner house, sat his second-hand desk, and on it his unused pen and prescription pads. Beside it on a stand were his books: his Gray's Anatomy, his Osler, a Gynecology, a Materia Medica and of course an Obstetrics.

He had come in unexpectedly a day or two before to find Katie poring over the latter, and had sternly ordered her to let his books alone. Standing there he remembered that, and frowned. Katie might be a problem. Certainly she was a nuisance.

He dismissed the Walters family with an effort and gazed about him. In spite of the dust, the ashes of yesterday's cigarettes and a soiled towel or two, the room to his critical eye looked entirely professional. In a corner was his surgical chair, ready at a touch to become a table; ready indeed, according to the agent who had sold it to him, to become everything but an icebox. Over the washstand was his medicine cabinet, and on the washstand was his small gleaming sterilizer. Against the wall was his instrument case, its glass shelves containing everything from scalpels and bistouries to a head mirror and his obstetric forceps; and scattered everywhere, short as the time had been, were the vials, boxes and small cartons of the sample men who had been his only visitors so far. Smiling and urbane they would walk briskly in, bag in hand.

"Good morning, doctor. Fine day."

"Very. What can I do for you?"

"Not a thing, sir. Just want to leave a few samples. You might try them out and see what you think of them!"

Out of the bag would come a profusion of liver pills in boxes, in bottles. Already he knew that there were usually only two guesses as to the contents of the bag: they would be either liver pills or baby food.

"I have some charts here, doctor, showing gains in weight of infants under this food. I'll leave some with you."

The desk would be littered with this and that. The sample man would talk, quickly and to the point. Then still cheerfully he would snap his bag shut, get up, take his hat and leave. He was not a salesman, he was a giver of largess. Generally he was portly, always he was benevolent.

"Well, good luck, doctor."

"Thanks. What on earth am I to do with all this stuff anyhow?"

"Oh, pass it out. People always appreciate something for nothing. Then if they like it they'll go and buy it. Try it yourself!"

Already he had discovered that these samples had an irresistible attraction for Lily Walters. Dusting the room—when she did dust it—she would inspect one of the cathartic bottles with rapt attention.

"I don't suppose you could spare this, doctor? I've had a headache coming on since yesterday."

"Let's see it first. You mustn't start dosing yourself with anything that comes along," he would tell her severely.

Usually she got it in the end. Already in two weeks she had had several bottles, as well as a box of malted milk tablets. "I find it rests me if I put one in a cup of hot milk." Later on he realized that his samples had gradually become one of the perquisites of her office. She even handed them out to the neighbors, as he learned when eventually they consulted him.

"I've been giving him that patent food of yours, doctor, but he doesn't gain on it."

"*What* patent food?"

"What Mrs. Walters gave me."

"Good God, woman, do you suppose that I—" And then suspiciously: "Did she charge you for it?"

"Oh, no, sir. I just told her about the baby, and she gave me the package."

Talk was no good. Lily would promise to be good, and for a day or two the samples would sit, on the mantel, on the top of his desk, undisturbed. Then by a sort of attrition they would begin to go again. She was incorrigible. . . .

Thus seen in the light of that Sunday morning, new necktie, shoes carefully brushed and his heavy hair slicked to the last degree of neatness, Chris Arden looked what he was, a tall good-looking young man with all of life before him, with a humorous quirk to his mouth, and at the moment a frown on his forehead.

"Damn the woman!" he muttered, and after weighing the disadvantages of calling in Lily or Katie and watching them shift the dust from one object to another, got out his handkerchief again and carefully set to work.

Outside the quiet of Sunday morning hung over the city. Below in the mill district tired workers slept; and above on the hill people slept also, trying to fill in the day. Later on he supposed they would rise and go out, to country clubs or to drive, or even to church. Their carriages or their cars would roll past his door, with its modest sign above the bell, "Noel Arden, M.D."; and, so far as he could see at the moment, would continue to ignore it and roll past. After two weeks of observation, Noel Arden, M.D., had learned that any excitement whatever induced by that sign was, to say the least, carefully controlled.

He finished his dusting, put his disreputable handkerchief back in his pocket, lighted the first cigarette of the day, and sat down to contemplation.

The fine flush of the early morning had gone. Suddenly it seemed strange that he should be where he was, sitting alone in that office, waiting for life to come to him instead of going out to meet it. He felt alone and extraordinarily useless. "Like a pulled tooth," he thought grimly. The waiting was sapping him, he considered. His confidence was going, and his confidence was all he had.

Sitting there cigarette in hand he went back over the steps which had brought him to where he was, to an empty office on a spring morning, with his small capital virtually gone and only his two hands and whatever he carried in his head to see him through. He was where he was, in a strange city, simply because he had served his internship there. And a damned lonely city it was.

He got up and went to the window. The house stood on a corner, and the city was rousing now for the day. There were people in the streets, holidaymakers were boarding the cars, and from the kitchen wing came distant sounds of loud noises. Katie and her mother again, he thought, and went back to his thinking. He had no immediate family, and outside of the hospital few friends. His vacations for years had been spent with an old uncle, a country doctor halfway across the state, but he had not seen him for a long time. Yet oddly enough it was to old Dave Mortimer that he owed the fact that he was sitting where he was that morning, his brass plate on the door and behind him some eleven years of college, medical school and hospital. Old Dave, breeder of tall taciturn sons, militant Christian, and doctor and father-confessor to an entire county, dumping his drugs and implements into his saddlebags and climbing on his big horse for his daily round.

"Buggy?" he would say. "What do I want a buggy for? I'm not crippled."

It was to old Dave that he had gone at sixteen with the question of his future, and old Dave had reached out and picking up a not over-clean hand, had examined it carefully.

"Good hands," he said. "Maybe do surgery some day. Why not study medicine, Chris? None of mine want it, but it's a man's job."

That had been the start. The big old figure on the tall horse, alternately profane and pious, had been romance to him. Sometimes he came in at dawn, gray-faced from some night of trouble, and everybody kept out of his way. But if there had been a death he would shut himself in his office for a while, and the boys said that he was praying. Then he would stamp out to his breakfast, truculent and vital once more.

"What the hell and damnation is wrong with this coffee?

Belly wash! Get me some whisky, somebody." And he would pour the whisky into his coffee and drink it down.

Yes, it was owing to old Dave Mortimer that he was where he was—wherever that might be. So far as Chris knew he had never boiled an instrument, and he had forbidden his wife, Letitia, even to look into his saddlebags. But Chris had done so once, and had found in one a chain from a bridle, a case of long-handled knives, a dentist's forceps, a splint or two, and a rusty horseshoe. In the other pocket was his drug case, wrapped in an old woolen muffler. Yet he had been enormously successful. His hands were big, gnarled but skillful. He had been the first man in the county to open an abdomen—doing it on a kitchen table while a member of the family poured chloroform on a towel—and the last man to accept the germ theory.

"Pus?" he would say. "Pus is healthy. Those fellows in the Civil War had the right idea. They packed an amputation in sawdust and let maggots clean it up."

"I wish you wouldn't talk that way, doctor," Letitia would protest. She had always called him doctor. "Nobody else can eat."

"You're a squeamish lot, aren't you? A good clean healthy maggot—"

Chris smiled at the memory. He had had something, the old boy. It was not only that he worked in widely scattered farmhouses, free from the infections of crowded cities. Even the tidiest farm had its share of organic stuff floating about. It was some dynamic force, some flow of vitality which seemed to spread from him to his patients. It was said that he had been known to sit silently for an hour holding an almost pulseless wrist; and that the pulse would grow stronger, minute by minute. It was, they said, as though he were fighting death by sheer will power. And after the crisis was passed he could scarcely stand up on his feet. . . .

He was still thinking of Dave Mortimer when there was

a knock at the door and Katie Walters came in, looking sulky and carrying a dust cloth.

"Mother said I was to do the offices."

"Not now, Katie," he said, with dignity. "*Before* nine. After that it's office hours."

"There's nobody here."

"There may be. At any moment the bell may ring, and some wealthy patient may step out of a carriage and enter. Never forget that, my child."

Katie, however, was not to be appeased. For one thing she was looking her worst, and knew it. She wore a blue blouse, not too clean, and a sagging skirt. Moreover, her hair was twisted over kid curlers, and to hide this she had hastily put on a boudoir cap. But he thought, idly watching her flick at the chairs in morose silence, that she was probably rather a pretty girl.

"Listen," he said, "do you always spend Sunday in hating the world?"

"I only hate my part of it."

"So?" He eyed her. "Just papa and mamma and little brother. Is that it?"

"And smart-aleck young men who spend all morning in the bathroom."

He laughed out loud at that.

"And how about little girls who use the tub and don't clean it afterwards?"

She flushed with anger. "I'm not a little girl. I'm seventeen, if that interests you."

"You surprise me," he said gravely. "I had no idea you had reached that extreme age. But to return you, so to speak, to the bathtub—"

Perhaps fortunately for him the doorbell rang just then, and Katie dropped her duster and flew to a front window.

"It's a girl," she said excitedly. "It's the Lewis girl, doctor! You know, the big stone house on the hill."

"Get away from that window," he said sternly. "And

for heaven's sake get out of sight. Where's your mother? She may look better than you do. She can't look worse!"

Katie gave him an infuriated look and disappeared, and—the bell ringing again with no sign of Lily—he opened the door himself. On the top step was a young woman, looking both embarrassed and alarmed, and under her arm she carried a dog. Years later he had only to close his eyes to see her there, direct-eyed, slim and lovely, gazing up at him with that absurd dog under her arm; and to struggle with an old hurt, a savage resentment against what life had done to them both. But at the moment he was merely apologetic.

"Sorry," he said. "My household is rather disrupted this morning."

"Are you the doctor?"

"I am indeed. Do you want a doctor?"

"My dog does. I do hope you don't mind, but he has a bone in his throat, and I can't find a veterinarian."

He stiffened slightly. Then he looked down at the black Scottish terrier in her arms and his expression changed. After all the dog was in trouble, and he liked dogs. He smiled cheerfully, and threw the door wide open.

"Come in," he said. "I'm no dog doctor, but I'll see what I can do."

She followed him, even in the emergency carrying with her a certain young dignity and the poise of good breeding; and Chris, hurriedly getting his head mirror and a forceps and turning on a light, was aware of it, and of her too. So this was Beverly Lewis, this girl with the steady eyes and the small determined chin. He shot a glance at her as he struggled into the white coat which was to protect his Sunday suit.

"Let's see him. We'll get it out; or at least we'll have a darned good try."

"I hate to bother you."

"No bother. Good thing to keep my hand in. Now, old man, let's have a look at you."

The dog himself was past caring. All that mattered to

him was the next breath, and for a moment or two there was no other sound in the room. Then suddenly that ceased, and Chris held out a small object to her and grinned.

"There you are!" he said. "Want to keep it and put it in a bottle?"

To his astonishment he saw that she was crying.

"Please don't," he said. "He's all right now. Look at him."

The terrier, as a matter of fact, was all right once more. Dog fashion he was prepared to forget the past and make the best of the present. He licked Chris's hand, gave a wiggle or two in her arms, and jumped to the floor. His mistress, however, was far from right. She was still silently crying, and at the same time fumbling for something and failing to find it.

"It's just relief," she said. "And of course I forgot my bag. I forgot everything. If you can lend me a handkerchief for a minute—"

Chris reached for his and brought it out. Then his horrified eyes saw its condition and hastily retired it. But the girl had seen it too, and smiled through her tears.

"Sorry," he said. "I was doing my morning housework with it. I'll get you a towel."

There was, of course, no towel. Strict orders that at least three clean towels hang by the corner washstand meant little to the Walters family. A hurried excursion up the front stairs to find Dick's door still locked, a rush down and up the back stairs to the bathroom, to find none there, and a brief and violent explosion from Chris in the kitchen finally produced one; but the fact that the dog had regarded it as a game and had rushed after him barking did nothing to ease the situation. When he returned to the office it was to find the girl more embarrassed than he was himself.

"I caught it," he said, holding out the towel. "It was a good run but I wore it down. Look at it. It's exhausted."

She laughed and wiped her face, and the rubbing brought

a faint color to her cheeks. Then she got up and looked at him uncertainly.

"I forgot my bag, doctor; but if you will take my name and address—"

"Nothing would please me more. But just why?"

"Don't tell me you won't make a charge for what you have done for Sandy. I couldn't bear it."

He eyed her.

"I did what any humane man would have done. If I'd seen your dog choking on the street I'd have done the same thing. So don't spoil it. I'm not a veterinarian, and I happen to like dogs."

"You make me very uncomfortable."

"That's ridiculous. I had nothing else to do. I was merely putting in time until I started out to fool the neighbors." And as she looked puzzled. "Pretending to be busy," he added, smiling down at her. "Every morning I pick up that bag over there and start out. The proper technique is to go out fast, as though in a hurry. Once around the corner of course I can slow down a bit, but I keep going."

She laughed again—she had a most delightful laugh—and took a quick comprehensive glance around the room.

"I know now who you are. You've been at the hospital, haven't you?"

"Only a trifle of three years! I had an extra year as chief intern."

He looked at her, but this impressive fact apparently had not registered.

"Then you are just starting?"

"Two weeks. Two endless empty weeks." She seemed so surprised at that, however, that he hastened to reassure her. "Don't let that worry you. We all go through it. But as you go out you might look at my sign on the door. It may be a trifle modest, you know. There's a chap over on Hill Street who has a tapeworm in a jar outside. They say he does a land-office business."

She smiled.

"It looked like a very nice sign," she said, and got up. "And now, doctor, if I leave my name and address, do please—"

"Don't be foolish. I'd have helped any dog. Look at him now!"

It was however an unfortunate moment to look at Sandy. For Sandy, comfortable at last, was giving himself his morning bath, and was not at that instant intended for observation. Chris flushed unhappily, but apparently Miss Lewis had not noticed. She was looking in fact rather annoyed.

"You make it rather difficult for me," she said. "I like to pay my debts, and my name—"

"I know your name," he said rather shortly.

"And you won't send a bill?"

"Certainly I won't send a bill."

Her chin went up, and he saw that her pride was affronted. He had, however, a very pretty pride of his own and a chin as stubborn as hers.

"No bill," he repeated, and she stiffened and moved toward the door.

"Then I'm sorry I've been such a nuisance."

"No nuisance either," said Chris. "And if you have any more dogs—!"

"Thanks," she said coldly. "I wouldn't dream of imposing on you again," and going out, the dog at her heels, slammed the door behind her.

"Now why the hell did I say that?" Chris thought as he went back to straighten his office. "After all she's a girl and a nice one. Stubborn too." He smiled at the memory of that exit of hers, but he was not too comfortable. Out of sheer blazing pride he had affronted her, and there was less than his usual truculence in his carriage as he sought out Lily Walters in the back of the house.

Once more, however, Lily defeated him by her very weakness and ineptitude.

"I'm sorry about the towels, doctor. I was washing some when you called."

"Well, just so it doesn't happen again."

She tucked up the loose ends of her hair and looked at him anxiously.

"I hope there's nothing seriously wrong with Miss Lewis, doctor."

"Never ask me questions about my patients—if I ever get any," he told her. "And Miss Lewis was not a patient. Her dog was."

"Her dog!"

Her face fell, and he saw that anxiety and not curiosity lay behind her faded eyes. Here at last, after God knows what tragedy of living, she had found sanctuary for herself and her family. His success would be hers, his failure hers also. Henry tinkering in a back shed with his useless inventions, Dick haunting billiard parlors instead of hunting for work, even Katie, sulky and lazy, going to the high school and eying boys with a distaste which concealed a keen interest, all of them were hung around his neck by that sheer necessity of hers. He leaned over and patted her shoulder.

"Cheer up," he said. "It's only a matter of time, you know. We'll carry on all right."

She hardly heard him. There was a sound of a door unlocking overhead, and then Dick's peevish voice. "Hey, mom. How about some coffee?"

Her tired face brightened.

"Coming right up, Dick."

When he left her she was busy at the stove.

He went back into the front hall, carefully straightened his tie in front of the mirror, picked up his black bag and started out on his daily round, this time for the hospital.

Before he started he looked about again and seeing nobody near on the street, got out his handkerchief again and rapidly and expertly polished his sign.

CHAPTER III

THE hospital was very old. It had grown, a bit here and a bit there, as the city had grown. Some parts of it indeed were fairly new; but the garage, where the ambulances spent their occasional leisure, was merely the ancient stable, equipped with cement floors but still on rainy days giving out the faint ammoniacal odor of the old days when fat John drove his team of big horses at a gallop through the city streets, his foot on the bell and an intern beside him on the front seat.

Nevertheless it was still useful, and largely dependent for its upkeep on one Staunton Lewis, local magnate and political power, whose enormous gray stone house crowned the ridge above the city, and who was popularly supposed—as to the hospital—either to be building a memorial to himself or buying favors of a God he had every reason to fear. Lewis or no Lewis, however, it was still the hospital. It welcomed to its doors all who needed it, prostitute and saint, rich and poor; and for a time they ceased to be either one or the other, and were reduced to the common level of the beds on which they lay.

It had changed with time, of course. The day was long gone when the new laparotomy room with its tile floor and glass operating table had been the admiration of the local press. The nurses no longer swept the floors with their long blue skirts; rubber soles had taken the place of the bandages worn over their shoes by the nightworkers. There were diet kitchens and dietitians now, and evening classes had superseded evening prayers. No longer did the tired nurses, off duty after long hours of labor, sit with folded hands, or kneel for the evening prayers:

"Fulfill now, O Lord, the desires and petitions of Thy servants, as may be most expedient for them; granting us in this world knowledge of Thy truth, and in the world to come life everlasting."

Perhaps only Miss Nettie Simpson, the head of the training school, felt these changes or missed the prayers. She had given her life to her work, ever since as young Antoinette Simpson, years ago, she had set out valiantly to be another Florence Nightingale. She was still working, ruling her school with a rod of iron, moving in her long flowing black silk dress from ward to ward, from bed to bed; and each night asking for and receiving strength for the day to come. But now she was old. Occasionally at the annual meeting, when she had made her report and departed, there was quiet talk of superseding her. But the hospital temporized and compromised. Her assistant was of the new school, brisk and modern. They let it go at that.

"Ladies and gentlemen: In view of her long and faithful service to this institution, and in view also of her advanced age—"

Miss Simpson knew. Sometimes, sitting in her quiet office, she felt slightly dazed. She wondered if science had not taken the place of service, and if the old days had not been best after all. She had turned out nurses then, young women who were accustomed to work all day and then to be called at night when old John with his foot on the bell brought in an emergency case. Now she ran her school like one of the mills down near the river, and there was even talk of three shifts and an eight-hour day. As for the operating room, it had its own staff. They worked hard, but while on duty there they did nothing else. When she went there nowadays she had to discard her black silk dress and put on a sterile gown.

It made her feel lost and without dignity. True, the old amphitheater remained, crowded with students. The table would be wheeled in, there would be an end to the shuffling and talking overhead, and under the brilliant light the operating surgeon would glance up at the young faces:

"We have here a case—"

But everything else was different. How far back she could remember! The day of the carbolic spray, and an odor that followed and stuck indefinitely. Like iodoform; carbolic and iodoform—they were an era in themselves. After the spray had come the irrigators, great glass bottles hanging over the operating tables, with rubber tubes from each, and uniforms and floor alike soaking from their contents, and pails and rubber blankets and mops everywhere. There had been, too, that time when the nurses had had to take bichloride baths and even wash their hair with the stuff. There had been almost a mutiny over that, she remembered.

Now she hardly knew the place, with men like ghosts walking, coated, capped, masked and gloved. Even the old bustle and hurry was gone. An operation was now a silent thing. It had lost drama. The tables were wheeled into silence and in due time returned from it. For good or bad the thing was done; like a business, she thought. Like taking a watch to be mended.

Yet she knew them all, these hospital doctors, from the chief of staff down, knew the fine ones and the mean ones, the generous and the nickel-chasers; knew too their tempers, their ambitions, even their jealousies. For medicine was a jealous profession.

She had liked a few, cared for only a handful, and come near to loving as a son only one, and that one was Chris Arden. His going had been a blow to her, although she had never even acknowledged it to herself. And on Sunday mornings ever since she had waited for him, clad in her best silk dress and austerely watching the door.

So Chris found her that morning, a little rigid old lady in a black gown, when having rapped at her door he opened it and entered.

"Is her majesty receiving?" he inquired.

"She is always in to you. Come in and sit down. Only don't smoke," she warned him, "or the hospital will say I've taken to vice in my old age! Well, Chris, how is it going?"

It was the first time she had called him by his first name, and he felt suddenly less alone.

"Fine! I had a patient this morning."

"Already?"

"Very interesting case," he said soberly. "A bone in the throat. Patient in bad condition. But by skillful manipulation—"

"What *are* you talking about?"

"It was a dog," he told her, grinning. "Quite a good dog, I imagine, belonging to a young lady whose name I gathered is Beverly Lewis, and who went out in a state of fury because I wouldn't let her pay me."

"Dear me. Beverly! It doesn't sound like her, somehow. What did you do, Chris?"

"I don't know. Probably I haven't the proper bedside manner. What about her anyhow?" His manner was carefully casual. "I know she can laugh and cry and get in a temper, but that's about all."

"That's about all you need to know about any young woman," she said dryly. "Well, she's Staunton Lewis's daughter, with all that that means. She's got her mother's eyes and her father's chin, and I gather that she's very popular in our local society; whatever that may be."

"Cuts me out, whatever it means! I wouldn't dare to lift my eyes to such a start. In fact, I don't look much above the curbstone these days."

He was still smiling, but now she looked at him closely. For all his bantering he looked tired, she thought, and his cheerfulness was obviously forced. She had seen a good many young men go through this period, and always it grieved her. They left the hospital arrogant and hopeful; then they started coming back, partly because for a time it had been home to them, but partly too because it restored their confidence in themselves.

"It takes patience, Chris," she said.

"I have plenty of that. It's about all I have got."

"And—are you comfortably settled?"

"I'm settled. That is, I have offices and a place to live. I suppose I'm comfortable enough. I haven't thought much about it."

"No," she said thoughtfully. "You wouldn't. Will you take the word of an old woman that it won't last? Like this, I mean. I've seen it happen so often. Men worked to death here, and then going out and having too much time. They all go through it, Chris. And—if you ever find that you need a little money until things are better—I've done it before, and been glad I did. I'm not young, and what I have will come to the hospital anyhow. It would be a loan, of course."

He got up and, going around the desk, put a hand on her shoulder.

"You're the salt of the earth, Miss Nettie," he said gravely. "But I'm all right so far. If the time comes—"

"You'll come to me?"

"I'll promise to think about it," he said, and stooping down suddenly he kissed her cool old cheek. "And that," he said gaily, "is the first time I've kissed a nurse in your hospital! What do you propose to do about it?"

He felt cheerful again when he had left her. At the office he learned that a railroad case had come in and that Bergman was operating, and he decided to go up and look on. But as he walked along the upper corridor he felt once again a nostalgia so great that it almost shook him. The combined odors of ether and steam from the sterilizers greeted him. A nurse intent on some errand hurried past. As he washed up and put on his gown and cap it was to remember that only two weeks ago he had belonged beyond the closed door, and that now he was not even sure of his welcome.

Bergman however was pleasant, if detached.

"Interesting case here, doctor," he said. "Glad you came in."

Then he bent once more over the table. The room was silent. At the patient's head sat the anesthetist, absorbed and watchful. The senior surgical assistant was at the instrument tray. Two or three nurses moved quietly about under the glare of the lights, and Bergman himself was working with his customary deftness, the small vein on his forehead standing out as it always did when he operated. Chris had a feeling of having come home again, accentuated to an almost lyric happiness when later on Bergman, having asked the time, suggested that he finish for him.

"I have a big day ahead. If you're not too busy, doctor—?"

Busy! At that moment he would have lain down and let Bergman walk on him. During his last year as resident he had done quite a bit of surgery, but it was rare for Bergman to turn over a case to anybody. Now as the chief of staff stood aside for him he was suddenly exalted, and happy as he had not been for weeks.

Later on, the work done, he found himself wandering through the hospital, aimless and homeless. He did not belong there. It might be years before he did. Even the nurses smiled at him with a new detachment.

"Good morning, doctor. Paying us a little visit?"

"Just looking in to see how you're managing without me. Hear it's not so good!"

"Well, we certainly miss you."

And then—that was all. Swinging along the hallways, head thrust forward after his old fashion, but not belonging, not needed. Meeting one of the interns, to be greeted warmly.

"Hello, old man. How's the practice?"

"I don't know. I haven't tried any yet."

Yet perhaps—he wasn't sure—a trifle of patronage, or worse still, of pity; of their security against his own insecurity, their activity against his enforced idleness. He had been popular there, he knew. Now he was no longer one of them. He had known that ever since he left. All he could do would be to find someone with a few minutes to spare and smoke a cigarette with him, or to wander into the newly installed X-ray room with its black walls and listen to the strange vernacular of Scott, the man in charge.

"Good God! A man certainly has to move to keep up these days! Here I am, barely out of school, and I don't even talk your language."

Scott would grin complacently.

"I wouldn't worry about that. This is highly specialized stuff, Chris. Send your people here and we'll tell you what's wrong with them."

"I'd rather hoped to find that out for myself."

"Go to it. Pretty soon you'll find that you need us a lot more than we need you, my lad."

As it happened, he saw Scott that day. And Scott, if arrogant, was vaguely uneasy. He had a dry spot on one of his fingers, and he led Chris into the daylight to look at it. "Fellows abroad have been having a lot of trouble," he said. "I don't suppose it means anything, but it heals and then dries and cracks again. And I've got a family. Trouble is, we don't know anything yet about the damned rays."

He talked on nervously. Even after fifteen years it was still a new medium, and protection was still inadequate. Men who had worked with it in the early days had lost fingers, even arms. And impotence was one of the results of carelessness.

"I've got a family," he repeated. "I suppose I could lose a finger, but a man doesn't want to be half a man. And my wife wants another baby. We lost one last year. I'm—by God, sometimes I'm frightened." Then his native caution reasserted itself. "I haven't talked around here," he said, "and I hope you won't either. You know how things travel."

"Of course not. But why stick, Scott? If you've got a burn already—"

"Oh, I'll stick. It's my job, and I know it. Besides, I need the money, and the hospital needs the work. Come in here, I want to show you some plates."

He was the enthusiast again, wrapped up in his specialty. He held the bad finger stiff as he handled his plates, but his face glowed; and Chris, standing big and vigorous beside him, thought of the woman who had lost a baby and now wanted another one.

"They're fine, Scott. But look here, have you talked it over with your wife?"

"Oh, forget that. I'm all right."

Chris could not forget it however as he started for home again that morning. A man had a right perhaps to destroy his own life, but what about others? What about Scott's wife? Or the children she should have? What about Scott himself? He, Chris, had passed the urgency of early desire when he fought and lost the usual battles; he had been too tired and too busy the last two years to let it worry him. But a man's virility was what made him a man. Sex betrayed him often enough, into trouble, into unwise marriages, into children he could not support; but it was the frame into which he fitted his existence.

Where did a man owe his duty, he thought. To his family when he had one, or to a profession eternally demanding and eternally ungrateful? He did not realize it on that bright day of May, nineteen hundred and ten, with the lilacs blooming in the park, fresh in spite of the city soot, and the benches peopled with young lovers; but years later he was still asking himself the same question, and still as far as ever from the answer.

He was in rather a somber mood when he reached the house, and the knowledge that his key in the door had caused some rapid surreptitious motion in the hall inside, followed by the discovery that his waiting room was filled with smoke, made him scowl. Already he knew that both Katie and Dick, against specific orders, used the room as a sitting room when he was out. His temper flared however when he saw that some of his new magazines were missing from the table.

He stalked back to the dining room, to find Henry Walters there, shoeless and collarless and absorbed in the morning paper.

"Sorry, Mr. Walters, but who has been in the front office?"

"Front office? Nobody that I know of, doc."

"Well, somebody has been there. And don't call me doc."

"Maybe Katie, doctor," said Henry vaguely. "She likes to look out."

"Then Katie was smoking. The place reeks of it. And just pass the word around that I want those magazines back, and want them quick. Also that room is not a sitting room. That's got to be understood."

He slammed out. There was nothing to be done with Henry Walters. He was too futile to fight. But he went white-lipped with anger when going into his back office he saw an envelope on his desk, enclosing a ten-dollar bill and the single word "Thanks."

He got an envelope of his own, placed the bill in it and sealed it. Then, still stiff with resentment, he addressed and stamped it, and carried it out to the mailbox. It was only on the way back that he suddenly laughed. He was thinking of Beverly Lewis when she received it the next morning.

Curiously enough, that evening marked a red-letter day in Chris's life, a day which had nothing to do with the Walters', or even with a stubborn and spoiled daughter of the rich. Between eight and nine two patients came in. One was the little seamstress from next door, who had run her machine needle through a finger.

"That's what I get for working on Sunday, doctor."

"Nonsense! It's what you get for being overtired and careless."

The other was a retired clergyman. The clergy being exempt, the total receipts for the day were one dollar, forced on him by Miss Sophia Barker, dressmaking and tailoring. However, he went upstairs that night to his sagging brass-bed with considerable cheerfulness. Even the fact that on his approach Katie slammed her hall-room door with violence did not daunt him. He was humming a song as he took off his clothes and hung them in the shallow closet next to the fire place.

Then, in pajamas and dressing gown, he started toothbrush in hand to the bathroom.

Early as it was the door to Dick's room was already locked, and still humming but with a gleam in his eyes, Chris simply hauled off and gave it a hard kick. The bolt flew off and the door opened. As he suspected, Dick was not inside. With a grin he picked up the bolt and put it in his pocket. Then he completed his simple ablutions, went back to bed and armed with a book on the therapeutics of diarrhea prepared to read himself to sleep.

He did not sleep immediately, however. Once again he was in the back office, with a girl confronting him with a flushed face, and a small Scottish terrier attending to his morning toilet. He chuckled to himself. Then his face grew serious.

He turned off his light and lay for a long time, gazing into the darkness.

CHAPTER IV

THAT was the year of Halley's comet. Chris always remembered that he and the comet, so to speak, had arrived together! At night it was clearly visible, a strange luminous streak in the sky, and all over the earth were people who believed that it heralded the end of the world. Down on the river, indeed, an old man in a shanty boat had gathered some believers about him. At dusk they would put on robes made of white muslin, and stand singing and praying on the open deck of the boat.

Joshua was the old man's name. He seemed to have no other. A crowd would gather on the cobblestoned wharf, to stand listening and laughing. But the watchers on the shanty boat did not hear them. They would stand there in their white robes, their eyes on the sky. "I'm ready, Lord, I am washed in the blood of the Lamb."

There was a story that this was literal truth, that old Joshua had killed a lamb and baptized his followers in its blood.

Chris, stopping one night on the wharf, had seen Katie Walters there, standing with another girl on the edge of the crowd laughing and joining in the shouting. "Go to it, Josh!" "Here it comes now, Josh! Watch out!" her shrill young voice rang out. She was enchanted, excited.

"Here's a policeman. Keep quiet, Katie."

"He can't arrest me for yelling."

He had never seen her before outside the house, and he watched her with amusement. Her sullenness was gone, she was flushed and gay. Then she saw him and edged off into the crowd, carrying the other girl with her. A queer furtive child, he thought, and forgot her.

It is a forgotten period now, as though the world had

slept between the turn of the century and that August of fourteen years later; but it was in fact a transition era, with iron hitching posts still in the streets, with country roads being paved for the new automobiles which still scared the farm horses, with electric coupés, slow and dignified, warning city traffic with their bells, with airplanes still clumsy but accomplishing flight in the air, and with new machinery competing with hand labor and inevitably winning the battle.

The jazz age was yet to come, as were shingled hair and the boyish form. Women wore feminine clothes and picture hats, men still expected six per cent on their money, overweight in either sex was still considered an act of God; and the dove of peace had hovered for a dozen years over the nation, and had apparently decided to build a nest and raise a family.

It was an active period in other ways also. Various research institutes had been established, their purpose scientific medical research. Men still largely unknown were struggling in their laboratories, later after years of labor to give their results to the world. For medicine had entered the scientific age. Already the expectancy of life had increased, and life itself was under the microscope. Not to be explained—perhaps never to be explained—but to be looked at, studied and possibly some day to be understood. To this end science worked, with rats, with mice, with rabbits and chickens, and not until it had checked and re-checked for years did it venture to work with the human race.

However, with all its activity industrial and otherwise, socially the world was still leisurely. Carriages moved along the street, sometimes with two men in livery on the box, regarding with contempt the purely utilitarian motors which chugged alongside. There was still elegance in living among those who could afford it. The telephone had not taken the place of formal invitations, men and women alike called and made calls, and the night club and the roadhouse had never been heard of.

It was to this world that Beverly Lewis had been formally presented the winter before; putting on her sheer white undergarments and her ruffled white taffeta petticoat, and then stepping into the dress Worth had made for her in Paris, long and feminine and young, and looking anxiously at her reflection in the cheval glass.

She was excited and a little frightened. This was the beginning of life, and she knew very little about it. She had had four years of boarding school, could speak indifferent French, play good tennis and fair golf, was amiable but had her father's temper at times, and was all in all rather a lovely thing as she surveyed herself in the long mirror that night under the admiring eyes of Martha, her mother's elderly maid.

"I'm scared, Martha."

"Nobody who looks like that needs to be scared," said Martha.

So she had gone down the stairs, her white draperies trailing behind her. The orchestra had come and was tuning up at the back of the hall, and the drawing room looked strange, almost empty of furniture and banked with flowers. For a moment she stood there alone, a little frightened. This was the beginning of life, and life was like this, an empty room waiting to be filled.

In the mirror over the mantelpiece she could see only her head, and she inspected that gravely. Once when she was a child a phrenologist had made a chart of her head and had told her not to be afraid of ghosts. Before he left he had turned and smiled down at her.

"And don't take things too hard, my dear. They pass. Everything passes."

He had gone, a tall lanky figure in a shiny frock coat. The chart was still somewhere about, however, and according to Martha it said that she was obstinate and proud. Funny that the very bumps on one's head—

When her father came in, fussily immaculate, she was still there. Then the orchestra began to play, and she was standing by the double doors between her father and her mother, shaking hands vaguely, changing her bouquet now and then from the table beside her, later on being whisked into dances with this young man or that. When she got into her bed toward morning she was merely utterly weary. The Worth dress lay over a chair, her white satin slippers had lost their freshness, and if life had opened any particular door she was not aware of it.

"Don't take things too hard, my dear. They pass. Everything passes."

What was there to take too hard in this pleasant but rather dull new world of hers? She smiled and yawned, and was almost instantly asleep.

Her flowers had gone to the hospital the next morning, and a jaunty young resident had pinched off a rosebud and worn it all day.

"What's happened, Chris? Celebrating?"

"I made my debut last night. Didn't you hear about it?"

She had a successful season, as Staunton Lewis's daughter was sure to have. If it bored her at times she said nothing about it. She wore her lovely dresses, danced incessantly, received and rejected several proposals of marriage, and was heart-whole and extremely weary at the end of it. Only one man was carried over into the spring, cheerful but insistent. His name was Jervis Ames, but he was called Jerry. Jerry Ames. He hovered about her constantly that winter and spring, tall, blond and debonair, proposing to her with cheerful regularity.

"What's wrong with me anyhow, Beverly? Most women rather like me!"

"Too many women like you," she would say. "I don't like competition."

He would throw back his head and laugh, but he never accepted his rejections.

"You know I'm frightfully in love with you, darling."

"You love yourself more, don't you, Jerry?"

He would laugh that off too. He liked the fact that she was difficult. It gave some excitement to the pursuit, for women had been easy for him always, as she had said. Nevertheless she attracted him irresistibly, her soft dark hair, her honest eyes, even that determined small chin of hers. She was a good playfellow too. She could ride a horse, play good tennis, was even surreptitiously learning to drive a car.

"We're made for each other, Bev. Think of the fun we'd have."

"Is that your idea of marriage? It isn't mine."

It had lasted all through the spring. Sometimes he drank. He would take too much champagne at a party, or too many highballs at the country club, and then he would be difficult to manage. Once she slapped him, hard, and he sulked for a day or two. Then he was back, devil-may-care as ever, and asking her to kiss the spot.

"Look," he said. "Right there. Mamma kiss, eh?"

"Oh, don't be such an idiot," she told him. "I loathe men who drink."

Upon which he had solemnly taken out of his pocket a small white ribbon and pinned it to his lapel, and she had had to laugh.

He was irresistible in some ways, this Jerry Ames, handsome, rich with inherited money, humorous after his own fashion, and not too scrupulous about a number of things. But it was a bewildered Jerry who confronted her that Sunday night after she had met Chris Arden, a Jerry resplendent in dinner coat and black tie, standing in front of her on the terrace and looking down at her young determined figure.

"I don't understand you, Bev. What's all this talk about work? I work, don't I?"

"If that's what you call it. You play at work and you work at play."

"Where did you hear that?" he asked suspiciously. "And anyhow, what has that to do with you and me? I can work if I have to. I will if you say the word. But if you care for me—"

"I'm not sure that I do. Not in that way. I've tried to, Jerry."

"Tried! Good God, if you have to try—"

He had gone then, with a sort of angry finality, getting into his car and driving furiously down the hill and past a lighted window where inside Chris Arden was bending over Sophia Barker's injured finger, and the small sterilizer hissed and steamed on the stationary washstand.

"Feel better now?"

"So much better. I've given you a lot of trouble, doctor. And—how much do I owe you?"

"Nothing, of course. Aren't we neighbors?"

"But I must pay you, doctor. I must indeed."

In the end reluctantly he took a dollar from her, which made two in his pocket and gave him a feeling of prosperity which had been absent for some time. . . .

That was indeed the all-time low in Chris's career. With the dropping of that envelope into the letter box Beverly Lewis had apparently taken herself indignantly out of his life, if indeed she had ever been in it; and a careful survey of his finances at the end of May showed his bank account dwindled almost to nothing, and his expenses carrying on.

"What do we do with all this light, Mrs. Walters? Does Dick read all night?"

"Not Dick." She was always on the defensive about Dick. "I'll speak to Katie. She's got a lot of that cheap paper-backed trash and she'll ruin her eyes."

"Well, ask her to do her reading in daylight. I'm no Croesus!"

Lily however had never heard of Croesus, and so Chris paid the bills, and had at the beginning of June some forty dollars in the bank, two furrows between his eyes, and a constant feeling that his big body required more nourishment than he was giving it. He ate his breakfasts, bad as they were, but other meals he took where he happened to be. Now he began to cut down on these. When as happened occasionally he was asked to a meal at the hospital, it seemed strange to him that he had ever railed at the hospital food. But he would leave at the end of the meal angry and humiliated. Cadging, by God!

It was at this time that he received a letter from old David Mortimer, written in his own crabbed handwriting:

"Dear Chris: I gather that you are out on your own now, and wondering just what to do next. This is to say that I would like to have you here unless you have something better in mind. It's a fair practice but hard work, and I've been living on borrowed time for a good many years. Think it over and let me know. Affectionately, David Mortimer. P. S. Do you need any money?"

He sat for a long time with it in his hand, tempted for the moment, and reading into it much that was not there; the disappointment that none of old Dave's tall sons had chosen to follow in his footsteps and his reluctance to leave his practice to some stranger. In the end he decided to reject the offer. "Just now," he wrote, "I could put my practice on a thin dime and have space left over, but nobody ever won a fight by running away from it. You know how I feel about your offer, and maybe I am only a stubborn fool. I'll stick it out on this line if it takes all summer. As to money, I have enough to carry me, but thanks anyhow."

Which pious lie he signed with rather a wry smile.

Money was not his only trouble, however. He had discovered that Henry Walters drank; not openly like Dick, but furtively, as though every so often he needed to escape from his own weakness, and to acquire a factitious temporary manhood. At such times he would be boastful and quarrelsome. Then the next day he would be his old self, ineffectual and incompetent, only now with a humility toward his family which only increased their contempt.

"I don't mind a lot of things," Chris heard Katie telling him angrily, "but I hate a bum. Where do you get it, anyhow? You never have any money."

After that Chris had a fair idea of where Henry got at least some of it, and he kept his whisky locked in his small drug cabinet. It was marked *spiritus frumenti,* but he suspected Henry of a fair education and probably rather better than fair antecedents. Somewhere he had begun to slip, probably when he met and married Lily, but more than that he did not know. Never was to know, as a matter of fact.

The comet was most brilliant during May of that year. Then slowly it began to fade, and although old Joshua still prayed and exhorted, the crowds on the wharf commenced to dwindle. Yet comet or no comet, the world seemed to have settled into a pattern which would endure, but in which Chris Arden had no vital part. By the first of June he had booked fifty dollars, of which he had collected twenty, and when he had paid the rent—in advance—he had exactly forty dollars left in the bank.

Nevertheless, he had made some progress. He was the young doctor now to quite a number of people; to Jake, the little Jewish tailor around the corner who pressed his clothes in exchange for services rendered; to Gus, the blond German who ran the Daily Market across the street and had cut his hand with a meat cleaver; to the druggist in the next block who filled his prescriptions, and to divers others. And at last to the Lewis household itself.

Impersonal in a way, that was; a message from Holmes, the butler, that one of the servants was sick and would Doctor Arden drop in. But Chris in his best suit climbed the hill that night in a fine state of perspiration and hope; later on to find that hope fulfilled, and a dignified young Beverly waiting for him in the hall. A Beverly who had certainly never sent him ten dollars and got it back again. A Beverly indeed with a faint smile and an air of letting the dead past bury its dead.

"I hope you don't mind," she said. "It's Eliza, the cook, and she's been with us for years."

"Mind!" he said. "But then I forget how little you know about this job of mine. We usually begin with the servants. After that if we're good we get the children. And of course in due time and if we're very, very good we get the family. Like trying it on the dog! By the way, how is Sandy?"

She flushed at that, but her smile deepened.

"Splendid. And your practice? How is it doing?"

"Equally splendid. I collected twenty dollars last month." Then, seeing her shocked face: "Don't take me too seriously. I booked more, of course."

She was still staring after him as, bag in hand, he went up the stairs. Something had gone out of him, she thought, since she had seen him before. He looked worried, even shabby. He still carried himself gallantly, but—twenty dollars! And he had an uncared-for appearance, for all his best suit and necktie. As though nobody looked after him, she thought.

When some time later, the cook being pronounced in no grave condition, Chris had gone down the driveway and out of sight, she went upstairs to her mother's room and carefully opened the door. Annie Lewis was in her bed, that wide bed in which these days she slept alone; a big handsome woman, her face carefully coated with cream. She stirred when Beverly entered.

"Are you asleep, mother?"

"No. Come in. What did the doctor say about Eliza?"

"She's all right. Mother, would you mind asking him to tea some day? I was frightfully rude to him about Sandy the other day."

"Ask him, of course. What is he like, Beverly?" she asked idly.

"He's presentable, if that's what you mean."

"I don't mean anything of the sort! Write him a note and ask him, of course. Look at my calendar and see when I'm free."

Beverly wrote the note that night, sitting at the desk in her luxurious gray and rose bedroom; wrote it carefully in her best hand, with her face slightly flushed and the wind from the open window blowing her loosened hair about her. "My mother," she wrote, "would like to meet you, especially since your great kindness on that dreadful Sunday morning. We shall be quite alone. If you can come on Thursday at five o'clock—"

She sat for a long time looking at it before she put it in its envelope. Then she went quietly down the stairs and along the drive to the mailbox on the street, and dropped it in. She had a strange feeling as she did so that she had taken some irrevocable step.

The result the next morning was the appearance before Chris at the breakfast table of a flushed and excited Katie, unusually tidy—for school—and carrying a heavy white envelope in her hand.

"It looks like a party!" she said, inspecting it.

"Most likely it's a bill, Katie. They do them up like that so you're sure to open them."

It was the note from Beverly, and he glanced up to see Katie's eyes on him, intent and curious.

"Not a party, Katie. I'm asked to tea at the Lewises'."

"Well, that's something," said Katie, slightly disappointed. "I'd better tell mother to press your clothes. And you need a new necktie."

"So Dick seems to think. He's left mine alone lately!"

He stuffed the note in his pocket and got up. Under all his calm he was excited and pleased, but he was also rather uneasy. And this uneasiness was not lessened as time went on by the sudden activity of the Walters family on his behalf. Under all their carelessness, their hit-or-miss living, he sensed an underlying kindness.

"Did you get the tie, doctor?"

"Not yet. What color do you suggest? Red? A nice, passionate red now—"

"You get a good blue. Blue's always safe."

"I don't think Dick cares for blue. You might ask him."

They were all gathered in the kitchen to see him in his magnificence when the day came. It was entirely typical of them that they immediately destroyed the thing they had created; for Lily had left a can of red paint on a shelf overhead, and reaching up for something it came down on him.

"Oh, doctor!" she cried. "Oh, doctor!" And burst into hysterical tears.

Chris stood there, dripping. The can had landed on his head and from there spread down to an incredible degree. Fortunately there was a moment when he was unable even to speak. Then having used considerable language for other purposes he demanded turpentine, gasoline or what have you, and Henry sprinted across the street to get it. The net result of all which was the presentation somewhat later at the Lewis front door of a breathless young professional man in his old clothes who smelled to high heaven of gasoline, his admission by a footman who audibly sniffed as he led him through the hall, and that same young gentleman's visible recoil when offered a cigarette and a match by the girl who greeted him inside a room beyond.

"Great Scott, no!" he said. "Take it away, or I'll explode!"

At least it was an informal opening, and she listened intently while he described the Walters' and their ways. But she did not laugh. Her eyes indeed were full of pity.

"They sound dreadful," she said at last.

"Not really dreadful." He smiled at her. "Only—casual."

"And how about the girl?" she asked. "I suppose she's in love with you, or thinks she is."

He sat up, startled.

"In love with me? Good heavens, she's a child. She's only seventeen."

"I'd been in love half a dozen times when I was seventeen," she told him; and then the arrival of Mrs. Lewis saved him.

She came in sniffing and she was still sniffing when, having shaken hands, she glanced around the room.

"What in the world do I smell?" she inquired, and was

startled to hear hysterical laughter from her daughter, and to see a sheepish grin on Chris's face.

"I'm afraid I'm responsible," he said, and had to tell the story all over again. All of which made the tea party a great success, although Chris left with the feeling that he had been led to talk rather too much about himself.

"It's a trying profession, I imagine."

"Well, it's a worrisome one. First you worry for fear you won't get into medical school, and then you worry for fear you won't get out. Then if you're lucky you get a hospital job, and you worry there for fear somebody will find out how little you know. You worry about your cases there, and then the time comes when you get out, and you worry for fear you won't have any cases at all. Great Scott, I didn't mean to impose all that on you!"

Left alone in the house on the hill after he had gone, Annie Lewis was watching her young daughter without appearing to do so, and stating flatly that she liked him.

"Not having too easy a time, either, I imagine," she added shrewdly. "He looks—not exactly defeated, but anxious. I dare say he's having difficulty in getting a start."

"He took in twenty dollars last month," said Beverly soberly.

"Good gracious! He told you that?"

"I think it was meant to be funny. . . ."

Late that night Annie took up the subject with her husband. Perhaps she was the only person in the world who was not afraid of Staunton Lewis, but she never quarreled with him. Long ago they had reached a *modus vivendi*. She knew now that those long years of semi-poverty had not been necessary, that he had pinched and saved during the best years of her life to lay the foundation of his fortune. She no longer resented that. His money was his, to do with as he liked; but her life was hers, and of late years her bed had been hers also. When he had built and furnished the big house she had found a handsome room there for herself, and a connecting room for him. She knew then that her married life had ended.

Sometimes when he was dressing or undressing he would wander in, dapper even under those conditions, and talk of this or that. But the old days of the double bed and its mutual confidences were gone, and she had welcomed the change. If she had ever loved him she had forgotten it. Now she liked him at times and disliked him heartily at others.

Much that she could see from her windows belonged to him, the traction lines, a bank or two, some of the mills, even a newspaper. To her he was merely her husband, a small not unhandsome man, greedy for money and for power, who no longer cared for her.

So now when he came in she merely put down her book and indicated a chair by the bed.

"Come and sit down," she said. "I want to talk to you." And when he had done so, not too willingly: "The young doctor who took that bone out of Sandy's throat was here to tea today. He's having a hard time getting started."

He stared at her.

"Did he say so?"

"Not in so many words. I gather he was rather amusing about it. But Beverly likes him, and—"

"What's the matter with young Ames?"

"I gather that that's over."

"Then she's a fool," he said shortly, and added: "I don't like doctors. They're a wishy-washy crowd."

"Not this one."

He had taken off his coat before he came in. Now he unbuttoned his shirt slowly, revealing a singularly hairy chest. There were men who said that Staunton Lewis had no blood in his veins, but none who claimed that he had no hair on his chest.

"How on earth do you know that?" he demanded.

"He is proud. I gather he was almost violent when Beverly wanted a bill for Sandy. Said he was no dog doctor, or something of the sort."

Her voice was casual, but she knew her man. Staunton smiled faintly. He liked men who did not truckle. God, he was surrounded by men who truckled. There was no pleasure in punching a pillow. He rose and yawned elaborately.

"It beats me how you women fall for the medical profession, Annie. Any young whipper-snapper who sits by your bed and talks in a soft voice.—"

"He never sat by my bed. And his voice certainly isn't soft. Perhaps you could do something for him. You might see him anyhow."

"How? Get a bone in my throat?"

He was rather pleased with that as he went out, and she let him go without comment. It was a long time now since he had kissed her good night, and she did not miss it. If sometimes she was lonely, lying on her soft bed surrounded by the luxuries he had provided without consulting her, she was not lonely for him. She would have liked a son, someone gusty with youth and laughter, wandering in to bring her little jokes, small unimportant confidences, even to laugh at her familiarly.

"How's the old lady tonight? Said your prayers and brushed your teeth?"

Beverly was a good daughter, but she was closer to her father than to her. Also she was another woman. Between them was the usual gulf between mother and daughter, the experience of the one against the militant virginity of the other. And she knew that to Beverly she was already an old woman. Sometimes at night, while she sat in front of her toilet table patting cream into her face, Beverly would be standing by waiting for her good-night kiss. At such times she was obsessed with age; the girl slim and young in her dressing gown, her hair in two long braids and her face shining with soap and water, seemed far away from her. She would wipe her face carefully.

"Good night, my dear."

"Good night, mother darling."

But the gulf was there. Only time and experience would

bridge it; when Beverly, herself a woman, would come back to her.

She dropped to sleep that night wondering if that time would be short after all. It would have to be short, or she would not see it. But that big heavy-shouldered young man was the sort Beverly should marry. He looked like the sort who would be the father of sons. Her prayers that night, which she now said comfortably in her bed, were rather incoherent. Naturally she wanted God to look after Staunton, although he seemed pretty well able to do that for himself; but they were also confused with a rather shabby young doctor who was to help God to look after Beverly, and not to be too long about it because there wasn't much time at the best.

For some time after that things looked rather promising. Chris, coming up daily to see Eliza in that small upper room of hers, was as likely as not to happen on Beverly, and Annie Lewis would see a light in her face after these encounters and make her small womanlike plans.

Then one day Staunton Lewis announced that they were going to Europe and sailing the next week, and she had a queer sense of apprehension, as though something lovely and hopeful was about to end.

CHAPTER V

THE summer was hot and dry that year. In her hall bedroom Katie, sweltering with heat, would linger impatiently until she heard Chris go into his room and close the door, and then open her own. Sometimes, waking early through sheer inability to sleep, he would find it so, and see her lying in her narrow bed, a small crumpled figure, its turbulence quieted for the time, and looking childish in its complete abandonment.

He would go down, take in the papers and the milk bottles, and wait for that uncertain hour when Lily Walters could be heard in the kitchen preparing a breakfast of sorts. Even the morning air was not cool. It came in short hot gusts, blowing dust over the offices and even into his instrument case and drug closet. The small back yard, where in the shed Henry carried on his desultory labor, was bare and baked hard, and the leaves of the ailanthus tree in the center crackled in the breeze.

He had not the heart to drive Katie away from the front office windows, and she sat there idly through most of the school vacation, her chin on her hand, gazing out at the blistering street.

"What's the matter, Katie?"

"I don't know. I wish I had a lot of money. That's all."

"What would you do with it?"

"Spend it. Get away from here. What else?"

The departure of the Lewises for Europe had left him lonely and deflated. True, his practice had commenced to spread, like the waves of a pebble dropped into a pond; but he had many empty hours, sitting alone in that back office of his, hours when he questioned not only his future but his very choice of a profession. What flair had he for it? Why had he thought that he could heal, or even help? And did he help? Nature cured or killed, and all he or any other man could do was to facilitate the one or ease the other.

If he missed Beverly Lewis he did not admit it, even to himself; but he was undeniably lonely. Even the hospital seemed empty, with most of the visiting staff away, and the interns idling through the wards.

"Business any better, Chris?"

"I'm still wearing out more trouser seats than shoes."

Miss Nettie Simpson had gone on her holiday, sitting under a tree somewhere with her memories, and when he walked past the Lewis house it was shuttered and forbidding, as though it had never housed anything so young and vital as Beverly. He would go back at night to his stuffy room, to sleep without the coat of his pajamas, or failing sleep to read. Even aspiration seemed dead of the heat, however, and his surgical books lay untouched on his table under the lamp. Not so long ago he had meant eventually to be a surgeon. Now it did not matter.

Through the thin lath-and-plaster wall he would hear Katie turning uneasily in her bed. "Poor kid," he would think, and remember Beverly, cool and comfortable in some European garden of the blest. Life was easy for her. It always would be easy. Then he would put her determinedly out of his mind. . . .

The drought continued through July and into August, and Chris watching it knew what it threatened. One day he saw it in a newspaper; not the one belonging to Staunton Lewis. "While the city fathers are safely in Europe or making holiday elsewhere, we are faced with a return of typhoid epidemic conditions. For several years this paper has advocated a new and better filtration system for the city, and adequate supervision of the rivers by the state. Now with the water low—"

Both Chris and the paper had been right. The river had dwindled until great banks of cracking mud bordered it on either side, and early in August the plague hit. It struck hardest among the poor, who would not or did not boil their drinking water. It hit the workers in the mills, hot and drinking from the nearest hydrant; hardest of all it hit the men in the Lewis plants, for the Lewis mill houses had neither city water nor sewerage, and water drawn from the wells was soon contaminated from the outhouses nearby. But Staunton Lewis was in Europe with his family, and Chris, working without pay day and night, hanging over beds in wretched unsanitary houses, would go home to such rest as he could get filled with an anger so violent that it shook him.

"The filthy grafting—!" he would mutter furiously, and recall that small pompous figure, arrogant and cold, moving about among his possessions as he had occasionally seen him.

He had little time however even for indignation. As the epidemic developed he began to lose weight, his eyes were sunken in his head, his cheeks hollow. There were nights when he got little sleep, and other nights when he got none at all. And nothing would make the Walters family careful, although they were kind enough.

"Here's a glass of lemonade for you, doctor. It's so hot I thought you'd like it."

"Thanks. Did you boil the water?"

"The lemon kills the germs, doesn't it?"

"Good God! No!"

He took to boiling the water himself, in odd moments. He would fill the wash boiler, set it on the stove, give orders that it should not be touched until he said so. More than once, however, he found it half empty, and an apologetic Lily Walters explaining that she had needed some for her washing; or—since it was too hot in the kitchen to keep the boiler going—that Dick or Katie had taken it for a bath. The Walters family, shy of the tub in the winter, seemed to have developed a taste for it during the heat.

In the end he kept a stone jar for himself in the corner of the office. It was tepid and tasteless, but at least it was safe, and he could not afford to be sick. Not only as to money, although that situation was grave enough; but he was needed, and needed badly. Many of the doctors were away. Some were down themselves. He was even filling in at the hospital, where the beds in the wards had been augmented by long rows of cots, and where the white screens went up with hideous regularity.

"In this day and age!" he would say, belligerently. "Other cities have handled the thing and got rid of it. But with Lewis and his rotten crowd in power, look what we have."

One morning Burnett, the hospital superintendent, sent for him. He was a thin, worried-looking man, soft-spoken and mild.

"Sit down, doctor. I thought we'd better have a little talk."

"What have I been doing?"

"Nothing, but you have been saying quite a lot."

"It's true, isn't it?"

"Well, it is and it isn't. Mr. Lewis has been a good friend to the hospital. You know what he has done for us, and he's likely to do more. He has practically rebuilt this hospital—"

"And damned well filled it!"

His truculence however got him nowhere. They must face the facts. It would be unwise to antagonize a good friend. True, the hospital cared free for cases from the Lewis mills, but Lewis paid for them indirectly. As to this matter of the water, it was too late to do anything now anyhow. Perhaps by next year—

Chris flung himself out of the office in a white-lipped fury. It was true, and he knew it. Moreover his entire future, or a large part of it, lay in his continuing affiliation with the hospital itself. As a result he was more careful after that, but his indignation was not lessened. If at night some thought of Beverly forced itself into his mind he fought it down, and when one sweltering day he found on his desk a post card showing a small Swiss village with snow-capped mountains behind it, he inspected it carefully and threw it into the waste basket.

"Such a quaint place," she had written. "Very cool too."

That was all, but his head went up with a jerk. How was he to know that the village meant nothing to her, or that she was wandering through Europe behind that small masterful father of hers, seeing Chris in every tall figure she saw, dreaming of him at night, and counting each day only because it brought her one day nearer to America and to him? He never guessed it. He wanted nothing to do with anything that belonged to Staunton Lewis. Fortunately he had little time to brood, over her or anything else. Day and night his telephone would ring. Sometimes it was a childish voice, some youngster sent to the grocery or the drug store with a message. "Please, doctor, mother says will you come?"

"Who is it?"

"It's Johnny O'Reilly, and father's bad."

Drugged with sleep he would pull on his clothes, catch up his bag and start out. The night cars ran only at long intervals. Frequently he had to walk. Then he would be admitted by some terrified woman and find himself beside a bed, once more to be king of some hot and pitiful domain, and too often to know that he was a king without power.

Twice he had perforations. He found his patients with the pinched features—clammy skin of profound shock; and in both cases, hurrying them to the hospital—time being the vital element—he had to operate himself. It was tricky work. There was no time for careful technique, for the leak had to be stopped at once. He sutured and drained, closed the wound and wiped the sweat out of his eyes.

"Got a bed for him?"

"We can give him a cot, doctor."

He was lucky with them both. Bergman, meeting him in a corridor one day, put a fatherly hand on his arm.

"That's the idea, doctor," he said. "Quick in and quick out. That does it."

Chris flushed with pride.

The hospital was suffering too, and in more ways than one. One or two nurses were down, and others of the personnel. One day Dickinson, the laboratory man, took to his bed; and Bergman himself looked sick and complained of headache. He called a meeting of the attenuated staff when he shrewdly suspected what was wrong with him, and brought up the need of young and courageous men to fill future vacancies. The staff listened uneasily. They were middle-aged or elderly men, trying to adapt themselves to a fast-changing medical world, and these younger men talked a language they did not always understand.

"You wouldn't put a youngster like Chris Arden on general surgery?"

"Why not, if a vacancy arises? Why wait until he's forgotten all he knows?"

He put his hand to his head, which was aching, and smiled grimly. "We are like an army," he said more gently. "We older ones pass on and the young must move up and take our places. Now as to the dispensary—"

The weeks passed. Chris learned more about the poor that year than he had ever learned in the hospital, and he was to learn even more before long. Ever after that he was to be gentle with them, compassionate and understanding. When toward dawn he would sit at some littered kitchen table, drinking coffee out of a tin cup, he no longer wondered that they were so often dirty and thriftless, or that drunkenness was common. Cleanliness cost money and time, and drink offered escape. They could build themselves an empire in liquor and be ruler of it. Then when they came shuffling home they could go to bed, shut out their troubles, their untidy houses, their noisy children, and once more escape into slumber.

Often they slept while he worked.

"Where's Jim?" he would ask.

"He's asleep, doctor. He's had a bit too much."

"Well, get him up. This child's bad."

He talked their vernacular to them.

Liquor brought its tragedies also. One night, working over a sick woman, he heard next door a shriek, the sound of blows and then a deathly unnatural silence. He ran, kicked in a door and confronted a scene which was etched on his brain for life. On the floor lay the body of a woman, killed with a hatchet; and on the bed lay a suddenly sobered man who had that moment cut his own throat with a razor.

There was an almost berserk fury in Chris's face when he straightened up from the woman on the floor and went over to the man on the bed.

"I'll save you yet for hanging," he said.

And he did. He got his bag, clipped the vessels, did some temporary stitching. When the police patrol came he was still working over the bed, and he waved the patrolmen back. "Let me alone," he said. "This bird wants an easy way to hell. I'm fooling him."

Had he been comfortable at home he would have stood up better under the punishment of that summer and early autumn. But with familiarity the Walters family had relaxed more and more. Days went by when his offices received little or no attention. Sometimes his bed was not made until noon. He would come back from his morning rounds to find it as he had left it. The modest brass sign on the door grew dingy for lack of polishing, the vestibule went unwashed.

"Why don't you make Katie do something?" he demanded of Lily. "She's young and strong."

"She works hard at school, doctor. The things they make them learn! It's too much. It really is."

He had his own opinion about that, for now and then he saw Katie on the streets, arm in arm with some other girl, giggling self-consciously and pretending to ignore the youths in front of the billiard halls or gathered at the corners.

"Well, I'd keep her off the streets, anyhow," he said.

"And where else has she to go?" Lily demanded belligerently.

There were times when he considered getting out and leaving them to their fate. Then two things happened which made that course practically impossible.

The first was the disappearance of Dick.

A tall impudent-looking boy of about twenty, Chris so far had paid little attention to him. He knew that he wore his neckties and took his cigarettes. He had even missed small change which he had left lying on his bureau. Outside of these petty annoyances however he had hardly spoken to him, save once when he missed his Gynecology from his desk, and found the boy poring over it, shut in Henry's shed.

He had controlled himself, recognizing the insatiable curiosity of youth about such matters; but he had taken the book with great firmness.

"Better come and talk to me some time, Dick," he had said. "You'll learn nothing out of this."

"A fellow's got to know something."

"Sure he has. And I'll tell you in words you'll understand."

Then, out of self-defense or some latent instinct of decency, Dick said: "Katie's always at that book. That's why I wanted to see it. Better lock it up, doc."

He had locked it away, although he had not much confidence in its security. The Walters family had little respect for locks.

Then one blistering hot September night he came home very late, to find Lily Walters sitting on the front steps, alone.

"Oh, it's you, doctor," she said tonelessly. "I thought it was Dick."

"Not home yet, eh?"

"No. Nor last night either."

He whistled. Then finding her faded eyes on him he smiled down at her.

"Boys do that now and then," he told her. "If anything had happened to him we'd have heard, you know."

She nodded. "He isn't hurt, or—anything else. Henry's been out all day. He's just gone. He did it once before. He gets a kind of feeling that he wants to travel, and there's no holding him back." She steadied her trembling lips. "Even when he was a baby he'd run away."

He took her into the back office and poured her some whisky. She did not want it, but he made her take it. "He'll come back sooner or later," he told her, "and in the meantime worrying won't do any good. Boys get these ideas, but I've noticed they're usually glad enough to get back to home and mother."

She was still a small figure of grief when he got her up to bed. Henry was already there, heavily asleep, and he had a vivid picture as he left, of her there alone with her trouble; of her crawling into the double bed, careful not to waken the sleeping man, and lying there, wide-eyed and stricken, until morning.

Dick's disappearance was the first blow to any hope of escape. For four weeks after he left the house brooded and even Katie was silent. Henry did his best. He visited hospitals and even the police courts, and Chris suspected that he rather enjoyed this new freedom of action; that it gave a point to his pointless days. Then one morning and without knocking Katie stuck her head into the back office.

"Mother wants to know if you'll look at dad."

"What's wrong with him?"

"That's what she wants to know."

But what was wrong with Henry was only too clear, and became more so as the days went on. Henry was down with typhoid, and down not to get up again. Chris fought hard for him, and since nursing was more important than drugs, he even took over a part of that. Henry, rousing from a stupor, would look up at him.

"Darned good of you, doc."

"That's all right, Henry. How about a little milk?"

Those were still the semi-starvation days of typhoid; and Henry, always thin, was now attenuated to skeleton proportions. Chris was filled with pity. He would come in, relieve Lily or Katie—the latter usually reading a book—sponge the bony body with alcohol and clean the dried and cracking mouth. Henry, at times delirious and raving, would grow quiet between his sheets, would even sleep; and it would be then that the battle would commence in that back bedroom, for it was with Henry Walters that, for the first time, Chris felt something akin to the force with which old Dave Mortimer had battled beside a bed; a combination of will power and pity so strong that it left him exhausted—the will power and vitality of one man against the weakness and defeat of the other.

Sometimes Chris would seem to win. Henry would open his eyes and look about him.

"Where's Lily?"

"She'll be here in a minute."

"Better get your sleep, doc. You look tired."

In a moment or two he would be gone again, back into that mysterious past of his. Once he asked for his mother, and again strangely enough he quoted: "The worldly hopes men set their hearts upon—" Chris, who had never read the Rubáiyát, was puzzled.

In those last days he developed a queer affection for the dying man; as though death, stronger than either of them, somehow united them. He would try to bring some order into the cluttered room, air it, straighten the bed. Every so often he would feed him the milk which was better than the wretched broths Lily Walters concocted in the kitchen. Then he would start out again on his rounds, small homes, slums, tenements, the hospital. Now and then a little money came in, but when one day he read in the paper that the Lewises were coming back it meant nothing to him but smoldering anger. He was tired, beaten. It was no use prescribing medicines when what was needed was care and proper nursing. Or when the thing should never have happened at all.

Damn Staunton Lewis and all his works. Damn all the rich, anyhow.

One day he came home to find a frightened Katie in the lower hall.

"He's had a hemorrhage, doctor."

He ordered ice and ran up the stairs. Henry was conscious and rational.

"I've been bleeding, doc."

"Yes, I know. We'll soon fix that."

"If I go you'll look after them, won't you?"

"I will indeed, Henry. It's a promise."

Henry weakly put out his hand and Chris took it. It was too late to operate, too late to do anything, and shortly after that he died. Lily stood by the bed looking down at him, more shocked than grieved, but Katie threw herself into Chris's arms and cried hysterically, her head on his shoulder.

"He's all right, Katie. He's comfortable now. See how peaceful he is."

She still held to him however, and he had an uneasy feeling that while she was grieving, she was also dramatizing that grief. He released himself and led her out of the room.

For a day or two Henry lay quiet on his bed in the back bedroom. Then in a casket of Chris's providing, he was taken down to the front office and there was a service. It developed oddly enough that Henry had once been an Episcopalian, and a young clergyman officiated in cassock and surplice. He gave an unexpected dignity to the service, but apparently the Walters' had no friends. A few neighbors came in, but that was all, and Chris wondered at a life which had accumulated so little.

He followed Henry to his grave. Lily and Katie were in the carriage with him, and it occurred to him then that he was all they had, and that he had promised Henry to take care of them. He glanced at them, at Lily, inert and listless in her shoddy black, and at Katie, taking what he suspected was her first ride in anything but a street car and furtively enjoying it. Then they were in the cemetery, and Lily was leaning heavily on his arm.

The next day he saw a small personal advertisement in the newspaper: "Dick. Father is dead. Please come home."

So far as he knew there was no answer.

CHAPTER VI

LIFE went on after that, but with a difference. Lily moved about like a ghost, starting when the door bell rang and even standing sometimes at the street door, looking up and down as though Dick would come at any moment. Chris was sorry for her, but Katie was impatient.

"Why on earth worry about him? He never worried about you."

"How do you know what he worried about?"

Chris, carrying this new burden as best he could, would hear them bickering. He had his own worries, as he soon discovered. Henry had had a small income from some obscure source, but it had lapsed with his death. Now Chris found himself entirely responsible for his wife and daughter; not only for the rent of the house but for everything else, even for their food. He ate all his meals with them now, giving Lily a small sum each week and spending his leisure time over his books, counting and figuring.

Fortunately, with the first heavy rains in late September the epidemic began to fade. Emaciated survivors in the hospitals began to eat, to move about. At first they could not stand. They would sit on the sides of their beds, carefully put their feet to the floor, and then attempt to rise. Their weakness shocked and alarmed them.

"I can't even stand up, nurse."

"You will tomorrow."

The hospital had taken a heavy loss. Dickinson had had a narrow escape, and Bergman, notoriously careless about himself, was gone after a long battle. When he knew that he was losing the fight he roused one day from a coma to ask that Chris be put on the general surgical staff to fill the new vacancy, and having thus dedicated not only the years of his life but almost his last breath to the hospital, lay back quietly and waited for the end.

Chris was not surprised therefore when one day early in October he got word over the telephone that at a meeting that afternoon he had been elected to the surgical staff. It was Williams, the chief resident, who called him.

"You'll get the official notification later," he said. "I thought you'd be glad to know."

"Thanks. I am, of course. A bit scared too. I'm as rusty as an old nail."

"You'll get over that," said Williams cheerfully. "How about a little party tonight to celebrate? I don't mind saying that a lot of us are proud of you."

It all warmed him, not only the appointment, but Williams' hearty voice and the applause of his fellows. For the first time in weeks he found himself whistling as he went up the stairs to look over his dinner clothes; and not even the discovery that moths had been allowed to riddle his fall overcoat entirely dampened him, nor the fact that his dress shirts had entirely disappeared. Business had fallen off since the end of the epidemic, he was saddled with Lily Walters and Katie for an indefinite time, and his bank account was negligible; but he was still whistling as he carried his dinner jacket over his arm to Jake, the little tailor around the corner, and utterly reckless when, on the way downtown, he bought a new overcoat and a new hat.

"Where shall I send them, sir?"

"Send them? I'm taking them, man! I'm wearing them."

He wore them home, and Katie in the front hall stared at him with open admiration.

"You're looking pretty grand, doctor, aren't you?"

"You're not so bad yourself, Katie."

He surveyed her, grinning. Certainly Katie had improved since Henry's death. She looked older in her new black—Lily of course had insisted on black—and rather subdued.

"Good heavens, Katie. I believe you are growing up!"

"It's time somebody in the family grew up. And I wish you'd call me Katherine, doctor. I hate Katie."

"Well, I don't hate Katie," he said lightly, and went on up the stairs. He did not see the look which followed him or the rise of color to her face, and in a moment he was calling down about his dinner tie. "What the devil's happened to it? I left it here."

"Mother's pressing it."

"Oh, all right. Thanks."

If he had happened to look down at that moment he would have seen that Katie was furtively stroking the new overcoat.

The party at the University Club that night was a great success. Speeches were made and drinks were drunk. Chris, slightly tight and making his modest reply to a toast, felt secretly exalted. Tremendous vistas opened before his somewhat befuddled eyes. He was going to be a surgeon, and there was no limit to what he could do. He would invent new operations, devise new techniques. He was overwhelmed with self-confidence. "The greatest profession in the world," he heard himself saying, standing up with a glass in his hand. "Try to be worthy . . . much to learn . . . great debt we all owe to the hospital. . . ." "Hurrah for Chris," they shouted. "Hurrah for the hospital."

He sat down in a glow. They were fine fellows, and nothing was impossible. He could even make speeches! Some day he would be speaking at medical conventions. "It is too early yet to draw any but tentative conclusions. Nevertheless, the results so far have shown—"

At something after midnight he found himself unaccountably on top of the club piano, while a dozen or more young medical men shouted that he was a jolly good fellow. And at two o'clock in the morning, he was—also unaccountably—alone on a bench in the cold autumnal park, while a stray dog of considerable size was sitting with its head on his knee. Both of them had apparently been taking a brief nap. Chris stretched and yawned, and then inspected the dog with interest.

"Well, Fido, where did you come from?"

For answer the dog wagged his tail, and Chris got slowly to his feet.

"All right, son," he said. "Better lay off the wagging and go home now."

The dog however showed no signs of going home. He too stretched and yawned, then galloped a few feet, crouched and barked. In effect he said that both of them having had a good rest, it was now time to run and play. Chris, who was dizzy, eyed him with envy.

"God, I wish I felt the way you do," he said, and started home. He skirted the small lake, once a thing of beauty where swans slid through the water and in the spring built clumsy nests on its infinitesimal island, but now a cement-bordered basin where children bathed in the summer and skated in the winter. The park at night was no new thing to him. Already his practice was showing its customary tendency to wait until the small hours and the usual night terrors before calling a doctor. That night in the cold starlight it seemed dark and funereal, with its trees dying or dead and the basin an opaque gray slate covered with floating leaves and the black scum of soft coal. His feet rang on the macadam walk, his brain seemed too large for his skull, and he felt lonelier than he ever remembered.

Even the day's triumph had died of its evening celebration. He was depressed and uneasy. If a man was going to do surgery he ought to do nothing else. He needed plenty of sleep, a clear head and a steady hand. But what chance had he for all that, obsessed as he was with the practical problem of sheer survival? Well enough for what's-his-name back at college to say that medicine was a career of service and a profession, and that good business men didn't belong in it. "If you are interested in the dollar, gentlemen, go elsewhere." But a man had to live, and when he had two women dependent on him—

He roused at the edge of the park, and glanced down to see the dog sedately pacing beside him. For some reason this restored his cheerfulness, and he stopped and looked down.

"You and I'd better have this out, Fido," he said. "I'm going home, and you're going home too, wherever that may be. Home!" he repeated, and waved a hand. Fido however merely wagged his tail again and looked up at him, delighted at this attention. Nor did a repetition of the gesture do more than make the dog blink, as though he expected a blow.

"I'm not going to hit you! Come here."

The dog came, this time tentatively watching him out of dark somber eyes. Chris bent down and patted the ugly mongrel head. "So that's it! Got your mind made up, have you?" He looked around him uncertainly. "All right then. Come along. We'll talk it over in the morning."

In the morning however they had something different to discuss. Chris, lustily splashing in the bathtub, heard Lily hurrying up the back stairs and her apologetic knock at the door.

"Did you bring a dog in last night, doctor?"

"I did. Or he brought me."

"Well, I hate to tell you, but he's chewed a hole in your new overcoat, and your hat's in pieces."

He swore violently, and scrambled out of the tub. Once downstairs however it was to find an unregenerate creature who greeted him as a long-lost brother, and he had not the heart to beat him. Instead he addressed him gravely.

"If this partnership is to persist," he said, "you must learn the law of *meum* and *tuum*. And don't wag at me. I'm serious."

"You're soft," Katie jeered, listening to all this with amazement. "Put him out. What business is he of yours?"

Chris grinned.

"Me?" he said. "Look at him! I am his father and his mother, my child. I am his whole darned family; and hereafter who loves me loves my dog."

She turned quickly and went away.

He kept the dog, calling him Caesar because he had come, seen and conquered; and later that day he lured him upstairs to the bathroom and lifted him into the tub. Lily down below in her kitchen heard a prodigious splashing and a wail or two, and knew then that Caesar had come to stay.

"I left a flea or two on him to give him something to do," Chris told her. It did not greatly concern her. Nothing mattered much to her since Dick had gone away.

Thus Caesar became a fixture in the house. Chris, putting his key in the Yale lock of the front door, would know that he was standing just inside waiting for him, and would feel more welcome and less alone. Frequently at night he and the dog made their calls in the neighborhood together, and at such times the dog took on an air of professional sedateness.

"I'll be here a good while, Caesar."

And Caesar would wag his stumpy tail and prepare to wait. Sometimes it was almost morning when Chris came out, but he was always there. He slept upstairs in Chris's room now, on the old dressing gown folded in a corner, and often they talked together. Katie would hear them through the thin partition, and listen to their one-sided conversations. She was jealous of the dog, of this conspiracy of the two males in the house.

"It's silly, the way you like that dog."

"Why silly? He likes me."

"Is *that* the answer?"

He had not the faintest idea what she was talking about. . . .

There had been no second post card from Beverly and the Lewis house remained stubbornly closed. Sometimes at night he and Caesar walked past the gates, but Chris's resentment at Staunton Lewis had not died, and he would go on, his jaw set and his mouth hard.

Then one day he came face to face with Beverly in the street, and felt a leap in his chest which most people would have considered was his heart; but which, had he been capable of thinking at all, he would doubtless have laid to the sympathetic nervous system or something similar. He was however not capable of thinking at all. He simply took off his hat and stood there gazing at her, while she gazed up rather shyly at his tired and haggard face.

"We've just got back," she said rather breathlessly. "You—you haven't been sick, have you?"

That brought him back to himself. Lovely as she was, young and appealing, twisting his very heart strings—or the sympathetic nerves or what have you—she was Staunton Lewis's daughter, and his face set.

"No. But a good many other people have."

"That ought to mean that the practice is growing," she said.

But he did not smile.

"If you can call it that. We've had a typhoid epidemic here. Perhaps you haven't heard about it."

"I heard something," she said uncertainly. "I don't think I understand."

"No, you wouldn't. Your father might."

She was gazing at him, incredulously. She knew nothing of what he had been through, of the hot nights and death stalking the streets, of his own exhaustion, of Henry's passing and the burden it had left him. All she saw was a tall young man in a faded shirt badly laundered and a tie which had once been joyous and was now anything else but that, staring down at her as though she had been guilty of something.

Her chin went up.

"What about my father?"

"You might ask him," said Chris. "Ask him about the water supply in the mill districts, for one thing. And about a proper filtration plant for the city. There are a few other things, of course. If you like I'll write them down."

"You needn't bother," she said, and turning on her heel left him abruptly.

He stood looking after her for a moment, his own head high. Then his anger died. He had been a fool. Curse and damn that temper of his. What did she know about the summer or the epidemic, or what had caused it? All those hot nights he had been waiting for just this hour, this meeting. Now he had ruined it. She hated him, and he deserved it.

Thoroughly miserable and alarmed, he turned toward home, or what for lack of something better he now called home. The trees in the park had lost most of their leaves, and he surveyed them moodily. Nature went about her business more methodically than mankind. There was no nonsense about romantic love, no upsurge of passion, no battle to fight. Quietly and systematically it reproduced its kind. Probably the very leaves under his feet carried seed pods. They would find anchorage somewhere, he supposed, and in due time there would be other trees. But men, men and women too—

He strode along, scattering the leaves as he went. His shoes were going; he would soon need new ones, but that would have to wait. Everything would have to wait. Who was he to think about romantic love, or any sort of love indeed, with Lily and Katie to support, and long years before he could even think of marriage?

He was no anchorite. Women had played their part in his past. Even in the hospital now and then he had been attracted by a pretty nurse, but as a rule they were busy and professional, and the regulations were strict. Once or twice he had found one alone and had casually put an arm around her, but it was a gesture, understood by them both. He remembered a talk after Henry Walters' funeral. The young clergyman had come back with him from the cemetery, and over a mild highball had opened up his heart.

"You're not married?" Chris had asked.

"No. I'd like to marry, but I can't afford it. Maybe in ten years or so—"

"That's a long time."

"It's too long. A priest is not like other men. Day after day he must say to himself, 'I am chaste. I am celibate.' That is the only defense he has. And in time that tells. One grows afraid to marry."

Chris had nodded gravely.

"That's not only true of the clergy," he had said. "Other men have their problems, too."

He remembered the women he had known, a girl he had loved long ago in the first urge of his youth, other girls in the houses which the college students had haunted, the casual contacts of his medical school days, the women who were brought into the hospital from the nearby red-light district, victims of a discouraged hour and poison, or of some brawl or other. Recovering they would ask him to visit them, but although some of the other men may have done so, he had never gone. Only one of them had ever interested him, and that was because her offer was entirely different. She was a big woman who ran a house a block or two away, and he had sewed her up after a hysterical girl had cut her badly with a razor.

"Any time you're in trouble, doctor," she had said, "just call on me. I know everybody, and everybody knows me."

Her name was Bessie Smith, and before she left she had given him a pair of cuff links.

"Just send me one of them if ever you need me," she told him, "and you'll find I'm not bluffing."

He had rather liked her. She was what she was, and she was no hypocrite.

Still and all, his record was pretty good. Some day he would marry, a sensible girl who wanted children and would bear them, a girl who would fight the way up with him. In the interval he had no time for romantic nonsense, and as for the Lewis family—

He was calm and even cheerful by the time he turned the corner to his front door, but he checked himself suddenly as he saw the Lewis car in front of the house and the chauffeur waiting on the step with an envelope.

"I rang, sir," he said, "but nobody's answered."

That was no surprise to Chris. He had often wondered

just how much work he had lost because Lily was talking over the back fence to Miss Barker. But the note startled him. He took it, yet he did not open it until he was in the back office with the doors shut. Then he did so, with hands that were not too steady.

There was no note, however. Only a new ten-dollar bill, and he stood looking at it, his face a study in anger and exasperation. Well, he had deserved it. And he could not send it back again. It was too final and too ridiculous. In the end he put it in his pocket and finding Caesar gazing at him with the instinctive knowledge of all dogs for a situation, leaned down and patted him.

"It's all right," he said. "Just a new pair of shoes, old boy. . . ."

In the house on the hill at that moment Beverly was confronting her father, shut into that handsome study of his where he sat as beyond a barricade behind his big desk, and eying her warily. Rather alike in some ways, the two of them, save that she was white with anger.

"I don't control the rivers of this state. If God chooses to send a drought—"

"Don't talk to me about God. I want to know the truth, for once. If we—if you are responsible for what happened here—"

"Don't be ridiculous."

"Then you are!"

It was then that Staunton rose from behind his desk and ordered her out of the room.

"Get out and stay out," he said furiously. "Or else go out and try to raise a new bond issue in this town just now. Try it and see what happens."

"You seem able to get money for everything else you want," she retorted, and going out slammed the door behind her.

She went upstairs and locked herself in her room. Months before she had picked out the ailanthus tree below which marked the shabby backyard of the Walters house, and now she stood gazing at it. A few yellow leaves still clung to it, otherwise it rose gaunt and ugly above its board fence. Soon she would not be able to see it at all.

Two weeks to the day after that debacle she walked into the Municipal Building and asked to see the Mayor; and half an hour later walked out again, slightly flushed, but with the air of one victorious. The Mayor, following her into the hall, looked rather less complacent.

"I've got a sneaking idea, Beverly, that you're putting something over on the old man."

"If I do I'll be the first one, Barney."

He laughed at that. He had known her for years, known her as a small child, when Staunton Lewis had kept his growing wealth to himself and while investing here and buying there had lived like a poor man. He remembered Annie in those days, struggling to get along, saving and pinching, and Beverly coming into his own kitchen for cookies. Now he patted her on the shoulder.

"Don't get any wrong ideas about him. He's been pretty good to you. It's just that he sees things different."

"He's not going to see this at all, Barney. You promised."

He was grinning to himself as he went back to his big office and his big mahogany desk. Two of a kind they were, that father and daughter, he thought; both obstinate and self-willed. Yet the girl was like her mother, too. He sighed a little. He had always had a soft spot for Annie Lewis.

CHAPTER VII

THE two weeks had changed Chris. He was still fighting for sheer survival, walking—in the new shoes!—to save carfare, and collecting far less than he needed, although he now had a practice of sorts. But he was irritable and impatient. He would come in, banging the front door behind him and Katie, reading as usual in the cluttered dining room, would cock an ear and listen.

"He'll break the glass in that door yet."

Lily, immersed in her own troubles, would retort sharply that it was his door now. Let him smash it if he wanted to. But both she and Katie stayed out of his way, leaving him to long hours of silence, or of pacing the floor, his pipe in his mouth—cigarettes were too expensive—and his mind ranging from Beverly Lewis to the hospital and his approaching service there.

The hospital was becoming an obsession.

His thoughts would go back over his days as an intern, seeing a thousand pictures; the staff men coming in, fresh, debonair and confident, and moving through the wards; the wards themselves neat and orderly for this great hour of the day, the beds tidy, and then the formal procession, the quick cocksure decisions.

"We'd better open up in the morning, doctor."

"Very well, sir. What time?"

They would walk from ward to ward together, companionable but serious. Some of the staff were small men. He would find himself slouching more than ever, attempting not to tower over them; and at the same time envying them their sureness, their long experience. Occasionally they stayed over for a meal. Then the housekeeper would get the word and there would be hurried changes in the food. They were grave men, absorbed in their work. Controlled, too. None of them had ever been known to throw a defective artery clip across the room, as he had done more than once! None of them shouted at the nurses in moments of excitement or anger. They went their way, medical side or surgical, made their rounds, consulted their small black visiting books before leaving, and then slipped into polished buggy or professional electric and went their way, still bland and sure of themselves.

Sure of themselves! Oh God!

He began to read surgery now with a vengeance; taking the books to bed and propping them on his chest with a pillow, while Caesar snored in his corner and Katie read her cheap romances in the next room. He was always tired, however. In the end he would doze off, and the book would collapse on him with a crash. He would mutter something and set to work again.

Then one day in the office, examining a heart with his stethoscope, he heard the telephone and let it ring for some time before he answered it. When he did an irritable voice at the other end announced that it was speaking from the Mayor's office, and that His Honor the Mayor himself and no less would like to see Doctor Arden that afternoon at three o'clock.

"What about?" said Chris, forthrightly.

"He didn't say," said the voice, with dignity.

Chris went back to his heart, puzzled but not excited, and at three o'clock he found himself in a crowded anteroom in the Municipal Building. The anteroom was nothing to boast about, being furnished largely with hard chairs and cuspidors, and a large clock on the wall which showed almost four o'clock before his turn came to enter the august presence. Chris, with some calls still to make, stalked into the inner office uncompromisingly and glared down at the man behind the desk; a heavy gentleman with an unctuous smile and a penetrating eye.

"My name's Arden. I believe you wanted to see me."

The Mayor nodded.

"Sit down, doctor. Yes, I sent for you. The fact is, we need another city physician, and you've been suggested for the job."

Chris looked hard at him across the desk. His mind, working quickly, was analyzing both man and offer. The Mayor he knew was largely a figurehead. The city was run by the local machine, and the head of that machine was Staunton Lewis.

"Where does that offer come from?" he inquired.

"It's not an offer yet, doctor. I sent for you to talk it over."

"Well, the suggestion then. If it's from Staunton Lewis or any of his crowd—"

The Mayor leaned back and took a cigar from his breast pocket.

"Mr. Lewis," he said carefully, "is a good friend to this city, but he has nothing to do with the running of it."

Chris grinned, but the Mayor was busy with his cigar.

"All right. We'll let that go. What I want to know is whether I'm being asked by the Staunton Lewis machine to whitewash it. If that's the case I'm not interested."

The Mayor sat forward and lost some of his unction.

"Look here, doctor," he said. "I don't know anything about you personally, or just why you resent Mr. Lewis. We need another city physician. We pay a hundred dollars a month, and if you don't want to talk about it there are about a thousand other young medical men who will. That's flat and that's all."

"All I am asking," said Chris, still stubbornly, "is how the lightning came to strike me, Mr. Mayor. It's a good offer, of course."

The Mayor was somewhat mollified. His full name was Barney O'Neill, and being what he was he rather liked a fighter.

"Well, I don't mind telling you that. We hear more things here than maybe you think we do, and one of them was the way you carried on during the typhoid epidemic. If you can work like that for nothing you ought to work like hell for twelve hundred a year!"

Chris relaxed. He was not being subsidized by Lewis and his crowd, then; and the money would be a godsend. He grinned across the desk.

"That's different," he said. "Am I to take it that it is still a suggestion, or is it an offer?"

"It's an offer."

"Then I'll take it."

Some time later he found himself out on the street again, one of the Mayor's cigars in his pocket, his bag under his arm, and a rather dazed look in his eyes. He never so much as saw a car which was parked across the street, and which had been standing there for more than an hour; nor did anyone emerge from it until Chris, still dazed with his new affluence, had turned a corner and was out of sight. Then Beverly Lewis got out and went into the building.

She was rather breathless as she entered the Mayor's office, to find him there alone, still grinning over his cigar. He jumped to offer her a chair, but she waved it away.

"I'm not staying," she said. "Did he take it?"

"He did. But I wish I knew what it is all about, Beverly. I can tell you this. There'd be the devil to pay if he knew. He's a suspicious young pup."

"I've told you why, Barney."

He eyed her shrewdly. "You've told me some rigmarole about a dog, and about this fellow last summer. Is that all?"

"Certainly it's all. I barely know him."

He reached over and put a hand over hers as it lay on the desk.

"All I'm saying, Beverly— Don't get interested in him. He's got a hate on your father for some reason or other, and a man's a fool to do a thing like that."

She colored.

"I like to pay my debts, Barney."

"Well, if that's all it is you've done it. Mind you," he

added, "we've looked him up. He's a worker, and we needed him. I'm not putting anything over. But don't you fall in love with him. A girl's a fool to marry a doctor anyhow; out at all hours, sitting by other women's beds and holding their hands—"

She laughed, unexpectedly.

"You saw him, Barney. Does he look like a hand-holder?"

"Every man's a hand-holder when he gets a chance," said the Mayor grimly.

Chris walked home on air that afternoon. The trees in the dingy autumnal park took on the glory of death awaiting resurrection; the bridge over the railroad tracks, rising in the center, might have been the bridge in a Japanese garden; even the one or two swans left in the sooty lake became creatures of exquisite majesty and grace. Now he could pay the installments on his chair, and the rent, and even on the new set of surgical books ordered from an insistent salesman in a weak moment, and over his own protest.

"I can't afford them. That's all."

"You can't afford not to own them, doctor."

So he had taken them, and one of the things he had learned from them was the rapid passing of time where such matters were concerned. But that day he was conscious of a vast relief, and of something more, of recognition. His sagging pride was bolstered. After all he had earned this job, and he would do his best to justify his appointment. He walked with a new confidence, and after a moment's hesitation near the house he went across the street to the Daily Market and Gus, and ordered a large and heavy beefsteak.

"Looks like you came into money, doc."

"Maybe I have. And don't weigh your hand! I can't eat it."

Gus grinned.

"Only do that on telephone orders," he observed. "Now there's a steak that will stick to your ribs all right. Eat that and you'll roar like a lion."

Chris took the brown-paper parcel under his arm and went out. The steak was merely a gesture. He knew well enough that it would reach him via Lily Walters a charred and blackened thing, extinguished under a thick flour gravy, but he was accustomed to such disappointments by that time. He bore it home in triumph, carrying it and his news back to the untidy kitchen with the air of a conqueror, or of a man who was about to roar like a lion.

But he never did deliver his news. Lily Walters, paring potatoes in a pan in her lap, was in tears, and he bent over and put a hand on her shoulder. It was shockingly thin, and shaking now with suppressed sobs.

"It doesn't do any good, you know, my dear. Boys are like that. You'll hear something before long."

"It's not Dick," she said astonishingly. "It's Katie."

She became hysterical after that, and he was some time in getting the facts from her. At last he had the whole story. Katie lately had taken to going out at night. "Nothing bad, but she's young, and she likes to dance, doctor." But the night before she had gone out, and she had not come back.

"I never knew her to do a thing like that before. Never. When I looked at her bed this morning and saw she wasn't in it—"

"Why didn't you tell me?"

"I didn't know what you'd think."

It came to him again as he listened, their dependence on him, the desperate clutch at the security he represented. His face was set as he straightened.

"Better give me a list of the people she knows and I'll look them up. Where was this dance last night?"

She did not know. She seemed indeed to know very little of Katie's movements outside the house. She did, however, give him the name of one or two girls she knew, and he immediately started out.

The next four hours were a nightmare. At first he was more irritated than apprehensive; hungry too, for he had started out without his dinner. As the evening wore on he became increasingly anxious. He found the girl with whom she had gone to the dance hall, but during the evening the two had become separated, and Katie had disappeared.

"Was she drinking?"

"She's no drinker, but she'd had one or two, doctor."

There was nothing to be learned at the hall either. The proprietor shrugged his shoulders. "We have maybe a hundred girls here in an evening," he said. "And we run a decent place. You can ask the police."

The last thing Chris wanted just then was to ask the police. He left the hall, however, with one clue, for what it was worth, and ominous enough it sounded. A waiter remembered that a girl answering Katie's description had felt sick and dizzy, and that a middle-aged woman had taken her out to the dressing room. Neither woman nor girl, so far as he knew, had come back again.

Chris went cold all over. He could not go home and face Lily Walters with that, and he doubted the usefulness of the police in such cases. He went out to the street again and stood there uncertainly. It was ten o'clock of a dreary November night by that time and a fine sleet had commenced to fall, but he did not notice it. Then he remembered Bessie Smith. She was no angel of light, was Bessie; but she knew her half-world well, and she might be able to help.

Nevertheless he felt rather absurd when at last he confronted her, in her tall brick house with the closed shutters, the heavy hall carpet and a lamp with a red globe burning overhead. She eyed him quizzically.

"Well, doctor, are you visiting us professionally? Or have you brought the cuff links?"

He gave her an uneasy smile.

"I've brought the links, Bessie."

"What's the trouble?"

"It's not mine. Somebody else. A girl."

"One of my girls?" she asked sharply.

"No. A girl who is missing."

He told her then, and she listened carefully. When he came to the woman seen with Katie at the dance hall, she merely shrugged her shoulders.

"I'm no white slaver myself, thank God," she said. "And I wasn't out of this house last night. You can ask the police about both those things. Last night was pay-off night, if you don't believe me. There were three of them here."

"I'm not accusing you, Bessie. I need help. And I rather think it's your sort of help."

She looked at him. Her eyes, tall as he was, were almost level with his.

"I might telephone around," she said, after a moment's hesitation. "After all you made a good job of me when I looked like a Hamburger steak, and treated me like a human being at that. If you're interested in this girl—"

"She's my landlady's daughter. That's all."

She left him abruptly and went up the stairs, the treads creaking under her weight. He sat down, exhausted but more hopeful than he had been. Somebody was fooling with a piano in the closed parlor beside him, but either it was too early or the weather was keeping clients away, for there was no other noise. Except for its closed shutters and perhaps the ceiling light overhead, it might have been any house anywhere. He was cold and wet, and Bessie was gone for a long time. When the mulatto girl brought him a brandy in a small glass he took it, but she would not let him pay for it.

"Madam's orders," she said, and disappeared.

It was a full half-hour before Bessie reappeared, her face as inscrutable as ever.

"Found her," she said laconically. "But don't get any wrong ideas in your head, doctor. She's all right. Friend of mine saw she'd had too much to drink and took her home to sleep it off."

He got up. He was slightly dizzy with fatigue, hunger and the brandy, but also with relief.

"Thanks, Bessie. I'll go and get her."

"You'll do nothing of the kind," said Bessie, brusquely. "You'll go home and wait for her. You've got my word of honor that she'll come, and that's enough."

He was conscious only of a vast relief, and that the brandy on an empty stomach had made him slightly dizzy. Bessie's massive outline was blurred, and he felt rather than saw her put out a hand and hold his arm.

"Steady, doctor," she said. "Better sit down a while."

He could not sit, however. He thanked her and went out into the night again, and the cold air cleared his head; but with his anxiety gone smoldering indignation against Katie began to take its place. "The little fool," he thought furiously. "The damned little fool. She ought to be whipped within an inch of her life."

There was, however, a practical problem to be met, and he forced his mind to it. Never must Lily Walters know the story. He must manage to see Katie before her mother did, and they could cook up something between them. Even this roused his anger again at the necessity for shielding a mother too helpless to face reality, too inept to manage a growing daughter. "A fine job Henry left me," he thought bitterly, and remembered furiously his lost evening office hours and his forgotten dinner.

He was both hungry and disgusted as with the stealth of a burglar he entered the house that night. Even Caesar had not heard him, and Chris did not turn on any lights. Instead he felt his way into the waiting room and to a window, and there he settled down in the darkness to wait. After a while he realized that the house was chilly, and he remembered that he had not attended to the furnace that evening. That would have to wait, however. He and Katie, if she came, must have their talk first.

He was shivering with cold when at last he heard hesitating steps on the pavement, and then a key cautiously inserted in the front door. He waited until the door had opened and closed again. Then he spoke very quietly.

"Katie, come in here, please."

She did not move. She stood where she was, a small dark shadow, with a whitish blotch above it which was her face. Then she made a quick move toward the door again, and he reached her just in time to prevent her escape. He caught her by the arm and jerked her into the room, closing the door after her and turning on the light switch.

"You damned little fool," he said furiously. "Do you know where you've been? And what I got you out of?" In his raw anger he shook her. "What business is it of mine to hunt the dives of this town for you? I've got something better to do."

"*You* got me out? Oh God!"

"Don't talk like that. If you were a year younger I'd turn you over my knee. Now by gad I don't know what to do with you."

"Why don't you send me out on the street again? I suppose that's where I belong."

He looked at her. Her face was swollen with crying, her eyes terrified, almost desperate. He released her arm and took a turn around the room. He was still angry, but she looked so despairing that he was ashamed of his anger.

"Get this," he said, "and get it now. I promised your father to carry on, and I've tried to do it. I've stood for dirt and disorder—look at this office. I've stood for bad food and forgotten messages and God knows what. I've seen you lying around while your mother has done what work gets done. But I've about reached the end, and tonight has finished me."

She went a dead white and caught at the table for support.

"You're not going to leave, are you?"

He swung on her.

"Leave!" he said. "How can I leave? Now listen to me. You were drinking last night. That's true, isn't it?"

"I never did before, Chris. I never drank anything."

"Well, you made a good start," he said savagely. He did not even notice her use of his name, nor probably did she. "And as a result— I suppose you know where you've been? Or did you know before you went?"

She shook her head.

"I got sick, Chris. There was a woman there, and she said she'd take me home. I didn't know until today when I woke up. There was a girl there and she came in and talked to me. I almost died. You've got to believe that. I was going to jump out the window."

He saw that she was telling the truth, although perhaps not all of it. There was a long scratch on her cheek, and another on one not very clean hand. She looked entirely exhausted. He pushed a chair behind her, and she dropped into it as though her knees would no longer hold her.

"Does mom know?"

"No."

"Are you going to tell her? It would kill her, Chris."

He considered that, his head thrust forward. Lily was too futile to expect anything from her but tears and recriminations, and the affair was too grave for either. Katie had escaped once, but another time it might not be so easy. And he did not want the girl driven to the streets.

"I'll think about it, Katie," he said, more gently. "But you'll have to fix up a story that she'll believe. What on earth made you do it, anyhow? Take those drinks, I mean?"

Then, to his utter horror, she slid off the chair to the floor at his feet and began to sob.

"I was so wretched, Chris. You never even see me. You look at me as though I wasn't there. And I'm so crazy about you. So crazy about you."

He was almost frozen with consternation. Then his quick anger flared again.

"You silly little fool! Get up and stop crying. What do you know about love anyhow? Get up and stop this nonsense." And when she did not move:

"What's wrong with you is the sentimental tosh you read, and I won't have it. Do you hear? I won't put up with it. That's the one thing that will drive me out of this house. Now get up and behave yourself."

He was crimson with indignation and embarrassment when she dragged herself to her feet, but she looked so crushed that for the first time he felt a faint stirring of pity for her. After all she was hardly more than a child, a foolish romantic child; and she must have had a pretty thin time that day, to say the least.

"Listen," he said. "When did you eat last?"

"I don't know. Last night, I guess."

"That's what's wrong with you. Suppose you sit here while I make some coffee and find some bread and butter. I missed my dinner, too."

"I'll do it," she said, and got up. "And—just forget what I said, doctor. I guess I was excited. I kind of lost my head. I didn't mean it, you know."

He was glad to let it go at that, to believe it was true. When the odor of boiling coffee brought Lily Walters down somewhat later, it was to find them companionably cutting bread and butter, and to listen to Katie's carefully invented story of having danced until morning and slept all day at the home of some girl she called Gert.

"You might at least have let me know."

"They haven't any telephone, mom."

And that was all! Chris, listening to this exchange, could only marvel at the ease with which Katie had covered twenty-four hours of sheer drama and near tragedy. It was fantastic, incredible. But then the whole situation was fantastic. Sitting there at the kitchen table, eating an incredible amount of bread and drinking vast quantities of hot coffee, he surveyed what now amounted to his family; a helpless woman, a foolish girl and a mongrel dog.

His family!

He did not go to sleep for some time that night. Beyond

the partition Katie was tossing restlessly in her bed, and he thought that she was crying. The little fool! The damned little fool! He rapped on the wall.

"Listen, child," he called. "It's all over and it's all right. Forget it and get some sleep."

"All right," she called back in a small voice. "Just so you're not angry."

"Who? Me? I'm never angry."

He thought he heard her laugh a little, and at that he turned over and went to sleep.

CHAPTER VIII

ON THE first of December the Staunton Lewises gave their first dinner of the season, three footmen and Holmes in the hall, a table set with purple and white orchids in the dining room, and the driveway filled with the miscellany of the period, sleek horses drawing sleeker broughams and carriages, automobiles, and even here and there a taxicab.

Annie Lewis, faced with filling a vacancy at the last moment, suggested Chris Arden, to have it vetoed promptly by Beverly.

"He wouldn't come. Why bother?"

"Wouldn't come? What on earth do you mean?"

"He doesn't like us," said Beverly succinctly. "We're the dust under his feet. Ask him if you like, of course."

"Why in heaven's name doesn't he like us?" Annie inquired, bewildered.

"I gathered that we had caused the epidemic last summer."

"Dear me," said Annie, still more bewildered. "We've been blamed for many things, but never before because it didn't rain. Are you sure?"

"That's what he told me," said Beverly, and went off to dress, leaving her mother to fill the empty place—which she finally did with Jerry Ames—and to realize that, what with travel and strange hotels all summer, she had not always remembered that prayer of hers. She dressed carefully, Martha helping her, powdering her face, getting into her handsome evening dress with its train, picking up her enormous feathered fan. She was thinking hard, and at the last moment she trailed into the dining room and changed the cards, putting Jerry the length of the table from Beverly. That was all she could do just then.

She went back into the drawing room and tried to ease her dress, which was tight over the bosom. Then Staunton came in, immaculate in black and white, and she tried to forget that nagging secret pain in her breast and that a young doctor blamed them for what she considered an act of God, and prepared to greet her guests. She hated these dinner parties, but she knew that Staunton enjoyed them. It pleased him to see at his table the wealth and power of the city, to offer them the best food, the best wine. Like his house they were the tangible evidences of his success.

"Best cook in town, Lewis," someone would say.

"She's pretty fair."

He would sit at the head of the table, watching the service, the people, the flowers. He seemed bigger somehow, seated there. Certainly he felt larger, dominating, important. It was at such times that he tasted to the full the flavor of his success. The big house, his handsome well-dressed women, the good food and wine, all these were his, fought for and earned. It was through the eyes of others that he enjoyed his possessions. Let them envy him, if not for what he was, then for what he had.

That night he saw that Jerry was seated far from Beverly, and Annie saw him frown.

Never mind. Don't worry about him. Keep them apart, Annie thought, and tried surreptitiously to loosen her dress.

Jerry, thus reinstated, was enormously cheerful however. His eyes were on Beverly as much as possible, and when the men had joined the women later he sought her out.

"Lovelier than ever, darling," he said.

"I'm not your darling, Jerry. I've told you that."

"No? Well, I'm a persistent sort of devil. Never give up, and that sort of thing. Can't we get away and go somewhere?"

She shook her head. He was young and good to look at, but he meant nothing to her. Nevertheless she smiled.

"You can't always get away and go somewhere, Jerry."

"Why not? I'd go anywhere with you."

She had a sudden impulse of frankness, to tell him that she was in love with a young doctor in a worn suit and a faded shirt who had a nasty temper and no manners whatever. But she controlled it. Jerry would only laugh again, and set to work with more determination. He was like that.

Later on that night she went into her mother's room. Annie, taking off her pearls and putting them into the wall safe, looked tired and not too well, and she lingered for a moment or two.

"It went well, Beverly. Don't you think so?"

"Very. But I wish—mother, are you sure you're all right?"

Annie controlled her voice carefully.

"I'm only tired."

"Do we have to have these parties?"

"Your father likes them. And I don't mind. Don't worry about me, Beverly. I'm all right What is all this about Doctor Arden? I liked him so much."

Beverly flushed, and for a moment it looked as though that gulf between them might be bridged.

"I like him too, rather," she said slowly. "But he doesn't care for any of us. Mother, if father says anything about Barney making him city physician—"

"What on earth has Barney to do with it?"

"I went to him."

That was the moment. They were closer then than they had been for a long time, the bars down, woman to woman. Then Martha came in to help Annie out of her dress, and Beverly made a small gesture and went out.

Annie lay for a long time alone in her bed that night. She was still awake when Staunton came in, and instantly alert when he mentioned Jerry Ames.

"It looks as though Beverly has come to her senses," he said, looking down at her, as was his habit, without seeing her at all.

She stirred uneasily.

"I don't think so. I don't know, of course. I doubt if she will ever marry him."

He scowled.

"What the hell does she want in a husband anyhow? She encouraged him for months."

"I don't think she cares for him."

"Care!" he said scornfully. "Lot of romantic tosh. What she needs is a home of her own and a baby or two. Ames is a good-looking fellow. What's the matter with him?"

Lying back on her pillows she surveyed him. He had been the center of her life for a long time. She had watched him grow from a sensitive ambitious underling to his present state, and had seen him hardening under the process. It was she who had paid the price for his success, she reflected. Then she had lost him. He had lost her too; although he probably did not know that, or care.

"She's in a curious mood these days," she said quietly. "I think she liked this young Arden, and for some reason or other they have quarreled. I don't know what it was about."

But Staunton Lewis suspected that he did know, and reflected grimly that this was the source of Beverly's information. He said nothing, however, and Annie went on:

"It's all rather tragic, for of course he won't marry her. He's too proud for one thing, and naturally he's too poor. It will be years before he can support a wife."

"More romantic drivel!" he said dryly as he prepared to go. "Men are heroic about everything but money. I notice he took the city job fast enough when O'Neill offered it to him."

So he knew that, too. He knew everything. He frightened her sometimes by the things he knew.

"It's just possible," she said, watching him, "that he took it because he knew you had nothing to do with it. Otherwise—"

He stared at her.

"Otherwise what?" he demanded.

She had made a slip, and she knew it.

"Otherwise I doubt if he would have taken it," she finished. "I gather that he doesn't approve of any of us; and that he blames you for a number of things. Probably you know what they are."

He moved rather pompously to the door. It occurred to her then that he was rather a grotesque figure, and that it did not really matter that he had not loved her for years.

"So that's what's the matter with her," he said, slowly. "That young fool's been talking to her. And now she wants to marry him! Is that it?"

She felt very tired. She wanted to be alone with her book, and the window raised and the cool night air blowing in.

"I don't know," she said wearily. "She listens for the telephone, but I don't think he's called her. I suppose he's busy."

He went out then, banging the door behind him, and she smiled. It infuriated him, she knew, that anything belonging to him should not be desirable, and it gratified her now and then to get under his guard and pierce the hard shell of his complacency. She had no illusions about him. If he had been faithful it was because power interested him more than women, not because of any great love for her. She knew now the story of those early days, when he had made her slave so that he might grow rich and then richer. He was still proud of her, of her looks and her fine strong body. He had a rather dreadful instinct of perfection.

She shivered, and lying back felt carefully the hard lump in her right breast. It had been there for a long time now, not particularly painful as yet, still to be concealed; but there, shameful but not to be forgotten. Never to be forgotten. She lay for a long time after she had put out the light, making her quiet self-contained plans. . . .

Chris Arden never knew of that discussion, although he read rather grimly about the party in the paper the next day. It was at that time that he took over the city work, and his first view of it was not encouraging. The Department of Health was still housed on a bystreet in a small two-story brick building a block or so from the Municipal Building; and the Department itself was the football of local politics. To it came the poor of the city, ready to sell their allegiance and their votes for a load of coal, a weekly grocery order or a doctor in time of need. Men, women and sometimes children, they came in through the double doors with their dirty glass and sat patiently on the hard wooden chairs until the gods behind the counter on the opposite side of the room were ready to hear their prayers.

There was no order, no particular organization, very little investigation. They came, presenting their letters from this or that society, or from ward bosses and politicians, and in due time they succeeded or failed. When they succeeded they went away triumphantly, carrying their orders for a dollar and a half's worth of groceries, or for a half-ton of coal. When they failed they went away to make again their dreary round, until once more they might make their pilgrimage to this shabby Mecca, where the prophet was a fat man named Jenkins, usually coatless and in a dirty shirt, dealing out his blessings from behind a counter.

Chris, walking in from the cold fresh air, was met by an atmosphere compounded of unwashed bodies, old clothes and the foul odor of a toilet room at the rear. The line of waiters on the chairs did not so much as look at him; but Jenkins hailed him with the hearty voice of comradeship.

"Hello," he said. "You're the new doc, aren't you?"

"I am. I don't know why."

The fat man grinned, rocking back and forth on his heels.

"Pull is the word, son. Why am I here? Why are you there? Pull, my boy."

Chris glanced hastily at the row of chairs, their occupants now interested and listening. But they did not rise and smite him, or Jenkins either. They smiled instead, for they too were there through pull of one kind or another.

"I suppose I'm reporting for work," he said tentatively.

"And work's the word!" said Jenkins cheerfully. "Work's what we've got nothing else but. Say good-by to a night's sleep from now on, doc. These folks here make it a rule to be sick all day and send for the doctor at night. As for the babies—well, they make it nine months to the minute, and you know what that means. Damn few babies born in the daytime."

Their god being jovial the line tittered, but Chris did not smile. There was something brazen and cruel about this exploitation of the wretchedness across the room. In the hospital they had at least received dignified handling. Their small jokes had been between doctor and patient, not between class and class. A woman in a corner, large with child, flushed with shame. It was as though a line had been drawn through the room, he and this fat man in his dirty shirt on one side and the city poor on the other. He was no crusader, but he felt uncomfortable.

"I suppose there is some sort of formula? I haven't an idea how one goes about this job."

"You'll learn, and you'll go about plenty," Jenkins assured him. Then he became businesslike. There was an order book with detachable slips. He—Jenkins—filled out the slips and the patients presented them. They were in duplicate and Chris gathered that this was the extent of the bookkeeping, on the medical side at least. There was apparently little or no investigation. He was supposed to make his own. In urgent cases the Department would telephone.

"Keep your slips and hand them in at the end of the month. That's all, doctor," said Jenkins, less familiar in face of Chris's gravity. "You'll earn your money and more. And," he added in a lowered voice, "if you have anything valuable about your office you'd better chain it! We get all sorts."

Chris smiled rather wryly.

As he went out he was aware that the line-up on the hard chairs was now eying him carefully, intently. Jenkins meant food and coal, but hereafter he himself might mean life or death to some of them. He felt heavy with responsibility as he went out into the street again. Also quite definitely he did not like Jenkins. He was the picture of the small bureaucrat, hard or patronizing to those beneath him and cringing to those above. Chris drew a long breath of fresh air.

That was in the morning. He was surprised to find that afternoon that his waiting room looked like a section of the morning line-up at the Charities office. Women and children mostly, they filled the room to overflowing, and one or two of them stood in the hall. Katie, standing in the rear hall, was scowling as he went back to leave his hat and coat.

"What's happened?" she demanded. "The whole place smells of them."

"Better get used to them, Katie. I'm a city physician now."

"Are we to let them use the bathroom? Two have been up already."

"In cases of emergency, Katie, I suppose we will have to."

"My God!" she said, and withdrew with outrage in the very set of her shoulders.

Later on he decided that that first day was the result of a perverted sense of humor on the part of Jenkins, for never again did the same thing happen. They came, of course; clutching their slips of paper, bringing their crying babies, using the upstairs bathroom, and in his absence allowing their small children to range the place and slide down the banisters. Lily took to locking herself in the back of the house, and as she usually mislaid the key there were long delays in answering the door bell. Katie wore an air of dignified resentment. But after that first day there was no small army crowding at his door.

As a matter of fact, he soon discovered that comparatively few came at all. The poor preferred sending for him to coming to him. The bell would ring, and some urchin would be on the doorstep with his slip.

"Please, mother says will the doctor come quick. The baby's sick." Or: "Father says to say mother's got her first pains."

He was busy, busy as he never had known a man could be. He slept in snatches, ate irregularly. Lily, trailing in in her eternal wrappers, would bring him a plate of dried and inedible food.

"I tried to keep it warm, doctor."

He would eye it. Sometimes he was too tired to protest, but once or twice he was moved to anger. "Why in the name of heaven can't you wait to cook it until I get here?"

Sometimes she wept, sometimes she clothed herself with dignity.

"I don't know that I undertook to cook meals at all hours of the day and night, doctor. Besides that I've got a growing child and she needs regular meals."

"Tell Katie she's a growing child, and see what she says!"

His anger rarely lasted. He was too busy and too weary those first days for much emotion of any sort. If he thought of Beverly at all it was to feel ashamed and even sometimes to smile; but she was too remote from this new world of the slums for him to think of her often. Only at night, with Caesar asleep in the corner near the old-fashioned register in the floor, she sometimes came to him; no longer angry, but rather gentle and lovely, to soothe him to sleep and to lie in some warm secret corner of his heart.

CHAPTER IX

EARLY December then, with Chris working day and night, and his three-months' service at the hospital soon to begin; with Lily despondent and slovenly; with Katie buying herself a pair of pearl earrings at the Five and Ten, and looking very pretty and almost mature in them; with Caesar growing fat and sleek by the kitchen stove while waiting, with the endless patience of all dogs, for his god to come back to him; and with Beverly Lewis, thinner than she should have been and rather quiet most of the time, once or twice on a free evening putting on her coat, and taking Sandy for a walk down the hill and past the corner house with the small brass sign.

They never came to anything, those small futile excursions of hers. Sometimes there would be a light in the offices, however, and once she saw Chris's shadow quite plainly against the shade. She was tempted to ring the bell that night, to go in and tell him that he had been right and that she was sorry. She stood for a moment, undecided. Then Katie opened the front door for some purpose or other and Beverly, standing on the pavement, saw her for the first time. For just a moment they confronted each other, the two of them, but Beverly was in the dark and Katie did not recognize her. The door closed again, and Beverly moved on, whistling to Sandy as she did so.

So that was Katie! And he had said she was a child.

She told herself fiercely that night that he was nothing to her, but as she walked on she knew that he had the fatal faculty of making other men look small and purposeless; and that, whether she was in love with him or not, he had made it impossible for her to love anyone else.

Chris of course knew nothing of all this. He worked to his limit, went to bed and was asleep almost instantly, frequently after an hour or two to be roused by the telephone and to have to go out again. Katie he hardly noticed; certainly he never saw the earrings. She was about, in and out, but she had become merely a part of the unsatisfactory background of his life. Now and then, however, rather like Caesar, she forced herself on his attention by her endeavors to placate him. She would follow him when he came in, and stand inside the office door.

"I polished your instruments today, doctor."

"Great Scott! What with?"

"Hand sapolio. That's right, isn't it?"

"Fine. Thanks, Katie."

His matter-of-factness would disconcert her, but she persisted. He would come home on a Saturday to find the office furniture turned out into the hall and Katie with a towel tied around her head and a broom in her hand, raising a dust which made him cough.

"What the mischief are you doing here?"

"The place is filthy, doctor." She had never called him Chris again after that one night.

"Well, take some time when I am out. I can't see people in this mess."

And she would look at him with eyes like the dog's, pleading and humble.

He was often irritable during those days. Katie annoyed him. Lily drove him frantic. And even his pity for the poor soon began to be mixed with resentment. They lacked consideration, and too often they were dirty and generally shiftless. Once, called at night to deliver a baby, he found nothing in the place ready for either mother or child. He discovered and cleaned a dishpan, set it on the stove and filled it with water to boil, took off his coat and rolled up his sleeves, and then set out to find a blanket in which to roll the baby when it came. He found no blanket, but in a corner a new upright piano.

"By God," he shouted at the husband, "if I did the right thing I'd stick this child in that piano."

"She wanted it," said the husband sullenly.

"And she didn't want the baby, I suppose!"

It was useless, of course. He was paid to attend to these people, not to reform them. And when at last he had safely delivered the child and held it in his arms, he had again for a moment that old feeling not so much of being God as of knowing what God had felt when He looked on His work and found it good.

Although he did not know it, he had in those early days something of old Dave Mortimer's dynamic quality; that quality which fought disease as a personal devil, and sent him rising from his knees after a night of trouble to stamp out to his breakfast, truculent and vital once more. "What the hell and damnation is wrong with this coffee?" Then to demand a stiff tot of whisky instead.

To Chris too there were times when death seemed to be a tangible thing, something less to be fought with drugs than by sheer will power. He would not dare to relax. When as happened once or twice he dozed out of pure exhaustion, death crept up; then he would rouse, shake himself and renew the battle.

"I'm going to die, doctor."

"Nonsense. We'll fight this out and win."

He did win sometimes. It never occurred to him that he was unconsciously drawing on anything beyond himself for his strength. The human body was still pure chemistry to him. As he matured he was to see it as pure chemistry plus life, and to remember some words of Bergman's a few months before he died. "It took four years of medical college to kill my belief in any sort of God, and forty years of practice to bring it back."

He seldom went to the hospital during that first month. Miss Nettie, hearing some determined step in the hall, would listen and wait, but for a long time he did not come. She sat in her office, with the daily bunch of fresh flowers on the desk, and with her only company for long periods the rows of photographs on the walls. Mostly they were pictures of surgeons, many of them long dead; and since beards and side whiskers predominated, her room was known to the training school as the monkey house. But to her they were the memories of more than forty years.

One day Chris did go in, to find her looking old and tired, and to realize that they represented the two ends of a long trail. She knew it too, for she turned her eyes to him from that wall of hers and smiled faintly.

"I suppose," she said, "that we are only young, Chris, so long as we can forget. After that we merely remember! But come in and sit down. I suppose you'll be coming on duty soon?"

"I get a cold chill every time I think of it. Hands shake too. Look at them!"

He grinned and held out his long surgeon's hands. To his immense surprise he found that they were unsteady and he stared at them.

"Must be smoking too much," he said sheepishly. "Been keeping up on coffee and tobacco. I'd better cut down a bit."

She eyed him, sitting across the desk from her, sagged deep in his chair and with his long legs stretched out before him. But she did not mention his hands.

"How is it going now?" she asked. "What about your work?"

"I have a little of my own, and the city job."

"And what are you learning out of it all?"

He was silent for a long minute.

"I hardly know yet. I'm sorry for them, if that's what you mean. When I fail I suffer damnably, but I suppose I'll get over that. As to the rest—" He grinned. "Well, I'm not subtle, I've got no tact, and I'll be eternally God-damned if I become a pillow stroker. Sorry! But that's about the way it is."

His language did not bother her. She had lived a long and vicariously violent life, so she merely ignored it.

"How are you living? Is it comfortable? Are you being looked after?"

"I'm all right. Not too good, not too bad."

It was probably, she thought, pretty bad; and in the end she made him tell her the story. She was thoughtful when he had finished.

"You can't go on indefinitely like this, Chris."

"No," he said. "No, I suppose not. But I happen to be heaven's gift to two women at the moment, and"—he smiled—"if you know any other answer I don't."

"Can't the girl go to work?"

He stretched and got up.

"I don't suppose that has entered her head," he said. "Rather a pretty head it is, too! No, the general idea seems to be that we carry on as is."

She sat still for a long time after he had gone. She knew men. She had seen them at their best and at their worst. Sick or well, living or dying, she knew them. Life had no secrets for her. Now she thought of Chris and wondered. A girl, a pretty girl! And he would take love hard and marriage soberly, as a sacrament—if there were such a word any more.

She was still sitting there when an assistant brought in some requisition slips, and she signed them absently.

It was that day that Chris met Annie Lewis in the hospital, leaving after a board meeting, and found her holding out her hand.

"Why, Doctor Arden!" she said. "Have you deserted us entirely? Or was Eliza our only attraction?"

She was smiling, and he tried to smile back.

"I've been frightfully busy. I'm sorry."

"But you will come?" she persisted, her handsome eyes on him. "After all, we are almost neighbors, aren't we? Come and dine with us some night. You do have to eat, don't you?"

"On occasion. You'd be surprised to know how often I don't!"

That was all, but she moved off feeling that he would not

come, and that after all perhaps Beverly had been right. There was a stubborn twist to his mouth now, and he looked definitely older, as though life had been doing things to him. As indeed it had.

Chris was uncomfortable after he left her that day. His feud was with Staunton Lewis and his crowd, not with his women. He stopped in front of a florist's shop and contemplated sending her some flowers as a peace offering, but the discovery that his total assets at the moment were a dollar and a half discouraged the idea.

He carried on. Now and then he went to see Jenkins to make some protest or other; but Jenkins was a realist and a cynic, and he cherished his poor because they gave him a job, and for no other reason.

"Listen, doc. You take all the money in town and divide it with these folks, and in a week the smart ones will have it all. Nobody's born free and equal. We start with different kinds of brains. That's why I'm here and you're there; and why those others are over there. Don't make any mistake about it."

"And that's why McCloskey's people get an extra ton of coal, and Staunton Lewis runs the city for revenue, I suppose?"

"And why you're getting a hundred a month, my lad. Don't forget that." . . . . . .

The days passed rapidly toward Christmas. The pile of slips from the Department mounted day by day, and there was a slow but steady increase in the number of his private patients. One month Chris, going over his books, made the surprising discovery that nine-tenths of his cases to date were women, and sitting back in his office chair, faced the fact with something like consternation.

It was true. Miss Andrews, the spinster from down the street, an unattractive woman of fifty who believed that she was the object of desire and pursuit by every man she saw; the Howard girl, running in day after day with imaginary ailments, taking up his time and eliciting a violent letter of protest from her father over the size of his bill; women who thought they were pregnant; women who wanted to be pregnant, women having trouble with their husbands, and here and there a woman really ill—this was his practice to date.

He was bitterly discomfited. He discounted or did not realize as factors his youth, his good looks, his singleness, and saw only women, sitting across from him at his desk or lying in their beds, women watching him with intent and hopeful eyes. Women. Old and young, attractive or otherwise, but always women! Betty Howard, for example, coming in day after day, eying him furtively, inventing symptoms of all sorts.

"I simply never get rid of this headache, doctor."

"I told you long ago you probably needed glasses."

"Spectacles! Now listen, doctor. You're not going to make an old maid out of me, are you? I may not be much to look at, but—"

He refused to follow her leads. There were times when, shut in the back office together, he knew that he had only to make a move and she would be in his arms. Once indeed she made an unmistakable overture, but he merely laughed at her.

"These are office hours. I never mix business with—anything else."

"Then why bother about business?"

He pulled himself together. After all, it was better than it appeared on the surface; and he was learning. This was his apprenticeship, and already he knew that, men or women, often what they wanted was something more than drugs and care. Dutifully they took his medicine and waited for the ritual of pulse and temperature; but the real moment came for them when, having put away thermometer and watch, he sat back in his chair beside the bed. They were rather pathetic then, he thought. This was their hour, the one time when as to a priest they poured out their anxieties and griefs, and even their sins.

"I suppose that's the reason I can't sleep. I get to thinking and I feel as though I'll go crazy. To have done a thing like that—!"

They wanted reassurance as well as confession. They wanted forgiveness. By some metonymy their doctors became to them almost a symbol of deity, and their confessions were like prayers. Often he failed them. He would go away feeling that he had failed, and be morose and curt at the table, so that Katie eyed him like a whipped dog. Now and then however he found the right answer. A face would brighten or relax, and he would leave with a new courage of his own.

One day he met Williams in a corridor at the hospital.

"How's the work?" Williams asked.

"All right. But only half of it is medicine."

"What's the rest? Babies?"

"Psychology."

"Sure. Tell 'em they're better and they get better."

He let it go at that. It was a much deeper and more subtle thing than that, this relationship between doctor and patient, but he felt somehow that it was not a matter for discussion. A man must discover it for himself. But it seemed a long time now since he had lived any personal life of his own, and there were moments when he wondered if this was all there was to be; hard work, wretched living conditions, and an inner loneliness with no time even to dream. One day the issue was put squarely up to him, and he had to decide between his pride—as witness Staunton Lewis and also a certain ten-dollar bill—and his inclination. For the morning mail brought him a surprise in the shape of a formal card, on which Mr. and Mrs. Staunton Lewis desired the pleasure of his company at dinner on Christmas Eve, December the twenty-fourth, at eight o'clock.

Katie had gone to school and Lily was in the kitchen. He sat alone at the cluttered table, turning the card over in his hands. To go was to surrender, but after all—why not surrender? Why not accept the friendliness in Annie Lewis's handsome eyes? Why not even see Beverly again, if only to realize how remote she was? Why—oh hell, why not go anyhow, and damn Lewis and all his works!

He was enormously cheerful after that, going up the stairs two steps at a time, running over his shirts and ties, getting out his old evening clothes and carrying them around to Jake for inspection and alteration. The little tailor put the coat on him and then eyed him.

"Grown some since you got it, haven't you, doctor?"

"I've had it since I left college. Seven years."

Jake stood off, his head on one side.

"Kind of a pity to spoil you with clothes at all," he commented. "Got a good body. Well, I'll fix it up, doctor. It won't be good, but it will be better. And you'll have it in plenty of time."

He always remembered Jake like that, with his head on one side and his tape measure slung around his neck; a short, kindly man with a wife and children he adored, and a canary singing in the window of the shop.

Chris was happier than he had been for a long time during those few remaining days, walking with a brisker step, even facing his approaching term of service at the hospital with more equanimity. After all, he had wanted surgery. The issues were cleaner cut. Drugs were uncertain, but the scalpel brought its own results. One could see them. With a bit of luck—

The day before Christmas found him rather complacent, especially after Jake that morning had returned his rejuvenated evening clothes. They looked better than he expected, and he hung them up with care, to turn and find Katie in the doorway watching him.

"So you're going out into society tonight!" she said.

"How do you know that?"

"I saw the card."

The card, as he knew, lay in a bureau drawer under his handkerchiefs, and he looked at her.

"I thought I'd asked you to let my things alone, my child," he said severely.

"Well, good heavens, somebody's got to straighten them for you! And I'm not your child. I'm nothing to you!"

She whirled and went out, leaving him in a state of acute discomfort; not only over that final shot of hers but over his entire situation, that he had no privacy, not even the decent privacy of his work. But his private life was his own, and he suspected both Lily and Katie of a consuming curiosity regarding it. He was in a state of violent revolt as he went down the stairs again, but neither one of them was in sight; and later on in the day, in a burst of remorse and Christmas feeling, he stopped and sent back to the house a small Christmas tree and a box of trimmings. Then, still under the spell, he bought a pair of gloves for each of them, saw them tied up with ribbon and sent them with his card. "To a Happier Christmas next year," he wrote on the one to Lily Walters, and did not realize until too late that he had virtually committed himself to another twelve months of the present arrangement.

He trimmed the tree himself that afternoon, and set it gaily in the center of the dining-room table.

"Very handsome, I call it," he said complacently. "I've seen worse done by Santa himself."

Lily had gone to the kitchen for something, and Katie and he were alone. He looked at her for approval, but she was not smiling.

"Why do you do all this for us?" she said somberly. "We're no good and you know it. Why don't you kick us out?"

Luckily Lily returned at that moment, and he did not have to answer her.

It was only a few hours after that that the accident happened to Jake Ettenburg, and Annie Lewis, after duly waiting as long as possible, saw her dinner party go in and Staunton scowling at an empty chair. Queer, all of it, Jake and Katie and the Lewises involved for one moment in some bit of what

Chris in after life was to call the pattern, but which was to be for one of them sheer stark tragedy. For Jake, hurrying home with an armful of parcels that night, had been struck by a street car.

Chris was upstairs tying his white tie when it happened, and Katie was sulking in the kitchen. Chris heard the brakes of a trolley car squealing outside, a woman's scream, and the loud voices of men.

"Get a doctor, for God's sake."

"Lift him up, somebody. There's a doctor right here."

He was on the stairs when the bell rang wildly, and at the door when a group of men had lifted an inert figure from the track and was carrying it across the pavement.

"Bring him in," he said, and stood back while the procession moved up the steps and into the house.

"Got a bed or something, doctor?"

"Not down here. Put him on the floor in the back office. He's better flat."

One look told him that the man would never be better, and told him too with a sense of shocked horror that it was Jake; that same Jake who that morning had proudly sent back his clothes. He stooped over the prostrate figure.

"Can you hear me, Jake?"

"Who is it?"

"It's Doctor Arden. Have you any pain?"

"No pain. I feel cold. That's all."

He lay quite still on the floor, small beads of cold sweat on his face, but his eyes open and his mind clear.

"I guess it's got me, doc."

"You'll be all right, Jake. Just lie still."

"I'm thirsty. Hate to trouble anybody, but—"

He was going fast, but Chris knew that the men around expected him to do something. They stood there awed and awkward, looking down and mutely demanding that he do the impossible. And he did what he could, called for jugs filled with hot water, prepared his hypodermic. A policeman had appeared and was taking names, an ambulance was sent for; but Chris, streaked by that time with blood and grime, knew that it would be too late. He was on the floor beside him when Jake spoke his last words, and like so many last words of the dying they were inconsequential, even faintly humorous.

"I certainly made a good job of that suit, doc," he said and closed his eyes, not to open them again.

CHAPTER X

THAT was Christmas Eve of Chris's first year in practice, and he never forgot it. Jake lived for a few minutes more, but he did not move again. The crowd drifted out, to be replaced by ambulance men. Katie was crying on the stairs. The policeman still stood by, his cap in his hand.

"Think he'd been drinking, doctor?"

"No," said Chris brusquely. "He lived near here. He has a family."

"Better send for them, then."

Chris shook his head. "No time," he said. "And they'd better not see him like this. I'll tell them later."

He did tell them, when Jake had drawn his last breath and relaxed into the comfortable arms of death; told them carefully and gently, and then remained until the first shock was over. He was deeply shaken himself, as he found when he was on the street once more; and it was only then that he remembered his dinner engagement and looked at his watch. It was after ten o'clock.

He went back to the house. Nothing had been done there, and he gathered up the blankets and jugs and carried them back. Lily Walters was alone in the kitchen, a shattered figure in a chair, holding to her nose a bottle of aromatic ammonia which he recognized as belonging to the office, and not even rousing when he entered.

"Where's Katie?" he demanded. "She might at least have picked up this stuff."

"She's in bed," Lily said, over her bottle. "She's young, and she oughtn't to have to see things like that."

"She'll see plenty in a doctor's house," he told her roughly.

"And she saw little or nothing. We can't always escape life," he added more gently, "or even death."

This brought a hysterical outburst from her. She hadn't known it was going to be like this; people dying on the floor and all sorts of contagion coming in, and as for the city poor—He gathered that she was and always had been a lady, and now to be at the beck and call of that scum, as she referred to them, was more than she could bear. If it wasn't that he needed looking after she would go at once and take Katie with her.

He heard her through quietly, although his own nerves were badly shaken by Jake's death. "I can manage for myself," he said shortly. "When would you like to go?"

That startled her, and she looked up at him with incredulous eyes. It was not the first time she had intimated that they might leave, but always before he had laughed it off. Tonight, staring at him, she saw that he meant it and was instantly terrified.

"I didn't mean that, doctor. You know I didn't mean it. And you can't turn us out. Where would we go? What would we do? Besides, you promised Henry. You said you would look after us. You told him on his death bed—"

"All right," he said, "I remember that. I have plenty of reasons for remembering. Was there any telephone message for me tonight?"

She was still engulfed in self-pity, but she roused somewhat.

"I think Katie got something," she said vaguely. "You might ask her, unless she's asleep."

Asleep or not he meant to ask Katie; and he did so, banging on her closed door in no uncertain manner and finally eliciting a sullen "What is it?"

"Did you get a call for me?"

"I don't remember. I was too excited. When he was carried in—"

"Listen," he said furiously. "Either you'll remember and

remember fast, or I'll break that door in and make you. Who called tonight?"

"It was the Lewis girl." Her voice was sulky. "She said they were waiting dinner for you."

"What did you tell her?"

"I told her you were busy."

"Is that all you told her?"

"She didn't ask any more."

He swore under his breath, confronting that closed door with a cold and bitter resentment. His inclination was to kick it in as once he had done with Dick's, to jerk her out and shake her. But he restrained himself.

"Very well," he said. "You've done a deliberately dirty trick tonight and you know it. Now I'm giving you five minutes to get into your clothes and go downstairs to clean up the office. If you don't do it, Christmas or no Christmas, tomorrow you and your mother can look for another place to live. I've had enough, and more."

He waited until he heard her moving about the room, and then with his watch in his hand he descended the stairs. It was less than five minutes when she appeared, a childish figure hastily clad and completely disarming in her youth and her evident fright.

"All right," he said, putting away the watch. "I'm going out. Let the hypodermic alone, but clean up the rest. And send your mother to bed. She needs it more than you do."

On the street his anger died. It was eleven o'clock by that time, and all he could hope was to explain what had happened. As he walked rapidly up the hill his spirits revived somewhat. After all, violent death was nothing new to him, and he could not bring Jake back from wherever he had gone, to a long sleep or to some new and better life elsewhere. Life went on, and he was still young and it was Christmas Eve. Here and there through a window he saw family groups around a tree, and he warmed to them. Just so in time to come would he gather his own about him, in some small house, some small and compact group. Just so would he and his shut out the world and be together and alone. In a few years, with luck—

He was very tired, and it was not until he reached the grounds of the Lewis house that he remembered the wreckage of his evening clothes. He stopped, straightened his tie and brushed his knees. It was only too obvious that the party was over. The front doors of the house were open and a line of cars and shining carriages was slowly moving forward. He hesitated and then went doggedly on. Women in sweeping evening dress and wrapped with furs were coming out, followed by the more somber figures of their men. A car or carriage door would slam, the line would move up, a footman would call a name. Chris stopped in the shadow of the shrubbery, watching this panoply of wealth and ease without envy, but with a sort of hard detachment. The contrast between all this and what he had just left was too great.

Almost at that point he turned back. He did not belong there, among people like this, devoted to the fine decorum of living. He belonged down the hill, where Jake lay still and rested, and his own small sign was the badge of service. He went on, however, doggedly waiting until the last carriage had swept proudly out into the night, and then presenting himself at the door to the eyes of a horrified manservant, dusty, untidy and with his white tie wildly awry.

"I'm sorry to be so late," he said. "I was expected to dinner, but I had an accident case. Will you say that I have come to make my apologies?"

"Certainly, sir. Come in. Mr. Lewis is just inside, sir."

He saw Staunton Lewis coming forward, inspecting him with penetrating eyes, but at least holding out his hand.

"Well, doctor, we had given you up."

"I'm frightfully sorry, sir. I was detained."

"You look to me as though you had been detained by a locomotive!" said Staunton, well fed and well humored for the moment, and still inspecting Chris. It was his first real view of Chris, and he eyed him with a certain amusement.

So this was the impudent young pup who had set Beverly on him, and who was according to Annie too proud to marry her. Well, he'd seen them like that before, young and uncompromising. It didn't last. Nothing lasted but place and power. He smiled.

"Beverly's in the drawing room," he said. "You can make your peace with her. My wife's gone up to bed. Nothing serious, I hope?"

"It was an accident case. A man struck by a trolley car."

Lewis became instantly alert. Men hit by trolley cars were apt to bring damage suits, or leave them behind them.

"Serious?"

"He died, I'm sorry to say. Nothing to do for him."

He told the story, and some of Lewis's after-dinner complacence faded, although he was still courteous as he led him into the drawing room and left him to make his apologies. Staunton himself went at once to his library and called a telephone number.

"Better get at it first thing in the morning," he said, after explaining. "Settle before some ambulance chaser gets to the family. And let me know what they'll take."

He did not rejoin Beverly and Chris. It did not occur to him to do so. He went upstairs and calmly and methodically prepared for bed. He was not particularly worried. He knew these trolley cases and the ease with which they were usually settled. If not, and it went to court— He yawned and wound his watch. He was not afraid of any court in the city, or in the state either, for that matter. Even that young fellow downstairs was on the city payroll now. Not a bad-looking lad, he reflected. If Beverly wanted him—

He wandered into Annie's room in his pajamas, still yawning.

"Young Arden's here," he said. "He was held up by an accident case."

Annie had taken off her dress. Now she held her negligee closely over her breast and looked at him. It was Christmas

Eve, and she always felt sentimental at that time; but to Staunton it was just another night after a dinner. Next year—but she would not think of that.

"Is Beverly still downstairs?"

"She is," he said, and going out again, closed the door between their respective rooms. It was always closed, that door. To him that was all it was, a closed door, to keep out Annie's reading light or to stop a draft. It was more to her, of course; it was a symbol, a dividing of two lives. Quite a handsome one, naturally, but there it was. She stood clutching her negligee and looking at it. Suppose she went in now, went in and told him her secret? Disturbed that smugness of his—for it would disturb him. He liked everything right and in its place. But she did not do it. Not yet, she thought. It was a weapon against him, and she might need it later.

When Martha came in she was entirely calm. . . .

Downstairs in the long drawing room Chris was being anything but calm, confronting a very lovely young woman in a rose taffeta dress who greeted him politely but without undue warmth.

"Well!" she said. "And is this the way you usually come to dinner parties, doctor?"

"Frightfully sorry again," he said. "I've already apologized to your father. If you say the word I'll go out and apologize to the servants too. I'd apologize to the dog if he was around. That's the state I'm in!"

She inspected him then, saw the tie, the dust, and even a small fleck of red on his shirt bosom. Saw more than that, for he was swaying slightly on his feet.

"Do you mind sitting down?" he said suddenly. "I've had a hard day. Sorry all over again."

He was still smiling, but she put him quickly into a chair and rang for some brandy. When she came back to him he tried to get up, but she held him down.

"Sit still and don't talk," she said. "You'll be all right in a minute. I'm the one to apologize."

He sat still, her hand on his shoulder, until the brandy came. Some day he would probably be ashamed, but now it was enough that she stood over him, her eyes anxious and certainly friendly. Oh, certainly friendly.

"Feel like a fool," he muttered. "Came up the hill too fast. But don't move, please! I'll faint on your hands if you do. That's a threat!"

That was how Holmes found them, coming in with the brandy. Being Holmes, however, he remained impassive under the strain, and when the brandy had revived him Chris told the story of the evening. She sat very still, listening, but when he came to Katie she stiffened slightly.

"She only said that you were busy," she put in.

"She was excited, poor kid. I gave her the devil, of course."

"But she's not a child."

The brandy on an empty stomach was having its effect, however. Chris felt extremely comfortable and relaxed.

"Let's forget her," he said drowsily. "It's Christmas Eve, and you're there and I'm here. What mortal man could ask any more?"

He leaned back and closed his eyes. The fire was warm and he felt very tired. He yawned and apologized.

"I've gone a little short on sleep lately," he said. "I'll be going on in a minute and let you get to bed."

He did not move, and Beverly sitting across from him was inspecting him closely. Thus relaxed he had changed, she thought. He looked older and not too happy, as though some of the relish had gone out of life for him. She felt a sudden tightening of the throat. Something had happened to him. Not only the accident that evening, but perhaps months of anxiety and hard work and—she suspected—bad food as well.

Suddenly she sat upright.

"Listen, doctor, did you have any dinner tonight?"

"I forget. I don't believe I did."

"You idiot! Why didn't you tell me?"

She disappeared, and he put his head back and closed his eyes. When she came back he was sound asleep in his chair. She sat down quietly and waited for him to rouse, watching him and protecting him, as women always protect their sleeping men. Yet there was nothing of that in her face when, at two o'clock in the morning, he opened his eyes and sat upright in his chair.

"Great Scott! How long have I been asleep?"

"Not long. And eat these sandwiches before you go. I've kept the coffee hot."

She was smiling, and he grinned back sheepishly.

"I ought to be shot," he said. "But not on an empty stomach. Even condemned men get a breakfast, don't they? And of course you are an angel of light and queen of all women."

He said it lightly, but she flushed as she poured his coffee.

"Have you forgiven us?"

"It's Christmas now, and all sins are forgiven on Christmas." He looked at her and dropped his bantering tone. "A very happy Christmas to you, my dear," he said gravely. "All that you want of life, and in abundance."

"And what shall I wish for you?"

He was still looking at her.

"That," he said, his lips smiling but his eyes still grave, "is a secret. A very profound secret."

She flushed again, but to his relief she smiled. They were back, thank God, back to the easy friendliness of the spring. Even as he thought that he wondered if it could mean anything to either of them. She was young, but how long would she wait, for him or any other man? And what had he to offer her, either now or in the future? Half a life. What was left from his own work. A tired man coming home, not even to her, but to anyone else who needed him.

It was almost three before he left. The servants had gone to bed, and in the hall he picked up his hat and stood gazing down at her. Then he stooped suddenly and kissed her.

"Sleep well, my dear," he said, and got himself out of the house. He heard the door close slowly behind him, and for a minute he was tempted to turn back. He did not however. He tramped down the hill to his own house, to find Caesar waiting for him inside, to discover in the hall mirror that his unruly hair was standing up over his head; and when he reached his room, to find that one of his socks was hanging to the mantel by a thumb tack, and stuffed with small lumpy parcels. Katie's work, he thought, and Katie's mute apology.

"The poor kid," he thought, and wondered if she was still awake. After all it was Christmas, and out of his superabundant happiness—

Katie however was asleep, and Caesar was shivering by the register in the floor. Then he remembered the neglected furnace, and swearing softly to himself went down the stairs to the dark and dirty cellar to stoke it furiously.

He carried two pictures to bed with him that night. One was of Beverly Lewis, closing her eyes under that kiss of his; a Beverly flushed and serious and always beyond his reach. The other was of a small shop and a squat middle-aged woman staring at him through the darkness.

"Oh, it's you, doctor! Is there anything wrong with the suit?"

"No, that's all right. Mrs. Ettenburg, I'm afraid I've brought you some bad news."

As he lay there in the dark, with that absurd sock hanging to the mantel, he could hear once again her voice, low, almost a whisper.

"Not Jake, doctor. Oh God, not Jake!"

Part II

THE TREE OF HEAVEN

CHAPTER XI

THE hospital treated Christmas with the proper combination of reverence and rejoicing. There were flowers on the center tables of the wards, and a small tree for the children's ward. The real celebration, however, took place in the big chapel on the lower floor. Here for days interns and nurses off duty had trimmed the big tree and wrapped small parcels; to each child a small toy and some fruit, to the men heavy woolen socks and to the women warm gloves or stockings.

There was a sort of frenzy of good works, a companionship shared by the engineer lighting the tree, by the head pharmacist who could play the piano, even by the orderlies, who slipped in on off moments to lend a hand on the ladders. There were rehearsals of carols too, and a relaxation of general discipline which did away for the time with the sharply drawn caste definitions of the hospital system.

Then, at ten oclock on Christmas morning, the lines began to form. Convalescents who could walk, convalescents in wheel chairs or on crutches, they waited their turn for the elevator.

"Merry Christmas, Joe."

"Merry Christmas to you all," Joe would say, grinning.

The nurses marshaled their motley crews; firm efficient young women in fresh uniforms, they were the captains of these irregular and shabby troops, the women in loose wrappers, the men in washed and faded hospital pants and shirts.

"Take your time, Lizzie. Don't push." "Watch yourself, Blake. This floor is slippery." "Make room for this chair, please."

Crutches, splints, wheel chairs, bandages, they moved

along. Here at last was a break in the monotony of their days, and once inside the chapel they eyed the tree with pleasure. It was gay and cheerful. It spoke somehow of hope, of life going on, and to a few perhaps of life everlasting. They were very quiet, content now to sit and look and listen. In the soft light from the tree their faces glowed with a new hope.

Chris, standing watching from the back, found them more touching than he would have a year before. He knew now from what they came, the pitiable background of their lives. He looked at the interns in their white clothes, so cocksure of themselves, each a ruler of sorts in his own small realm, and wondered about them. In a year or two they also would be on the outside looking in, looking back too, on the days when they were so confident of themselves, so cared for.

The service began. "Almighty God, Who hast given us Thine only-begotten Son to take our nature upon Him—"

He glanced about him. He saw Miss Simpson in the front row gazing intently at nothing, four of the interns anxiously clutching the sheet music of their quartet, the nurses unobtrusively keeping order, the rows of patients and of wheel chairs. It was familiar and yet strange, as though it had changed, or he had.

The staff came filtering in, to stand at the back of the room, and he ran his eyes over them; tall and thin, short and stout, he knew them all. Soon he would be one of them. How had they felt when they first went on service? Were they frightened, as he was? It was hard to believe, seeing them there. Perhaps in time a man developed an immunity, or a philosophy, to carry him through. But at first? The first day? He wondered.

The quartet was singing now. They sang very well, he thought. And there was a slight surge of motion among the patients, a relaxation, as though the morning's business would soon be over and the real excitement begin. Behind him in the hall was the muffled sound of small bells, and he knew that the hospital Santa Claus was waiting outside. When he turned he saw Beverly beside him.

She gave him a quick smile.

"I overslept," she whispered. "How pretty it is!"

"My fault. I must have nearly killed you last night."

She shook her head.

"You needed the rest. I didn't."

They stood side by side, friendly but silent, while excited sounds from the hall and the louder noise of the bells indicated the approach of the high point of the morning. When he glanced down at her he saw that she was very sober.

"They get so little," she said in a low voice, "and it means so much to them."

He saw that there were tears in her eyes, and that she was fumbling for a handkerchief. He got out his own, held it to show that it had not been used as a duster, and gave it to her. She was smiling when she returned it.

"I always cry at this," she whispered. "Excitement. I'm perfectly all right."

Santa Claus came in, portly with pillows and wildly jingling, and Christmas had come to the hospital. Stockings and woolen gloves, handkerchiefs and mufflers, toys for the children and an orange for everybody,—the largess was poured out and passed around. It was not much, but it was enough. It marked Christmas as a day of days; and when the lines re-formed each one carried something away with him, a gift and a memory. It was enough.

Some time during that confusion Beverly slipped away. Chris, turning to smile down at her, found her gone and knew that the day was over for him. He went about as usual, made his belated calls, and at noon sat down with Lily Walters and Katie to a dried and over-cooked turkey and what was meant to be a plum pudding. At his suggestion Miss Barker from next door had been invited, and he stood over the turkey flourishing his knife.

"Don't all of you ask for legs. I'm not carving a spider!"

But he could not upset the terrible decorum of the table. They spoke in low voices and used their knives and forks warily. And it ended in Lily insisting on reciting the morbid details of last night's tragedy, and on Katie hastily leaving the table. All in all the remainder of the day was a failure, but that night for the first time in weeks he dreamt of Beverly. It was hardly a dream. It came between waking and sleeping, when his defenses were down, and mixed up with his last thoughts, emerging from the rigid censorship of his conscious mind as it gradually let go, there came once again that old picture of her; not as he had seen her the night before, or that day, but as he had first beheld her, standing on his door step with that absurd dog under her arm and gazing up at him with her direct and honest eyes.

The next day he went again to see Jake's widow, and to feel bitterly that Staunton Lewis had again raised a barrier between Beverly and himself. For Rachel told him that the case with the traction company had already been settled, and he stared at her with blank eyes.

"Settled?"

"Yes, doctor. There was a man here early yesterday morning. And I needed the money."

"How much did you get?"

"Five hundred dollars."

As clearly as though he had been present he saw Staunton Lewis leaving him in the hall two nights before, and not going up the stairs. Going back instead to that library of his, and closing the door so that he could telephone. Telephone and settle—for five hundred dollars.

He looked around the empty shop, where a black cloth covered the canary's cage. Then with anger almost choking him he went out again. . . .

He made no attempt to see Beverly during the week that followed. Fortunately he was busy. Christmas had brought its toll to the city poor. Men had been drunk and abused their families, and children were sick of cheap candies. There was an epidemic of births, too; new lives coming in with the New Year.

"You've got a fine little girl."

"A girl! And some day she'll have to go through this!"

He would prop his feet on the side of the bed and sleep between pains. At night, with the brass ball on his bed anchored with adhesive plaster and his hands stiff with cold from the open window he would read surgery with fierce determination. "Following a longitudinal incision on the anterior wall—".

He carried on somehow, study, city cases, private work. Old Colonel Lee across the street, in the house with the immaculate curtains, secretly drinking himself to death and hiding his bottles against his two watchful daughters. "We don't know where he keeps it, doctor. We've even stolen his keys, but we can't find anything." Or he would come home with an hour or two for study, to find Miss Andrews, peering prim and angular out of the front office window from behind the curtain.

"Do you see that man standing across the street, doctor?"

He would look, obediently.

"Don't you think he's waiting for a street car?"

She would purse her lips, drop the curtain. "He followed me here, and I'm afraid to go out."

She was definitely psychopathic, but as she harmed no one except herself he could do nothing. Already Freud had delved into the mystery of the human mind, and recognized many of these border-line cases as wish fulfillments of one sort or another. He recognized her as the sexually starved creature she was, and giving up any hope of work, would talk to her gently and let her go.

She would go, as warily as she had come, into the desperate adventure of the street. Sometimes he went back with her, and safely home again she would lock her door, slip another bolt and running to a window peer out again.

"Mary, come here."

The maid would come on the run.

"Isn't that the man who tried to get in last week?"

"He's just the man who sells brushes, Miss Andrews. Now you take off your hat and I'll get you a cup of tea."

Chris would watch her, taking off her hat obediently, even relaxing after the strain of the last hour or two. But soon she would be up again, listening, looking out.

"Who rang the door bell, Mary?"

"The man to look at the gas meter."

"Are you sure that's what he is?"

"Well," Mary would say prosaically, "he's in the cellar now. I reckon he isn't after the coal."

When she seemed quiet again Chris would leave her and go back, but his hour was lost.

During that week also Betty Howard again offered her own and different problem. Having taken time off for Christmas, she came in gaily.

"Don't I get a big kiss for being a good girl?"

"Do you happen to think that's funny?"

She eyed him delightedly.

"I believe you are afraid of me!"

"I am indeed," he told her. "You aren't sick. It is merely playing a game, and a rather dirty game at that. How do you think I like sending bills to your father for this? I've been tempted more than once to tell him that it isn't honest money I'm getting."

She stayed away for a day or so after that, sulking. Then one day he came back to find her waiting for him and slightly defiant.

"You needn't look like that," she said. "I've got a cold this time. If you don't believe it, look at me!"

It was poor preparation for the work ahead, and that time after she had gone he found that his hands were shaking with pure nervous irritability, and surveyed them glumly.

"Good God," he thought, "I can't go into the operating room like that."

He gave up smoking that day, and as a consequence was

irritable to the point of frenzy. Caesar, sensitive to all his moods, retired to the kitchen and lay resignedly under the stove there. Lily Walters, moving about her duties, attempting to escape attention and become invisible by walking on her toes, drove him distracted.

Late in the afternoon of the last day of the year, with the prospect of going on duty at the hospital the next morning, before him, the unmarried daughter of old Joshua decided to have a baby on the shanty boat. Leaning over the side of the deck and dipping a pail of water for boiling out of the icy river, Chris articulately damned his job, the poor, the prophet, and the human race in general.

He was gentle with the girl, however, and when later on after a long struggle he had delivered a strong boy he held it so she could see it and smiled down at her.

"You'll have to tie a rope to him before long!" he told her. "This is no place to raise a baby."

"Father says he'll drown him anyhow. Maybe I'll save him the trouble. I've thought of it, for both of us."

It was late that night before he dared to leave her. She was quietly desperate, and he waited for Joshua until midnight. In the interval she told him her story. She had believed that the comet had meant the end of the world, and she had wanted to live before she died. But the comet had come and gone, and so had the child's father. Life was a dirty mess, she thought. Joshua had beaten her when he found how things were, and now—

Not until the midnight whistles had brought in the New Year and the old man had come back and been cajoled and threatened into reason did Chris leave her. The din was still going on when he reached the house and found a note in Katie's unformed hand on the battered hall table. "Please call Miss Lewis."

He looked at his watch. Characteristically Katie had not given the time of the call, and it was well after midnight. All at once he wanted to hear Beverly's voice; wanted it so much that it shook him. He picked up the receiver and made the call, to hear her voice at once and to fancy it rather unsteady, as was his own.

"Hello," he said. "I'm sorry to be so late. Is anything wrong?"

"Wrong? No. I thought—I wanted to say Happy New Year. That's all."

"The same to you, my dear, and many of them," he said soberly.

"And good luck tomorrow!"

"How can I help it, after this?"

It was not much. Certainly not much to cherish through the years, but he went upstairs that night with a feeling of renewed strength and a deep contentment; as though he no longer stood alone, as though indeed she had put a sword in his hand with which to conquer whatever lay ahead.

He was never to forget it. . . .

He was still calm the next morning. The nervous tremor had gone from his hands, and he shaved and dressed with unusual care. Katie, in the lower hall, saw him coming down and inspected him critically.

"What is it? A party?"

"You could call it that. I go on duty at the hospital today."

"And what might that mean?"

"All sorts of things you wouldn't like, my child. Two or three operations, probably, for one thing."

"And you're going to do them?"

"I am indeed," he told her solemnly.

"Then heaven help them!" she said, and slammed out the front door.

But he had other things than Katie to think of that morning. To the eye he might have been any young business man, walking briskly through the bracing winter air on his way to an office somewhere or other. To himself however he was taking the first step toward a larger and fuller life, a life not only of service but of gratified ambition; of going on and up, taking some time in Europe, being called in consultation, reading papers before the medical society. "In an experience of forty-odd cases, the following facts apparently developed—"

So grandiose had been his thoughts that he was shocked when, a block or so from the hospital, he found himself with a bad attack of nerves. His heart was beating wildly, his hands were damp with sweat. He stopped an steadied himself.

"Good Lord," he thought, "I'm scared. Scared as a kid."

He looked at his hands, which were shaking, and felt that his knees were uncertain under him. He was even slightly nauseated. He lighted a cigarette and went on, but the tobacco sickened him still more and at last he threw it away.

"A fine surgeon I am!" he thought disgustedly. "Sick. Sick at my stomach, by God! I'd look well, losing my breakfast on the street. What's the matter with me, anyhow?"

He straightened and walked on, but he did not entirely recover from his funk until he reached the hospital. Then suddenly he was himself again.

"Morning, Dave. How's the family?"

"Morning, doctor. Glad to know you're back, sir."

Yes, he was back home again, and the hospital reached out and welcomed him. In the office where he checked in was his name, new on the board, and Burnett, smiling and shaking hands.

"Congratulations, Arden."

"Thanks. I've been scared as hell."

"You'll be all right. Everybody goes through that, I expect. But there's a bit of bad luck; Doctor Grant meant to clean the operating slate for you so you'd have a day or two to get your bearings, but he's sick."

"Well, I suppose one way to learn to swim is to jump off the end of the dock!"

The first operation had been scheduled for ten o'clock, and it was almost that now. He found Williams in the hall waiting for him, and they went up together in the elevator. The usual hospital smells surrounded them, a mixture of disinfectants, drugs of all sorts, carbolic acid, hot water and strong scrubbing soap. Pungent and sharp it penetrated the cage, and went to Chris's head like wine.

"Getting off at the corner of the park, Joe."

"Yessir. And I'm surely glad to see you back, doctor."

"Still drinking the whisky out of the medicine baskets, I hear."

That too was an old joke between them. The Negro chuckled.

"Ain't none been missing that I hear of since you left, doctor."

They got off at the top floor. Chris was smiling, his hands steady, his head thrust forward. Williams, watching him, wondered if he had any nerves.

"Sorry you had to be pitchforked in like this, Chris."

"Probably the best way. Tell me what I've got."

He had, it appeared, three cases that morning, and Williams launched into explanations as Chris scrubbed up and got into his linen clothes, his cap and mask. Chris listened and nodded. It seemed amazing to him now that he had been afraid of this thing. It was his work. It was to be his life work. He drew a deep breath and threw out his chest.

"Ready? Come along," he said.

The operating room was waiting, spotless and gleaming. It looked like a stage set, with the nurses scattered here and there and Chris the star actor making his entrance. For a moment all movement ceased, all faces turned toward him. Then Miss Clarke the head nurse moved forward, quiet and competent.

"We're ready, doctor, and—we're all delighted to have you back."

He glanced around him. For a time now each year this was to be his kingdom. His word would be law, and these subjects of his in blue and white or in white would rush to obey it. He knew too that he was in their hands, as they were in his. They were friendly, these interns and nurses, but where once they had been indulgent now they would be watchful and critical. It was a closed world, protecting its own, and the staff men did not entirely belong. They came and went, the overlords of this small world, but they belonged outside, beyond its walls.

There was this knowledge in his eyes when they met Miss Clarke's, and she colored faintly under his quizzical gaze.

"That's very kind of you," he said. "I'll try not to throw things. All right, Williams."

The table was wheeled in, the anesthetist bending over it as it came. To the odors of steam and fresh linen was now added that of ether. The action on the stage accelerated, the characters moved swiftly for a moment. Then, as suddenly as it began, it ended. The movement froze about Chris, about the table, and about his first operation case as a member of the staff on that table. He lifted his head and looked about him. Everything was there. Everybody was ready.

He reached out his hand in its rubber glove and Williams handed him a scalpel.

CHAPTER XII

ON A MARCH night toward the end of his first term of service at the hospital, Chris sat at the desk in his back office and over a pipe reviewed his situation. The pipe was an indulgence, only to be used after the work of the day was over, and preferably with a window open. One window was opened now, and through it came on the brisk cold air the sounds of the street. They were familiar sounds now, the grating of stopping cars, the shouts of children playing in a late snow, even the bang with which Katie shut and locked the kitchen door for the night.

Around him the house was quiet. It exuded the odor of the Walters' old dusty carpets and a faint musty smell of mold from the uncemented cellar below. When he put his hand on his desk it encountered the familiar gritty film of dust, and after what had become a habit now he took out his handkerchief and wiped it. For the problem of the Walters family had not changed. It was what it had been, unsatisfactory and expensive; and in some ways it was worse. Katie had discovered the telephone as a means of communication and now spent long periods on it. He would call up his office to find the line busy, bang up the receiver, wait and call again. Once she was talking to a boy, and he was cut in on the line.

Here was a new Katie, coquettish and slightly affected, and he listened to her grimly.

"I don't see how you can say that. I thought I looked terrible. Say, listen, Jim. He's out tonight at a meeting. You can come around if you like. I'll have the front office."

He had read the riot act to her when he got home that day, and she turned on him furiously.

"What do you want me to do?" she demanded. "Sit on a park bench?"

"You have the dining room."

"With mother sitting there all evening! Thanks."

In the end he had compromised. She could use the waiting room after office hours in the evening, but it was to be tidy and aired before he came in. In her way she was living up to the agreement, but the room had about it now a consistent aroma of cheap perfume and cheaper cigarettes. Nevertheless he was relieved. Better for her to see boys of her own age than to cherish any silly romantic dream about himself. Well, that was over, thank God.

He would have been shocked had anyone told him then that it was far from over, so far as Katie was concerned. That lying awake in her tumbled bed above she was listening as usual for the sound of his feet as he came up the stairs, for the final closing of his door. Or that only then, with the comfortable sense of his nearness, she would turn over and go to sleep. Nevertheless he was disturbed about her. She was growing up. Even he could see that. And she was always somewhere underfoot. It was as though by saving her he had bought her.

She amused him at times. He treated her as he would treat a child, usually with the facetious cheerfulness she loathed.

"Still pouting, Katie! You'll spoil your mouth, you know."

"It's my mouth, isn't it?"

"Other people have to look at it!"

It was like a battle between them, light-hearted on his part but a thing of deadly seriousness to her. Alternately she hated and adored him.

"He thinks he's God Almighty, and we're just dirt," she would say to Lily.

"Don't talk like that, and pull that kimono around you. Have you no modesty?"

"He never sees me. Don't worry."

At the first opportunity she would be back in the empty office again, touching softly his old pipe, his office coat, his pen. She was Katie, of course. She would follow this by reading his case records in their filing box, and glance through his books for pictures; for she was intensely and insatiably curious. Chris, coming in, would find things out of place and surmise what had happened, but he felt helpless; and that night, sitting there alone, he dismissed the whole Walters family with a gesture. Good or bad he had them, to feed and shelter and even to clothe. He had them. They could not have him.

It was bill night. Before him lay his small day book, his big ledger, and the blanks which read "To professional services," and in a corner, in very small letters, "an itemized statement will be rendered if desired." He made no move to fill them in, however. It was work he hated, this appraising of his labor in dollars, the reduction of the vast drama of living and even dying into terms of money. He pushed them aside impatiently and sat drawing at his dead pipe.

Professionally he was doing better than most. He had his city job and the hospital work. He was even solvent, although he had been obliged to sacrifice the suit he needed to buy Katie a winter coat. He grinned at that memory, for a day or so later he had seen Katie in her new finery on the street accompanied by an apparently infatuated youth, and had bought himself a new dollar necktie immediately afterwards, as a sheer act of self-assertion.

He was doing well at the hospital. Nothing startling, but substantially well. The winter service was always a heavy one, fractures on the ice, skidding automobiles, even now and then some poor devil found almost frozen, and perhaps an amputation to follow. The mills and the railroads too contributed their quota; and one night there was a train wreck and he lost four out of six cases, and found himself toward dawn standing by the bank of the river, undecided whether to give up surgery altogether or to jump into the icy stream and give up everything else.

He had learned a lot, and had kept his head and his temper—except for that one time when, about to close an abdomen, the sponge count was verified and only his quick eye discovered the corner of a bit of gauze before it was too late. He stiffened and looked at the nurse who had made the count.

"Sure of that, are you?"

"Yes, doctor."

"Then you're a fool, and a goddam dangerous one at that."

He pulled out the gauze sponge and the nurse had an attack of hysterical crying in the hall. He was still shaking with anger while he finished his work, but later on he interceded for her with Miss Simpson.

"She'll be safer now than she ever was before," he said. "And I lost my temper. I'm sorry about that."

"Better your temper than a patient," said Miss Nettie drily.

He loved his work. He had the hands of the born surgeon, both gentle and strong. And, although he was unconscious of it, the dramatic side of the business appealed to him. When at night he rode up in the elevator past the silent floors to the operating room the sense of being a part of the drama of sheer survival was strong in him. He worked better at night; as though the interference of the world outside had ended with its noise, and there was only himself and the job to be done.

Under the glare of the dome over the table every detail stood out in strong relief, the yellow waxy look of hands in rubber gloves, the fine red line following the knife, the sterile towels, the long retractors, the sponge holders, the neat row of artery clips laid back as the work went on. The room would be hot from the sterilizer room next door, the carriers would come and go with their heated burden of towels, sheets and dressings, and all movement was silent and deliberate and careful. Outside people were living casually, were sleeping or dancing or praying, but here nothing must be casual.

"All right. Sutures."

"Silk or catgut?"

"Gut."

He would straighten, draw a long breath, bend again. Sutures, dressings, adhesive, bandage. Then slowly he would come back to the world again, grin at the assistants, slip off his gloves, wait until the tapes at the back of his long operating coat had been untied.

"How long?"

"Forty minutes, doctor."

It might have been ten minutes or ten hours; so had his world contracted.

Sometimes after it was all over, he would light a cigarette and go onto the roof; wanting to be alone under the stars, or at dawn to see hope coming again with a new day. All around him lay the quiet city, like a world to be conquered, and for a moment or two he would feel that it lay at his feet. Then he would draw a deep breath, to get rid of this delusion of grandeur as well as the sweetish ether in his lungs, and go down cheerfully to drink endless cups of hot coffee.

He would stretch and yawn luxuriously.

"God, I'm tired. I could sleep for a week."

Going home through the night or the gray early morning the exaltation would die, and as he neared the house he would become once again merely an everyday young man, worrying about coal for the furnace or the rent, and with a feeling that the curtain had rung down on something rather magnificent and had left him somewhere outside in the dark.

That was the professional side of his life. What about the other?

He stirred in his chair. The street was quiet now, the children gone, and the snow had turned to a fine rain and was beating in at the window. He got up and closed it, and took a turn or two about the room.

Somehow, somewhere, the brief intimacy between Beverly Lewis and himself had been lost. For one thing, he had been incredibly busy; and for another, it was the season and she was popular. Now and then at night on his way home he saw some house lighted, an awning at the door and the usual line of cars and carriages waiting; and surmised that she was inside. Once indeed he even saw her, a festive figure in an ermine wrap, with two or three men putting her into her car. Chris, stopping in the shadow across the street, had watched her until the car had picked her up and gone on.

"That's her life," he thought as he went on, "and this is mine. Well, to hell with it!"

He had seen her, of course. Once or twice he had gone to the house, in response to a call or a note, but the season was on and she was never alone. He would go in, very stiff and straight in his old clothes, to the sound of talk and laughter and the cheerful tinkle of ice in glasses. But although she was glad to see him and showed it, even his youth and his good looks could not entirely offset the fact that he was a worker among the drones.

"What? No liquor? Not sick, are you?"

"Working hours," he would say, with his disarming smile. "I do my hard drinking at night."

She watched him. He towered over their silliness and frivolity like a young giant, but when they found out what he was they affected to find it slightly humorous.

"My God, a doctor! You don't look like one."

"Why not?"

"Well, where's the good old beard, or whatever it is?"

"Give me time, can't you?"

He was indulgent, like some big mastiff with puppies playing about him, but he was not entirely comfortable among them. It was not only that they disliked illness and therefore his profession, or even that laughing at a thing the mind does not comprehend is one method of overcoming a sense of inferiority. It was because they had nothing in common with him, or thought so; as if he belonged to a class apart, he thought resentfully. As if he never had played a game of golf, or football at college; as if, indeed, having become a doctor, he had in some strange way become less a man.

Looking back later on all that he was to see was that he had not been entirely fair to them or to himself; and that the real gulf lay, not in their failure to recognize that medicine was a science—they respected science—but between their frivolity and his own life-and-death obligation to society.

"I'm afraid to talk to you, doctor!"

"Why?"

"You'll think I'm so frightfully silly."

"Try it and see!"

They would drift away, those pretty girls in the Lewis house, to watch him from a distance, to admire him—although he did not know that—and to discuss him at length among themselves. They did not come back, or when they did it was to be demure and tactful.

"Do tell me about your work. Do you really cut people open?"

"Not always. Quite a lot escape me. Of course now and then—"

"I knew you wouldn't take me seriously."

"Great Scott, am I only a man or only a job?" he would say, exasperated.

Girls and young women drinking tea or sherry, men with highballs in their hands, someone banging a piano, abstracted couples in corners or on the stairs, and a tall devil-may-care youth called Jerry Ames hanging over Beverly as though she belonged to him—that was his memory of those afternoons at the Lewis house. Then one night he was to go there alone and Beverly had promised him a quiet evening; and of all things on earth he had fallen asleep on a street car and wakened at the end of the line, miles out of town.

He telephoned as soon as he could, but she was annoyed, and showed it.

"What in the world happened? Where are you?"

"I don't know, exactly."

"You don't *know*?"

"Only approximately. You see, I was on a car, hurrying home for an evening with you. Then I shut my eyes for a minute—only a minute—and when I opened them again I was here. The magic carpet. No less."

"You went asleep?" she said incredulously. "That's not very flattering to me, is it? Of course, if you think it's funny—"

"Funny! My dear girl. I'm laughing for fear I'll weep."

She had laughed too at that, but he knew her pride, and she had not repeated the invitation. Well, to hell with that, too. What was he to her or to that group around her, but something between a butcher and a glorified midwife. Young Ames grinning at him:

"How's the baby business these days?"

"Still paying dividends."

"By Jove, you fellows have a cinch. You get us coming am going. Even nature works for you!"

"We have to help her a bit now and then."

Idle talk. Young Ames smiling over his glass, but watching him, eying him, appraising him. Not unamiably, but as one opponent might measure another.

"Better change your mind and have a drink."

"I have some calls to make. I'll take tea instead." And even that, his inability to drink during working hours, marking him off, setting him aside.

Not coherent thinking, all this. It was a series of pictures in his mind; of Beverly, cool and lovely, trying to marshal her disorderly horde, of occasional glimpses of her mother, and even one encounter with Staunton Lewis in the hall, and his own sudden rigidity when he remembered Jake.

"Pretty noisy crowd, doctor."

"They seem to like it," said Chris drily, and passed on.

Oh, for God's sake stop it, he thought. She's not for me, nor I for her. But his mind went on, automatically. It was not that she would take the high road while he took the low. It was the question of two lives with different objectives, not to be reconciled. Every woman, Beverly or any other, would demand time, claim the right to a love and her own romance. And what could he bring her? A tired man, irritable at times, worn with the burden of other people's troubles; a man who battled all day for power over sickness and death, and only dared to abdicate at night when at last he slept.

He remembered one of the interns months before, laying down the law after the fashion of all interns.

"We doctors make rotten husbands."

"The hell we do. Who told you that?"

"Well, look at it. A man who is really set on getting somewhere in medicine or surgery can have only one job, and that's it. He can't strike a balance. Either he's a good husband or he's a good doctor. He can't be both."

He grunted and got up. The room was cold, and after damning the furnace he went down and stoked it. It did not soothe him to find that the light in the cellar had been left burning, or that the coal in the corner was getting low again. Nobody had taken out the ashes, and after a momentary hesitation he took off his coat and did that also. But the contrast between his recent memories of the Lewis house and his present occupation set him to grinning.

"I'll be a damn good wife to somebody if I keep on," he thought, and carried the ashes up the cellar stairs. In the kitchen as he turned on the light there was the usual soft scuffling of cockroaches on the linoleum as they fled to shelter, and an unwashed coffee pot sat on the stove. There was nothing new in all this, however, so he merely shrugged and, opening the door, carried the cans out onto the back porch.

He put down the ashes and standing there proceeded to dust himself as well as he could. Outlined against the soft snow in the yard was the shed where Henry had pursued his futile experiments, and he stood gazing at it and thinking of the legacy he had left him. It was strange, he considered, that Henry dead should be so much more potent than Henry living; that he had passed on comfortably through some mysterious door to freedom, and by the mere act of doing so had left him in chains.

He stared at the shed more closely. Certainly it had an unusual aspect. The next moment Caesar growled, a figure detached itself from the shadows and stepped into the light, and a familiar voice spoke.

"Hello, doc," it said. "Family still here?"

It was Dick. A different Dick, nattily dressed, but looking up at him with shifty eyes and his old impudent grin. "I've been throwing pebbles at the window up there, but they sleep pretty sound. Old man's tight again, I suppose?"

Chris looked down at him with shocked distaste. "The old man's dead, Dick."

"Dead! When'd that happen?"

"Soon after you left."

It was characteristic of Dick to express no grief, nor to feel any. He looked thoughtful for a moment and then came up the steps.

"Might as well see mother. She still here?"

"She is still here."

He looked relieved at that, and stepped past Chris into the kitchen. "Same old smell," he commented briefly. "Jeez, I'd know mother's kitchen with my eyes shut. Well, I'll go up, doc. 'Night. I suppose my old room's still there?"

Sudden anger flared in Chris. He blocked the way to the back stairs with his body, and confronted Dick with his hands clenched in his pockets, afraid to draw them out.

"The room is there, but you're not using it. Get that, and get it now."

"Aw say, doc—"

"You can see your mother and sister, and then you're getting out. I'm supporting them, but I'm damned if I support you too."

"Who asked you to?"

"That's fine! And that's all there is to it. If I find you sleeping in that room I'll drop you out the window. That goes for tonight and all the other nights."

He waited until Dick had gone up the back stairs. Then he moved forward, putting out the lights as he went, and climbed rather heavily up the stairs. At Katie's door he stopped and rapped.

"Yes?"

"Dick's back."

"Oh, my God! Did you let him in?"

"He's with your mother. I've told him he can't stay."

"You bet your life he won't stay," said Katie. "If he tries it I'll let you know."

Dick did not stay. Chris, falling into a heavy sleep after an hour or two of waiting, wakened in the morning to find him gone, and that his own pockets had been neatly rifled of all the money he possessed.

He went down to his breakfast in a fury of indignation, slamming his bedroom door behind him and stalking down the stairs like the very majesty of the law itself. Nevertheless Lily defeated him that morning, as up to the very end of her life she was to defeat him. She was overflowing with happiness. Her faded eyes shone, and she had even tried to make herself neat. She beamed at him as she brought in his coffee.

"Wasn't it wonderful, doctor? And he looked so well, too. Did you notice that suit he had on?"

"Very good suit. Better than mine! Is he working?"

"He has been. He's a good boy, doctor. He even left me a little money. And he says there will be more where it came from."

Chris smiled grimly.

"Did he tell you to tell me that?"

"Well, he did. He said—"

But Chris was laughing. The impudence of Dick's farewell was part and parcel of his whole domestic situation. He laughed helplessly and almost hysterically, until even Lily became suspicious.

"I don't see what's funny, doctor."

"I'm sorry. I'm not laughing about Dick. Heaven forbid that I should laugh about Dick. He's been no laughing matter."

He sobered, but she was still puzzled when she left the room. And Chris knew then that he could never tell her the truth. She had too little to take away what was left.

CHAPTER XIII

FOR all its apparent gaiety, the spring opened rather cheerlessly in the house on the hill. Beverly, watching her mother, found her languid and withdrawn, and suspected that she was sleeping badly. She was eating very little too. Beverly would go in after breakfast to find the tray untouched beside the bed, and her mother's eyes gazing intently at the new green buds on the trees outside.

"You ought to try to eat, mother."

"I'm not hungry. I had some coffee."

Later in the day she would get up, bathe slowly and carefully, dress meticulously. She had lost weight and her handsome dresses hung loose on her, but her pallor was so marked that she had bought a box of rouge and kept it carefully hidden. Now when she sat in front of her dressing table she rubbed in a little of the color, smoothing it carefully with her well-kept hands and then examining herself in a strong light. She could deceive Staunton—he had not really seen her for years—but she was afraid of Beverly's young eyes. Her fear of discovery was far greater than her fear of death.

How long she could keep up the masquerade she did not know. She was a strong woman and all this was new to her. But it would last for a while, and in the interval—

She made her decision carefully. There had been a time when something might have been done, but it would have meant mutilation and there was no guarantee of cure; so months before she had sat in her chair in a New York surgeon's office and had calmly shaken her head.

"Not now. Perhaps later. You see,"—she paused, groping for words—"it isn't only that I hate the idea. I'm afraid, of course. But even you admit that it is rather late, and I should like to go on as long as possible. Maybe you find that hard to understand, but a woman might, I think. You see, the instinct for perfection can be a very terrible thing."

He stared at her.

"You are not telling me that you are weighing your life against a slight mutilation!"

She smiled faintly.

"A chance for life, and not a good one. No, doctor, I was thinking of my husband."

She went away then, without giving her name, and walked the streets for hours. Not that she cared so greatly to live. The zest for living had left her with her youth. Staunton could waken in the morning to a new day, a day in which to renew his battle for place and power. She rose only to another day in which to do him honor; the house, the grounds, the heavy ponderous dinners were obeisance to him. She had never resented it, although sometimes she had wondered if he knew the size of that burden or her own lack of interest in this panoply of living.

She walked along in her handsome furs; block after block, stores and people, carriages, wagons, automobiles, a wedding party coming out of a church, a woman shaking a crying child, a hand organ and a small monkey. Life all around her, and death in her breast. Staunton, fastidious and resentful of anything that disturbed the order of his days. Beverly, vaguely suspicious and alarmed. Old Martha, who knew now and was praying for her in silence and alone. And a small stabbing pain which made her draw back from her clothing and stop in a drug store to buy the bromide which would do little or nothing to allay it.

That was when she had bought the rouge.

She went home after that, outwardly unchanged. She was essentially a simple woman. For years in her leisure she had made layettes for the nameless babies born at the hospital, and some of her thwarted maternity went into those small garments. Now she turned to them again, sitting all day by her window, sewing her fine stitches and making such plans as she dared. When spring began to come she watched it from her window, knowing that it was her last one, as though to carry away with her some indelible picture. But she was practical too, and her time was getting short. One night she mentioned Chris to Beverly; sitting at her toilet table, creaming her haggard face carefully and avoiding Beverly's eyes.

"I liked your young doctor, Beverly. What's become of him?"

"He's busy, I suppose. And he's not mine, mother."

"Doctors make good husbands."

"Good gracious, mother," said Beverly, and colored hotly. "He has no idea of marrying me."

"I don't see why not."

"He has no intention of marrying anybody. He won't be able to marry for years."

"Not even if you—had an allowance?"

Beverly's face set.

"Do you think he would live on our money, mother? He would starve first."

"Has he said that?"

"He doesn't have to say it. I can see it. And he detests father. I'm sorry, mother, but that's true. Even if he cared for me, which he doesn't—"

"He wouldn't be marrying your father, Beverly."

Beverly leaned down and kissed her.

"Look here," she said severely. "He'll marry when he wants and whoever he wants. He's that sort. And don't throw me at his head. You'd only get me back again, in a hurry."

Nevertheless, something of precisely that sort was forming in Annie Lewis's anxious mind, and one night soon after she slipped out of the house and went down the hill. She moved slowly, looking down at the furnaces where a blast now and then shot a red glow into the sky, smelling the fresh spring she could not see, and stopping every so often to hold that pendulous troublesome breast of hers. She was trembling when she reached Chris's house, and she waited a moment on the door step before she rang the bell.

When Chris opened the door, however, she was smiling.

"I'm frightfully late, doctor. If you are busy—"

"Come in," said Chris. "I'm not busy at all. But don't tell me you are a patient!"

"I really came to talk to you. But I suppose I am, in a way."

He inspected her as she moved in her trailing dress into the back office. He saw at once that she was thinner, and that she moved carefully, like a woman who was saving herself from something. But she was still smiling as he put her into a chair.

"I have disturbed you. Look at that bag."

"Doing my spring house-cleaning," he told her cheerfully. "I didn't find a rusty horseshoe, such as an uncle of mine carried in his saddlebags; but I found almost everything else."

She glanced at the articles spread out on the desk, the obstetric forceps in their towel, the stethoscope, the hypodermic case, bandages and dressings. And from them she looked up into Chris's face. Something there gave her confidence. It was a grave dependable face, already etched from nose to mouth with faint lines. She could trust this man, and all at once she felt an overwhelming desire to trust somebody. She kept her eyes on his.

"I want something for pain, doctor."

"What kind of pain?"

Her determination weakened. She hesitated.

"Do you mind terribly if I don't tell you? Just pain. I need sleep, doctor, and I don't know what to take."

He shook his head.

"That's not fair to either of us, Mrs. Lewis. Pain means something. It's a symptom, not a disease. To relieve it for a few hours isn't to cure it."

She had gone even paler, and now she made a half-movement to get up. Then she thought better of it.

"Perhaps I'd better tell you," she said. "But before I do that I want your solemn promise to keep my secret. That sounds rather melodramatic, but—I mean it, doctor."

"That's understood, of course," he agreed, quietly.

"I'm afraid I want more than that. I don't want Beverly to know, or Mr. Lewis. Not yet, at least. And I must be certain they won't."

He stared at her. He saw that her hands were shaking and that her mouth was quivering. But she steadied her voice.

"It is too late to do anything," she said quietly. "And Beverly is young. Also my husband has a horror of anything of the sort. I would like them to—I would like to carry on as long as I can. Surely you can understand that."

"I can understand it. Don't expect me to agree with it. If there is anything to be done—"

"There is nothing to be done."

"Won't you let me find that out for myself?"

She was stubborn, however. She had not come for a diagnosis. Unfortunately she already knew what was wrong. She had seen a man in New York. She had come for relief, something to stop the pain. And there were ethics in his profession, weren't there? He could not tell unless she gave him permission. All this in her quiet voice, with Chris puzzled and anxious across the desk.

"There are no ethics to permit anyone to commit suicide," he told her bluntly. "What did your New York man say?"

She paused before she answered.

"He thought it might possibly be operable then. But I refused."

"In God's name, why?"

She had thought there might be some other way out, it appeared. She had tried some advertised cures, but they were painful and useless, as she knew now. Chris, listening incredulously, saw behind all this something more than the eternal shame and secrecy of women in her condition, and was filled with consternation. What sort of man was Lewis anyhow, that he must be saved a knowledge like this?

"He doesn't suspect anything?"

"Nobody suspects. Martha knows. That's all."

However, he would give her no opiate until he had examined her, and at last reluctantly she allowed him to do so. When he straightened it was to find her watching him with her faint smile.

"You see, I was right, wasn't I?"

"I'd like another opinion on it," he said cautiously. "In any event something ought to be done, and done at once. At least it—"

"At least it would give me a few more months of this! Do you think I want that?"

"You have no right to commit suicide."

"That's rather a debatable point, isn't it?"

He made an angry movement. These soft obstinate women, with their gentle faces and implacable determination! And Beverly's mother; Beverly with this ahead of her! He sat frowning across the desk, and once more she smiled at him.

"You don't approve of me, do you, doctor?"

"I don't understand you. That's all. To let yourself go like this, when you have a husband and a child—surely you owed them something."

"I wanted Beverly to be happy as long as possible, and I had hoped she would marry before this became—acute. Nature does a great deal for us, doctor. If she could have married and had children of her own it would have been more bearable. I had even hoped—"

He glanced up at her. She was still smiling, but rather diffidently now.

"Yes?"

"I had even hoped that you and she would care for each other. I suppose I am very foolish, but at least—as things are—I can afford to be candid."

He knew then why she had come. The pain was real; the condition was there. But it was Beverly and Beverly's problem which had brought her to him. For the moment his surprise was dominated by his pity for her. She sat across from him, one hand laid lightly across that breast of hers, and watched him with eyes that were as candid as Beverly's and even younger in their pain.

"I am shameless, of course, doctor. But at night when I can't sleep I lie awake and worry about her. My husband"—she hesitated—"my husband will do very well. He will miss me in some ways, but he has his business and his friends. He—" She smiled again, her faint apologetic smile. "It is a long time since he has really cared for me."

She glanced at him, but he said nothing.

"I have always wanted a son," she said. "I think things would have been different if I had had a son. Beverly is closer to her father than she is to me. She loves me, but girls are often like that." And when he still said nothing, for sheer lack of anything to say: "That is why I have talked like this tonight, doctor. She is like her father. She wants a great deal out of life. She needs a man she can look up to, and someone who will look after her. The ones she knows—"

Then she saw Chris's face, and her voice trailed off. She pulled her wrap around her shoulders, and prepared to rise. Her eyes were tired and defeated.

"I suppose I have made a mistake. I often do. I am not a very clever woman, doctor. Please forget all this."

He was on his feet instantly and around to where she sat. With a queer boyish awkwardness he stooped and put an arm around her shoulders.

"Mistake? What mistake? Why not be honest? You know I care for her. You know that I'd ask nothing better than to care for her all her life, if she would have me. But—"

"But what?"

"I suppose it's my damnable pride," he said. "I want

to support my wife when I marry. A few years and I could do that, but now—"

"I cannot wait a few years," she said quietly, and got up. "I have suffered a long time for one man's pride, doctor. It has done many things for him, but it has not made him happy. Or me."

He hesitated, looking at her.

"I can't make terms with you," he said. "Not with things like this. You know that I care for her, and that, God willing, I'd care for her to the end of her life, or mine. If I want to do that in my own way—"

"Why not do it in your own way?"

Then, and only then, he agreed. Looking back he was to see that scene as a strange one, and his own part in it not particularly noble. But the whole situation was unreal. He was slightly dazed. Even when she swayed slightly and he held her in his arms to steady her, he found his new status difficult to comprehend.

"I shall sleep tonight, doctor."

"She may not take me. Remember that."

"I think she will. You are big and gentle. Big men are always gentle, I think."

"I'll do my best, my dear. You can trust me."

It was still unreal to him when he took her home that night, going slowly so as not to tire her. Now and then he stopped, on one excuse or another, to let her rest.

"Look at the city lights. Like stars in a pond, aren't they?" Or: "I'm sorry. I'll have to tie my shoe." Not a word of what was uppermost in both their minds, until at last they reached the door of her house. Then she put out a hand and laid it on his arm.

"Good night, Chris. May I call you Chris now? And God bless you."

He did not let her go at once, however. They stood in the driveway like two conspirators, the night wind blowing her light draperies about her, while he urged her to get another opinion, to do something, anything.

"Why not try Grant? He's a good man."

In the end she agreed; but as he went down the hill again he knew that she expected nothing from another opinion, nor indeed from life itself. Not any more. She was clearing her way, laying her course to the end. He was so absorbed in her problem that he was halfway home before he remembered Beverly and his promise.

"To marry her and take care of her!" he thought. "On what? With what? Not with Lewis's money, by God! Not with his dirty money."

He walked the floor of his office that night for hours, an empty pipe clenched in his teeth. Sometimes he thought of Beverly, trying to fit her into his house and into his life, but he had had no preparation for what had happened, and no assurance whatever that she would accept him. Curiously enough, she had never seemed so remote as on that night when he had promised to marry her if she would have him; as though his dream had been more real than reality. He was thinking of her, but he was more aware of Annie Lewis, going back alone to her room and her bed, to be still alone when she had reached them. A door shut somewhere, and her husband beyond it, small and tight and comfortable, while she lay awake in the dark.

Perhaps all marriage was like that, the man caring most at the start, giving up his liberty and doubling his burdens. Then as the years went on the woman growing accustomed to his caring, more and more dependent on him, and then watching him escape her, leaving her in the end alone.

He registered a small vow that night that if Beverly cared for him life would not be like that for her.

CHAPTER XIV

IT was shortly after that that old Dave Mortimer died. Chris, going home after his morning calls, found a letter from Letitia, written in her crabbed old hand. "Doctor," she wrote, "is not so well this year. He is over eighty now, and as he often talks about you I know he would like to see you. He has made no calls for a year or so, but people still come to the office and they tire him. I wish you could come and talk to him, Chris. It's time he took a rest."

Over eighty and still working. Chris stood still, the letter in his hand, and considered that. Some of his arrogance of youth died in the face of that sixty years of service. He felt guilty, too. He had not written since his reply to David the summer before, although somewhere there was a letter from Hiram stating that his father had bought a car and that he drove it exactly as he had ridden his horses, into and over ditches and across fields. "Every now and then he gets into trouble and has to be hauled out," Hiram had written; and Chris had a vision of that indomitable old figure, going hell-for-leather by the straightest route he knew to trouble, any trouble, all trouble.

He took a train that same night, having arranged with Jenkins for his city work and with young Lawrence—a new man down the street—for emergencies; and the next morning he was getting off at the small country station, hardly more than a platform, and shaking hands with Hiram Mortimer.

"Well, Hi!" he said. "How are you? And how's the family?"

"Fine," said Hiram. "Old folks are getting on, of course."

That was about all. Hiram was taciturn as usual. His mother wanted his father to rest now, but there wasn't a chance.

Old man wanted to die in harness and likely would. Always had done what he wanted anyhow.

The car bumped along the dirt road and into the village. It looked small and shabby to Chris; surely a narrow field for sixty years of effort. He remembered that old Dave's field had not been the village, but the county.

"Remember the night we found your father in the ditch, Hi?"

"Which one was that? He's been in ditches all his life. Ain't more than a year since we pulled him out of one with this car on top of him."

"Great Scott, was he hurt?"

"Not so he couldn't swear," said Hi with a modest pride.

The house was on a dirt road leading from the end of the main street, with the big farm behind and beyond it. House and farm looked well kept and thrifty, and two or three cars parked by the office door showed that old Dave was still in harness. Nevertheless Chris was startled when he saw him. His big frame was as huge as ever, but the flesh had gone off it. Only his eyes, piercing and direct, were still young.

"Well, Chris, grown up, haven't you?"

"Time passes, sir. I'm almost thirty."

"Thirty!" said old Dave. "You're a child, Chris. A babe in arms. A man doesn't know anything until he's sixty. He's got women out of his blood by that time."

He shouted with laughter as Chris flushed.

"Hit you there, eh? Sit down. I suppose Letty sent for you. Well, it's no good, Chris. I owe these people something. Some of them owe me too! Always have and always will. But I'm not quitting until I have to. Now what about yourself?"

They talked a good bit through the day. Now and then a car or buggy would drive up and once Chris was called in to see the result of a Colles's fracture of the wrist, finely set and mended. Old Dave watched him with twinkling eyes.

"Just as much skill required if a man falls off a haystack

as if he'd slipped on a city pavement," he said cheerfully. "And when I've got to use a machine instead of my fingers to tell me where the break is, then I'll retire and go to knitting socks."

"Not all men have your hands."

"Why not? They ought to have. Lot of young cubs these days, depending on serums and vaccines and laboratories and God knows what, instead of using their brains."

Later on he sobered, and Chris was surprised at the breadth of his knowledge. He took and read the medical and surgical journals, and he had evolved theories of his own which Chris always remembered.

"Take the quacks," he said. "We can learn from them, if only where we are failing. Every successful quack is an admission of failure by our lot. Why? Because they claim to do what we know we can't do."

He had other ideas. "Look at germs," he said. "Why aren't we all dead of germs? Because we set up an immunity to them? Well, maybe. But maybe the Big Man has got something else too. Maybe he's put something into Nature to kill them. Sunlight? I don't know. Some principle or other, anyhow. They'll find it some day. I won't live to see it, but you may."

And years later, watching the laboratories laboring over their various bacteriophages, Chris remembered old Dave Mortimer, sitting back in his chair with a halo of sunlight around his head and a toddy at his elbow, vigorously prophesying.

Only before he left did Dave touch on Chris's personal life. He did it with his customary directness.

"What about women? Trouble you?"

"I've been too busy to worry much."

But he colored, and David laughed.

"Just be careful, boy," he said. "Most of these city hoity-toities won't ever know what you're thinking about. Or care. Get a wife who'll travel the whole road with you. And it's no easy road."

After supper the two men sat together on the porch. Inside the house Chris could hear Letitia moving about. She was past seventy, but she still did her own housework. Old Dave seemed to be listening too, as though the sounds were a part of the familiar background of his life but now newly significant.

"She'll take it hard when I'm gone, Chris."

"You're good for a long time yet."

David shook his head, but he did not speak of Letitia again. He watched the sun disappear and the golden afterglow which followed it.

"If I'd been God," he said rather somberly, "I'd have fixed a lot of things that need fixing. I'd like to have been God, Chris."

Chris never saw him again alive, but going back on the train that night he felt humble before those long years of service. What was he, with his ambitions and hopes, but a man in what might some day be a good business. Lying there in the smoky darkness of his berth, his long body at an angle to accommodate it, he thought of Letitia; her small indomitable old body, bent with a thousand burdens not her own; saw her face when the mare came home that night years ago, with a saddle but no rider; saw her indomitably bearing and rearing tall sons, working in the house, helping in the office.

"Pour some more chloroform on that towel, Letty." Or: "For God's sake, can't you hold the end of that bandage?" Not a fair picture, perhaps, but there it was. Meals delayed or never served. Getting up at night to give old Dave some badly needed food. Sending the boys hotfoot to find their father in some emergency or other. She had lived a vicarious life always, the life of her children and of her husband, but also the life of the town and of the surrounding countryside. There was a story that more than once old Dave had taken the very blankets off her bed and carried them out to some poor household or other.

Nevertheless, Chris felt that David Mortimer had left behind him something of triumph, of victory. It was in them both, that look of work well done and now harvest and the setting sun.

"God bless you, boy. I may not see you again."

"Don't talk like that, sir. You're a better man than I am. Arteries of a boy."

"Well, perhaps. . . ."

Chris went back, to his work and to occasional visits to the Lewis house, now desolate and quiet; for Annie had sent for Grant as she had promised, and a blight had come down from the sky and lay heavy on that hilltop. Beverly was sad and remote, and not a little terrified. It was no time for love-making. Sometimes they hardly spoke, but she seemed glad to have him there. Or again they would walk the paths of Annie's garden, companions rather than potential lovers, and in the bright spring light he would see the dark shadows under her eyes.

Only once in those days did she mention the end, and then it was with trembling lips.

"Will she suffer, Chris?"

"They'll look after that, my dear."

Living was a small thing just then compared to dying, and he was content to have her there, close and warm, beside him.

Looking back on those months later he remembered them as a jumble of hard driving work, of hasty and sober hours with Beverly, and of quiet intervals in a cool and orderly hospital. He was not on duty now, but he was still called on in emergencies. The big door would open and he would step into his own world again.

"Where's the case?"

"Gone up to the operating room, doctor."

Or it would be the emergency room, four beds in a row covered with brown blankets, a figure on one of them, and maybe a policeman or two standing by. He would make his examination, his big hands gentle, his face betraying nothing.

"Not so bad, old man. We'll fix you up in a hurry."

Sometimes, of course, it was not like that. A priest would come, or a clergyman, and for a time the ward door would be closed and another door opened into some far-distant place. Chris was always obsessed with his own futility at such times, and the hospital had learned to let him alone.

"Where's Doctor Arden?"

"I don't know and I don't care. He's looking for somebody to bite."

Occasionally he operated. The man on duty would be playing golf, be out of reach or busy. He was utterly content then; scrubbing up, once more the good feeling of hot water and soap on his hands, the smell of steam, the sound of rubber-shod feet on the tiled floor, the very feel of the instruments, still warm from the sterilizer and lying neat and orderly in their trays.

"Clamp."

"Here, sir."

"Wipe my face, somebody. It's hot as hades in here."

Sterile nurses and non-sterile nurses. Orders given by signs and gestures. Gauze sponges, clips, forceps, scissors, knives; threaded surgical needles, curved and shining.

"All right. Dressings, please."

Dressings proffered on a towel. Miss Clarke teetering on heels too high for her. The sun boiling in and sending a wavering heat line shimmering above the radiators. And then Chris straightening up, his back tired and aching, with a small return of that early feeling of his, not that he was king or God, but that some of that power on which old Dave had depended had for a time passed into him and through him.

And then old David died, and not from age after all. He received a telegram from Hiram: "Father killed last night, automobile accident. Mother asking for you. Can you come?"

He went at once, shocked and stunned. A day or two later he saw old David laid away in the country cemetery where he had always said he had buried all his mistakes. The crowd was enormous, and in the forefront stood Letitia surrounded by her boys. She did not look down. She stood with her head thrown back and her eyes on the sky; as though she saw David riding in triumph there, looking after his own somewhere beyond the clouds, and perhaps helping small sick angels to use their wings again.

That night, lying alone in her big bed, the other side hollow with the weight of that missing body, she sent for Chris. The boys had gone back to their houses scattered over the big farm, neat white wooden houses, each with its wood lot, its barn, its chickens and its well-cared-for beasts. David Mortimer had never wanted any land, they said, but what lay next to his! So there was plenty of land. And Letitia lying there alone was thinking of all this, that the boys had plenty and would have more and that Chris, who was also one of her boys, looked worn and not too prosperous.

"Sit down, Chris," she said in her thin voice.

He sat down and took her hand with its knotted veins. She was like David himself, still indomitable, still undefeated.

"I'm lonely tonight," she told him, "but I'm not grieving, Chris. Not for him. He's all right. He would be glad to get rid of his body. It had troubled him a lot lately. I suppose," she added, "men like him oughtn't ever to have had bodies at all. It holds them back so. Many a time I've thought, when he was going some place, that it was a pity he couldn't just flap his arms and fly."

"He'll be doing that now," said Chris, not too steadily.

"Yes."

She came at last to her reason for sending for him. She was like the doctor in some ways; her body was troubling her now, and she didn't care how soon she could cast it off. No, nothing wrong. Just a nuisance. But the point was that she had saved a little money of her own, and when that happened it was to go to Chris. There were no grandchildren. David had always hoped for them, but it hadn't happened. And the boys were well-fixed.

"What I thought was, maybe you'd take it and go abroad to study, Chris. It might be enough."

He protested, but she was firm. None of the boys had studied medicine, and that had disappointed their father. He would like to feel that someone was carrying on, and he had been very proud of Chris. He had always hoped secretly that

Chris would follow him, there in the country. It was only when at last he agreed that she relaxed, and he left her there with that hollow beside her. He noticed that one of her small hands lay there, as though perhaps she felt closer to old David now that he was gone than she had ever dared to be while he lived.

The next day he went back to the city again, self-confident and perhaps the better for Letitia's confidence in him; back to his work, to seeing Beverly, and to face again the problem of the Walters'. Life was a fixed thing, and after all, all rivers run to the sea.

Not that the rivers in that part of the state were running much, at that. May ended in a burst of heat. It hung in visible waves over the car tracks on the street and set the paving soft under the feet. Only the Lewis garden, where he sometimes sat with Beverly, was an oasis of green in the general drabness and heat. Caesar went about panting, and more than once Chris took him out under the drooping ailanthus tree and turned the hose on him. And again there had been little or no rain. The dust whirled in at the open windows of his offices, and down below the mills the river shrank, leaving its mud banks cracked in shallow patterns. The city work increased, but his private practice had shrunk, leaving Chris anxiously examining his books and his bank account. One day he came home to discover the ice left on the back porch melted and almost gone, and found himself confronting Lily Walters and suddenly shaken with anger.

"Why on earth can't you take it in? Show a little common sense anyhow."

"I didn't hear it come, doctor."

"If you were paying for it you would hear it come."

He slammed out and left her there, only to see her later on staggering across the street from the Daily Market and carrying a huge lump of ice wrapped in a newspaper. He went out grimly and took it from her. He could not be angry with her for long. She was too helpless.

His nerves began to go under the pressure. Grant was in

charge of Annie Lewis, but now and then she asked to see him. Chris would find himself in the big bedroom, holding the thin hand she extended to him and trying to answer the question in her eyes. They were almost never alone, however. Nurses came and went, Martha hung about, and the panoply of living seemed rather less than the panoply of dying.

"How is everything?" she would ask in her faint voice.

"Fine. Don't worry, my dear."

That was the nearest he could come to reassuring her. His presence seemed to comfort her, however. She would doze off, holding to his hand, and he would sit quietly until she wakened again. Then he would get up.

"Do you have to go, Chris?"

"I have calls to make. I'll be back tomorrow."

Then one day it happened, and he told her in a half whisper that afternoon. She stared up at him from her pillows and suddenly her face looked relaxed and content.

"My son," she said. "My son, Chris. I have always wanted a son." . . . . .

It had been quite simple in the end, as such things are. He had found Beverly in a secluded part of the garden, crying as though her heart would break, and he had merely put down that inevitable bag of his and taken her into his arms.

"Darling!" he said. "My own girl. Don't cry like that."

"I can't help it."

"I know, sweet. I know."

"I can't cry in the house. I daren't let her see me with my eyes swollen."

"Let me kiss your poor eyes, darling."

Bright sunlight all about them, the imposing grounds around them, and nobody in the world but the two of them.

"I love you so desperately, darling."

"I didn't think you did, Chris. I've been so terrified."

"I'll take care of you now, darling. Take care of you all my life, God willing."

It was as simple as that.

CHAPTER XV

HE was utterly happy after that. He could not save Annie Lewis. No power could do that. He could not even think of ways and means, although now with the summer coming and what private practice he had departing for seashore and mountain things were urgent enough. In the mornings as he shaved and bathed Lily Walters below would hear him singing, and would listen with a trembling mouth. "Your father used to sing in the mornings," she said once to Katie. "I can hear him now. He used to sing 'After The Ball Was Over' until it broke your heart."

"Oh, for goodness' sake stop it, mother. What's the use anyhow?"

One morning Lily turned on her.

"What's the matter with you anyhow? Can't he sing if he wants to? You're so crabbed these days I don't know what's come over you."

But Katie knew. She was both jealous and suspicious. Her mother could hear her now and then over the telephone.

"I don't know where he is. You might try the Staunton Lewis place. He's mostly there now."

"You ought to be ashamed of yourself, talking like that," Lily would protest.

"Well, it's true, isn't it? Have you thought of what's going to happen to us if he brings her here?"

"Brings her *here?*"

"Marries her. What do you suppose I mean?"

"Marries her?" said Lily blankly. "What on?"

"She's got money, hasn't she?"

To Beverly during those days Chris was a rock in a weary land. She was more nearly demonstrative than she had ever been. The small casual caresses of most families had never been hers, and her kisses were still the kisses of the child rather than the awakened woman. But there were times when in his arms he felt her sigh and relax, and his heart leaped. She was his. She was lovely and lovable, and she was his.

"You do love me, darling?"

"I adore you, Chris."

But their times together were brief. The telephone would ring, or he would look at his watch.

"Well, I'll have to go. City case."

"But you've just come!"

"It's a strange thing, my child, but a woman having a baby just naturally wants a doctor around. Nine times out of ten she could do just as well without him, but there you are!"

He would go, and she would try to fill in the time until he came again. It was not easy. Once or twice she told him that he cared more for his work than he did for her, but he only laughed. He realized the strain she was under, the strange mixture of tragedy and happiness which was her life just then, and he was doubly indulgent. Once he sat her down in front of him and talked to her soberly of their future.

"We have to have this out, Beverly," he said patiently. "My life divides itself into two parts. One of them is the service part. It belongs to my work, it takes most of my time, and it makes me damned difficult to live with. The other part is you. That's vital, so vital that I'm afraid to think about it. And somehow we'll have to reconcile the two."

"I'm to get what's left over. Is that it?"

"That's not fair, my dear."

"If I cared less I'd be more fair, Chris. I'm sorry."

Nevertheless she was happy in her engagement, fiercely and possessively happy. He would belong to everybody before he belonged to her. For richer or poorer, in sickness and in health, she would be his and he would only now and then be hers. But she put that thought away from her. She was enormously proud of him. She spent hours watching for him from an upper window, staring down to where the tree in the back yard marked his house, hurrying downstairs when he came and then receiving him with the odd little dignity which was always a part of her.

"Sorry to be late, my dear."

"Just so you're here!"

Her happiness followed her even into Annie's room, where Annie lay now content to live and quite prepared to die. Her child had come back to her a woman, and now she would be safe. She had been frightened to her very soul since she had gone to Chris, for it was a dangerous thing, this trying to mold human lives. She had seen Staunton doing it too often. But now it was all right.

"Beverly."

"I'm here, mother."

"If anything happens to me, I want you and Chris to live your own lives. Not—your father's."

"Chris will always live his own life, mother. He's like that."

"And you? You have had so much, Beverly. You will have to take Chris as he is. Don't ask too much of him."

"I want him as he is, mother."

They never talked for long. The morphia sent Annie off into little naps in which her body rested but her mind raced on in her dreams. Beverly would sit alone beside the bed. She felt wicked to be happy, but perhaps death was easier when one had lived a long time. So she too dreamed, but awake and glowing with young life, seeing the years ahead with Chris beside her, big, stalwart and dependable; Chris coming and going, a telephone ringing and calling him away; Chris in a white coat in the operating room, forgetting her until the work was done, and then coming back to her, weary and needing her.

But always coming back to her.

There was no announcement of the engagement, and for a day or two Beverly did not even tell her father. He was unapproachable now, fastidious and dapper as ever, but shutting himself into his study in the evenings and looking older, as though a blight had suddenly withered him. Each evening he went in and sat with Annie, and these visits now were longer; but he could not entirely conceal his fear of these hours with her, or his resentment that now at last she was failing him. Annie waiting for him could hear him in his room, fussing about, prolonging the interval until he must open the door and come in to her. The nurses had learned that these visits must be prepared for, the lights softened, the room aired and fresh, the rose silk blanket cover smoothed. Then they would slip out, and he would come in, with an air of ease which never deceived the sick woman.

"How are you tonight?"

"Comfortable," she would whisper. "What sort of a day did you have?"

He would tell her, and she would listen. The morphia made her mouth dry, and now and then she would take a sip of water. But he would not stay by the bed. He would move uneasily about the room, picking up this and that.

"Where'd that come from?"

"You bought it for me in Naples. Don't you remember?"

Or he would stop by a window. "Better get the screens in. There's a fly."

"I rather like the spring air."

He did not love her, she thought. He had not loved her for a long time. Nevertheless she was a part of him, a part of the comfortable background of his life. Sometimes she felt that he was silently enraged against her, as though she made him feel sinful merely because he was alive and well. Yet he was gentle enough after his fashion. He was even less angry than she had expected on the night when Beverly finally told him of her engagement, although his face was set as he came into her room afterward.

"What's this nonsense about Beverly and young Arden? Is it serious?"

"She's in love with him."

"And what about him? Is he in love with her?"

"So I gather."

"A doctor!" he said. "What kind of a life will she have? At everybody's call, all hours of the night and day. And no future in it. Why the hell couldn't she have picked somebody worth while?"

He was jealous of Chris. She saw that. But then men were often jealous where their daughters were concerned. He had never been jealous of her.

"What do they expect to marry on? He's got nothing."

She tried to moisten her dry lips.

"They haven't talked of marriage yet. Of course she'll have what I leave her."

It was the first mention between them of what was coming, and she was surprised to see his face twist, as though she had hurt him. It couldn't be possible, of course. Not after all those years, but how ironic if he still cared about her, and now she was going on somewhere else, where it wouldn't matter at all.

"We're not talking about that yet," he said, and stooping over kissed her for the first time in years. Then he stalked out of the room, ashamed probably, but leaving her faintly smiling.

She was not surprised however when he came in again, late that night, in a dressing gown over his pajamas, and his softened mood definitely gone.

"Are you trying to tell me that that young whippersnapper will refuse to let Beverly have an allowance from me?"

"I don't know," she said wearily.

"Why? What's wrong with my money?"

"Look back, Staunton. You didn't ask for help when you married me."

"There wasn't any. I'd have taken anything I could lay my hands on. God knows I needed it!"

He went out on that, leaving her puzzled and anxious. For the first time she realized that there might be trouble ahead;

the clash of two men, each determined, each proud, and Beverly somewhere between them; a Beverly without her, and being pulled two ways. As a result she was restless all that night, and at dawn the night nurse wrote on her chart: "Unable to sleep. Considerable pain. Also headache." Then she put it into a desk drawer and going into the bathroom, prepared her face and hair for the light of day. . . .

June came and went, with Annie slowly sinking and Chris put to it sometimes to find time for her, or for Beverly either. The heat increased his city work. Milk soured in hot rooms, babies were sick and wailing. Now and then a worker in one of the mills keeled over and lay like a felled ox. When and if Chris got to the Lewis house he would be tired and dusty, too weary even to talk. Sitting on the terrace, the light showing his shabbiness and the tired lines of his face, he would look far below to the mills by the river and wonder why he was there at all. As though he did not belong in that coolness, that luxury.

Then suddenly Katie, submerged for weeks under his work and his engagement, forced herself on his attention again.

One night late in June he found himself sitting beside Lily in the hall at the High School, a Lily surprisingly decked out for the occasion, while on the platform sat Katie in a new white dress, very composed and looking entirely grown up. Not only grown up. When she got up to receive her diploma he realized that she had become a very pretty girl. She was more slender than she had been, and her hands and feet were small. Katie, he thought idly, was a miracle in her way; to have brought anything so young and lovely out of that background of hers was surely a miracle. Beside him Lily was twittering with excitement.

"It's the best dress there," she whispered. "Miss Barker made it, out of the money Dick left me. Isn't it pretty?"

"Very pretty," he said gravely.

And it was that night, with Katie brave in her new finery and Lily in the kitchen preparing a supper by way of celebration, that the girl walked into his office and confronted him with his engagement. Chris looked up to find her staring at him with reddened eyes in a small white face.

"Engaged? Who told you that? And why don't you knock before you come in, Katie?"

"I heard it. That's all. Is it true?"

"It is true, of course. That needn't make any difference as yet to your mother or to you, Katie. And you looked very sweet tonight."

Katie however was past compliments.

"Are you in love with her?"

He smiled.

"I'm very fond of her, Katie. Do we need to go into that?"

"And you're really going to marry her?"

He kept his temper, although his color rose.

"It hasn't come to that. Maybe, a long time from now, when I can afford it and you are grown up and married yourself—"

"Grown up! Listen, Chris Arden, I'm eighteen now, I'll soon be nineteen, for that matter. And I'm more grown up than she'll ever be. She's been pampered all her life, and I've had to look out for myself. Oh, I know I'm dirt to you, but she's all wrong."

"That's enough, Katie. Stop it."

"What are you going to do? Live off her? Or turn us out and bring her here?"

"I can't discuss it with you, Katie. Nothing's settled anyhow."

"A doctor's wife!" said Katie. "Running to answer the telephone and trying to catch you some place for a baby case! How long would she do it?"

"I don't need any help in managing my own affairs, my child," he told her stiffly. "Let's forget it. As I said before, you looked very pretty tonight."

"And much you care!" she said, and banged out of the room.

It was the next day that she asked him for a letter to Miss

Simpson at the hospital. He was startled into speechlessness.

"Why shouldn't I be a nurse?" she said sharply. "If you think I'm going to stay on here now and live off you, you can think again. Anyhow, if you're going to be married—"

"Listen, Katie. If you imagine that a nurse's job is to smooth pillows and stroke foreheads—"

"I know all about it. Don't be funny, Chris. I'm no brow-stroker, but I'll do the job all right. You won't be ashamed of me. But if Beverly Lewis is coming here I'm out, and that's flat."

He thought it over that night, lying awake in his hot room. For the first time he faced, not only the problem of Katie and Lily, but the concrete fact of his marriage itself. To be in love with Beverly was one thing. To marry her was another. How adaptable was she? Could she fit herself to his scale of living, or to being only a part of his life? Yet other medical men managed it, he thought; carried on their work and reconciled it with marriage. He ran over the list in his mind. Grant, childless and with an elderly wife who both bullied and adored him; Wheeler, newly wedded and hurrying home, but carrying on contentedly with limited means; even Morrison, whose wife had believed it wicked not to bear his children and who had died giving birth to the tenth. Chris had been in the hall when that happened, and Morrison had staggered out and almost fallen into his arms.

"I've killed her, Chris."

"Get some brandy, somebody. And don't say things like that. She wanted them, you know."

"If I'd been half a man, Chris—"

Morrison had slipped since then, but for that one there were a dozen happy marriages which he could think of, men and women who had effected the necessary compromise. "Mostly the women," he thought, and remembered Letitia Mortimer. She had accepted her life tranquilly, borne her children as she had borne with old Dave's irregular hours and tumultuous temper. He remembered that household, the untidy abundant meals, the overgrown boys, Letitia's crowded mending basket, even the night when old Dave's saddle horse came home alone, and the search which found him in a muddy ditch with a broken leg.

"Get me out of here," he shouted. "I've had a frog sitting on me for three hours."

"Are you hurt, father?"

"No! Just lying here because I like it. Where the hell and damnation is the buggy?"

They had got him home somehow, and Letitia had ducked the boot he threw at her with the ease of long practice.

"If you're able to do that you're all right," she said. "And now stop that yelling. You don't scare me a mite, and I value my ears."

Yes, David and Letitia had managed it; but they had started together from the same level. "Had two of everything when I got married," David used to boast. "Two socks, two boots and two feather beds! Letty here, she had the same. Looked for a while as though we'd have to eat feathers!"

It was a long time that night before Chris slept. One thing was certain. He must get Katie out of the house and out of his life as soon as possible. He had no illusions about her. She was young and attractive, but she was undoubtedly dangerous.

He went to Miss Simpson the next day and laid his problem squarely before her. She listened carefully, watching him.

"What sort of girl is she?"

"She's straight, if that's what you mean."

"And she's fond of you?"

"She thinks she is. She'll get over it."

"I don't like it, Chris. How do I know she'll behave here? I'm particular about my girls. They're straight and they're—ladies."

"She has good stuff in her," he said sturdily. "She's never had a chance. That's all."

"And you're still supporting them?"

"Such as it is! I'm a sort of licensed victualer these days. But I'm anxious about the girl. She has no chance where she is. As a matter of fact, she almost got into trouble last fall. Maybe I oughtn't to tell you, but I want to start straight."

He did tell her, saving nothing, and at the end she looked more than doubtful. But she was fond of Chris, and the picture of the family he had drawn had been, she imagined, a masterpiece of understatement. She needed no description of that household to tell her what it was, and she had whipped unpromising material into shape before this. Anyhow the girl would better be taken away before she did any material harm. She had seen a good many medical men ruined by the women they married; common wives, jealous wives, over-ambitious wives. The ordinary man could leave his wife at home and go to his business. The average doctor could not. His offices were in his home. There was no such dissociation.

Better perhaps to get the girl away from him and see what she could make of her. But she was still uncertain.

"You said she'd been drinking that night?"

"For the first and last time; so she says, and I believe her."

She fingered the letter opener on her desk. She had her school to think of, and she preferred her girls to come recommended by their clergymen, and not saved by the Bessie Smiths of the world. In the end however she compromised. She would see Katie and let him know.

That was toward the end of June, and on a blistering day early in July Katie carried a small bag into Chris's office and closed the door behind her.

"I'm going, Chris."

"Well, good luck to you, Katie."

"I'll not bother you any more. You know that?"

"You never did, my dear. I've been no angel of light myself, have I?"

She stood close to him, her face a mask of tragic indifference.

"I suppose you wouldn't kiss me for good luck?"

"Kiss you? Why not?"

He bent over and kissed her gently, as a brother might, or a father. Then she turned and went out.

CHAPTER XVI

LIKE everything else in that transition period before the World War, medicine was moving rapidly. The isolation period in surgery had ended. There were still vast systems of medicine on the market, but faith in empiric prescribing was rapidly dying; scientific medicine was taking its place, and specialization was coming like an army with its banners.

Chris, reading his medical journals that summer when he had the time, tried to adjust to the new trend and told Ted Lawrence down the street that he felt outdated already.

"Another few years of this," he said, "and we'll be as extinct as the dodo!"

"Not you," said Lawrence philosophically. "You can always take a knife and do a little carving. It's the general fellows like me who'll be ringing a bell and carrying a tin cup!"

It was a mighty movement now, this forward surge of science into the human body and its ills. Improved machines had come in; for metabolism tests, for graphing the heart, for blood examinations, for a thousand and one uses in the laboratories. "Dead bodies are pure chemistry. Living bodies are chemistry plus life." Disease was a chemical injury, followed by invasion. Men bending over microscopes and Petri dishes, studying cancer, studying everything under the sun. Preventive medicine, scientific medicine, public health, public welfare; and even a new type of public conscience which denied that rivers were meant to be both sewers and sources of water supply, and that tuberculosis, like overweight, was an act of God.

"The unfit are a burden to the State. Cure them."

It was hard on the older men and difficult even for the young ones. Later on Chris saw that period in its true perspective, and realized that disease could not be regimented; or cure be reduced to pure science. Disease was always more than the sum of its parts. A dozen, a hundred intangibles entered into the picture of every case.

He was tired that summer. The dry heat rasped his nerves like a rough finger on silk, and that last prolonged agony of Annie Lewis's seemed unnecessary and beyond bearing.

"Some day, by God," he said to Grant one day, "we'll be too civilized to allow it. It's inhuman. It's refined cruelty."

"Dangerous thing," said Grant drily. "Can't take over the power of life and death, Chris. That belongs elsewhere."

Grant was right, of course, but the days of waiting were endless. Beverly looked like a thin ghost; and still Annie held on, opening her eyes each morning in the hope of Paradise, and seeing only her familiar room once more.

"There isn't a God, Chris," Beverly said violently one day. "You don't believe a God could be so cruel. You don't believe it, do you?"

"I don't know," he said slowly. "There's order. There's a pattern, darling. That's as far as I go."

He was desperately in love by that time. What had started more or less as a romantic dream had become a reality which was bone of his bone and flesh of his flesh. Her picture sat on his old bureau, and his good-night to it during those days was more of a prayer than he knew. He managed to keep his head and his integrity, however, went prosaically enough about his work, stormed as usual at the conditions of his poor in the blistering heat, fought Jenkins for ice, for milk, for whatever he could get, earned a little, even slept a little; but he knew then that his feeling for Beverly was the strongest actuating motive of his life. He never questioned that.

"I'm frightened, Chris. Come over here and hold me. Don't let me go. Never let me go."

"I'll never let you go," he told her gravely.

That was his courtship, a somber affair at best, with her holding to him like a scared child and a hush over the house as though it waited for something. As of course it did.

He still saw Annie now and then. She would send for him and he would go in alone to sit by her bed. Sometimes she roused enough to put out her hand, and he would hold it. Neither of them talked, but there were times when he wished that he had had old Dave Mortimer's faith in God and a hereafter, so as to reassure her. He was too honest, however, and the dissecting room had cost him his orthodox faith. After cutting through the tissues of a human body he had found it impossible to believe that it had ever housed a human soul. Life seemed totally dissociated from it. God's image, and a group of rowdy students jumping rope with twenty-odd feet of intestine! What could he promise her?

"You'll be good to her, Chris?"

"You know that."

She had better days, days when she would get Beverly in and plan her trousseau for her, even order her linens. One day in July Beverly asked him up to her sitting room, and he saw lying on a couch an old-fashioned wedding dress of ivory satin and a long tulle veil. Beverly stood over them, looking down.

"She had them brought out today, Chris. She wants me to wear them—later on."

They stood together, gazing at the dress; its long train lined with lace ruffles, its high neck, its narrow waist. The veil had a satin band over the head, and a bunch of osprey at the side. Beverly was crying.

"She must have been so happy when she wore them, Chris."

"Don't think about it, darling. Don't think. Just love me and let me love you."

She matured at that time, confronting raw life and suffering as she was for the first time. One day she told Chris that she wanted to make him a home and bear his children. She wanted sons, fine big sons like himself. He was touched beyond speech. But later he talked to her about their marriage in more practical terms.

"I'm a poor man, darling. You won't like that."

"I'll not be poor, Chris."

"Listen, darling. I can't let your father support me, or you either. If you take me you must take me as I am."

"Then I take you as you are," she said, softly.

He knew that she had no idea of what he meant, no notion of real poverty or of struggle of any sort; but he was too deeply in love by that time to insist further. It was not until soon after that, when she showed him her linens, that he felt that something would have to be done. They lay everywhere, great piles of shining damask embroidered with her monogram, linen sheets, napkins, towels, tablecloths. They covered the chairs, the couch, the tables, and even overflowed on to the floor, and Chris had a fleeting memory of Lily Walters' table with its spotted cloth and its napkins in their wooden rings. He smiled, but his eyes were serious.

"Great Scott, do I have to live up to that? Who's going to wash them?"

"You're too practical, Chris. That's my business."

One day Staunton Lewis sent for him, and he found himself across the desk in the library from a devitalized little man who regarded him with blank eyes but intense dignity.

"I have been waiting for you to come to me, doctor," he said. "Since it is a question of my only child—"

"I thought it could wait, Mr. Lewis. This hardly seemed the time."

"It was not a time for Beverly to become engaged, for that matter," said Staunton coldly. "Nevertheless it is time we came to an understanding. If you intend to marry her she must be supported, naturally."

"I had hoped to do that, sir."

"With what? On what?"

"On what I earn, or will earn."

"Nonsense! If you want to starve that's your affair. Beverly is another matter." Then his voice changed. "She has—she will have—some money from her mother. I suppose that will help?"

"Not to support her. If she wants to buy her own things

with it that's different. I must support my own wife, Mr. Lewis. I can't live on her money, or on yours."

"Better men than you have done it."

It ended where it began, both men determined and Staunton blowing hard with anger. Toward the last he called Chris a stubborn fool, and after that he was barely civil to him.

All in all, life was not too comfortable for Chris that summer. Downstairs Lily without Katie about had slumped into a comfortable lethargy and the house was in chronic disorder. The heat was terrific in the mill district, and men were drinking water from a river which, as Ted Lawrence said, was too thin to plow and too thick to drink. Chris was too busy sometimes even to see Beverly at all.

Then one day out of a clear and boiling hot sky Jerry Ames came back from wherever he had been, arriving armed with flowers for the sick woman and a ring in a box—hopefully—for Beverly, to learn of her engagement.

"Engaged?" he said, white-lipped and incredulous. "Who to?"

"To Chris Arden."

"The doctor fellow! I don't believe it. You're not serious, are you?"

"Very serious."

"But it's preposterous. It's ridiculous."

"Not to me."

He lit a cigarette with unsteady hands.

"I don't get it," he said finally. "It isn't you. What sort of a life will you have?"

"The sort I want, Jerry. I'm sorry."

"How do you know what you want? I suppose this is your mother's work. She never liked me. Anybody else, but not me."

"What do you mean by that?"

He laughed.

"Listen," he said. "Are you telling me that this fellow

without a nickel to his name simply walked up here and asked you to marry him? I don't believe it."

She sat very still for a long time after he had gone, slamming out of the house and into his car, his face still rigid with anger. It wasn't true, of course. Chris had come to her because he loved her. Jerry was angry, that was all; angry and unreliable. When Chris, exhausted with his day, discovered her on the terrace that evening he found her slightly aloof, somewhat constrained.

"Tired, darling?"

"A little."

"Anything happened to worry you?"

"Nothing new."

He reached out and took her hand, content merely to be with her. But he was tired and the terrace was cool. He dozed off, sitting there, and when he roused she was gone.

He telephoned her from his hot office later that night.

"I'm groveling, darling. If you can't hear me it's because I'm flat on the floor, with ashes on my head."

"Why?"

"I don't know. I thought you did!"

She laughed then.

"If you *will* go to sleep—"

"Only when I'm happy and at peace, darling."

It was all right, she thought. She had been idiotic. What did Jerry matter, or what he said? And down in his room Chris, preparing for the night, found that Lily had put a battered book of Henry's on his table, and carried it to bed with him. It was the Rubáiyát, and his eyes fell on the line Henry had quoted: "The worldly Hope men set their hearts upon, turns Ashes—"

He read the rest of it. "And anon, Like Snow upon the Desert's dusty face, Lighting a little Hour or two—was gone."

He put the book down and stared for some time at the disfigured paper on the wall.

He was more cheerful the next morning, making his rounds

contentedly enough, walking in the heat, climbing into tenements where the air felt like a hot stove. Toward evening he turned down the coverings from a feverish child to examine some faint pink spots on the abdomen, and then straightened with a set face.

It was typhoid again.

CHAPTER XVII

KATIE had become Miss Walters. She had done so as easily as she had slipped between the clean sheets of her hospital bed that first night and ultimately gone to sleep.

In her closet were hanging her striped uniform dresses, the skirts made by Miss Barker to escape the floor by two inches; below them sat her high black shoes with rubber heels, and on the closet door hung a paper bag marked "Laundry." The room was new, the furniture new also, since this was the new Lewis nurses' home for the training school. A bed, a bureau, a table and two chairs furnished it, and a scrap of rug was placed in its exact center.

She was excited and more than a trifle suspicious of her surroundings. The glimpses she had caught of the nurses had showed her a sober and efficient group, and the appalling order of everything rather disturbed her. Already that first evening she had decided on several matters. One was that she disliked Miss Simpson, sitting behind that desk of hers with her black silk dress swirling about her and keeping her standing while she inspected her through her glasses.

"You will be given three months, Miss Walters," she had said. "In that time you will have to show whether you will be competent to finish your course or not. The work is hard and exacting. We can afford no mistakes. You will be given orders, and it is your duty to carry them out."

"That's all right with me."

Miss Simpson eyed her carefully.

"My name is Simpson, Miss Simpson."

"Yes, Miss Simpson," said Katie, suddenly meek.

"Another thing. I have accepted you on probation, young as you are, because Doctor Arden thought you would do well here. I hope you will live up to that, but you understand that there are very rigid regulations as to nurses, interns and the staff. No former acquaintanceship with any of them means anything while you are here. The doctors are your superior officers, nothing else."

"If you mean Chris Arden—"

"*Doctor* Arden. No. I refer to all the men connected with the hospital."

But she had meant Chris. Katie knew that and writhed under it. She was to let Chris alone, was she? Maybe, she thought shrewdly, that was why Miss Simpson had taken her; so that she would be cut off from Chris. Well, she was cut off anyhow. That old cat needn't worry.

She lay unhappily in her bed, listening to the sounds outside. Across the hall was the bathroom for that floor, rows of washstands on one side, rows of cubicles on another, each containing a tub; and there was a constant procession to and from it, a splashing of water and the odor of soap. Evidently it was the thing here to bathe often. She tucked that away in her retentive mind.

Some time later she heard the ambulance driving in, and got up to see what was happening. She saw orderlies emerge from somewhere, the careful sliding out of a stretcher, an intern dropping from the front seat and throwing away a cigarette. She remembered Jake and felt a little sick. Then she crawled back into her bed again, trying to orient herself, to remember what the matron had said to her. She liked the matron of the nurses' home as little as she liked Miss Simpson; a short heavy woman with her hair parted and drawn back into a knot on her neck, she had shown Katie to her room and issued her instructions in a sharp staccato voice.

"You will be called at six, Miss Walters," she had said, "and you will leave your bed made and your room in order. Also the window open. Your laundry will be collected on Monday mornings, and must be listed. You will find lists in your bureau drawer. Take your own towels to the bathroom and bring them back with you. I think that is all."

Nevertheless Katie, lying in her bed that warm summer night, felt a faint pricking of excitement. They did not like her, those two old women, but she would make good in spite of them. She would work and learn, and some day she would wear a cap and be accepted. Then Chris would see what she was. She closed her eyes and thought of Chris.

It was a bright early morning when she wakened and got out of bed. Nurses were already bustling through the halls, into the bathroom and out again. She dressed quickly, put on a kimono and went across to wash. The young women eyed her, and one or two spoke to her.

"You the new probationer?"

"Yes. Name's Walters."

But they were in a hurry. They scurried about without giving her much attention. "Who's got my towel?" "What time is it?" Only one tall dark girl stopped to speak to her.

"I'm on probation too. It's no fun, you know."

"I didn't expect it to be fun," said Katie briskly.

"The probationers get all the dirty work. If it isn't sputum cups it's delousing heads. I'm pretty well fed up with it."

"I didn't come to be a pillow-stroker," said Katie, quoting Chris.

The tall girl only smiled and went out.

Breakfast was a hurried and sober meal. Prunes, cereal, bacon and eggs and weak coffee. Katie, surveying the long tables, saw about her serious-faced young women bracing themselves for the long day ahead. Already they were mentally in their wards, poised and ready for flight toward them. The night had been theirs. Now the hospital claimed them again, with its rules, its emergencies, its crowded wards, its problems of life and death. They looked at their watches, got up, went out. Promptly at seven they reported to the weary night nurses, took over keys and glanced at reports.

"Adams died last night."

"Then we've got an extra bed."

They were not calloused, not hard; but Adams was a number, a chart, a cot in a crowded ward. The hospital had no time to weep for its dead. Its policy was purely pragmatic; it fought for the living. When that fight was lost there were always replacements.

"I had to tie Jones last night. She was out in the hall twice, crazy as a loon. And Blake's pretty bad."

Katie stood by, listening. Beyond lay the ward to which she was assigned, a woman's medical ward. The night nurses had given it a perfunctory straightening, but now it lay open to the morning sun, an ugly remnant of the night, draggled and weary like some tired woman of the streets.

The night nurse got up. She had unlaced her shoes, and her ankles showed swollen when she stooped to tie them.

"I can't sleep in this heat," she said, to nobody in particular. "I haven't really slept for a week."

The day nurses had taken over. Nobody heard her, and she trailed off, her face gray with fatigue.

By noon that day Katie was dropping on her feet. She had carried innumerable trays, bed pans and feeding cups. She had been taught to change a bed without lifting the patient, sheet, rubber sheet and draw sheet; to make one side of the bed, roll the remainder against the patient's back and then turn her over the low mound and make the other. To fold in corners, drawing everything snug and tight. "All that fuss about making a bed!" she thought.

Her back was aching from leaning over beds, and her head heavy from hospital odors, drugs, disinfectants and others less pleasant. But she was young and quick. Miss Simpson, making her morning rounds that day, stood in the doorway and watched her with the eyes of long experience.

"How is she getting on?"

"Very well, so far. No hysteria, anyhow."

"No," said Miss Simpson, slowly. "No. She wouldn't. I imagine she knows what she wants and goes after it"; and left the head nurse staring after her as she went calmly on to the next ward.

It was a hot and wilted Katie whom Chris found when he came in that afternoon. Long before he came she had recognized that slightly arrogant step of his in the hall, and had hastily run her hands over her hair. But he only nodded to her. He had a case in the ward, and he went directly to it. On his way out however he stopped for a moment.

"Well, Miss Walters," he said, "how does it go?"

She flushed at his impersonal tone.

"All right, doctor. It's pretty messy, but I'm learning."

"Good," he observed and went out again, leaving her resentful and hurt. He had kissed her good-by, and now she was Miss Walters and a stranger to him. She went back to her work, her mouth set and her head high; but that night she sat for a long time in a bathtub, soaking her tired muscles and aching feet. And for almost the first time in her rather detached young life she shed bitter tears, alone and in silence.

It was within a few weeks of that time that the typhoid hit, and hit hard. The heat had continued, and with it the drought. Once again the river receded, leaving exposed its dried and cracking banks. Trees turned brown in August, and Annie Lewis, lying in her bed, saw her world of the window slowly dying. It was strange, she thought, that her world showed now through a window, a tall rectangle of sky and tree-top. So life contracted, grew small and yet smaller, until finally it ended. Not only her life. All life. And Chris, after that first case of his, had carried some samples of water to Dickinson at the hospital and got his report. It was a grim one, and he took it to Jenkins at once.

"Looks like a problem in arithmetic to me, son. What's it about?"

"Typhoid. That's all."

"Well, tell 'em to boil their water. That's the idea, isn't it?"

"They won't do it, Jenkins."

"Then they deserve what they get," said that gentleman tersely.

Before he left however Chris had blocked in a huge card

and hung it on the wall. "Boil all water," it said. "By city order." Jenkins queried the last three words, but Chris was adamant. "I'm part of the city," he said, "and I order it. What's wrong with that?"

"You won't be part of it long if you raise a fuss, son. Get this, Chris. Either you're with the crowd or you're not. If you're not you're on the skids so fast it will burn the seat out of your pants. Look at me! I'm here because I keep my mouth shut. Some things I don't like any more than you do, but I've got more sense."

There came a time when even the Lewis papers printed daily the order that the city water be boiled. A major catastrophe was threatening, and Lewis and the machine were beaten and knew it. There was no escape this time, no comfortable trip to Europe, no cure at some spa or other. The opposition press was bitter and outspoken; pointing out again that the river was a sewer, that the city had no proper filtration plant, and that many of the houses in the mill district were largely dependent on wells, and had no sewerage system whatever. It was tragedy, no less.

Cases poured into the hospital. Katie, rushing from this to that, had to make her way around the cots which sat everywhere, even in the halls with screens around them. She learned the very smell of typhoid, and one day she took her off-duty to buy a bottle of Eau de Cologne, and was sent out of the ward to bathe as a result.

For Chris it was merely a repetition of the year before, coupled with a fresh indignation. It was hard to face Lewis those days, or even to conceal his resentment from Beverly.

"You don't believe all this stuff in the papers, do you, Chris?"

"I have to believe it, Beverly. It's a fact. One doesn't have to believe a fact."

"You talk as though you had a personal grievance."

"Come with me some day and I'll show you that I have. And why."

But there was no time for quarreling, no time even for love-making. Days went by when Beverly never saw him, or when he dashed in to hold her for a moment and then dashed out again. When he had an hour with her he was worn and haggard, too tired to talk, too tired even to notice her increasing aloofness. Actually he lost the battle during those weeks, although he did not know it until later; for Beverly needed him and needed him badly. She was worn to a thread, high-strung and taut. Her mother, rousing out of a stupor in the middle of the night, would find her beside the bed, a haggard young figure of despair in a dressing gown over a thin nightgown, and try to send her back to bed. She would go obediently; then in an hour or two she would be there again.

"Is she any weaker?"

"About the same, Miss Beverly. I'll call you if there's a change."

Annie herself was only half aware of her, occupied as she was with the tedious business of dying. She had no curiosity now, only an infinite patience. Sometimes Staunton sat by her bed, but it was rather late to make much difference, save that it was interesting to see him facing something at last that he could not dominate. Sometimes she played with the idea that it was a son who sat there, and that at any minute he might grin and say:

"See here, old girl, snap out of it. Where's that hand of yours? Hiding out on me, aren't you! Such a pretty hand, mother. Nobody has hands like yours."

She would lift a hand and look at it.

Once or twice she asked for Chris, and by some miracle he found time for her. She would doze off and rouse to find him sitting quietly beside the bed. He had very little to say, but sometimes he would reach over and lay his hand over hers; and once he said that she had beautiful hands. It was like her dream come true, and she always felt better after he had been there, as though some of his strength had gone out to her.

"Haven't you something you ought to do?" she would whisper.

"Not a thing," he would lie, cheerfully.

Once he even dozed, there beside the bed. It gave her a sense of comfort to have him sleeping there. A son might have done that. . . .

If there was no time for love-making during those days, there was no time even for sleep or for decent living. People were dying like flies, in hot tenement rooms, in shabby little houses. The hospital mortuary was crowded, and still they came. Alcohol sponge baths, mouths to be cleansed of sores, temperature charts soaring, nurses running about with feeding cups, interns sleeping in their clothes and going about badly shaved and with eyes sunk in their heads; and still the river taking its toll. "Boil your drinking water. Boil the water for dishwashing." And the mill district not reading the papers and drawing water from the pump in the yard as usual.

The end of September saw Chris worn in body and in mind. He had hardly seen Beverly for a month. He worked furiously, but always with a sense that the battle was lost before he began. Nursing, not drugs, was the answer, and outside of the hospital there was still no nursing to be had for the poor. Then on a bad day about that time, eyes red from sleeplessness and revolt in his very soul, a brisk young man walked into his office and asked him what he thought about it.

"Think about it? I think it's murder."

There was more of it. He attacked the local administration; the water supply, the rampant graft which kept the city too poor for proper reforms. He sat back in his chair and unloaded all his fatigue, his helpless wrath and his indignant pity. It was probable ruin, but he did not care. And ruin in a sense it proved to be. An evening paper that night ran a three-column headline: "Epidemic Is Murder, Says City Physician."

Chris did not see the paper. He seldom saw newspapers at all in those days. He knew nothing about it until that evening when, office hours over and about to start out on his endless rounds, Staunton Lewis walked into the back room and slapped the paper down on his desk.

"Did you say that?"

Chris glanced at the paper.

"I did. What's more, I meant it."

Lewis said nothing further. He looked around the shabby room, gave Chris a hard sharp glance, and turning on his heel went out as abruptly as he had entered.

CHAPTER XVIII

CHRIS worked almost all night, and turning in toward dawn was wakened at eight by the telephone and Jenkins' voice.

"Look here, you damned young fool, what do you mean by that stuff yesterday?"

"I meant it. That's all."

"That's plenty. You've got them in a hot spot. But you're in one yourself. They can't fire you now. But this fall they'll gently ease you out of your job, son. That's sure as shooting."

"That's all right with me," he said, and replaced the receiver. He did not sleep again however. It would happen, as Jenkins had said. In a way he had known it all along. As he lay back he realized that the situation involved more than his city job. It would worry and upset Beverly, at a time when she was bearing all she could, and the loss of his salary would certainly defer his marriage. He ran a hand through his heavy hair and stared at her picture on his ancient bureau. Damn it all, a man couldn't even be honest in this business without hurting somebody.

At nine o'clock he called her by telephone, to be told that she had been up most of the night and was still sleeping. He tried again from a drug store later in the morning, but Holmes answered that she was with her mother and not to be disturbed. Save for that, the morning was much as usual. He went about, into houses, up the stairs, into bedrooms. "What sort of a night?" "He was bad, doctor. We could hardly hold him in bed. He was out of his head." Medicine, largely for the sake of the family, orders as to care; then out again into the hot sunlight and another house. Flies buzzing through unscreened windows, boiling heat, tired women, glimpses of unwashed dishes in cluttered kitchens, crying babies, sick children.

But sometimes a bit of cheer. "How's the boy?" "He seems better. The fever broke this morning, and he's sleeping." Relief then, and a feeling of victory. Standing by a bed and looking down at a sleeping child, and a small humble feeling of having been just possibly a viceroy of God; provided of course there was a God.

There was nothing to warn him, nothing to tell him of that short sharp interview between father and daughter the night before.

"You wanted him. Now you've got him, and I'm warning you. I'll follow him up if it's the last thing I ever do."

"Maybe he's right."

"Right! The impudent young pup. What does he know about it? I'm telling you. If he ever sets a foot in this house again I'll have him thrown out."

She went upstairs and into her mother's room. Annie was fully conscious, and she stood beside the bed looking down at her. No, she could not ask her, she thought. There was no one she could ask. After a while she went away again. . . .

All Chris knew, when he entered by the kitchen door that afternoon, was that he was dirty and hungry, that Lily was out, and that what might have been lunch at some time or other was now something dried and brown on a cracked plate in the oven of the stove. He needed food, however, and so he took it, carrying it forward to the back office and swearing softly under his breath.

It was not until he had set it down on his desk that he saw Beverly, a dry-eyed and white-faced Beverly who stood in the doorway, tight and unsmiling.

"My darling! Why didn't you send for me?"

"I think you ought to know that," she said uncompromisingly.

He stared at her.

"Meaning—?"

"Meaning that you can't expect to be very welcome after yesterday, can you?"

He was fairly close to the breaking point himself. He stiffened slightly.

"That, I imagine, would depend on who is doing the welcoming," he said slowly. "If it's that newspaper story, I'm sorry, of course. I suppose I was tired. But why not tell the truth, Beverly? After all it was my duty."

"Even if it separated us? You would still feel it your duty?"

"Why should it separate us?"

"But if it did?"

He hesitated.

"Perhaps—even then," he said slowly. "But it can't do that, my darling. Not if we love each other."

She passed that over.

"You owe a duty to the people who pay you, don't you?" she demanded. "The city—"

"Oh, damn the city," he said savagely. "What's that got to do with you and me?"

"Because I got you on the city pay roll. You needn't look like that. It's always done that way. I've known Barney O'Neill for years."

Suddenly he laughed, mirthlessly.

"By God," he said, "and I thought it was because I was a good doctor! It's funny. And so it's always done that way. That's good, too. And me telling Jenkins I had no pull!"

She ignored that.

"You've always hated my father," she said. "But to take a cheap revenge, and at such a time—"

"Precisely," he said drily. "At such a time is right, with things as they are. But hardly a cheap revenge, my dear. It's costing me my job, isn't it?"

"Hasn't it occurred to you that it may cost you more than your job, Chris?"

He stared at her, uncomprehending. She was tired, exhausted like himself, and facing a tragedy also. It was incredible that they should be quarreling, incredible and absurd.

"My darling," he said gravely, "I'm sorry if I hurt you.

I told you long ago that I am not easy to love or easy to live with. I've earned my money, however it came, but I have my work to do. I can't compromise with that. You've known that all along, my dear."

"And your work will always come first. Before me. Before anything," she said. "That's true, isn't it?"

"No, by God," he said violently. "But it's got its place."

She stood, looking about her uncertainly, at the dust, at the mail he had had no time even to open, at that wretched plate on the desk; and from there she looked back at him and anger rose in her again, that she should care so much, and that he should be looking at her with eyes that were hard and uncompromising.

"Life," he said, "has been easy for you, my dear. It isn't all like that. It won't be easy with me. But I'm prepared to put into it all I have, if that's enough."

"I'm not sure that it *is* enough, Chris. Maybe I want too much. Maybe I'm selfish, I don't know. But this last month or so, and with father and you feeling as you do— Chris, did mother ever talk to you about me?"

"Plenty of times."

"I mean, before we were engaged."

He hesitated, and that hesitation was his undoing. She did not wait for him to speak. Her head went up, her color rose. She was sorry, she said, but she had not thought it would be like this, especially as things were at home. She had thought that he would at least have some time for her. Perhaps she was jealous of his work. She didn't know. But in that case she was not cut out for a doctor's wife, was she? Anyhow her father would soon be alone, and he would need her. When she married, if she ever did—

Chris heard her through, his jaw set hard. He made no defense. Only at the end he sat up in his chair and smiled at her across the desk.

"My dear girl," he said, "you needn't either attack me or defend yourself. You are right as you see things, and maybe

I am right too. I'm never sure of that, of course. But if you want to be free, darling, you are free."

Perhaps she had not expected that. She went rather white again and got up, and Chris leaped to his feet.

"Only if you want it, my dear—"

She stood quite still, and he had the feeling that there was something she had not said and that should be said. But she did not say it. Instead she smiled faintly.

"I'm afraid I do want it, Chris."

She gave a curious, almost a heartbreaking glance around the room, and then turned and went out. He followed her, but he found nothing to say. When he had closed the door behind her he found that he was shaking. He shut himself into his back office and sat down again. His knees would not hold him.

For a day or two his pride kept him away from her. He was working at terrific pressure, too, and perhaps he hoped that given time Beverly would see reason and send for him. But nothing happened, and at last he put his pride in his pocket and climbed the hill.

Holmes answered the door, however, and one glance at his face was enough.

"Things pretty bad, Holmes?"

"I'm afraid she's going, doctor."

He did not ask to go in, and so Annie Lewis died that day without him. She went very quietly at the end, only once she muttered something that sounded like his name, and tried to hold out her hand. Beverly, a white ghost beside the bed, had gone even paler. Then it was all over, and Annie had gone probably to the same heaven as little Jake the tailor; although she lay in state for two days under a pall of orchids, whereas Jake had been worth all told only five hundred dollars to the traction company.

Not that the orchids mattered to Annie. They never had mattered.

On the day after her death Chris resigned from his city job, at least saving himself the stigma of being ousted, and two days later he sat in his office and faced his successor, a heavy young man named Barrett. Chris did not like him. He was cocksure and arrogant, and there was nothing in that meeting to show that their lives were to be mixed in any fashion whatever. Barrett at once stated that he was not in medicine for his health, and that as for the city poor, they were dirty and thriftless, and so what could you expect?

Chris, who had expected little and received rather less, listened to him carefully, his face slightly averted. He had done this to them, handed to this cocksure youth his children of the shadows; and as Barrett talked he saw them again. He was climbing long flights of dingy stairs to the aeries where they lived in crowded misery. He was seeing children pallid for lack of sun, and the grown men and women who had looked to him for help and even for life.

"You'll find they're not all bad, Barrett."

"Well, they are good clinical material, anyhow," Barrett grinned. "Jenkins says you spoiled them."

"I treated them like human beings. Not scum."

Barrett was unimpressed. He went away still smiling. The dingy office had not been lost on him. That damn fool back there had no idea of public psychology. Look prosperous and you became prosperous. Already he had furnished his own place handsomely on the installment plan, and some day he would have a nurse there, a good-looking girl in clean white. He might even wear a white coat himself. A man he knew in Chicago had gone in for smocks and served tea in the afternoon. He was coining money.

Chris felt rather lost after that, as though he had suddenly changed the open road for a cul-de-sac and confronted a blank wall. He had a queer feeling of detachment too, as though Annie and not Beverly had been the tie to the big house; as though indeed he had been for a time the son she had never borne, and she the mother he had lost so early.

One day soon after the funeral he went out to the Lewis mausoleum and sat for a time on the marble bench outside.

But Annie seemed far away. The cemetery was very quiet, and after a while a man working nearby came up and spoke to him.

"Pretty fine building," he said.

"Very handsome," Chris replied.

The man took off his cap and rubbed his head.

"Me," he observed, "I like the earth best. They seem closer somehow."

That was it, Chris thought. He could have found her perhaps had she lain in the ground. As it was, the Lewis marble and the Lewis money cut him off. It was years before he ever went back there again. . . .

It was perhaps a week after Annie's funeral when Katie came home from the hospital for her half day, to sniff the musty odor of the house as she stood in the hall, and to see on the table a small black-bordered envelope addressed to Chris. She stood looking at it; then she wandered back to the kitchen and surveyed it with distaste. Lily was not around, but the stove was going and a kettle was hissing on top of it.

She took off her hat and called up the back stairs:

"Mom! Hey, mom!"

There was no answer, and after a moment's hesitation Katie went back to the front hall and picked up the envelope. It was lightly sealed, and with a little steaming— She went cautiously back to the kitchen again and held it to the spout of the kettle; and she was still holding it there when she heard Lily on the back porch.

She was frightened, for Lily had her own code such as it was, and there was no time to escape. She did the only thing she could think of, jerked the kettle aside and dropped the letter into the fire. She was putting the kettle back when Lily came in.

"What's all the fire for, mother?"

"I was going to have a cup of tea. Better have one."

They sat together at the kitchen table and had their tea, and within a day or two Chris saw in the paper that Beverly and her father had sailed for Europe. It was the first time he had really believed that his engagement was over.

Part III

THE DOCTOR

CHAPTER XIX

IT was probably about that time that Chris ceased to be called the young doctor by the neighborhood, and became Doctor Arden, or often merely the doctor. The youth had gone out of him, and Katie, coming home once a week, watched him uneasily.

"He looks sick, mother. Is he still worrying about her?"

"I don't know. All I know is there's no pleasing him. He found the cellar lights burning the other morning, and he shouted so you could hear him a block away. How are you getting on?"

"All right, I guess. This kitchen is a sight, mother. Don't you ever wash the dishes?"

For this was a new Katie, not only a Katie who had so to speak burned her bridges behind her, but a Katie alternately frightened at what she had done and secretly exultant. Probably neither then nor later did she know the full extent of that infamy of hers. What was a note? But then, what was anything now compared with the fact that Chris was free again?

She was a new Katie in other ways also, although Chris hardly noticed it; a Katie familiar with neatness and even cultivating it, a Katie who had already seen tragedy and death in a variety of forms, had been accepted—with mental reservations—by Miss Simpson, and was receiving the ten dollars a month which did not buy her thermometers and pay for her uniforms and rubber-soled shoes. A Katie now definitely more cheerful and with a new hope springing in her practical young breast. Neater too. Chris found her one day in his bedroom, giving her mother a lesson in bed-making.

"No wonder he doesn't sleep," she was saying. "You can't just pull the covers up and give them a jerk. Look here. Watch how I fix the corners. You take the sheet like that—"

"I haven't time for all that nonsense. If that's nursing I'm sorry for people."

Katie ignored that. "Like this, mother. It's easy when you get the hang of it."

His bed that night was properly made, but the next day it was only too obvious that Lily had again reverted. She was hopeless. She had always been hopeless.

He accepted that, as he had accepted everything else, as stoically as possible. Life had become very simple again, and very bare; the mere skeleton of existence. For a time he thought that Beverly would surely write to him, and he would hurry home from wherever he had been to look at the hall table. No letter came however, and so in time he stopped looking for any. The epidemic was over with the fall rains, and he went back to the old round, or what was left of it. It was at about that time that he began talking to Caesar, putting his case, as it were.

"We've been a pair of damned fools, old boy," he would say. "'Snow on the Desert's dusty face,' that's the idea. Nothing lasts, old man. Nothing lasts, does it?"

Except of course the Walters'.

It was during that early fall that Katie and Lily had a talk one day. It started innocuously enough, for Katie with a new hope in her heart since Chris's engagement was broken, was wanting some clothes. Yet that talk with all it implied was to change the entire course of more than one life.

"I've got to have a suit, mother," Katie said. "I can't go around ragged."

"Well, what are you going to do about it?" said Lily, indifferently. "Ask *him* for it? If you'd gone to clerk in a store—"

"Well, I didn't, and that's that. If Dick was worth anything he'd help us. But he's too busy helping himself. To anything that's handy!"

It was a moment before that registered with Lily. Then she turned on her a terrible face.

"Just what do you mean by that?"

"You know as well as I do. Where do you think he got that money when he came here that night? If you believe he earned it I don't."

"He's your own brother, Katie. You ought to be ashamed."

"Well, I'm ashamed all right," said Katie. "He got out good and early the next morning, didn't he? And when did he ever do that before?"

"If you're saying that he took—"

"I'm guessing, but that's my guess."

Katie was frightened after that, but it was too late. There was something ominous in her mother's face. She moved about like a woman in a dream and she ate no dinner that night. If she had wept Katie would have understood, but her usual facile tears were dried up, her eyes blank and staring.

"Maybe I'm wrong, mother."

"Of course you're wrong. He's had hard luck, and you've always been down on him."

Chris was out that night, on one of the interminable walks by which he tried those days to earn a night's sleep, and after Katie left, Lily went into the office and examined the sample bottles carefully. Finally she took one of sleeping tablets and shook a couple into her hand. She replaced the cotton in the neck carefully and carried the pills up to bed with her.

She slept that night. Also she had learned something. In that bottle in the office lay peace and forgetfulness, a comfortable oblivion, and after that she never slept without them. She would take her pills and sit by her window in her nightgown until her head began to droop. Then she would crawl into her bed and be instantly asleep. Once or twice she overslept in the morning, and Chris had to rouse her. She would hurry down, looking pale and unrested, and bring him his half-cooked coffee, a slice of burned toast.

"I'm sorry, doctor. Seems as if I never get enough rest somehow."

One day he took her into the office and went over her. Her pulse was slow, but otherwise she seemed to be all right. He took that occasion to tell her that things were not to be different after all.

"I have changed my plans," he said, not looking at her. "If you have been worrying about that—"

She had not, as a matter of fact. She had known of that change almost as soon as he did; but it no longer seemed important to her. Nothing mattered but Dick; a Dick stealing at night into that upper front bedroom and rifling Chris's pockets, and then making her *particeps criminis* by giving her a portion of the loot; coming into her room and waking her at dawn.

"Here, buy yourself something pretty, mother."

"Are you sure you can spare it, Dick?"

And Dick grinning down at her as she lay in her bed, and saying: "Plenty more where this came from!"

She roused herself. "I'm sorry your plans are changed, doctor."

"That's all right. These things happen."

The truth never occurred to him. He was busy that fall, after a fashion, although he was doing a great deal of work without pay. Many of his city patients still called for him, and he had not the heart to turn them away. They did not like Barrett, for one thing. He would not make night calls, and when he did come he scolded them for their slackness and their squalor. "Look at that floor. Why don't you scrub it?" What did he know about the cost of soap, or the effort required of tired arms and underfed bodies merely to do the routine work of living? Or:

"Why don't you keep those children out in the air?"

"Where?" they would ask. "On the streets, to be run down by automobiles? Doctor Arden was trying to get that empty lot at the corner for them to play in, but now that he's gone—"

One day Chris had to call on Barrett himself. A big

Negro from the South had come up on one of the boats and was taken sick. Chris found him in a shack on the river bank, surrounded by other Negroes, and broken out with a peculiar rash. He went home, got out his books and then called Barrett.

"Smallpox!" said that gentleman. "I don't believe it, Arden. We've got no smallpox here."

"You will have. All those darkies ought to be vaccinated, for one thing, and this fellow should be sent to the municipal hospital."

"Got it all fixed, haven't you?" said Barrett in his jeering voice. "Well, he's your case. Why call on me?"

"I can take care of him, but the rest is up to the city."

Barrett however did nothing, and a telephone message to Jenkins only amused that cheerful gentleman. "Say, listen, son," he said. "Every case of measles we get in town is smallpox, and I've never heard of one yet. We miss you, boy. What the hell made you fight with your bread and butter?"

"It's smallpox," Chris persisted. "Confluent smallpox, if that means anything to you. It isn't nice and it isn't pretty, but I give you my word that if this fellow dies and is buried and the thing spreads, I'll have him dug up and invite you to be present."

"I have another engagement," said Jenkins promptly. "I'm booked solid for the next year. I—"

Chris hung up the receiver and went back to his case. He took all possible precautions, kept the shack quarantined, changed to old clothes for his visits and vaccinated himself and Lily Walters, who bore the indignity with resentful fortitude. But the man died, and half a dozen new cases developed after his burial.

One day Chris found himself in the Mayor's office, facing a Barney O'Neill who was half quizzical and half annoyed.

"Smallpox!" he said. "My God, doctor, does trouble just follow you or do you go hunting for it?" He pointed to his crowded desk: "That's your work, or part of it," he said.

"The country's going crazy. I eat and drink sewage and garbage disposal, and by the Lord Harry, they're trying to hand me the State watersheds! Now you bring me smallpox. I don't want it. I won't have it."

"You've got it," said Chris grimly.

Before Chris left Barney dropped his banter and stared at him squarely across his big desk.

"What made you do it, Arden? You knew the old man."

"Somebody had to do it."

"Not," said the Mayor, "that I care so God-damned much about him myself. But Annie Lewis—Well, no matter about that. You did your duty, and look what it cost you!"

Chris got up, still smiling.

"It cost me more than I expected," he said. "Well, what about these cases?"

He got an exhumation order finally, and the State sent a representative. But it was a bad job. Barrett, sent by the city and sweating profusely, stood by. The State representative was calm and watchful. Chris was quiet. He had staked his reputation on the result, and a half dozen newspapermen standing at a safe distance were there to witness his success or failure. When the casket was opened the State man required hardly more than a glance.

"Smallpox," he said laconically to the reporters. "All right. Close him up again."

There was no epidemic, save of sore arms. If it added anything to Chris's reputation it damaged his practice, and even his regular patients, the Lees, Miss Andrews and Betty Howard, stayed away from him that fall. Not that Betty abandoned him even then. She would call over the telephone.

"Hello! Any pimples yet?"

"Covered with a rash! Come and see it."

She did not come, of course, and there were days that late fall and early winter when he wondered whether a purely pragmatic sense of duty, like O'Neill's, was not better than his own.

One night Katie, finding him alone in the back office, wandered in and sat down on his desk.

"I thought you needed company, Chris."

"I'm not good company for man or beast these days, Katie."

"You're always good company for me, Chris." She leaned over suddenly and put her cheek against his. "I've never changed," she said. "You know that, don't you? Never have and never will, Chris dear."

He put his arms around her. He did not love her; there were many times when he disliked her and more when he forgot her altogether. But for that moment at least she was something young and friendly to soothe his wounded pride. When he released her and got up, she remained on the desk watching him.

"And so—what?" she inquired, smiling up at him.

"And so nothing, my dear. I was low and you have cheered me. Isn't that what you meant to do?"

"What about me in all that?"

"You? You'll forget it and go back to work. I hear good reports of you."

"And that's all, is it?" she demanded angrily, and got off the desk. "I'm like your dog. You pet me when you feel like it, and kick me when you don't."

"I've never kicked my dog."

She flew out of the room and left him standing there. He had been foolish, and he knew it.

That winter was cold, with deep snows. He would come in late, go down and shake the furnace and shovel in coal for the night. It ate coal voraciously, and he watched the dwindling pile with apprehension. His practice had picked up again, but when he made out his bills at the end of the year he found that he had earned outside of his city work less than two thousand dollars in twelve months, and sat back to face a future which seemed less promising than ever.

He lighted his pipe and confronted the facts. He went

back in his mind to a class room long ago, and a big booming voice:

"The doctor, if he makes a discovery of value, does not own it. He must pass it on that all may benefit. And he must be prepared to give away without cost four-fifths of his time, his skill and even his bodily energy. That is the practice of medicine, gentlemen."

He had smiled then. Now he knew that it was true. But at least he was thankful that he had work to do. It was good to be tired, to drop into his bed and go to sleep at once. Like Lily in her drugged rest he asked only to forget; not for a moment did he realize that the unpolished stove in the kitchen had been the dingy crematory of his dead hopes.

He went back on duty at the hospital at the beginning of the year, a serious man who had lost his spontaneous smile and who carried himself like the overlord he was. Even his occasional outbursts of anger had been a part of his youth, a quality of his vitality. Now he went back a tired man, discouraged and heavy-hearted. Miss Nettie, meeting him in a hallway, was saddened by the change in him. He had never told her of his engagement, but she was no man's fool and there had been rumors of it.

She went back to her room and inspected a picture of Annie Lewis on the wall there—among the side whiskers and others—and then sat down and wrote to Beverly in Paris.

"I am an old woman, my dear," she wrote, "and I have no idea what has happened. But Chris Arden is one of my boys and the salt of the earth, and I loved your mother very dearly."

She re-read it carefully, having got so far. Then she tore it up and, having about as much privacy as an elephant in a zoo, she also burned it. She had played many parts in her life, she thought, but young love had not entered into them; and the good Lord had a way of attending to such affairs Himself.

Nevertheless, letter or no letter, Chris got through his first two months creditably. Weary as he was, the familiar sights and smells of the operating room never failed to rally him. He would scrub up, be put into his operating coat and wait until the tapes at the back had been tied; glance at the trays, draw on his rubber gloves. Sometimes the patient was already there, sometimes he waited. There were times now and then, as in his days as an intern when he had been wakened out of sleep, when he felt that he was actuated by a sort of automatism; going through the proper motions, but working with his spinal cord rather than his brain. He would shake his heavy head, as though to clear it.

"Get some air in here, somebody."

He was doing well in spite of that. Now and then Grant or one of the other men would scrub up, put on coats and wander in to watch his work. He was a fast and certain worker, and they were proud of him. Perhaps there was also a natural envy, for most of them were no longer young, and surgery was moving fast. It was beginning to be a young man's world now, this world of the knife. They knew their work, knew it well. But the new men thought less of life and more of blazing a new trail, were willing to take a chance, to experiment, that the world might ultimately gain. To some of the older ones even their masks and rubber gloves were irksome.

"Don't bother with that stuff," they would say. "I'll only be here a minute or two."

"Sorry, doctor."

In the end they would submit, speechless with resentment. "Damned lot of nonsense. We used to have cuspidors in here for the chewers! Now by God it's as much as your life's worth to sneeze!"

Chris was modest, and they liked him for that; but when it was all over they would go down in the elevator to their waiting cars, feeling as though they had built up a competent young Frankenstein to destroy them.

"Works too fast," they would say to themselves. "Brilliant, of course, but reckless too. He'll get into trouble some day."

He got into trouble during the third month of his service.

CHAPTER XX

HE had gone down to his usual cheerless breakfast, to find a trembling Lily waiting for him in the doorway. Someone, she said, had got into her room during the night and stolen the rent money from her pocketbook.

"Got in?" he said incredulously. "How?"

"By the shed roof," she said tonelessly. "I never heard a thing, doctor. Believe it or not, that's the truth. My window was open, and you can see the marks in the snow."

She had many faults, but she was no liar. Chris, examining the roof, saw that she had told the truth; but he suspected her of guessing the identity of the thief, as he did himself. He said nothing, however, and ended by forcing her to take some coffee and stating that he would not go to the police.

"Not a chance in the world of finding who ever did it," he told her. "But I'd open the other window hereafter."

It was disturbing; even serious, but he picked up his newspaper to avoid her tragic eyes, and saw confronting him the announcement of Beverly's engagement to Jerry Ames, cabled from Paris. He sat quite still, holding the paper in front of him. He had the usual capacity for belief in what was printed, but he knew also that this was true. Perhaps he had never entirely abandoned hope until that moment. Now, dizzy and shaken, he realized that that particular page of his life had been turned over and the book closed.

He carried the paper into the office and read it again. There across the desk Annie had sat, holding that breast of hers and saying: "I had even hoped that you and Beverly would care for each other. . . ." Here Staunton Lewis had stalked in: "Did you say that?" "I did." And then that last day with both of them exhausted and not normal, with Beverly divided in her allegiance and terrified of life, especially of his life: "Only if you want it, my dear." "I'm afraid I do want it, Chris."

The fool he had been! The doubly damned fool, when he might have taken her in his arms, remembering how tired she was and the horror waiting for her on the hill. But he had let her go, and so—

He crumpled the paper and threw it across the room. Then with a set face he picked up that everlasting bag of his, got his hat and coat and started for the hospital. He was apparently quiet enough. Men after long strain await the inevitable with the calm of exhaustion. Nevertheless the nurses stared at him as he went into the operating room, his head thrust forward, his jaw set. He did not see them. He did not know that he was colorless, and his hands as he drew on his gloves were steady enough. He did a double hernia quickly and skillfully. He dragged out a spleen, packing the cavity against bleeding with hot moist gauze. He worked better than he knew that morning. Then suddenly with the third case, a woman, in front of him, he knew that he was losing control.

He would have stopped then, but the case was prepared, the woman already anesthetized. He went to a window and took a few long breaths, went back to the table. Nobody had apparently noticed any change in him, and so he picked up the knife and drew the first red line.

It was a simple case, an ovarian cyst. Ordinarily it would have been over and Chris shouting for sutures in a short time. But somewhere in that dissection his knife slipped and he knew he had cut the uterine artery. Instantly the place was flooded with hemorrhage. There was no chance to stop it. The field was obscured; there was nothing to see, nothing to catch hold of, and when the sucker was brought the tube promptly jammed. The operating room ceased then to be static and became bedlam, but it was too late.

Chris, gray-faced and tight-lipped, looked up at the anesthetist.

"How is she?"

"I'm afraid she's going, doctor."

But she was not going. She was gone. And Chris, stained from head to foot, said nothing whatever. He stood for a second or two, looking down at the dead woman. Then he turned heavily and went out of the room.

He did not go home that day at all. Patients came and went away again. The telephone rang. A small girl brought a note. Gus at the Daily Market cut his finger with his meat knife and came over with it wrapped in his white apron. Caesar waited in vain at the front door, and back in the kitchen Lily sat with her dishes around her, absorbed in her unhappy thoughts.

Late that night she took an extra sleeping pill and went to bed, with Chris not home and no message from him. . . .

Chris was walking the streets. How many miles he walked that day he never knew. Once—after dark that was—he glanced up and saw Bessie Smith's house beside him, and paused at the steps. Inside there was warmth and drink and forgetfulness. There would even be a welcome of sorts. Yet in the end he decided against it and went on. Again at a coffee stall he stopped and got a cup of coffee; it warmed him, for the night was cold, but he could not touch food. Late in the evening he found himself outside of Grant's imposing home and was admitted by Grant's imposing butler.

Even Grant, who already knew the story, was startled at his face and even more startled by his first words.

"I'm quitting, Grant. I'm through. I'm resigning. You're chief of staff, so I'm telling you now."

"Don't be a fool, Chris. We all lose cases."

"Not like this."

"How do you know?" Grant demanded. "We don't all go around shouting our mistakes to heaven, as you're doing. She was a ward case, wasn't she?"

"What's that got to do with it? She had a right to live, whoever she was."

Grant, seeing that strong measures were required, leaned forward across his imposing desk and said:

"It's up to this, Arden. If you've lost your nerve—"

It answered. Chris jerked up as though he had been slapped.

"Lost my nerve! Hell, I haven't lost my nerve. I've lost a woman, damn it, not a case. I've killed somebody. I knew I oughtn't to operate today. I went ahead anyhow."

Grant got up without a word and producing a bottle from his medicine cabinet, poured him a substantial drink.

"Maybe I'm as stupid as you think I am," he said, "but I still know when a drink is indicated. Stop shouting and take this."

He was a busy man with calls to make that night, but he did not go until Chris had relaxed in his chair. In that interval he told Chris certain things which he was always to remember.

"We can't be gods," he said. "We are only men, so we have to draw a balance. You've the making of a fine surgeon, Chris, and to throw that away is to lose the balance. You'll always save more than you lose; but you will always have losses. Better think of them as cases, not as men and women. Then you can carry on. You'll do that eventually anyhow—or you'll break. And what good will it do to anybody if you break?"

It was sound stuff, but he was talking against time. He too had seen that notice in the paper, and he had not been in and out of the Lewis house for months without recognizing the situation there. It was not however until Chris, agreeing not to resign and slightly dizzy with whisky on an empty stomach, had risen to go that Grant touched on the matter.

"I understand you sent Annie Lewis to me. Thanks for that, old man. It was too late, of course. Just why women commit that sort of suicide—"

"I don't think she was particularly happy."

"Perhaps not. Still—" He paused. "She was fond of you, Arden. She'd have liked that marriage."

Chris stiffened. "That's over," he said. "All over. I was a fool there too, but in any battle between Lewis and me he was bound to win."

"Beverly's young, of course, and an engagement isn't final. She's come through a bad time, and she probably doesn't know yet what she wants."

"She knows well enough what she doesn't want," said Chris without bitterness, and went away.

Grant watched him out and then went back to his handsome offices. Around him was his expensive house, and somewhere in it was his expensive wife. But he was not thinking of these visible symbols of success; rather Chris had carried him back again to his own youth, to his first death on the operating table, to his first love affair and its failure, and to the struggle of those early days. He had lived through them all, through death and failure, through success and reputation, even through the urgency of passion and the physical distress of sex.

Now he and Janet had settled down. He was making a large income but saving very little of it. There were no children, and Janet fretfully wanted him to retire. He could not afford to retire, and tired as he was, retirement was like suicide, a confession. A confession of weakness, of inability to carry on. He would make no such confession.

He moved around his consulting room, preparing for his evening calls. He did not hurry, although his car and chauffeur were at the door. It was at such times, when his nurse had gone and his rooms were empty, that he seemed to recapture his practice, as though only at night could he strip it of its trimmings and once more could hold it in his own hands.

Perhaps Chris was lucky, in one way. Women could play the devil with work. He remembered the first case he had lost on the table after he had married Janet; how he had walked the streets all night without coming home, and in the morning she would not speak to him. When at last he had told her, stripping his soul bare, she had not believed him.

"And you walked all night, without even sending me word?"

"I felt like a murderer, Janet."

"Nonsense! Do you think I believe every cock and bull story you tell me?"

He had never done that again. Now he had a fashionable practice. Sometimes he hated himself for it, but Janet liked it. It gave her prestige. He had even, like editors and ruling sovereigns, learned to say "we." Bustling into a room, gazing down at some supine figure on a bed:

"Well, how are we this morning?" he would ask.

"I was awake practically all night, doctor."

"Well, we'll have to see to that. We certainly can't go without sleep."

It was good business. It identified him with his patients, made a small partnership between them as against an outside and healthier world. He was a sound man for all that. Long ago he had dreamed of giving up general practice and doing only surgery; but Janet had needed many things to keep her contented, so he had never done it. He had lost something, he knew. He thought about it that night. The thing which had set him to walking the streets long ago, or into a desperation like that of Chris's that night, was gone. Nowadays a call was a sum of money, to be tidily recorded in his ledger by his secretary, and a death was bad luck or the will of God, according to the status of the family. Yes, he had lost something; but he was too old to change, and too comfortable.

He picked up his black bag and went out to his car. His brief discontent was over, and so he settled back into a corner and closed his eyes. Very soon he was asleep. He often slept like that nowadays, between calls.

Late that night Chris unlocked his front door and entered his house. He was tired to the point of exhaustion, but the hall was cold, and he went down and put coal on the furnace.

The cellar was dirty and cluttered with the odds and ends Lily Walters obstinately refused to throw away, old crates, empty paint cans, broken chairs and tables. The light was burning too, and he swore angrily when he saw it. Sitting under it was some of Henry Walters' futile paraphernalia, and with the coal shovel in his hand he stood staring at it. No, by God, he would not be defeated like that. He would go on, fight his battle, carry his own load. Henry had quit, but he would not.

He operated the next day as usual, his hand steady, his technique certain, his face impassive. Toward the end Grant came in and stood by, watching. The eyes of the two men met for a moment, then Chris bent over his work again. When he had finished he looked up, but Grant was gone.

CHAPTER XXI

SPRING of that year came much as usual. There were lilacs on the ancient bush in the back yard, and in the ailanthus tree—the "tree of heaven"—newly arrived birds sang, not the songs of love but of conquest. This branch is mine. This bit of air is mine. Keep off. Keep out. Keep off.

The park was green again, with children playing there, and at night Caesar would be let out to disappear mysteriously. In the morning he would be lying guiltily on the back porch, and more than once he bore the scars of dishonorable battles. Lily, admitting him, would eye him with disfavor.

"Shame on you, acting like that!"

For Beverly the fall and winter had been endess. She had been dragged from one place to another, as though her father was trying to escape from himself. But he could not leave himself behind.

"I think we'll go on tomorrow."

"Where?"

"Berlin. I've wired the Adlon."

And the next day, in a stuffy overfurnished room at the Adlon she would be unpacking her clothes again, and instead of Monte Carlo or the Nevsky Prospekt in Saint Petersburg she would be gazing at Unter den Linden and the Brandenburger Tor. When she was settled she would go out, holding her big fur muff against her face, for the wind was cold, walking briskly so that she would be weary enough to sleep. Then back again, to the long heavy German dinner, to a silent father, to bad coffee later in the lounge or a liqueur at a table in the small bar.

Now and then she was accosted on the street. Some resplendent officer would drop into step beside her and address her in English: "Pardon, Fräulein, but have we not met before?"

"Not before, and not now."

He would salute her gravely and go on. One of life's little failures, but there were other women. Plenty of women, in that gay and decadent prewar Berlin.

She had no time to make friends, no lightness and laughter in her life. When one day near the Gate she came face to face with Jerry Ames it was like recapturing her youth; and Jerry, smiling down at her, proceeded to tuck her arm under his and do some capturing of his own.

"What in the world brought you here?"

"I like that! I've chased you all over the map and onto the margins. And now that I've found you, my dear—"

She was very lovely, there in the cold with her muff against her cheek, with her face flushed in the wind and her skirts whipping around her slender legs. He eyed her with appreciation.

"Now that I've found you I'm not letting you go, Bev."

She said nothing to that. He was young and gay and possessive. He took her to tea, came to dinner that evening, got up a theater party later and sometime that night she found herself dancing in his arms, the long slow German waltz, to a band playing the Blue Danube. Jerry holding her and whispering in her ear:

"I love you, sweetheart. Love you. Love you."

She went back to bed and to sleep with that ringing in her ears, the music, the soft lights, and Jerry's handsome head towering over her, whispering to her. The next day he sent her a huge bunch of violets, and she pinned them to her black fur coat. She had worn no flowers since Annie's death.

Later on they went to Paris, and he went with them. While Staunton slept in the compartment of the train Jerry came over and sitting beside her, reached out and took her hand.

"You do care for me, don't you, Bev?"

"I don't want to think about love now, Jerry. Not with mother—"

"I know, sweet. I'll not bother you."

He made Paris possible. She was not in love with him, but she was fond of him. Staunton was seeing his foreign agents, buying pictures and old French furniture, keeping busy to fill a strange emptiness in his life; and Beverly, facing a lonely day, would hear Jerry on the telephone.

"How about dinner and a dance?"

"I was going to bed early."

"Time for that when we're old, my child. Come on; put on something pretty and let's go somewhere." He was always wanting to go somewhere.

One night in a taxicab he slipped something on her engagement finger and leaning over, kissed it gently. She looked down at his bright head and, when he straightened, up into his blue eyes.

"Do you mind?" he asked, smiling.

"I don't know. Give me time, Jerry, won't you? I feel so lost."

"Lost? Not with me around, sweetheart. Never with me."

She kept the ring, and her father seemed pleased when she told him, or as pleased as he could be just then, with the order of his life altered without his consent; and at his suggestion she began to select her trousseau, going from shop to shop with a small worried frown, determinedly putting away that young past of hers, her youth, her mother, and of course, Chris Arden. That sense of practicality she had inherited from Staunton told her that Jerry fitted into her scheme of life, whereas Chris never had and never would; and she was fond of Jerry. In time, she thought, she would probably love him. Marriage was more than romantic sentiment. If people liked the same things, lived the same lives, they grew together. And Jerry was cheerful, cheerful and rather demanding. She would come into the hotel from a long day to find him there, smiling and fresh.

"How about dinner and dancing somewhere?"

"Do we have to, Jerry? I'm so tired."

"Change of occupation is rest, my love! Hurry now, get a hot bath and you'll be ready to go."

They would go, and after a cocktail and food she would feel better. It was good to feel Jerry's arms around her, close and protective. It was good not to worry any more, to have discarded her past and not to think too much about the future. But Jerry was tireless.

"What? Going home already?"

"I have a big day tomorrow."

"Come on, just one more dance. It's still the shank of the evening."

One night she said to him: "We can't dance all through life, Jerry."

"Who wants to! But we're only young once, and it's spring, my sweet."

Some time toward morning she would get back, to crawl into her bed in her hotel room and fall asleep at once. She saw little of daylight Paris outside the shops, and almost nothing of her father, meeting his business associates and in his leisure studying books and catalogues. If he was lonely he said nothing, but sometimes Beverly thought he was anxious, for all his spending. Business was not good, had been on a declining scale for some years. Only the automobile had saved it so far, and there would be a saturation point for that. One day he told Jerry before her that a European war would help, and that there was one in the making.

"They'll have to buy from us," he said. "And they have money or credit to do it. It would take care of our surplus anyhow."

"But you don't want a war, father?"

"What has that got to do with it? If these fellows want to cut each other's throats—"

It seemed of no importance to her.

It was that spring in Paris that Jerry got a letter from America. He read it twice and then carefully destroyed it, and after that he took a drink to steady his nerves, and then another. Beverly waited for him until late in the evening, and then went to bed. He turned up the next morning with a cut lip and a story of a taxi crash, however, and she believed him. She had to believe him. He was all she had.

That was in Paris. In America too spring had come. It had come to the park, with small black and green buds on the trees and the yellow of the forsythia sprayed like golden plumes among the shrubberies. It had even come to the old ailanthus tree, joyously young each spring and welcoming back its birds after their long pilgrimage. "Business as usual," it said to them, waving its branches. "Stop and rest. Stop and rest your tired wings. It's been frightfully dull all winter."

"Drat the birds," said Lily. "A body can't sleep for their noise!"

In the yard Chris scattered bread crumbs and seeds, and kept an old tin pan of Lily's filled with water; and in the hospital the spring and new hope had put a little dance into Katie's step, and a trifle of coquetry when an intern idled into her ward.

"Looking very gay this morning, Miss Walters. Got a new young man?"

"No, but I'm looking for one, doctor," she would say demurely.

She had an animal vitality which made men always aware of her. It went no further than that, however, for Katie was watching her step. She had her own plans that spring, and she was aware that she was not too popular in the school. She was competent and willing, but she was too self-contained, a trifle hard. Perhaps that hardness of hers was a defensive mechanism, set up for her own protection, but psychiatry was still feeling its way, and to the other nurses she was merely a compact efficient little machine, doing her work but no more, and singularly callous.

"What on earth are you crying about?"

"That baby in G is dead."

"Probably better off," Katie would say, and move along

briskly. The hospital as such barely touched her. She saw it as work to be done, hours to be kept. Never once did she see it as more than a job, or as having any spiritual overtones whatever. By the end of her first night duty she had stood by a half-dozen deathbeds and duly recorded them on her charts, but she kept herself detached from them. It never came to her with a shock—as it had to Chris—that she had seen a human soul pass on in the night and had gone to bed the next morning and forgotten it. She would fix the screens, call the orderlies, go about her work. If death did not shock her, however, birth did. Her first obstetric case sent her horrified out of the delivery room, to burst into tears in the corridor. Chris, on his way to the operating room, happened to find her there.

"I never knew it was like that. It's horrible, Chris. Dreadful."

"What's dreadful about it, Katie? It's rather grand in a way, isn't it?"

She never became accustomed to it. She hated the whole business of gestation. She hated the sight of the women in their loose wrappers waiting in the ward for their hour to come, and sitting and rocking placidly their grotesque and distorted bodies. She loathed their swollen faces, their swollen legs and feet. And when at last a child had come she saw in it no miracle, but a small red animal sucking at a full overflowing breast, and hated it for being what it was. The other nurses, especially the older ones, took a certain pride in their babies. They would pick up and hold the little squirming bodies, satisfying some deep maternal instinct by this contact, looking at them with pride and affection.

"Look, my Jimmy is going to have brown eyes."

"*Your* Jimmy!"

She was conscientious enough, but always after a seance in the delivery room she would go to her room as soon as she was off duty and stare at her own slim body with terrified eyes. Never, never would she bear a child; and long after that assignment was over she would waken at night in a hot sweat.

For a minute or so in her sleep she had been one of the women in the obstetric ward, awaiting her hour, or she had been on the table and a new life was being wrenched from her. She would open her mouth to scream, and then the familiar light coming in over the transom would show her her own room, her uniform flung over a chair, her cap on the bureau, and she would turn contentedly and go to sleep again.

Never, never would she bear a child.

She seldom saw Chris. He was busy again; his practice growing, spreading beyond the block into the ward, and from there slowly extending. On her afternoons at home he would come in, eat hurriedly and go out again, closing the door into the back office with firm finality. Sometimes she did not see him at all, and the house without him meant nothing to her. It seemed untidier than ever, and after a visit home she would go back to the hospital, grateful to it for its order and quiet, for the linen folded and piled on the shelves, for the plentiful hot water, for the neat medicine closets, for the regular hours and for her own room at night, where she could close the door, live her own life and dream her own dreams.

One afternoon when she was at home Betty Howard came in and spent an hour in the office, and Chris was astounded to have Katie march in after she had gone, her face white.

"I suppose you know your own business, Chris, but everybody knows what that girl is. She's been in here for an hour."

"And what," said Chris coldly, "is that to you?"

"Nothing at all, except that the neighbors are talking."

"I think that that is a lie, Katie."

That roused her to fury. She had fought for him like a tiger, she said, when that woman had died on the table. She spent her half-days off trying to make the house tidy for him. But any girl could walk into his office and be shut in there for hours, and nobody knew what went on. If that was the sort he was— Then she broke down and said she was a fool, and he had to soothe her as best he could.

"I wish you'd get that nonsense out of your mind, Katie."

"I wish I could, Chris."

And for a few minutes she was something young and helpless again, gazing at him with tear-dimmed eyes while he puzzled over the problem she presented.

Her visits home always upset her. She would go back with her nerves on edge, and for days her patients would watch her warily.

"Get back into bed, Smith. If you get up again I'll tie you."

Or she would find after visiting day some small cache of fruit or tobacco in a bedside stand and confiscate it peremptorily. It became a game with them, this hiding of contraband from her. In vain she sent grinning orderlies to search the men's toilet and bathrooms. They never found anything, and she would feel frustrated and indignant.

"But I saw smoke coming out, Briggs."

"Nothing there, Miss Walters."

One day Miss Simpson sent for her, and eyed her as she stood across the desk.

"A hospital, Miss Walters," she said, "is a curious thing. It is a machine, and an efficient one. But it is more than that. We have somehow to put a soul into it."

"I don't know what I've done, Miss Simpson."

"If you don't know I probably can't tell you. You are an efficient nurse, but nursing is more than efficiency. It's a matter of tempering justice with mercy, and perhaps—compassion. I don't want to turn out merely machines from my school. Even good ones."

"I've done my best. If that's not good enough—"

Miss Nettie sighed. She was dealing with intangibles, and they were hard to put into words.

"What I am trying to say," she said patiently, "is that we have to heal minds here as well as bodies. We don't need to be sentimental, but we must not allow ourselves to grow hard."

But Katie, leaving with a strong sense of grievance, knew

better than that. She knew better than to feel. If other people knew they could hurt you it gave them a hold on you. And Miss Simpson, sitting thoughtfully in her room after Katie had gone, knew that she had not reached the girl at all; had merely antagonized Katie and gained nothing. . . .

Chris knew nothing of this that spring. He was mentally wretched and physically highly uncomfortable, for Lily had lapsed even from her previous state of inefficiency. Her wrappers were more bedraggled, the accumulation of unwashed dishes and dust everywhere greater. There were times too when she acted like a woman drugged, although she angrily denied it.

"Drugs? What sort of drugs, doctor? And where would I get them?"

He took to locking his medicine closet then, but Lily knew a trick worth two of that. There were always the samples left in Chris's absence, and one day also she got in a locksmith and had a second key made to the closet.

"The doctor's lost his," she said, and paid him a dollar out of the house money.

Now and then Chris brought in a colored woman from the alley behind the house to clean up, and for a day or two the brass plate on the front door would shine and the house be orderly. But soon it would lapse again and Lily be shut away in her upstairs room, rocking slowly in her comfortable daze.

He worked hard, walking his district sturdily, reading the stories of many houses as he passed them, or going in, had climbed stairs, to find himself in some upper room where he ceased to be Chris Arden and became both doctor and priest. He began to know the insides of many houses and many lives; that behind the neat windows of the Lee house old Colonel Lee was quietly drinking himself to death because the army had been his life, and because the fretful wife he had lost had made him get out of it; that Miss Andrews was what she was because long years before she had loved a man who jilted her; and that the chronic invalidism of Mrs. Betts, who had not left her bed for five years, was due to her terror that her only son would marry and leave her. "I can't let him go, doctor. I can't. It would kill me. He is all I have left."

"But don't you want him to be happy?"

"He'd never be happy with her."

One day he lost his temper. "You mothers!" he said. "Some of you would mentally castrate your sons to hold them. Don't you want him to be a man?"

He had accepted his life. Sometimes he wondered whether the people he struggled to save were worth saving, but not often. Now and then too his long continence bothered him, merely as a physical fact. But in the main his defenses held. He never let himself be idle. When he had an hour to spare he posted his books; or he would wander down the street to where Ted Lawrence was wearing his clothes shiny waiting for practice and making a joke of it.

"What are you doing?" Chris would say.

"Looking at the map. This place is too healthy for me. Where's the malaria district anyhow?"

"No good. They all take quinine anyhow."

"Well, speaking of that, let's take a little something ourselves."

He would set out a bottle and two glasses, and often they talked late into the night. He was good for Chris; small, cheerful, eminently practical. If he suspected or knew of the tragedy of Chris's broken engagement he never mentioned it, unless indirectly.

"Come on and take a walk. Your face is as long as a wet day in the country."

Together, having tramped all day, they would take a busman's holiday and tramp some more. It was Ted who found a field outside of town where the tall dried stalks of some sort of weed still stood, and initiated the game of throwing them like spears.

"If we ever get in a war," he boasted, "I'll be chief of the javelin throwers."

CHAPTER XXII

ONE day Chris saw the Lewis car on a downtown street, and knew that Beverly was back from Europe. It made no appreciable difference in him, save that he began then to develop those deep lines from nose to mouth which were so characteristic of him as he matured. But very soon after that he had one of those experiences that set many a medical man to wondering just where right and justice lay, and which caused him many a sleepless night for weeks to come.

He walked into his office one night to find a young woman waiting for him. She had an intelligent face and was well dressed, and he had no suspicion of the situation when she followed him into the consulting room. Her first words enlightened him.

"I am in trouble, doctor. I suppose you know what that means. And I imagine you will refuse to do anything about it." She smiled gravely. "I know, because I've tried before. There's a law against it, isn't there?"

"It's rather more than merely a law, isn't it?"

She nodded.

"Much more. I know all the arguments. I've had several months to think them over. Alone," she added with a slight emphasis.

"Then the father of the child—?"

"Has been away. He didn't know about it, you see. Not that that would have made any difference. I thought once he would marry me eventually, but—well, that doesn't matter now. I think now that I will have the child, doctor." She smiled again. "I'm not being particularly noble, but you see I happened to care for the man."

She was so carefully matter-of-fact that he kept his own face impassive.

"You are being very brave now. It's the best thing, of course; the only sensible thing."

She had not finished however. She was still calm, but he saw that her hands were clenched tight on the arms of her chair.

"What I want, and what I think is fair, is that the—the man in the case shall see me through it, and support the child later. That's not being mercenary. I support myself—I'm a stenographer in one of the mills—and I shall have to go somewhere else to live. Unfortunately he does not see it that way. He thinks it will give me a hold on him, be a sort of blackmail." She flushed. "In other words, now it might be anybody's child. If he sends me money or checks, it is his."

"And what else does he suggest?"

"He thinks I need not have it at all."

Chris was puzzled. Apparently she wanted nothing from him; but there was a determination in her voice, a purpose, that put him back in his chair observing her with level eyes.

"I see. There is no hope that he will marry you, I suppose?"

"None whatever. He is about to be married to someone else."

Suddenly she sat forward in her chair. "I don't need a doctor," she said. "Not yet, at least. But I want someone young enough to understand and interested enough to help me, Doctor Arden. And I chose you because the man is Jervis Ames, and I think you know the girl he is going to marry."

He said nothing, and after a quick glance at his set face she went on.

"You see, I have two courses open, and only two, doctor. One is to go to Miss Lewis. I don't want to do that. The other is to hand Jerry his part of this problem and make him take it. So far I've failed. He is frightened, but he is still not frightened enough. You see, he knows me. He knows I won't tell on him, and he's banking on that." And she added: "It's just his bad luck. But it's mine too. I fell in love with him, and that was that."

Chris still said nothing, and she went on. Of course Jerry was "a bad man with women." She knew that now. He would never be faithful to a wife; but he had his good points too. He was kind. He had been both kind and generous to her until now. He would be good to a wife, even while he was being unfaithful to her. "Even more then, probably." He thought she was a fool for having the child, and he was furiously angry with her.

"You see, he's very much in love with Miss Lewis. I suppose he was in love with her even when—" She stopped, then added: "Men do queer things in situations like this, doctor. I don't suppose he'd murder me, but—"

Chris had had time to pull himself together. He smiled dryly.

"I suppose any man who is capable of passion is capable of murder, but I doubt if Ames would even think of it," he said. "I imagine you want me to see him. Is that it?"

"I thought," she said calmly, "that you would rather go to him than have me go to her."

He sat back in his chair. The room was silent, the desk under his hand as usual gritty with dust. He was no moralist, condemning Ames for what he had done, but in a way his hands were tied. The secrets of the consulting room were like those of the confessional. But if this girl was right there was more at stake than the birth and care of a child. There was Beverly's whole future.

"I'm to see Ames and try to fix this up?" he asked heavily.

"He'll fix it," she said with practical assurance. "Just now it's between him and me. He thinks I won't talk. If he knows I've told you—"

"I see," he said, still heavily. "It's the devil of a thing to ask me to do."

"He's more afraid of you than of anyone else," she said simply; and sat quiet, her hands folded in her lap.

He agreed finally, jotting down such details as she gave him; her name, Ursula Martin, the sum she would require and the approximate date of the child's birth. When she had gone however he sat for a long time thinking over the situation. He resented being pitchforked into a position like this, but more than that he wondered if the Martin girl was merely bitter, or if she had been right. To let Beverly go blindly into a marriage with a man who would not be faithful . . .

He glanced at his watch and got up. If it had to be done better do it soon, he thought, and wondered how to go about it. Since Beverly was back Ames would probably be at the Lewis house now, and he might catch him on the way out. The best thing of course was for Ames to tell Beverly and then let her make her own decision. But he would refuse, almost certainly, and in that case what?

He lighted a cigarette and saw that his hands were unsteady. It was the devil of a mess to be in. Either he saw Jerry or she would go to Beverly. Well, why not let her go to Beverly? If Ames was what she had said he was it might be better in the end. But the girl, for all her poise, was in real trouble, and he had promised to do what he could. At last he threw away his cigarette and got up.

The evening was warm as he climbed the hill. Up that hill he had walked with Annie Lewis. "I have always wanted a son. I think things would have been different if I had had a son." And then later: "Good night, Chris, and God bless you." Up that hill too he had gone to Beverly. "Don't let me go, Chris. Don't ever let me go." And his own voice replying: "I'll never let you go." Only a year ago, all that, and now his worldly hopes had indeed turned to ashes, and his mouth was dry with them.

At the top of the hill he stopped and looked back. Somewhere down there was old Joshua, with his white ascension robe now folded away in a box. Perhaps men had always wanted a hereafter to compensate for an unsatisfactory here. Somewhere down there too were those children of the shadows, as he always thought of them, left to the indifferent care of the Barretts of the world. And gleaming in the red and yellow flames from the mills was the river, the river which had divided him from his past as definitely as it separated its now untidy banks.

He turned and went on. The past was past. Now Beverly was in love with somebody else, and his only job was to preserve her happiness if he could. . . .

The driveway was familiar even in the dark. It was almost a year since he had been there, but the very odors from Annie's garden were reminiscent; the scent of newly-cut grass, the heavy sweet smell of the lilacs. He stumbled on, homesick for old familiar things, for the blaze of light as the hall door was opened, for the sharp greeting of Sandy, for Holmes' welcoming smile, and then at last Beverly herself. "Don't let me go, Chris. Don't ever let me go." It was she who had gone, taking herself out of his life with a cool definiteness that had left him no recourse. And now—

He saw as he made the turn in the driveway that he had been right, and that Jerry was there. His car was parked not far from the house, and Chris stepped into the shadow of the trees and waited. He had not long to wait. The door opened and Jerry came out. As he left the house behind him he began to whistle cheerfully, and he was still whistling when Chris confronted him. He stopped and stared.

"Who is it? Oh, it's you, Arden!"

"Do you mind driving me around a bit? I have something to say. I don't want to say it, but it's been put up to me."

Ames was not whistling now. He eyed Chris with suspicion.

"Why not say it here?" he said truculently.

"Not here, if you don't mind."

"All right. Get in."

He let in the clutch with a jerk, and Chris lighted a cigarette. In the light of the match he saw the other man's handsome face, set and hard, and knew he had guessed his errand. It was not until they were in the street however that he spoke.

"I find myself in a situation I don't like, Ames," he said. "In a way it has nothing to do with me; in another way it has. The Martin girl was in to see me tonight, and I agreed to see you."

"What the hell have you got to do with it?"

"Nothing, personally. It's not my business. But she gave me two alternatives, neither of them pleasant; and here I am. I can induce you to see reason, or she will go to Beverly. That's the way she put it, and I think she meant it."

"The little bitch!" was Jerry's furious comment. "She threw herself at me, and now she's blackmailing me. That's what it is. Pure blackmail." He glanced at Chris. "See here, Arden, you're a doctor. If you're so interested in her why don't you get her out of this mess?"

"She doesn't want out," said Chris quietly. "And I'm not interested, as you call it. I never saw her until tonight. I wouldn't do it anyhow. Aside from the risk to her, it's against the law."

"Is it against the law if there's enough in it?" Jerry said nastily.

Chris kept his temper with difficulty.

"I'll let that go," he said. "She's going to have this child, Ames, and she isn't asking a great deal. She doesn't see it as blackmail, nor do I. After all, it's your child."

"So she says!"

He was badly frightened, however. After a time he stopped the car at a curb and lighted a cigarette. Chris saw that he was white and twitching.

"What in heaven's name does a man do in circumstances like these?" he demanded. "I'm to be married in a few weeks, Arden, and you know Beverly. She'd throw me over in a second if she knew."

"I suppose if that happened you wouldn't marry the Martin girl?"

"God, no."

"Then," Chris said gravely, "I'd pay up like a man, Ames. And I'd tell Beverly before I married her. She might"—he hesitated—"she might be more understanding than you think."

Ames laughed without mirth.

"You know her," he said shortly. "Do you think she would be understanding, as you call it? You know damned well she wouldn't, she nor any other woman. No, that's no good, Arden. I'll pay up, but I'll not tell Bev. Not now. Nor ever."

Chris opened the door of the car and put out his long legs; then he turned his body and looked at Jerry, sulky and defiant.

"That's fixed then," he said. "But by the living God, if you're not good to her I'll make life a hell on earth for you."

He walked home, unhappy and dissatisfied. He had saved Ursula Martin—so far as she could be saved—but what about Beverly? This reckless defiant boy was not the Jerry Ames he had remembered, and his heart sank. To give her over into such hands—

When he reached his door again there was a messenger boy on the step, and he signed for a telegram. It was from Hiram Mortimer and it read: "Mother sinking. Would like to see you." . . . . .

Letitia was dying. There was no particular trouble, as Hiram said when he met him at the station. Nothing that anyone could find out. It was merely as though she didn't care to live any longer.

"She misses father, I guess," was Hiram's laconic statement.

Later on Chris, having gone over her, was inclined to agree with Hiram. It was as if old Dave, always lavish with vitality, had imparted to her something which now was gone. She lay on her own side of the wide bed, so small and light that her body hardly raised the bedding, with that hollow space beside her, and with her mind quite clear and fearless.

"I think Dave needs me, Chris."

"Don't you think you're needed here too?"

"That's different. The boys are married and have their own. They'll be sorry, but that's the way of life. Dave always had to be looked after."

It was that night however, with the "boys" sitting solemnly downstairs in the old house and the daughters-in-law bustling about in the kitchen, that she really opened up her heart to Chris as probably she had never done to anyone in her long life.

"Life is queer, Chris. Dave wasn't in love with me when he married me. There was a girl he wanted, but she went away."

"He loved you all the rest of his life, my dear."

"Maybe. I never did know, Chris. He wasn't much for talking. But he needed me, and I made him a good wife."

She would drowse, waken, sleep again; but always she held to his hand. It was as though she could say to him the things she could never say to her sons, things that she felt must be said. Once it was about Dave's faith in God, and there was something about a time long-ago when a strange woman had come to the town and he had been infatuated with her for a time. "He was always there when he had any time. But I always knew he would come back to me." Then after an interval there was a long story about a boy out in the country who had got drunk and killed his young wife, and was known to be hiding somewhere near; and of Dave's getting on his horse and riding madly for hours to get there before the posse which was out to lynch him.

"He shut himself in before he left and prayed, Chris," she said. "And so I suppose what he did was right. But I've worried about it sometimes."

What Dave had done, however, startled Chris. He had found the boy, slinking into his father's farm house just before the dawn, and they could both hear the horses of the posse as they came pounding along the road. Old Dave had said a quick prayer, holding onto the boy with all his strength, and then taken his loaded revolver from his holster and held it out.

"Better go behind the barn, son, so your mother won't hear it."

The boy had gone, and the posse had heard a shot and came on a gallop. Nobody had ever known until now that the gun had been Dave's.

"He'd have been hanged anyhow, Chris. Not only the posse. The police were on their way, too."

"Yes. Probably that was the only answer."

"It wasn't taking a life, or helping to."

"No."

"There were times later when Dave wasn't sure, you know. He was a strong man, but sometimes he distrusted himself."

"He was strong, my dear. Don't be afraid for him. He's all right."

She died a week later, her sons standing tall and diffident about her bed and their wives respectfully in the background. Chris was astonished and touched to find that she had left him five thousand dollars, "to be used for study abroad or elsewhere."

He left with a sense of having once more turned over a page which could never be reopened. Before his departure he went into Dave's old offices, carefully kept as he had left them. They seemed singularly bare now; a table and a few chairs in one, a desk and a chair or two in the other. In the consulting room was the sagging leather couch where he had so often thrown himself down for some badly needed rest, and beside which undoubtedly he had prayed when in doubt. Chris had a momentary vision of him on that night of which Letitia had spoken, kneeling there and wrestling with his God; and then rising from his knees, getting his old revolver from his desk and hurriedly loading it. What answer had he had to that prayer? What answer did any man have to any prayer? . . . . .

It was during that absence of his that the date and details of Beverly's approaching marriage were announced, and he knew then that it was too late to do anything. He was tempted to take Letitia's money and go abroad at once, before it took place. Even then he knew that flight was not his answer. Also he had promised to see Ursula through her confinement in the fall.

There was no escape for him during the days that followed. The papers were filled with details of the wedding. Names of the bridesmaids were given, marquees were described, gifts apparently were pouring in. A silver coffee set had been presented, it appeared, by the Mayor and the City Council. One day he saw that Beverly's wedding dress had been made in Paris, and he was standing once more with his arm around her, gazing down at an old-fashioned white satin gown, its train lined with lace ruffles, its neck high, and a tulle veil with a satin head band and a bunch of osprey at the side.

"She wants me to wear them, Chris. Later on."

He had not been asked to the wedding; he had not expected to be. Nor had he seen her since her return. Late on the night before it was to take place he was sitting at the desk in his office when the telephone rang and he heard her voice, rather breathless.

"Chris?"

"Yes."

"It's Beverly."

That old tightening of the throat, an inability to speak when suddenly moved, kept him silent and she said. "Are you still there, Chris?"

"I suppose I'll always be here when you call me, my dear. Is anything wrong?"

"No. That is—Chris, are you still angry with me?"

"Angry? Never. I want you to be happy in your own way. If that didn't happen to be my way—"

"And you are all right?"

"Fine. Even busy."

She said nothing to that and it struck him suddenly that she was crying.

"See here, my darling," he said, "if you're not sure of this marriage it's not too late. Be very sure of yourself before you go ahead. Don't make a mistake."

She did not answer that, and once again she seemed to be waiting for something, although he only realized that later.

"Look here," he said, "you're tired and nervous. I'm going to send you something to give you a night's sleep. You'll take it, won't you?"

"Yes," she said in a small voice. "You're sure you're all right?"

"Perfectly."

"Then good night, Chris. And—good-by."

He was pale but collected when he walked to the drug store and sent her the promised tablets. He took one himself when they were being measured out, and the drug clerk grinned at him.

"Optimistic, aren't you? No babies tonight, eh?"

"This is one time when I intend to sleep," he said grimly.

"Well, pleasant dreams!"

"No dreams at all," said Chris, and walked out again.

Beverly married Jerry Ames the next afternoon in the Lewis garden in a blaze of sunlight; a Jerry who, along with his ushers, blinked at the glare with eyes slightly congested from his bachelor party the night before. Beverly was white but composed. Nearby was the place where Chris had found her breaking her heart a year before and had caught her in his arms. She did not look at it, however, and her voice was steady when she made her responses during the ceremony. She liked Jerry. They would grow together. And she had her father's stubbornness. She had agreed to do this thing. Now she was doing it.

The next morning's papers showed pictures of her in her wedding finery, standing at the end of the green alley, with the fountain behind her and Jerry beside her in spats and a morning coat, with a gardenia in his lapel. She looked very beautiful in her heavy white satin with its long train draped about her and a band of orange blossoms over her dark hair to hold her real lace veil. She was holding her head high and smiling faintly into the camera.

CHAPTER XXIII

CAESAR was killed that summer, run down by a limousine belonging to one of the local magnates. He was romping with another dog in the street and the car, running well above the city speed limit, went over them both. Went on without stopping too, leaving Chris to carry in the one creature which had loved him, and later to give him decent burial under the tree in the back yard.

Lily did not dare to speak to him that day, and she told Miss Barker later on over the back fence that he was acting very queer, and that he had thought a lot of the dog. She was dozing in her chair late that afternoon when Chris, having seen the car on its way home, deliberately put on his hat and started after it. He knew where to go, and he moved on as relentlessly as fate itself.

The garage was on an alley behind the house, and he was white and tight-lipped as he turned into it. The chauffeur was there, kicking his tires and smoking a cigarette. He was a big man, and he knew trouble when he saw it coming. He threw away the cigarette.

"You killed my dog today," said Chris.

"Yeah. Why didn't you keep it out of the street?"

"Killed it and went on," said Chris inexorably.

"You and your damn dog! If you're looking for trouble you've come to the right place."

"That's precisely what I'm looking for," said Chris, and hauled off with a straight right which landed on the chauffeur's jaw.

Five minutes later he picked up his hat and departed. He was considerably battered, but he felt better than he had for days. The fact that he had left his opponent sitting on the cement floor, groggy and bloody, was comforting. He turned in the doorway as he left.

"Perhaps that will teach you something you needed to know."

"For God's sake," said the man, "where do you pack that wallop anyhow?"

Chris felt rather better as he went home. Some of the accumulated fury of days and weeks had exploded during that epic battle; and Ted Lawrence, wandering in that evening for a talk and a drink, found him surveying himself in his head mirror, and turning toward him a whimsical eye which was already black.

"Hello!" said Lawrence. "Run into a door?"

"Ran into a fist."

"How's the fist?"

It was probably Lawrence who saved him during those first weeks after Beverly's marriage. He knew what the trouble was, and often he stayed until late in the night, discussing and arguing.

"Pretty soon we'll be a profession of specialists, and it will take a dozen or two of us to know what's wrong with any case." Or: "You're lucky. You know what you want and are going after it. I'm no surgeon, and pretty often I think I'm no doctor."

He was highly controversial.

"Why not State medicine anyhow?" he would argue. "About nine-tenths of what I do now is free. I'd better be paid something than nothing. Sure it would ruin us as a profession, but it ought to make us into a lot of damned good business men."

But he was a romanticist after his own fashion. He saw nothing humdrum in his work. "We don't only patch bodies," he would say after a drink or so. "You and I, Chris, patch human lives."

Chris liked him. The human race, he considered, was the most badly handicapped of all God's creatures; not only in its social and moral laws, but in everything else. And the higher the civilization the greater the handicap. The savage woman gave birth as easily as an animal; and the lowest of all in the scale, the insects, merely laid their eggs and forgot about them.

"Even the lowly cockroach," he would say, "has it all over the rest of us. Give him a warm kitchen and a few scraps on the floor and he flourishes."

"He does indeed!" said Chris grinning, with Lily's kitchen in mind.

But Lawrence considered the movement toward specialization a mistake, and Chris a fool for making it. "What will you be?" he would say. "A plumber! We general men will tell you what's wrong, and all you'll have to do is to go in where we show you and do the dirty work!"

"You have to have us."

"Sure, but where are you without us? A man gets a pain these days, and he can run around to a dozen fellows before he hits the one who knows what it is. That's not medicine; that's shopping."

He was good for Chris, and he was wise beyond his years. He knew that normal men did not carry disappointment all through their lives. Women cherished griefs but men forgot them. They would not willingly be unhappy or even uncomfortable. And as a matter of fact Chris, having accepted Beverly's marriage, was doing his best to forget her that summer. Alone on hot nights he was quietly preparing for Europe and study on Letitia's five thousand dollars. He was freshening his college German, and even studying a small phrase book of common medical terms: *Zeigen sie mir, bitte, ihre Zunge,* which was merely a request to show a tongue, or *sich operieren lassen,* which was much more grave and meant to undergo an operation. He was reading surgery again also, and spending time now in the operating room watching other men work. Katie, on the operating-room staff now, would see him coming in with that eager thrust of the shoulders as though his mind was traveling ahead of his body, and would watch him surreptitiously. When he smiled at one of the other nurses she would grow hot with jealousy.

He played golf that summer, as he wanted no idle time in which to brood; and now and then when things were slow in the evenings he went to the club. If he drank more than he should at such times he would temper it with a period of abstinence. It was in August that he took off Scott's finger.

"It's got to go, Scott."

"Go ahead, but I'd like to save the hand."

Chris, with Scott on the table, surveyed the dried and burned tissues and knew that eventually the hand would go also.

"Why don't you quit, Scott?"

"It's all I know. I can't let my family starve."

One day, however, going unexpectedly into the X-ray room, he found Scott practicing writing with his left hand. Neither man said anything, and Scott put his paper aside and showed him his fish in the anteroom. Lately he had taken up the raising of small tropical fish as a hobby. They required considerable care, and Chris surmised that by filling his leisure they helped him.

"Very handsome," said Chris. "Look as though they're increasing."

"Oh, they're prolific enough," said Scott grimly.

His face was a mask of tragic patience.

Ursula Martin's boy was born early in the fall. Chris attended her himself. She had insisted on going into the ward. Now and then he saw her there, rocking quietly among the others and awaiting the miracle of birth. She sewed a great deal, taking fine careful stitches and occasionally showing him some small completed garment. At times when the nurses were busy he would find her holding some fretful baby, and would marvel at the tenderness in her face.

She was still calm when preparing for her labor. She took

down her long heavy hair and braided it into two plaits, and she walked quietly to the delivery room when her time came.

It was a hot day, and the birth was slow and difficult. Chris, leaning over her after it was over, was dripping with sweat. But she was smiling.

"A boy?" she said feebly. "I wanted a boy. I shall call him for you, doctor."

Noel. Noel as a baby, red-faced and shrieking in his arms. Another signpost that along the road, although he did not know it. He put the child down in the crib.

"Then I'll keep an eye on him for you," he said. "We'll make a good job of him, Ursula."

She looked happier after that. She could depend on him. She had felt weak and alone. Now she was not alone. And Chris, stopping in Miss Nettie's room on the way out, told her a little of the story.

"She wanted the child," he said, "and now she has it. The father will pay her something, so that's all right. But I'd like to feel that someone knows about her while I'm away, in case of trouble."

"You know who the father is?"

"I know," he said briefly, and she eyed him.

"You are an incurable sentimentalist, Chris," she told him. "What on earth is this girl to you? And haven't you enough on your hands without her?"

However she agreed, and he left more easy in his mind. Later on he told Ursula, and she thanked him gravely. "But nothing will go wrong, doctor," she said. "I'm strong and so is he."

"And you won't make any trouble?"

"Why should I? I have my baby."

The next morning he saw in the paper that the Jervis Ameses had returned from their honeymoon and were to live in the Lewis house. He was prepared for it, so it gave him no particular shock. Beverly married was not his Beverly, was no longer the girl he had worshipped and adored. It was ridiculous to suffer now, when she belonged to some one else. . . .

Beverly however was not so sure of where she belonged. She had come home—with Jerry of course—to Holmes smiling at the door, to her father, formal but apparently pleased in the hall with his new tapestries on the walls and flowers everywhere, and later on to her own bedroom, where a new bed had been installed for Jerry and one could see from the window the top of an ailanthus tree far below among the housetops. Martha was there, unpacking her wedding finery, and Beverly took off her hat and then went to the window. The tree was there, but it was early autumn now and already its leaves were falling. Soon they would be gone, and she would not see it at all. Perhaps it was as well. It had belonged to a part of her life which she had put behind her; to the days when her mother lay in her bed and looked out at what she was never to see again; to youth and romance in a garden against the stern reality of her marriage.

Chris had been sanctuary, she thought. She had needed him and he had come. Now she did not need him. Her life was fixed. There was Jerry's bed behind her to prove it, his dressing room beyond. She was not unhappy. Jerry loved her, after his fashion, but she had no feeling of belonging to him, or indeed to anybody, even to her father. That small dapper man, cool and aloof and obsessed with his own affairs, seemed to her now an absurd figure around which to have built a furious loyalty; and that night, looking at him over the long length of the dinner table, she knew suddenly that she had thrown away the substance of living for this shadow, arrogant in his dinner clothes, critical of his meal, impatient at the service.

"For God's sake, Holmes! Get some food in here."

"Yes, sir. In a moment, sir."

The footman hurrying in, Holmes impassive, Jerry hungry and drinking too much, and herself alone in her mother's place, isolated from them both, from them all.

"That's your fourth glass, Jerry. And you had a lot of cocktails."

"Don't come home from a wedding trip every day, honey."

She was not actively unhappy, sitting there in the candle-light, with her arms bare and her mother's pearls gleaming on her neck. Facing her situation with her usual honesty, she knew that if she did not love Jerry she was fond of him. He was cheerful. He sang in his bath, whistled while dressing. If his superabundant vitality tired her at times, there were others when she was grateful for it. And he was proud of her. On that trip of theirs he had found friends in the most unlikely places, would immediately plan a party and survey her carefully after she had dressed for it.

"You're looking very beautiful, sweetheart."

He would kiss her passionately and she would do her best to respond. But it was acting, and he knew it. He had never really won her. He would release her and go away, drinking a cocktail or two to restore his self-respect and lessen his sense of failure. He was still courting her, she knew; still trying to win her. She would be very gay after that, and he would smile at her with approval.

"Lovely wife you have, Jerry," someone would say.

"You're telling *me?*"

But she had remained curiously inviolate, even after three months of marriage. She still wondered why what was so important to him meant so little to her. He would leave her, angry and frustrated.

"By God, I'll make you care for me."

"I do care, Jerry."

"You call that caring!"

Yet she was not cold. It was simply that Jerry excited no response in her. She had accepted the implications of marriage without question. If Jerry was irresponsible he was at least tactful. There had been no shock. And at first he had rather liked that fundamental virginity of hers. It gave him the pleasant illusion of violation, as though he held in his arms an untouched girl. Now it merely annoyed him, she knew. He hated anything that seemed beyond his reach.

Sitting there playing with her food she wondered just what there was to hold the three of them together, her father, Jerry and herself. For years her mother had sat where she was sitting. Had she wondered that too? She could remember long silences at the table, broken only by the cautious movement of the men who served the food. Now even Jerry seemed daunted. He caught her alone in the hall after dinner and grinned at her.

"Cheery little meal, eh?" he said. "Are they all like that?"

"Pretty much. You'll get used to it."

"Will I? Not if I can help it. Let's get the car and go somewhere."

"Our first evening at home?"

"What can we do here? Sit and twiddle our thumbs?"

In the end they went. They would always be going somewhere, she thought as she got a wrap. He was tireless, filled with animal energy. His cheerfulness was a part of that vitality of his, and already she knew that if she did not go he would go alone, and she was determined to make her marriage a success. She had paid a high price for it. It must succeed.

Neither of them knew, that first night of their return, that in an upper ward in the hospital Jerry's son was lying in his mother's arms, and that she was holding him almost savagely to her breast. He was hers; nobody should take him from her, not now or ever. The lights low, women tossing in their beds, the night nurse tiptoeing in to take the child. And Ursula holding to him.

"Just a little longer, please. I want to feel that he is mine."

"Of course he's yours! Do you think we mix our babies?"

Nevertheless, Beverly saw both Ursula and Jerry's child before they left the hospital. She had taken up her mother's work of making layettes for the babies in the obstetric ward, sitting in the garden sewing, or cutting flannel into absurdly tiny garments. The sewing soothed her nerves, already tired with Jerry's febrile activity and her father's lacquered inflexibility. She dreamed no dreams, sitting there on those bright autumn days. Rather she lulled herself into acceptance with her needle. This was her life, the only life she had ever known or, she thought, she ever would know.

When she had finished her first layette she took it to the hospital, going up in the elevator, walking along the corridor and feeling rather like her mother, substituting good deeds for happiness. But she was startled to find Katie Walters there, very neat and competent, and she was aware that she was being subjected to close inspection from head to foot.

"I brought some clothes," she said. "My mother always did it, and so I would like—"

"We're glad to get them, Mrs. Ames," said Katie, slightly patronizing. "I'm only relieving here, but I'll take them if you like."

Beverly glanced around the ward. Her mother had known how to greet these women, had moved smilingly from bed to bed, admired the babies, talked to the grotesque waiting figures in the rocking chairs. She did not know how to begin, but in a bed near by lay a girl with a child on her arm, and Beverly—and Katie—moved toward her. For an instant then the three of them were together, Ursula smiling with her baby beside her and her long brown braids on the pillow, Beverly shy and rather at a loss, and Katie, businesslike and alert under her cap, saying:

"Let Mrs. Ames see the baby, Ursula. Then I'll have to take him away."

"It's a beautiful baby," said Beverly, and was instantly conscious that the girl in the bed had frozen into immobility. It was curious. She felt more shy than ever. "Is it a boy?"

"A boy," said Ursula out of stiff lips. "Maybe you'd better take him now, Miss Walters. I think I'll go to sleep."

Beverly felt rebuffed. She moved on, miserable and bewildered, to the next bed.

CHAPTER XXIV

CHRIS had no illusions about his future as he prepared for Europe that early fall. He knew that even with the prestige of Vienna behind him it would be a long uphill climb, and that only gradually could he abandon general practice for surgery. His money would go so far and no further. It would provide for Lily Walters while he was gone, and with care furnish a downtown office on his return. Nevertheless he went about his preparations blithely, got his steamer ticket, bought a trunk and some clothes to put in it. Katie, taking her two weeks' vacation at that time, watched his preparations with tragic eyes.

"You'll never come back, Chris. Not to us, anyhow."

"Nonsense, Katie. It's only for a few months."

It was vaguely upsetting to have her there, sleeping in her small room so close to his that at night he could hear her turning in her bed. Sometimes he would meet her in the upper hall, clad only in a kimono over her nightgown, her small breasts sharply outlined and about her the smell of soap and bath powder. He was not in love with her, but she was a disturbing element in the house. Like the Howard girl he knew she was his for the taking, and one night he roused to find her actually in his room, a small scared creature at the foot of his bed. He sat up and she retreated toward the window.

"Your shutter's banging, Chris. I came in to fix it."

He was tempted then. The shutter was not banging and he knew it. As she passed by his bed on her way out he put out a hand and caught her.

"Listen to me, Katie," he said, "I'm only human, and you're being very foolish. You're not that sort of girl."

"How do you know what sort of girl I am?"

He had himself well in hand by that time. There were too many things at stake, his position at the hospital, his conviction that Katie was fundamentally straight, even his promise to Henry. He grunted and let go of her.

"Run away and go to sleep," he told her. "And for God's sake don't come back. You make me feel like a fool."

He breathed easier when she went back to the hospital at the end of her two weeks. She was prettier than she had ever been, and while he could grin over that ridiculous episode there were a good many times when he felt that he had somehow impeached his own manhood.

"The damned little idiot," he would mutter.

He had not seen Beverly since her return, and his preparations for Europe kept him from brooding. Even Lily entered into the spirit of them, and one day he actually found her with a sewing basket, mending his underwear and stockings.

"You might be in an accident over there," she said, "and I'd hate you to be found with holes in your socks."

She had a terror of Europe, a terror of anything unknown and unfamiliar. Nevertheless she was more cheerful during those last weeks, and Chris wondered if she had been hearing from Dick. Then one morning she met him smiling at the foot of the stairs and showed him a registered letter containing five ten-dollar bills.

"I always knew he was a good boy," she said. "No matter what Katie says, he doesn't forget me."

"That's fine," he said with all the conviction he could muster. "Spend it on yourself. You must need a lot of things."

She was very happy that day. She ran next door to tell Miss Barker, and Chris coming home at lunch time found his bed still unmade and a sketchy meal left for him on the table. He ate it philosophically, and said nothing when later she came in with her arms full of bundles. Soon he would escape all this, and when he came back he would make some other arrangement. He would continue to take care of her, but he himself would get away.

Then suddenly and without warning it was Lily who went away, taking herself out of life with a finality so unlike her that even Chris, accustomed to such matters, went sick and cold over the sheer despair of it.

One night she got a telegram saying that Dick had been arrested for burglary in Chicago and was being held for trial. She read it in the hall, read it over and over. Then she carried it in to Chris's back office and laid it on the desk for him to find in the morning, and carried off with her a bottle of sleeping tablets left by a sample man that day.

She made no other arrangements, left no letters. Apparently she had simply shaken out of the bottle enough tablets to be sure that she would never waken, and then gone quietly to bed. When Chris found her she was lying there, her untidy room littered with the clothing she would never wear again, and on the dresser the faded picture of Henry in its broken frame.

It was too late to do anything. She was gone, and Chris stood for some time looking down at her, wondering if he could have prevented it, recalling his own impatiences, feeling guilty—as only those who have faced such situations can feel guilt. In this room and this bed Henry had died. "If I go you'll look after them, won't you?" And he had promised. Mingled with this was a terrible anger at Dick, his young callousness, his cool selfishness. "Dick. Father is dead. Please come home." And no Dick, until he had wandered in to steal from him; Lily watching and waiting, and no Dick.

He could have killed him with his bare hands that morning, with that pitiful wreckage before him; killed him for the weakness which unfitted him for anything but crime; killed him for his cruelty, for his slyness, for being Dick Walters.

Katie, blank-eyed and dazed, came home from the hospital that day to move like a shadow through the house. She seemed incapable of thought or of action, and Miss Barker, bustling about with the morbid activity of lonely women suddenly thrust into life, finally put her to bed.

"I wish she would cry," she said to Chris, out of her new importance. "It's always better if they cry."

Chris was busy. There was the inquest, the thousand and one details of a death in addition to his own work. When he went in to see Katie it was to hurry out again. And under Miss Barker the house was in confusion, curtains being taken down, washed and hurriedly being hung again, furniture polished, and the dust of ages being removed from dark corners. It was as though she expected an investigating committee instead of a funeral, and it was in this chaos that Chris saw Beverly again, for the first time in more than a year. He came in to find her standing in the back office, a ladder nearby and pails around her and her face white and tired. So unexpected was the sight of her that he could find nothing to say.

"You don't mind, do you, Chris? I thought, if I could do something—"

"Mind? No, but I imagine everything is being done. It looks like it!"

She was looking at him as though she could not look away, but he was busy pulling out a chair for her.

"Sit down," he said. "I haven't seen you for a long time. How are you?"

"Very well," she said. But she did not take the chair. She was hearing his voice over the telephone that last night before her marriage: "See here, my darling, if you're not sure of this marriage it's not too late"; and trying to reconcile it with his present one, carefully casual as it was and without feeling.

"I hear that you are going abroad." Her own voice was breathless, but he did not notice it.

"Yes. Very soon."

"You'll like Vienna. Everyone does."

"I hope so. My German's pretty rusty."

Why had he never answered that letter of hers? If only she could ask him, even now! But she could not ask this new Chris, casual and polite and detached. He was too far away.

"Would you mind if I sent some flowers from the garden? We still have a good many."

Ah, but that was a mistake, that mention of the garden. Chris finding her crying there and taking her in his arms. Her mother's garden, and her mother saying: "If anything happens to me I want you and Chris to live your own lives." She saw him stiffen.

"Thanks. That would be fine."

It was over and he was seeing her out, friendly and smiling. She was smiling too. They even shook hands, and she wished him a good journey and a good winter. Then she went back up the hill again, to her friends and her dinners, to occasional silent meals with her father at the head of the table and to more than occasional nights when she lay awake for hours listening until Jerry's car came in. For she knew now that this was the way it was to be, and that it would not change.

She did not go to the funeral the next day. For an hour or so Lily was brought down to lie in state in the front office, a few neighbors gathered, and in the back room Katie sat beside Chris and listened to the service, holding tight to his hand.

"Only the two of us left, Chris!"

"She's all right now, Katie. Asleep or awake, she's all right."

"But I'm alone, Chris. You're going away, and I'll be alone."

"Hush, dear. Listen."

"I am the resurrection and the life, saith the Lord. He that believeth in me, though he were dead, yet shall he live." Lily lying there in her new dignity, unshriven because she had dared to take what was of no value to her any more, but with a kindly clergyman found to do her that last honor nevertheless; Katie holding Chris's hand and more conscious of it than of her mother in the next room; and Chris, looking back at his failures and forward to God knew what—that was Lily Walters' funeral. When it was over he stayed behind in the cemetery, to put those flowers of Beverly's on the mound and to gaze across to where Annie Lewis lay in majestic pomp in her marble tomb.

Two women, far apart in life, and now meeting in this common resting place.

Katie stayed home for a day or two, her exuberant vitality gone, eating little and sleeping badly. For the sake of propriety Miss Barker remained in the house at night, using Dick's old room; but in the daytime Katie was there alone, a pathetic figure wandering about the house and watching Chris's preparations for departure with desperate red-rimmed eyes.

"You can't go and leave me like this, Chris."

"Nonsense. You'll be busy, my dear. I'm not leaving you homeless."

"A hospital isn't a home."

He was relieved when at last she went back. They had kept the secret of Dick's arrest, and she had nothing to fear from that. Although the cleaning woman from the alley behind came in daily, it was a strange feeling, coming into the empty house at night from his evening calls; no movement of life, no sounds save those from outside, the scraping of the brakes of the streetcars as they stopped, or faint footsteps on the pavement. Sometimes the silence beat on his ears like a sound, and to escape it he took long walks, up the hill, past the Lewis house and on; but he could not leave his ghosts behind him. He would go back again into the silence, taking them with him.

He was relieved when the night came for him to go. Ted Lawrence was taking over his practice for the period of his absence, and early in the evening Chris had handed him his keys and his lists. Lawrence scanned the latter with uplifted eyebrows.

"Still doing the city work for nothing, aren't you?"

"You can hand them to Barrett if you want to."

"That skunk! Not on your life."

They had a farewell drink out of the medicine closet; then Ted left, with a final cheerful word of warning as to the women of Vienna and a miserable sense of helplessness as he closed the door behind him; as though he had lost a crutch on which he had leaned, and would now have to walk alone.

In the quiet house Chris made a final inventory: luggage, tickets, cash, letter of credit. Miss Andrews had been in, bringing him for some unknown reason a large bunch of roses, and he eyed them wryly. Betty Howard had brought him a leather case containing hair brushes, and on the strength of it he had kissed her good-by. Harriet Lee had knitted him a sweater for the ship, and Nancy Lee a pair of heavy socks. "Europe is so cold in winter." He felt warmed by all this, and by the whisky, and if when he tried the kitchen door for the last time he stopped to look at the ailanthus tree and Caesar's mound beneath it, it was only for a moment.

Everything was done. He had seen Ursula, strong again and proud of her baby. "He looks like you, doctor. And he's gaining every day." In Chicago Dick was safely in jail and awaiting sentence. Chris had even ordered a small headstone for Lily's grave. Now the past was behind him and he could look ahead. He had run that part of his race, had reached this particular goal, had even achieved a measure of hope again. If it was the hope of ambition rather than the hope of fulfillment, he had accepted it. Now, in an hour or less—

He was looking at his watch when the doorbell rang, and he opened it to find Katie in the vestibule with a suitcase at her feet. He knew before she spoke that here was trouble, for she looked crushed, defeated, and she was swaying slightly on her feet.

"What's all this?" he demanded.

"I've left the hospital, Chris."

"What are you talking about?"

"It's true."

"They would have put me out anyhow, so I left."

She explained, standing among that luggage of his and desperately trying to be coherent. She had made a mistake in the medicines that day; nothing fatal, but they had acted as though she had killed the man. She had stood all she could; then she had told them what she thought of them and had packed her bag and left.

He stood staring at her, unable at first to face this new problem. A moment ago he had been free. Now—! What on earth to do with her, with that empty house behind him and—remembering Lily—that desperate look in her eyes. He temporized.

"You've been very silly," he told her. "But you're going back, of course. I'll call up Miss Simpson."

"She wouldn't take me back. Anyhow, I'm not going."

He tried to reason with her, still standing in the hall. She couldn't stay alone in the house, and Miss Barker had gone to the country. He'd leave her at a hotel for the night, and arrange for money until she could manage for herself. She was not listening, however, and at last his frayed nerves gave way.

"Listen to me," he said savagely. "I've had enough. I'm fed up, and more. What is it to me that you've made a fool of yourself? I haven't adopted you. I'm not married to you. And by God if this is some scheme of yours to interfere with my plans I'll leave you here. You can get along. You're young and strong. You can manage. I'm going."

"Some scheme!" She gasped. "You can't think that, Chris."

"What am I to think?"

In the end he believed her, however. There was desperate truth in her voice. She had been through a lot, she said; her mother and Dick, and now his going away. Especially his going away. She had hardly known what she was doing that day. He had to believe that. She was no killer. Her record was good. But to be left alone, like this— He still wanted to shake her, but he modified his tone.

"The taxi will be here in a minute. I'll take you back and see Miss Simpson. That's all I'll have time to do."

She stiffened stubbornly.

"I'm not going back, Chris. I'll kill myself first. Or go on the streets."

"Don't talk like that," he said impatiently. "You don't mean it for a minute."

"I do mean it. I know the ropes now. Probably it's all I'm good for anyhow."

In that too there was the ring of despairing truth. She was capable of anything, this Katie. She was Henry and Lily and even a part of Dick. He stared down at her. She was beyond coquetry. There was even a hint of the old slackness in the way she had thrown on her clothes, in the very set of her cheap hat. Suddenly he was profoundly sorry for her.

"You'll let me take you back, won't you, Katie? When I tell Miss Nettie the reason for all this—"

"Not about Dick! I'll jump off a bridge if you do that."

"Not about Dick, of course," he told her gravely.

In the end she agreed to go, although she shivered as she did so. Gradually however she became quieter, and Chris was relieved to see her straighten her hat by the hall mirror when the taxi driver rang the door bell.

He consulted his watch. There would be just time to go to the hospital, and he put her in the cab and threw in his bags in a sort of frenzied haste. But in the taxi his anxiety and anger returned. He sat in furious silence, hardening his heart against her swollen eyes, her white and frightened face. Now and then he looked at his watch again, calculating minutes, and once when she put her hand over his he shook it off.

"None of that, Katie. You've damned near wrecked me, and you know it."

He left her outside in the taxicab and strode back to Miss Nettie's familiar office. She was still up, looking old and tired, and when she saw him she needed no explanation.

"I have tried and failed," she told him. "That happens now and then. I can't take her back, Chris."

She went on. Katie's mistakes had been more grave than she had said, and her attitude later one of bitter defiance. For the sake of the school—Chris listened with his eye on Miss Nettie's clock.

"Then what in heaven's name am I to do with her?" he asked helplessly.

"Let her find her own way out. She's young and strong. Surely she can't be entirely friendless."

"Not the kind of friends to help her in a situation like this. I don't want her to kill herself, or to go on the streets."

"Did she threaten that?"

"She intimated something of the sort."

"Oh, Chris, Chris," said Miss Nettie helplessly. "Why take on the troubles of the world? She's young and she's ambitious. She's practical, too. She has tried to scare you, that's all; and she's succeeded."

"You're darned right. I am scared."

She compromised finally, offering to keep Katie for a few days until she had found something to do. But Chris, going out to the taxi, faced a Katie who refused to do anything of the sort. He looked at his watch and at the taxi meter, clicking away cheerfully and expensively, and made a desperate effort to control the situation.

"All right," he said. "Then here's where you get out."

He swung her bag on to the pavement and stood waiting, but she did not move.

"I'm not going in there," she said quietly. "You can leave me here if you like, but I'm not going back."

Her very quietness was alarming. He stood on the pavement staring at her, at her white face and blank eyes. Then he slung her suitcase back into the taxi and got in himself.

"To the station," he said, and sitting back in a corner, doggedly faced his problem. He was savagely angry, at Katie, at the hospital, at life itself for this scurvy trick it had played on him; and he knew too that there was but one thing to do, and that was to put the girl out of the cab and go on with his own work, his own life. He knew it even when she slid over to him and put her head on his shoulder.

"I do love you so much, Chris."

"Don't be an idiot, Katie."

"And I have nobody else. Nobody in all the world."

"What am I to do with you, child?"

"Take me along," she whispered. "I'll kill myself if you don't. I'll do what mother did. I'm not just talking. I'll go to a drug store and—"

"Stop it! Stop it, I tell you."

"I'll love you all my life, Chris. Take me with you. I'll look after you. I'd do anything. You don't have to marry me. Just let me go along. If you don't I'm gone. I'm no good without you. I'm nothing. You can't just go away and leave me. You can't."

It was within fifteen minutes of train time then. He said nothing, and at the station he got out and stood looking at her. She did not move.

"If you leave me now it's good-by, Chris. I can't go on; not alone."

He was white to the lips when he reached in and taking her suitcase gave it to a porter.

He sat up all night in the smoking compartment of the train, his old pipe clenched in his teeth. Katie had his berth, and whether she slept or not he did not know, or care. Toward morning he got out his German book of medical terms and tried to forget that once more life had trapped him. On the leather seat nearby the Negro porter slept, and after a time the darkness outside the window turned to gray and then to brilliant daylight. Perhaps a man's life was like that. After all Beverly was gone, and he still had his work. Thank God for work. He put down the book and slept the sleep of profound exhaustion.

He married Katie in New York the next morning, an hour before the ship sailed. He did not love her, but almost in spite of himself as he sat doggedly beside her in the cab on the way to the ship he was aware of her youth and her soft young body. He did not love her, but he would be good to her.

He was not unhappy on the voyage. Katie stood up well under the merciless intimacy of the ship, where they were crowded together in the small cabin; even under the merciless intimacy of marriage itself. During the day she left him alone, to endless pacing of the deck while she lay inert in her chair, watching for him to pass her. Then at night she took him into her arms and held him there, offering him peace and forgetfulness.

He was hers then. Nobody could take him away. She held him fiercely.

CHAPTER XXV

PROBABLY Chris never really faced that marriage of his during those early months. Katie had been for so long a part of his background that it was not strange to have her continue there; as though she had merely passed through the wall which had so thinly separated them before. She was Katie, that was all. A better Katie, perhaps, fastidious now in the care of her body, doing her hair in a new fashion and carefully polishing her nails; but still untidy in other details. The cabin on the ship was always littered, and he stayed out of it as much as possible.

She found him one day hanging up some of her clothes, and flushed.

"I was going to do that," she said.

"I've waited for two days for you to do it," he said, not unamiably.

After that she did somewhat better, but to Chris's orderly mind those small matters were more imminent than the much greater fact of the marriage itself. Now and then he heard someone call her Mrs. Arden and it always startled him. He would look at her quickly. She was his wife; not a companion for the night or for the voyage, but his wife. Possibly even the mother of his children, although already he knew she would be an unwilling mother.

"Not yet," she would say, and shiver. "Give me a year or two, Chris. After all I'm young, and a baby—"

Vienna was not much better, so far as she was concerned. From the beginning she loathed the pension, small and inexpensive as it was. It was in the eighth district near the *Allgemeine Krankenhaus,* and it occupied the fifth floor of a tall and dingy building on a side street. There was no elevator, and its guests were compelled to climb up the stone staircase flight after flight with only an iron balustrade to hold to. Even when reached it was slightly daunting to the eye. There was a salon done in brown plush with antimacassars, an upright piano and a center table ruined from many beer steins. There was a dining room with a long table with a cloth changed once a day, a bunch of dusty paper roses in the center, and a sign on the wall which said: *Nicht Rauchen.* Also there was a bathroom with a water-tank and a small coal stove under it, but as baths were extra the stove was only lighted when one of the guests—usually an American—wanted a bath. Then the tank hissed and boiled like a tea-kettle about to explode; and there was a story about an American girl, a piano student, who had been in the tub once when it did explode, and who had sought the safety of the salon *in puris naturalibus* as a result.

Katie loathed it all; loathed it from the *Guten Morgen* with which the overworked housemaid brought her her *frühstück* of two hard rolls, a pat of butter and a cup of coffee extract colored with raisins, to the cold night when she crawled into her narrow bed and pulled over her the short square feather comfort which would cover either the lower part of her or the top, but never all of her at once. She would lie there awake, listening to Chris's heavy breathing, with the feeling that in sleep he escaped her, and that he welcomed that escape.

"Good night, Katie dear."

"Good night, Chris."

Then he would be asleep and far away, beyond her; beyond even her genuine love for him. She would lie awake, staring at the tall heavy wardrobe, at the wooden washstand, with its bowl and pitcher, at the heavy cushions between the inner and outer windows to keep out the night air, and cry for very homesickness and helplessness.

Nothing was as she had expected it to be. She had to sit in silence through the heavy meals: the two o'clock dinner of soup, meat, salad and fruit compote; the late supper. The polyglot table chattered, Chris cheerfully practiced his German, and she could speak to no one. Then, the meals over, they all disappeared. It was as though a temporary death had descended on the place, save for the women polishing the floors with their feet, and that too was a *danse macabre,* hopeless and without grace. Chris, having eaten, would hurry out and the long hours faced her, dreary and empty. She would ring for the maid, have the tall tile stove in the corner filled with briquettes and sit over it alone, hour after hour. When she went out to walk, the rough cobbles of the small streets nearby hurt her feet in their tight high-heeled shoes, and she would have to come back. At night Chris was tired, too tired to take her out.

"I'm sorry, Katie; I'm all in."

"Well, I'm not. I have to sit in this rotten place all day alone. I can't even find any books to read. As for talking to these people—"

"Why don't you learn some German? That might help."

"I didn't come over here to study."

"Well, I did, my dear."

He would be cheerful and friendly, but by that time she knew she did not matter. He might come to her with his physical needs, but in the real essential—which was his work—she did not figure at all. Gentle as he was with her, he was there for a purpose and pursuing it with deadly earnestness. His marriage had doubled his costs and lessened his time, so he filled his days to overflowing. He took a lesson in medical German early in the morning, and the rest of the day was devoted to lectures, to clinics and operations. Sometimes he felt that he had gone back once more to his college days: the intent faces of the watchers, and over the table an authoritative figure with a beard—almost always with a beard—saying in German, or perhaps in English: "Gentlemen, here we have a case—"

There was a difference, of course. The order and decorum of America was missing; often the operating rooms looked like shambles. And the men were different. No young students these, but men from all over the world, although Americans strongly predominated. Old men and young ones, successful or on the edge of failure, they had come for some purpose of their own, to learn and to carry back that knowledge, to gain prestige, to specialize so that they might have more business and more money, or humbly enough to be able to help more people. They stayed, some for months, some for a few weeks. They went to the American Medical Association—familiarly known as the Club—for advice, since in every case the time element counted.

"I'm here for nose and throat, and I've only got six weeks. What's the best thing to do?"

Sometimes the classes were full, and they would have to wait their time, sitting worriedly in coffee houses, reading the Paris edition of the "Herald" and surreptitiously counting their money. A considerable majority did as little work as possible, picked up a bit of technique here, saw a few clinics, heard a half-dozen lectures, and went home to join the gay procession of specialists who had their evenings and Sundays to themselves.

They were popular, these Americans. It was not only that they brought in money. Vienna was Anglophile. Its children had English governesses, its men aped English clothes and English sports. Even the dogs in the Prater were of favorite English breeds! And what were Americans but younger and more joyous English? It was American ragtime music now which the Hungarian orchestras played in the cafés at night, and American Negroes who danced there, grinning, showing white teeth in black faces, throwing about their lithe black bodies and in the intervals sitting at table with tall Austrian officers. These blacks too were Americans, and joyous.

"What is your name, little black girl?"

"Gladys."

"I drink to you, Gladys. I offer myself to you. We

shall marry, and have little brown children who will dance all day and have teeth as white as milk."

The *Hofraths* and *Docents* were different. They took their work seriously. It was incredible to them that these foreigners should come to learn in a week or a month the experience and technique of their own painful years. Their standards were high. The University was only a beginning. After that they had hung around the hospitals and the clinics possibly for years. When at last they became *Docents* in a hospital they were paid three hundred dollars a year and their board, and they were not allowed to marry. Not at least until the *Hofrath* consented, and that might not be for years. To them the Americans were a godsend, for they paid; a godsend, but still incredible.

"You are fortunate, you Americans. You already have a wife, *nicht wahr?*"

"I already have a wife," Chris would say, and find it strange in the saying.

He was finding what he had come for. There was material there. God, how much material! Life was cheap in old prewar Vienna. Fifty thousand patients a year in the one hospital alone, and two hundred thousand outpatients. Hour after hour the bell tolled another death, and it was hardly possible to move about the streets without encountering a funeral cortege, the draped funeral cars, the professional mourners in black carrying their lighted torches. And there was a post-mortem after every death. It made for careful diagnosis, that. Men could not afford to make mistakes which were certain to be discovered.

He had to get all he could in the time at his disposal, and within his means. Nothing was free, except possibly death. He was paying thirty dollars a week for Katie and himself, with coal extra. Meals too sometimes, for he could not always get back to the two o'clock dinner at the pension. Sometimes he went to the Club, where the lecture courses were posted, and ordered up what he needed from the restaurant below. He was soon working eight hours a day and often more.

He would go home to Katie tired and often impatient, to find her alone in that dreary room and huddled over a stove which she keep blazing hot.

"Haven't you been out?"

"It's been raining. I suppose you didn't notice that!"

She was like a cat, hating rain, and it was almost always raining that fall. Hardly a rain; a sort of mist which condensed rather than precipitated. Even the beds were damp, and the days too were growing shorter. The room would be dark, except for the light from the stove, and Chris would press the switch, kiss her hastily, and begin his preparations for dinner.

"I suppose there's no use asking if we're going anywhere tonight," she would say dully.

She had begun to sink into a morass of self-pity. She had been gay enough in Paris, suspiciously tasting new foods, trying to like champagne, window-shopping along the Rue de la Paix, even buying a little here and there. But the old medieval city frightened her, and Chris seemed detached and far away. There were nights when she said she was cold and crawled into his bed with him, and his tired body tried to respond. More than once he dropped asleep as soon as she was settled beside him, and she again would lie awake, alarmed as well as sulky.

There were better days, of course. Days when Katie went out, to sit in some storeroom made into a movie, where men wore their hats and smoked, and between reels an usher went about with a spray gun, clearing the air. Then Chris would go home to find the room lighted, and maybe some flowers on the table, and Katie herself carefully dressed and waiting.

"Anything new today?"

"Nothing much. A *Docent* shook a nurse." He would grin.

"He wouldn't dare!"

"He did. They don't mind. They're used to it."

Chris did not always sleep at night, however. Sometimes

he lay awake, trying to look ahead. One part of his life was made. It was there asleep in the next bed, soft and young and still malleable. If it was not what he had hoped, it was at least done and he could forget it. The other was still ahead, years of work, gratified ambition, success. If once more he had chosen the shadow for the substance it was too late to change.

And he was learning; learning not to hurry, to go slowly and carefully, to use new techniques. These men worked cautiously and deliberately. They disliked so-called brilliant operating. When they had to use haste they explained it; so many cases waiting, or the patient taking the anesthetic badly. Life did not matter greatly, but the success of the operation was a different thing. One and all they were materialists. But also, here as all over the world, they were explorers. For thousands of years the human body had kept its secrets. Now under the lights overhead these secrets were exposed, an apparently disorganized jumble, soft and yielding to the hand, neither ugly nor beautiful, but with the strange power to function, to support life. It could even restore itself; the blood went quietly and intelligently about its business of restoration, building itself new channels, and through those new channels carrying food and building materials.

There was no such factory in the world. One did not heal it. All the surgeon could do was to cut and bring together. The body itself did the healing. The jumble functioned again, the chaos was order. A pattern.

The work and the vast amount of clinical material began to obsess Chris, and one day he realized that he was neglecting Katie. She played so small a part in his active life that there were long hours when he forgot her entirely. Then at the end toward evening he would suddenly remember her with a feeling of guilt. She was his wife, he would think. He did not intend her to be his victim. On those evenings at home in the pension he would try to be amusing, even loving. It was not easy, but

Katie had by that time a strong sense of grievance, not unjustified.

"I'm nothing beside your work."

"You are apart from my work, my dear. That's all."

Sometimes he tried to tell her about it and she would listen, pretending an interest she did not feel, and Chris would realize that he was being self-centered and incredibly dull at that, and stop. In the back of his mind he knew already that this marriage, comparatively unimportant to him, was a tragic failure to her; and that the failure was his.

He tried bringing her things, after the agelong habit of guilty men. Sometimes she kept them, sometimes she exchanged them for something else. One day, finding she had nothing to read, he sent her a set of Lafcadio Hearn, and found her struggling with it that night.

"What on earth *is* this stuff, Chris?"

"It's pretty good. Try it and see."

That night he heard her crying. He went over to her and sitting on her bed, groped for her hand and held it.

"What is it, Katie? If it's anything I've done, my dear—"

"You think I'm a stupid fool, don't you?"

"Never in the world."

"I'm not. I'll show you some day."

"You're my very lovely young wife, my dear. If it's those ridiculous books, throw them away."

She did not throw them away, of course. She went to sleep in his arms that night, and the next day she took them back to the shop and bought herself a hat instead. It was an enormous hat with a bunch of ermine tails on the brim, and that afternoon a tall Austrian officer bowed to her on the street. She went home to the dreary pension, fluttered and flattered and considerably happier. . . .

A month before Christmas Chris found himself, to his surprise, on the executive council at the Club, and asked to help prepare for the Christmas dance. They might have been in Vienna a year instead of a few weeks, and America was far behind them. It was like a voice from the past to receive a letter from Ursula Martin telling about the baby and herself: "I am sure I chose wisely and I wish you could see him. He really looks like you, or maybe I imagine it. I have a position now, and a woman to mind him during the day. . . . I do hope you are having a happy Christmas, and I shall never forget you. Never."

Katie found the letter and read it.

"You'd think it was your child," she said resentfully.

"It's certainly not mine, my dear."

"That's what you say!"

She was not really suspicious, however. She was busy getting ready for the dance and Chris was watching himself now and trying to make her happy. One day they learned that Dick had gone to the penitentiary for two years, but she took it better than he had expected.

"After all noboby knows about it," she said, and even agreed at Chris's suggestion to send him some money for tobacco and other small luxuries.

One day at that time Chris stopped in a shop and bought a purse for Miss Barker and had it sent to her. She would like it, he thought. After a moment's hesitation he put a bill inside, and wrote on the card: "An empty purse is bad luck. This is to break the jinx! Merry Christmas." But these fine threads were all that held them to America and home. A hand could have brushed them away, and yet it was at that time that somewhere between sleeping and waking that old image of Beverly rose out of Chris's buried mind and confronted him, so to speak, on the doorstep again.

"Sorry," he said, quite articulately. "My household—"

His own voice roused him. Katie was sitting up in bed staring at him.

"What about your household?" she asked sharply.

"I don't know, my dear. I suppose I was talking in my sleep. . . .

He and Katie were dancing at the Club on Christmas

Eve when, on the afternoon of that day in far-off America Beverly took her usual flowers to the cemetery. She had her own key to the mausoleum, and she opened the door and went in alone. It was bitterly cold inside, and she drew a fur coat around her as she sat down on the marble bench. After a time she slipped down on her knees and made her usual prayer there, which was to the effect that Annie was to be busy and not alone, wherever she was.

She went out after that, locking the door behind her. The car was waiting, but she stood for a few minutes looking down and across to where Lily's small headstone rose above the snow. Then she got into the limousine and was driven home. Jerry was not there, as usual. She went up to her room and getting out the gold cigarette case she had bought him, tied it up carefully in white tissue paper and red ribbon.

She gave a dinner that night for her father's friends; and she was sitting, dutifully smiling, over the flowers, the silver and the hothouse fruit when the *Votivkirche* with its twin Gothic spires was acclaiming three o'clock of a Vienna morning and the birthday of the Christ Child, and Chris, having had too much sweet champagne, was taking home an irate Katie.

"You've had too much to drink."

"It's only Christmas once a year, Katie."

"And don't call me Katie. My name is Katherine, if you can pronounce it."

"Merry Christmas, Katherine, my dear."

He went asleep in the taxi, and in his sleep he was back in the Lewis house on a Christmas Eve long ago. Jake was dead, and Staunton Lewis was slipping away, going to the telephone. Then he was sleeping and Beverly was trying to rouse him for hot coffee.

"Chris! What's the matter with you anyhow. Get out and pay the cab driver."

The *Portier* let them in. During the week he was a humble little man, but on holidays and Sundays he blossomed suddenly into a semimartial figure with a fiercely upturned mustache. Now he wore only his nightshirt and his mustache bandage, a black arrangement which fitted over his ears and tied at the back with tapes. He was shivering as he lighted the small candles which were to see them up the stairs, and he received his ten hellers—or two cents—with a muffled *Danke*.

Chris climbed rather uncertainly behind Katie. She was a few steps ahead, small, indomitable in her own way, ruthless. It seemed incredible that they should be there, climbing that staircase together. There was something wrong about it, he thought dizzily; Katie carrying her determined little candle and he following it. He had never meant to follow Katie. He had never wanted to follow her. But at the top, because he had had too much wine and because he was sorry he had ever married her, he took her in his arms and kissed her.

"A Merry Christmas, darling."

She relaxed in his arms. She was not defiant now, or determined. She was his, and for what it was worth now and forever, he was hers.

"You looked very lovely tonight."

"Did I, Chris? I thought you hadn't noticed."

He did not go into their room at once, however. He wandered into the salon and turned on the light. The Christmas tree which had been lighted earlier in the evening was still there. It sat in the center of the table, with the stein marks covered now by a plaster crèche, the wise men, the Mother, the shepherd and his sheep, and in a small wicker cradle the Child Himself. But the candles had melted and run down, and some vandal had set a wine glass near the cradle. Chris carefully removed it. There might be a God after all. A good many people still believed it. In that case one must not offend Him, even in small matters.

CHAPTER XXVI

THERE were plenty of straws in the wind that year, with Europe an armed camp, watchful and wary. German bands in the streets of London: "Don't give them money. They're all spies." A small secret cabal in Vienna, secret even from the old man who drove out daily from the *Hofburg* in an open carriage, wearing a cape and a military cap, and left behind him for that hour or two his dead son, his dead wife, his dead hopes.

Plenty of straws, with a kindly little man in Russia wearing a beard to hide the weakness of his chin, sleeping in an alcove at the rear of a room in a great palace, his wife beside him, his uniforms in rows outside in closets with sliding glass doors. Two bowls and two pitchers on the washstand, the two narrow brass beds pushed together, figured curtains to shut out the light, and so he slept. Next to his uniforms in wardrobes with glass doors hung his wife's clothes, and in the adjoining room they sat together; a dreadful room, a German room, cluttered with hundreds of family photographs, with ugly chairs and tables. Like the bedroom it had windows only on one side, but the afternoon sun came in there, and then it was cheerful, almost gay.

The next room, on the corner, belonged to the children. There they played. Once there had been a wide staircase there, but now it was boarded over and had become a slide. Under it stood the children's bicycles and sleds, and all around were their toys. The little man with the beard could sit in his office beyond and listen to them playing.

Plenty of straws, with the German Emperor being deftly shoved into action to proclaim his greatness; with Poincaré coming from France and being acclaimed as he drove with the King along the streets of London; and with Prussian soldiers strutting along the narrow streets of Berlin and shouldering off the pavements the Englishmen and Americans who looked English. The goose step, the tireless French marching step, the sturdy tramp of the British. And spies, spies everywhere.

One day Katie told Chris that they had a spy in the pension.

"A spy? Who told you that?"

"It's the fat little German."

"Nonsense! Don't believe all you hear, my dear."

The spy was a quiet square little man, pleasant but silent. He had a job somewhere, and in his room he kept a bullfinch in a cage. When he came home he would put a cloth on his shoulder and the bird would sit there for hours. Sometimes he whistled and it sang a German folk song, in a soft sweet piping voice. He seemed to live for the bird.

One evening, coming home after dark, Chris met him on the staircase, carrying the bird in its cage and stumbling down the long stairs. Chris put out a hand to steady him.

"Go easy," he said. "These stairs are bad. Not leaving us, are you?"

The little man stopped and wiped his forehead with his handkerchief.

"I leave the bird with some friends," he said hoarsely. "I go away for a time. Yes. You—you have been very kind to me, Herr Doktor."

Then he was gone, stumbling down the stairs with Chris staring after him. They found his body the next day in the Danube, but nobody ever heard of the bird again.

Spies. Airplanes. Submarines. Poison gas. War. Ridiculous. Nevertheless there will be war. But why? Why in the name of the good God a war?

In America business was not good, with production still overcoming consumption, and Staunton Lewis fighting a strike now; locking his mills and sending men in by the river. The strikers discovered the boat that night and fired on it, but the city went on about its business. In the hospital the interns went about, their stethoscopes hanging from the pockets of their white coats; and in the Lewis house nothing was changed. Jerry at the table would try to make talk with his father-in-law, but Staunton was busy with his own affairs.

"Those fellows in Europe seem set on having trouble."

"Looks like it."

That would be all.

Nevertheless, it was that winter that the Annie Lewis Research Laboratory was established, its primary purpose the study and possible cure of cancer. Beverly knew nothing of it until she saw it in the newspapers, but it touched her deeply. She saw behind it her father's loneliness, perhaps even his remorse. One day he brought her the plans of the building, and a sketch of the bronze plate which was to be set into the wall inside. It was a profile view of her mother's face. She looked up.

'It's a fine thing to do, father."

"Somebody had to do it," he said gruffly.

She felt closer to him after that, not so alone. Now and then when Jerry was out—he was out a great deal now—she would take her book or her sewing and go into her father's den. He never greeted her, but she thought he was not unwilling to have her there. One day they laid the cornerstone of the new building, and at the last moment he gave her a small locked box and asked her to place it in the stone.

"They've cut a place for it," he said. "Just put it in."

She never knew what was in the box.

She went regularly to the hospital, for she had taken her mother's place on the Women's Board. The room would be set with chairs in rows, the business would go on: "In view of the cost of the new sterilizing plant it will be necessary—"

Her mind would wander. The hospital seemed empty and silent without Chris in his long white coat, striding along with his head thrust forward. She would stir uneasily in her chair.

"I have to report, from the Needlework Guild, the receipt of ten dozen roller towels, ten dozen tea towels, ten dozen—"

Why had he married that girl? How could he? He had not loved her, surely. That time in the hospital she had not been like the other nurses. She had been—what? She did not know. Her mind would make the circle, come back again to the starting point. Why had he married that girl?

"Ten dozen dusters, ten dozen napkins, ten dozen—" She would rouse suddenly and look about her at these middle-aged and elderly women in their furs, with their folded hands and calm eyes. One lived through all sorts of things, she thought. Life went on, terribly, inexorably. There was no defeating it. Only death defeated it. They must have lived through a great deal, those women there, before they came richly clad and impassive to do their duty as they saw it and to ask nothing more than peace and a sense of work well done.

Some day she too would be like that. She might rebel, but life would do that to her. She would be old and past caring; would have paid her youth for peace.

After the meeting there would be tea. They would go downstairs to Miss Nettie's sitting room, and the tea table would be there; the big old silver urn, the sliced lemon, little cakes, sandwiches. Miss Nettie in a black silk dress behind the table, for she poured her own tea, roses on the desk, the clatter of cups and saucers, and over all the hum of soft elderly voices. Beverly was a child among them, for all her new status of marriage. They made a fuss over her, these older women, flattered that she cared to be with them.

"You set an example, my dear. If only my girls were interested!"

Tea over they would rustle out, well-dressed, well-bred women, going back in their cars, to what? Were they happy? Was anyone really happy? She would smile at them, her wide young smile, and they would smile in return.

"You are like your mother, Beverly."

"I wish I were."

Then one cold day when the snow lay heavy in the courtyard outside the windows and the car was late in coming for her, she found herself by Miss Nettie's fire in a low chair, and all the others gone. She turned suddenly and faced the older woman.

"Why did he do it, Miss Nettie? Why did he ever marry her?"

"Chris?"

"Yes, Chris. She wasn't the wife for him. He must have known it."

"Perhaps we are both to blame, Beverly. He was so much in love with you. When you let him go—"

"I wrote him. He never answered."

"It doesn't sound like him. He must have been terribly hurt. He is proud, my dear. You know that."

Beverly said nothing for a moment. She sat looking at the fire, shielding her face from it with the hand which wore Jerry's two rings. Then she stirred.

"I was in love with him, too. I suppose in a way I always will be."

Her face was somber under her wide hat; and Miss Nettie, who knew as much about Jerry as most and perhaps more, felt her heart contract sharply. These two young creatures, so unnecessarily suffering. Time would heal it, of course. They would live on and forget, and some day even smile over it, but not now.

"Perhaps it's better for him as it is, Miss Nettie. His work would always come first with him, and I wanted to be that."

"Yes. His work would have to come first, of course."

"Then when he attacked father—"

"He was right to do that, Beverly. It had to be done. Have you never thought of that?"

"But at such a time?"

"That was the only time, to be effective."

Then and there she told her of Chris's marriage; of that wild last night of his, with Katie suddenly on his hands and no place for her, and his promise to Henry. Standing there at her door, with his ticket bought and his ship sailing the next day, and that girl outside in a taxicab.

"He went out to get her, and when he didn't come back—If I'd only known. If I had dreamed for a moment that he would do what he did—"

"But why? Even then why marry her?"

"I think she had threatened something desperate. Probably to kill herself, or to go on the street for a living. Well, it's done now. No use worrying about it. Once in a long time I get a girl like that here, but not often. And she may be good for Chris. She's young and ambitious. She'll want things, and he'll have to work to supply them. That is better for a man than not being able to give a wife anything she couldn't have without him."

Beverly flushed.

"I see," she said slowly. "Even you didn't think Chris ought to marry me."

"He is a man, my dear. He would always want to make his own way."

She got up, drawing on her long gloves, picking up her handsome fur coat.

"He must have cared for her. I still think that."

"Cared for her? There are a dozen ways in which a man can care for a woman, and not be in love with her. You know that." Miss Nettie hesitated, looking up at the face out of which all the carefree youth had already gone. "I'm an old woman and I've seen a lot of living, Beverly. Let him go, my dear. He has his work and he has a wife. Don't hurt him again."

"I'll never hurt him. How can I?"

Long after she had gone Miss Simpson sat alone by her dying fire. She could not reconcile herself to Chris's marriage, or forgive herself for it. Men could be made or broken by their wives in his profession. She had seen it happen. Medicine was not an academic science. It was too close for that, too personal. They still worked, most of them, in their own houses. They might close off their offices, lock them away; still the character of the house was there, and of the woman behind it. Some of those early pictures of Chris persisted in her mind; that time when he had looked badly fed, shabby and uncared for; of Katie, crude and inclined to defiance when she first entered the school; of the matron calling her one day to view Katie's room, incredibly untidy in that place of neatness. And now she was Chris's wife.

She was still in the dark when her assistant came in.

"I'm sorry! Were you sleeping?"

"No. What is it?"

"I've sent your tray down here. Dinner's over. And do you remember that Ursula Martin who had a baby here in the fall? She's back. It looks like pneumonia."

Miss Simpson sat up suddenly.

"Where is she?"

"In C ward. She didn't want a room."

"I'll go up. And cancel that tray. I've had tea."

Ursula Martin lived for three days. She lay in her bed; bed, mattress, sheet, rubber sheet, draw sheet. On either side of her stretched a row of similar beds. They stretched on and on, thousands of beds, millions. They went out the window and around the world. Sometimes she slept, but not often, and a time came when her breathing seemed to her to fill the ward. She could hear it herself, breath, pain, breath, pain. She had none to spare for talk, so she lay silent, saving her breath. Sometimes, day or night—she did not know—she would see a dark figure sitting erect beside her, an elderly woman with her hair brushed back from her face, and one day she found herself shut in with that figure, the other beds wiped out. They sat together in a small white-muslin world, the two of them, and Ursula knew that the screens were up, and what that meant.

She made a terrific effort then, and whispered.

"Give my baby to Doctor Arden."

"I'll find a home for him, Ursula. You can trust me."

She shook her head.

"To Doctor Arden," she persisted in that difficult whisper. "You heard me?"

"Yes. I'll tell him."

She died that night, and the next day Miss Simpson wrote to Chris. "I have the baby here," she said, "and we can keep him for a while at least. But I do feel, Chris, that this at least is not your problem. I can find a good family to adopt the child, and I beg you to let me do it. I must however fulfill my promise to her, and tell you that she left the child to you."

Three weeks later Chris received the letter in Vienna, and felt dull and dispirited for days. Ursula had deserved to live. She had courage and will power. But she had not lived, and she had left her child to him. In the end he went to Katie and told her the story.

"She left it to *you*?" she said incredulously.

"So Miss Nettie says."

"It's ridiculous. Why would she leave you a baby?"

"God only knows," he told her heavily. "I suppose not literally. She meant that I was more or less to look after it."

"Not in my house! You don't expect to hand me a baby like that, do you?"

"No," he said. "No, I suppose not."

"And you are to support it?"

"I imagine the father will do that."

"Oh! So you know who the father is. Well, that's something."

There was evidently to be no help from Katie, and in the days that followed she seemed to be oddly jealous of the child and even suspicious. One day she said out of a clear sky: "Chris, is this baby yours?"

"You know well enough that it isn't. I never saw the girl until a few months before he was born."

"Then who is the father? Tell me that and I'll believe you."

He was tired and irritable, and suddenly his temper flared.

"I haven't any intention of telling you, and I don't give a good God damn whether you believe me or not."

Undoubtedly he was difficult during those days. He was exhausted with the endeavor to get all he needed in a shorter time than he had planned, and the courses were proving more expensive than he had anticipated. Now he had a baby on his hands, and it annoyed and puzzled him. One day he wrote Jerry, to that business office of his where he played at working.

"I have as you know no responsibility for this child. Ursula asked me to look after him, but that is your job, not mine. In the meantime I suggest that, if you have nothing in view, you leave him where he is until I come back. I know a childless couple in the country who might take him and rear him. They are cousins of mine and prosperous farmers, and they have no children. I doubt if money would enter into such an arrangement, but my own idea would be that you continue your monthly checks, and that the money be banked for his education later."

He wrote the letter in a coffeehouse in the Alserstrasse late one afternoon. Wrote it in his small neat hand, to the noise of billiard balls clicking, to the rustle of the *Fliegende Blaetter* and the Vienna papers being read about him, to the clatter of coffee cups and the hum of conversation. Wrote it away from Katie and her jealous eyes, and having dropped it in a street letter box felt somewhat relieved.

He walked back to the pension that night, along the Ring and finally into the meaner districts of the older city. He walked heavily now, as though the youth had gone out of him; or like a tired man, planting his feet squarely and doggedly along a dull familiar road. The *Portier,* smoking a cigarette in the doorway, saw him coming and went back to his wife, who was frying meat in the kitchen.

"The big *Herr Doktor,* he is troubled in his mind," he said.

"So? And why?"

"One knows. That is all."

"He has a pretty young wife."

"Women do not make a world," he said darkly. "Nor looks a woman."

CHAPTER XXVII

WINTER lasted long that year in Vienna. Katie bought a hot-water bottle and at night took it to bed with her. The fuel bills for the tile stove mounted high. The *Portier's* wife, washing down daily the long stone staircase, was enveloped in a cloud of steam from hot water against cold stone, and outside the smoke from the small coal stoves in the street cars blew down in the wind from the mountains and set the passengers to coughing. Women carrying bricks in hods up stepladders steamed like cattle, horses slipped and fell in the half-frozen ooze of the streets, and now and then a fog turned the gray medieval buildings of the old quarter into pale ghosts of a long gone past.

Chris noticed none of these things. He was working furiously now. Everything was grist that came to his mill. He was taking an X-ray course, all the surgery he could find, even bronchoscopy. For the equivalent of twenty-five cents a woman came to the clinic and almost daily went through the exquisite torture of the bronchoscope.

One day Chris spoke to her about it.

"One must eat, Herr Doktor," she said quietly.

He and Katie had established a *modus vivendi* of sorts. The week was his for work, but Saturday nights and Sundays were hers. On Saturday night he would get into his worn dinner clothes and they would go to the Bal Tabarin or somewhere else. It was for these nights Katie lived. She would sit at the table sipping her sweet champagne and stare round-eyed at the boxes a few feet above the floor, filled with cocottes and gay with flowers and uniforms.

"Are those women really bad, Chris?"

"I don't know. What does it matter?"

He was conscious that he himself was interested. The women were beautiful and the gaiety and laughter made him feel old. He would take Katie on the floor to dance, and near the boxes he would try not to look.

"You're a very good dancer, Katie."

"You're pretty good, too."

The eyes of the women in the boxes on them, and Chris aware of it.

"Who is the big man with the girl in blue?" they would ask.

"Probably an American doctor."

Their interest would lapse. These doctors, they were either poor or highly virtuous, or both. The officers were poor too, but not virtuous.

Now and then there would be a stir, and some royal highness or other would enter his box, bringing with him the lady of the hour. Then the flower vendors would hurry, and he would buy great armloads of exotic blossoms and pile them around her. Katie would watch, filled with envy. The jewels and dresses made her feel cheap and shabby, and one day, after such a night, she went boldy to the Kärntnerstrasse and ordered some expensive clothes. She was terrified afterwards, but the thing was done.

"I've bought some clothes, Chris."

"That's right, if you needed them."

"But I mean *clothes,*" she said desperately. "Good clothes. They cost a lot."

They had, as a matter of fact, cost five hundred dollars, and he tried that night to explain his financial situation to her, but she only cried. In the end he paid the bills, not only because he had to but because as the days went on he had that increasing sense of guilt toward her, that she meant practically nothing to him. Later, looking back over those first days of his marriage he was to wonder whether those weeks and months in Vienna had not been a mistake. There was good material in Katie, and at that time at least she had loved him. He might have made something of her. But he had never been in love with her, and if she had eased the loneliness of the first few weeks she still lived her strongly self-concentrated life.

He would come home to find her running ribbons through her underwear, her hair in curlers and her face covered with cold cream, and no chair in the room available.

"I didn't expect you so soon, Chris."

"It's dinner time. Better hurry."

There would follow the minor discomfort of two people dressing hastily in the small room, with Katie pre-empting the mirror and Chris tying his tie over her head.

"You take so much room, Chris. Can't you stand back a little?"

He considered taking an adjoining bedroom for himself, but to Katie that would be the unforgivable affront and he did not do it. He went on, afraid that she would break through his pretenses and see the stark facts of their mutual failure.

For his work was his real love now. To that he gave all he had. Lessons, clinics, lectures, operations. Abdominal surgery. Brain surgery. Simple amputations. Technique. A new instrument for stones in the kidney. Reading X-ray plates or, protected by lead aprons and lead screens, working with the machine itself. A great day when Chris used the bronchoscope and recovered a toy whistle from a child's throat. A dryness on one finger, and a secret terror that he had a burn. It passed and there was no burn. Better and easier medical German now, a feeling of belonging. Being an old and important member of the A. M. A., and even confronted with a strike of the *Docents* who wanted to form a union of sorts, and who had to be told that they would either keep open shop or the Americans would go elsewhere.

Katie had no place in this world of his.

He had no time to remember Beverly. He had almost forgotten America. Now and then he used the excuse of work for a night off with some of the other men. There would be poker then in some upper room, with beer steins on the table and a supper of cold ham and bread and cheese to follow. It was a bit of home for a few hours.

"I'll raise that a *Krone.*"

"Let's see what you've got."

After the game they would drink beer and reminisce. Their talk invariably was medical shop; their hopes, their ambitions, even their memories seemed limited to their work.

"Remember the time we put that cigar-store Indian in the hospital chapel, Bill? When the sisters came in the next morning there was old Sitting Bull among the saints, holding out a box of cigars! Crazy thing to do, but it seemed a good idea at the time."

Chris would stay late. There was nothing to go back to but that dreary room in the pension. Also he was essentially a man's man, and he liked the company of his fellows; too he had begun to dread the long hours alone with Katie, the attempt to meet her on her own ground. Even in the daytime he would go into a coffeehouse sometimes on his way back, to escape the long hour alone with her until the little maid, her felt slippers now changed for shoes, would rap on the door with her *bitte zum speisen.* The coffeehouse would be alive and cheerful with American doctors, with students and officers, with substantial citizens and their wives, drinking beer or coffee with whipped cream and thriftily slipping into their pockets the extra lumps of sugar provided. There would be a haze of tobacco smoke and a sense of relaxation and peace.

Once he fell asleep there and awakened at nine o'clock, to go home to a frightened Katie who turned angry when she saw him safe and sound.

"Where on earth have you been?"

"I'm sorry, Katie. I fell asleep."

"That's a nice story! Where?"

"In a coffeehouse."

She did not believe him, but he let it go. He did not care enough even to quarrel. He picked up his hat however and slammed out the door, to eat a solitary meal at a restaurant down the street. She was repentant when he got back, and he was obliged once more to go through one of those reconciliation scenes by which she tried to bring some drama into her dull life.

Late in March, with the snow melting from the hoary head of the Rax and the grass growing green in the Prater, Katie came to him with the announcement that she was pregnant, and that he would have to do something about it.

"Do something? Do what?"

"You know I don't want a baby. I won't have one. Don't make me have one, Chris! Don't make me have one."

She was so alarmed that he had to hold her until she stopped shaking. Then he tried to talk to her.

"It would be something to live and work for, dear. Don't you see that? I'd like it, myself. You would too, once it was over."

That was unfortunate, for she wriggled out of his arms and confronted him in furious anger.

"Once it's over!" she said. "You'd let me go through with it, wouldn't you? *You* don't have to have it. It's easy for you. But I won't do it. I'll go somewhere else if you won't help me."

It turned out to be a false alarm, such as he was to know frequently so long as they lived together. Katie, after a sullen silence, was bright and happy when he came home one night. Apologetic too, trying in a dozen ways to make amends for the past week.

"I'm sorry, Chris. I was just scared. You don't hate me, do you?"

"Of course not, my dear," he said patiently. "I'm glad, if you are."

She crawled into his lap and he held her there. He did not hate her. It was nothing so simple as that. There were even times when he was fond of her. He would come home to find her struggling over his mending, her mouth set, the needle tight in her unaccustomed fingers, and she would look like a child over a lesson.

"I'll darn this if it kills me!"

She was only twenty to his thirty, and life had not been easy for her. He would have a moment of real tenderness then, would stoop and kiss her shining hair, soft and young under his lips.

"We can't let that happen! Throw it away and I'll take you for a walk."

"Like taking the dog out! Is that it?"

But she would go out happily, hanging on his arm, looking at the wild game hung up for sale in front of the shops, and hoping that other passing women knew that he was hers and she was his.

"Chris, look at the dolls! I never had a really good doll."

"Shall we get that one?"

They did one day, a doll dressed in short full skirts and boots, like the nurses in the park, and with two long blonde braids of hair. Katie called it Lena.

No reply had come from Jerry Ames about Ursula's boy, and in April Chris wrote to Hiram Mortimer and his wife: "I hardly know how to make the suggestion, but I remember that at one time you contemplated adopting a child. I know of one now, a boy, with good blood on both sides but born last fall of an unmarried mother.

"He was a wanted child, which means something, and as the mother is dead he needs a home. I believe a small sum would be paid monthly, although that may not matter if you later adopt him. What could be done, if you are interested, might be to take him for a few months without any obligation. After that—"

He ended by telling them where the boy could be seen, and sent his letter off without much hope. Hiram and Amy were no longer young, and it was asking a good bit of them; might even revive the old bitterness of their childlessness. Late in May he got an answer from Hiram.

"We have the boy, and Amy is like an old hen with a chick. He is a good boy, and I rather like him myself. It looks as though we will keep him, and I'm going to the city tomorrow to see about the necessary steps."

Chris was greatly relieved. For the first time in months he felt that Beverly was safe at last. She need never know. The Mortimer farm was far away; and the child would be safe too. Sitting back in his chair, his long legs stretched out in front of him, he thought again of old Dave and Letitia who had sent him here, and of old Dave's disappointment that none of his sons had followed him along his road. Perhaps this boy would do that. If he were to have no son of his own—

They went back to America in the late spring of that year. Katie was relieved and happy to be going. On the Siebensterngasse she found a trunk covered with a thin skin of black leather and built like a small chest, and in that she packed her new clothes and Lena, the doll. Except for those small items she was taking nothing with her from Vienna, nothing of its age-old culture, its art, its luxury behind stone walls, or even of its music. The opera had bored her to tears.

Watching her at her packing Chris wondered what was going on in that small tight mind of hers.

"You're glad to be going, aren't you?"

"They could burn this town up and I'd never miss it."

What was she going back to that she was so eager, he wondered, and decided that it was merely to familiar things, familiar living. He himself was eager, but he had something to look forward to, work and eventual success. But was that any better than Katie's simpler demands? Was his ambition any better than hers? Hers was the instinct of the cat for the familiar hearth; his was ambition now, the desire to rise above his fellows, to do good work and have it recognized.

On the last day in Vienna he went back to the Club, the lounge, the reading room, the small room for the secretary, the women's room. The place was empty. In the lounge American papers and magazines littered the table. The bulletin board was posted with lecture courses. It had become familiar territory by that time, and he was aware as he wandered that he was seeing it for the last time, and that when he left it he would be leaving his youth also.

When he returned to the bulletin board a bright-eyed youngster was standing in front of it.

"Something you want to know?"

"Plenty! I've got six weeks and a lot to learn."

It was no use protesting, he knew by that time. God only knew by what triumph of thrift or luck these men got over here at all. But the youngster grinned.

"Listen," he said. "I know it's funny. So do you. But out where I live it's Europe or nothing, and the last job I had was pulling a tooth for a pet monkey."

"Well, I started with a dog myself," said Chris, and was suddenly aware of a tightness in his chest. Beverly and Sandy. Beverly on his doorstep that first day. What a fool he was to remember. Oh God, why can't I forget the whole damned business? Forget it. It's over. It's done.

The youngster was lonely, and Chris took him to the restaurant below and ordered beer. He had about decided on nose and throat. "You can get that quicker, and my town is hell on the good old sinuses." But under his cheerfulness Chris sensed fear and almost desperation.

"I thought of obstetrics," he said, "but I look too young. And everybody's got tonsils. Not everybody has a baby!" He grinned.

Before leaving for home Chris had fixed him up in an inexpensive pension and found some vacancies for him in different courses. Then he forgot him, but a few years later he saw him again in a lieutenant's uniform in an army camp, arguing with a bearded young Mennonite conscientious objector on the advantages of a razor, and of buttons over hooks and eyes. He saluted Chris debonairly.

"If you'll hold him, Captain," he said, "I'll shave him."

Chris saw him only once again after that. He was dying on a dirty blanket on the floor of a dugout in France. He grinned and made a move to salute, but the gesture was a failure.

"We never shaved that fellow," he said, and lapsed into a comfortable eternity.

Part IV

THE DOCTOR'S WIFE

CHAPTER XXVIII

CHRIS was going through the process of reorienting himself after a night's sleep. He had been doing that now for several days. He would open his eyes, gaze for a second or two at the bedroom and then close them again. There should be a wardrobe, a wooden washstand and double windows with red cushions to keep out any possible fresh air; and pretty soon now the little maid in her list slippers should be carrying in his coffee and rolls, and Frau Wagner should be waiting to give him his German lesson.

He stirred, suddenly aware that he was occupying the center of the sagging bed, and that Katie was lying on the edge. She did not waken, and he settled down to doing some serious thinking. He lay very still, partly in order not to waken her and partly because the brass knob on the head of the bed had come loose again, and he had not had time to fix it. It had been a difficult week. The house had been familiar but not welcoming, and although it had been cleaned before they arrived, there still hung over it the odor of dust and mildew.

But he was glad to be back. The hospital had welcomed him warmly.

"Well, what's new, Chris? Got a lot to show us?"

"Got a little beer fat I'll have to take off."

Only a few of them mentioned his marriage, although he did not notice it. The sensation it had caused was over. If the nurses wondered about it among themselves it was quietly, behind closed doors. Only Miss Simpson, eying him on that first visit of his, asked him bluntly if he was happy.

"Happy?" he said surprised. "Happy to be back? I am indeed."

"And your marriage?" she persisted. "I have sometimes wondered—"

"Nothing to wonder about," he said, curtly.

"Then it's working out all right?"

He flushed.

"I suppose the idea of marriage is always more romantic than the fact itself," he said lightly. "Certainly it's all right."

The old affectionate intimacy between them was gone. She had many pictures of him, but not this one, and she knew unhappily that she had lost him. She and Beverly had both lost him. And Chris, swinging angrily out of the hospital that day, was furious at her without knowing why. "What business is it of hers?" he thought savagely; and did not know that he was blaming her for his marriage, for Katie, for the general wreckage of his personal life.

There in the bed with Katie beside him he was remembering that, but his anger did not last long. He put his arms under his head and planned. He would keep this house and this office, for he would still have to carry on his general work. But somewhere in the heart of town he would have an office for consultations. Already as he lay there he was furnishing it.

Lying there, he seemed to have traveled a long distance since he had first occupied the room. He looked at the blue china clock on the mantel, at the corner where Caesar had slept uncounted ages ago; and by shifting his position carefully, at Katie. It was at such moments that she got under his guard, when she looked small and defenseless. Now she lay on the edge of the bed, soft and relaxed, and he felt a wave of pity for her. He knew that he confused her, confused her thinking, such as it was, confused even her living; and he realized uncomfortably that he was doing the unforgivable thing, and making her feel inferior.

Her very sharpnesses were the retaliation of the weak against the strong.

"Can't you let that sweeping go until I am out of the house, Katie? It's covering me with dust."

"Then why don't you get out? You've been dressing for hours, and I have my work to do. If you think it's any fun running a doctor's house, with meals at all hours and the telephone ringing every minute, you can think again."

Not a shrew, Katie. A rather scared young woman, likable most of the time, trying to live up to him as best she could. He moved uneasily, and the knob fell down and hit him on the head again.

"Damnation!" he said, and Katie stirred and wakened.

"I do think, Chris, that you might let me have my sleep out."

"Sorry, my dear. It's that knob again."

Sounds and the odor of bacon and coffee were coming from the kitchen, where a heavy-footed German girl had scrubbed Lily's dirty tables to the whiteness of snow. Now he heard her on the stairs.

"Breakfast's ready, doctor."

"Why on earth doesn't she tell *me?*" Katie said fretfully.

"That's easy. Because I usually eat before you do."

He bathed and dressed carefully, a white shirt, a blue tie, a light suit, as the weather was warm. Katie watched him from the bed. Later on he knew that she would throw a kimono over her nightgown, thrust her bare feet into slippers and go down to her breakfast. Now she followed his every movement with her eyes.

"You're very fine today. What's it all about?"

"Going to look at some offices, my dear."

"Is that all? I thought you might be meeting your old sweetheart."

He turned quickly and glanced at her. Only once or twice since their marriage had she mentioned Beverly, but since their return she had brought her up several times. He saw that her jealousy, latent while at a distance, had been aroused now that they were back on the scene of that early defeat of hers.

"I haven't seen her, Katie. I don't expect to see her. And why should you worry about her?" He grinned at her. "She is married, I am married, you are—"

"As though that counted!"

"Doesn't it count with you?"

She was silent. He always managed to silence her. But she knew. He might grin all he liked, but she had got under his skin. He was still crazy about Beverly Lewis. Let that get out, and where were all his fine schemes for the future? That small vindictive streak in her which sought to hurt him when she could not reach him urged her still further.

"I've been thinking, Chris. I'm going to sell this furniture."

"Sell it?" he said blankly.

"Well, it's mine, isn't it? Or mine and Dick's, and he doesn't matter. It won't bring anything, but it's disgraceful. We ought to have at least a decent house."

He thought, carefully tying his tie: "She is trying to make me angry. And it is her stuff. I'd forgotten that. Good God, I don't want to be dependent on her. Let her sell it. What's the use of telling her I've bought it over and over?"

"That's your privilege," he told her evenly. "I can't refurnish the house and have a downtown office too, of course."

"Then why have a downtown office? What's the matter with these?"

"We've been over that before, Katie. You must do what you like, of course."

He looked at no offices that morning. Luckily he had calls to make, for business was better than he had expected. His old patients greeted him happily, and there were even one or two new ones. Clearly there was prestige about Europe. When he went back for lunch he found Katie busy with a secondhand dealer, a small heavy-set Jew, and arguing with him acrimoniously. In the end she made a deal with him and came in triumphantly to lunch, breathless but exultant.

"He's a robber," she said. "But we have two weeks to get ready for him."

"I hope you remembered that the offices are mine."

"Don't be idiotic. But I wish you'd do them over, too. They're terrible. Chris, could we have our bedroom for a living room and use mother's room? We ought to have one somewhere."

The idea revolted him. He did not want to sleep in that room where Henry had died and Lily had lain down for the last time on the bed among her littered possessions. But he looked across the table at Katie and realized that her ambitions were as legitimate as his own.

"Of course you should have a living room, my dear. Why shouldn't you?"

"I'd like to have a place to see people."

"So you shall, if you want it."

Yes, she ought to have a place to see people. Just what people, he wondered. He remembered those telephone conversations of hers, the girl who had been with her at the dance hall. But he agreed, and she went around the table and kissed him. Olga, coming in with the potatoes, stared at them. These American men, so easily cajoled! Not like the Germans. There a man was a man, and a woman looked after him and bore his children.

Chris was stubborn too, in his own way. He might yield to Katie, but he would not let her defeat him; and that afternoon he saw Grant and borrowed two thousand dollars from him.

"I've no collateral, no security," he said. "But if I live I'll pay you back. That's all I can say."

He did not tell Katie, busy now buying her new furniture; wearing her Vienna clothes, and moving with an air from shop to shop. He took his downtown offices, furnished them, and one day installed himself there. Only when they were ready did he take her in to see them, and although she accepted and even admired them, she knew that from that time on he would live a part of his life to himself. She was beaten.

"I suppose you'll have a nurse here?"

"Not yet. I can't afford it. Some day, of course."

Shut in there with a nurse, some pretty girl in a uniform,

winning him in a thousand different ways, admiring him, trying to get him away from her. Her mouth tightened.

"Why couldn't I do it?"

"That's out of the question, and you know it."

She had however taken it better than he expected, and later on he had to admit that she had done wonders with the house on very little money. The dining room was cheerful with new paint and paper and a set of imitation mahogany, and the front bedroom seemed larger and had gained dignity in its new status. There was a big chair by the fire for Chris and a reading lamp on the table beside it, and even a rather hideous miniature beer keg on the table to hold his pipe tobacco. One day coming home he found a group of men trying to get a new upright piano around the turn at the head of the stairs, and stood watching them with some amusement.

"Going to take music lessons?" he asked Katie.

"No, but it furnishes. I only pay a little every month."

He was busy, however, with his own work and his new problems. In the weeks since his return he had not seen Beverly, and there were times when he forgot her completely. Then he would see some young woman who held her head as she did and she would come back, as if she had walked into a closed room. There was a day, too, when on a suburban street car, he saw Jerry pass in his automobile with a young woman beside him. It was not Beverly, and he wondered if Ursula had been right. "He would never be faithful to a wife," she had said. In that case—

He was irritable that night, and Katie watched him nervously. Life was not too easy for her just then, struggling with her furnishing, with Olga, with Chris's uncertain hours, with all the problems of a doctor's house. The doorbell and telephone rang interminably. She would go up to the attic for some purpose, or down into the cluttered cellar, to be called for this or that. Olga's English was worthless for messages, and by evening Katie's legs would ache and she would be too tired to dress for dinner. She would wash hastily, brush back her hair and go to the table, only too often to have Chris detained in the office until the meal was spoiled.

"I'm sorry about the steak, Chris."

"My fault. It doesn't matter."

Nothing mattered but his work, she told herself angrily. He did not need her. Even his occasional caresses were furtive and half-ashamed, and it was during that period of readjustment too that she staged another of her alarms about being pregnant and was hysterical for days. She was conciliatory afterwards, but Chris was impatient. He hated himself for it, but there were times when he felt that she had blocked every road into the future, even the hope of a child, and was deeply and silently resentful.

"I wish you'd *say* something, Chris."

He would rouse.

"Yes? What about, my dear?"

Now and then he had a patient in the downtown office. Now and then too he and Ted Lawrence found time for golf, or for a long walk to the javelin field. One day he told Ted that he was a rotten husband, and was surprised to find that young gentleman agreeing with him.

"She's pretty young, Chris. Maybe you forget that. And why not praise her now and then? She's trying, you know. She's done a good job with the house."

"I've told her I like it."

"Damn it all, man, she's not a clerk in a store. She's trying her best to live up to you, but you're always a mile in front with your head in the clouds. You might at least stop and give her a hand now and then."

Chris nodded gravely.

"Right, of course. I suppose no man can do two jobs well at the same time, or travel two roads at once."

"Not if he takes the high one and leaves his wife the low!"

Chris was thoughtful after that. A long time ago he had said that about Beverly; only then she was to take the high road and he the low. Ted watching him saw the guarded look in his face and wondered again about his marriage. Why had he married Katie? He had said good-by to him alone there in the house one night, and the next morning he was married. Without a word. Without, so far as he knew, an intention. Had he been forced into it? Were the stories true? And if they were, then what?

"The poor devil," he thought. "It's changed him, whatever did it. He looks damned unhappy."

It was early summer by that time. One day Chris saw in the papers that the Jervis Ameses had taken a cottage at Bar Harbor and felt that the city was suddenly hot and empty. But there was no drought that year. The park was green and gay with playing children, rain fell and broke the heat, and Vienna, like Beverly, was once more far away like a half-remembered dream.

He would sit across from Katie at the table while the candles—she used candles now—flickered in the evening breeze, and try to talk, try to be kind and gentle.

"What sort of day, my dear?"

"Nothing much. Harriet Lee was in."

She had struck up a friendship with Harriet, the younger of the Lee girls.

He could not keep it up for long, however. The bell would ring and he would be wanted in the office or at the telephone, and Katie would sit there in lonely grandeur, under her candles, with the heavy-handed Olga to bring her food and the surreptitious cigarette she had learned to smoke abroad. Her jealousy of Beverly was dying of sheer inanition, and if she thought of her at all it was to see her going about from one great house to another, and living a fairy-tale life of luxury and ease. . . .

Something of the sort was happening to Beverly, of course. There were evenings when she and Jerry dined out, young and handsome and popular, among their kind; Beverly exquisitely dressed, Jerry in his carefully-fitted evening clothes.

"You're gorgeous tonight, sweetheart."

"Am I? That's nice, Jerry."

Eating and drinking and dancing, while the old mountains looked down on them and the sun set red across the bay. Yachts in the harbor, a British battleship coming in and men in uniform at the parties, urbane and apparently not thinking about war at all. Any war. And then going home again to the white house, where Sandy barked a welcome and Jerry would see her safely inside the door.

"Aren't you coming in?"

"There's a moon. I think I'll take a ride. Any objection?"

"Certainly not, if you want to go."

She never knew where he went on those rides of his. But sometimes he came home in the small hours to find her still on that upper balcony of hers, a flowered silk shawl about her, gazing out over the water to the islands, tree-covered shadows dropped as by some casual hand.

"What's the matter? Not waiting for me, are you?"

"It's so lovely. I didn't feel sleepy."

She did not think consciously as she sat there, letting the night soothe her spirit. She did not even think on those long mountain walks of hers, when Sandy stirred up small wild creatures and the hills gave her something of their peace. But she took to going to church again that summer, as though she needed something to lean on, something stronger than herself and stronger than Jerry. Certainly something stronger than Jerry.

CHAPTER XXIX

CHRIS did well that autumn. His general practice was growing, and already several men had sent operative cases to the downtown office. For the first time he had private surgical cases in the hospital; patients in private rooms with private nurses.

His arrival would cause the usual stir. "Here's Doctor Arden. Where's the dressing table?" "It's in 36. They're about through with it." He would go into the room, made ready for his coming; the high bed neat and white, flowers on the table, an earnest young intern behind him, and the nurse standing ready with the record.

"And how are we this morning?" he would say.

He was entirely unconscious of that "we." He would stand, big and smiling, over the bed, his competent hands ready, his eyes steady and keen.

"Let's see it. Ah, that looks better."

They trusted him, these men and women. He was solid and dependable and gentle. When he was going to hurt them he said so, and they understood and got ready.

"Now! Just a minute and it's over."

And it would be over. It had come and gone, and they were still there, looking up at him.

The hospital was proud of him after its own fashion. Already he was producing revenue for it, operating room charges, anesthetist's fee, room and board for his patients. The hospital had trained him and now he was repaying it. No patient, private or otherwise, ever paid his full cost, but at least Chris was helping them to lower the deficit. And after a talk with Grant one day he charged more adequate fees than he had at first.

"You're not charging for the operation," Grant said. "You're charging for the dozen years or so it took you to be able to do it. And you'll have to make those who can pay for those who can't."

He repaid half of his loan that fall, and told Katie one day that if things kept up he would soon be needing a nurse at the downtown office.

"A nurse!" Katie said when he told her. "Already? What in the world do you want with a nurse now? You're not as busy as that, are you?"

Because he knew her he replied whimsically that he might need a nurse, but that she would be a nurse and not a mistress, and that when the time came she might come and see for herself. "I shall choose her with great care," he said. "Not for pulchritude but because she knows her business." And Katie, uncertain as to the word and highly suspicious of it, was silenced.

He was watching himself now with her; had done so ever since the talk with Ted Lawrence. Because he was busy and glad to be busy, and also because he felt guilty of many things, when Christmas came that year he bought her a solitaire diamond ring.

"A ring! Oh Chris, how I've wanted one! I can say it's my engagement ring, can't I?"

She was very happy all that day, but he was busy and out until evening. Coming home late he was touched to hear her upstairs at the piano, picking out with one finger the air of "Stille Nacht, Heilige Nacht." He went up and put his arms around her.

"I'm sorry, dear. It hasn't been much of a day for you."

She burst into tears. "Do you remember last Christmas, Chris? The Bal Tabarin and the dancing, and the way they threw flowers? It was so cheerful."

"You should have asked some people in."

"How could I, with Olga out, and not even knowing whether you'd be here or not?"

He made any number of good resolutions that night, lying

in one of the twin beds in Lily's old room and remembering Henry and other things. He would take her out, go to the theater now and then, bring men there, make a common life for them both. But he did not keep them. Grant went to Europe the first of the year, coincident with Chris's period of service at the hospital, and Chris took over his private work. Grant had not been well. He had taken to falling asleep at all sorts of odd times; even in the office with a patient there. He was a bad color too, and he could not eat. One day he went to Dickinson in the laboratory, and some time later Chris found him with a laboratory report in his hand and his face a sickly yellow.

"Look at this," he said. "Nothing much to do, but I'd better make the gesture and go away for a while."

So he went, and with him Chris's resolutions. The double job, with his own work, proved to be a day and night matter. Katie was peevish, but Chris was happier than he had ever been. When he went home, usually late at night, it was to be called frequently for a night operation.

"Good heavens! Aren't we ever going to have a night's sleep?" Katie would say drowsily. He would not answer for fear of rousing her. He would carry his clothes into the bathroom and dress there, go into the alley where in an old stable he housed the small car Grant had left him, crank it and be off into the quiet night; aware that he was vital to some life, and conscious still of a small thrill of excitement. Sometimes it was a private case. Sometimes it was some poor wreck from the mills or the railroads or a motor smash. Whatever it was it was the same to Chris. He would scrub up, put on his mask, his cap, his long sterile gown again, and set about the business of saving a life if possible. . . . .

He took off Scott's hand that winter. The hospital always cared for its own and so Scott was to remain, but he had an assistant now.

"I can do without the hand," he told Chris quietly. "It

hasn't been much use lately anyhow. But I'm less than a man now, Chris. That hurts."

He was up and about soon however, feeding his fish, showing the new stereoscopic plates. "Three dimensions instead of two," he would say. "We'll be showing you fellows the soft tissues soon, and you can stop guessing."

That winter Chris began to watch himself. It was too easy to regard these people as cases, too easy to see the operating room at night as the stage setting for a good job well done, and not as a bit of human tragedy. Going out after the work was done to some silent, waiting group, and facing them.

"I'm sorry. He'll probably get over this, but he had to lose that leg."

"Now, mother, don't look like that. The doctor says he's going to live."

"But his leg! What will he do without a leg?"

It was too easy, after such a scene, to go back to his house, to put away his car and undress in the bathroom and then fall asleep filled with self-confidence and pride. A man had to build defenses or he could not carry on, but it was a devilish thing, the practice of medicine. He would look at Katie, still sleeping, and realize that she was losing him, not to Beverly or any other woman, but to his work itself.

All the women who married into the profession took that chance, of course. Their men lived vicariously a thousand lives, but they lived only one; and it was only when night came, when every soul is a lonely soul and a tired man turned to some woman for comfort, that their men were their own.

Not that he put it that way, or even that he turned to Katie for comfort to any great extent. She was too tightly bound up in her own affairs now for that, making friends, building a life of her own. Rather to Chris's surprise people called, especially the ones in the neighborhood. Some of them were merely curious, but some liked Katie and came again. He would see Olga carrying a tea tray up to the living room, and more than once he found some women around a card table, teaching Katie bridge.

It relieved him, took some of the onus from his own shoulders. But one day he found Barrett there drinking a highball, and was conscious of sharp annoyance.

"Good liquor you keep, doctor."

"I don't keep it long." Chris smiled with faint irony.

"Aren't you having any?" said Barrett hospitably.

"Thanks. I don't drink in working hours."

Barrett was unmoved.

"Thank God I'm not a surgeon," he said, and helped himself to another of Chris's cigarettes. . . .

Grant was away all spring, and by summer Chris was an exhausted shadow of himself. Ted Lawrence, who had become deeply attached to him, protested.

"You're not superhuman," he had said, "and you've been doing three men's work all winter. What have you got but your nerves anyhow? You're not a factory. How long is it since you've had a real night's sleep?"

"I don't remember. Grant's back now. I'll be all right."

But he was not all right. He was irritable, impatient, and on edge, still carrying many of his old city cases, nursing his practice, making out his own bills; and at night remaining downstairs in the office until all hours, smoking his pipe until his tongue felt burnt and dry, reluctant to go up to the room which he shared with Katie, but unwilling to hurt her by suggesting another one.

"I'll be all right, Ted."

"Nonsense! Look at your hands."

Chris had held them out, and they were not steady. He was thunderstruck.

"Funny!" he said. "Smoking too much."

"Better get away."

"Get away, with bills all over the place and two rents to pay?"

That was the nearest he had ever come to disloyalty to

Katie, that mention of her bills. For Katie was spending money now, upholding her position, talking about buying a car, patronizing beauty shops and spending hours each day on her dressing. Two maids in the house, one wearing a uniform and cap and opening the door unwillingly to the city cases. Candles on the table for dinner, big and still bigger bills at the Daily Market. And collections poor. Chris sending out his bills like shooting an arrow into the air, and times hard. Bread lines in the lower part of town near the river, a few near-riots, a deputy sheriff brought into the hospital badly beaten.

Then one hot day in the operating room, closing up after an appendectomy, Chris had felt himself go dizzy, as though all the blood had left his head. He finished and went out, to find his legs soft under him and the floor apparently receding.

"Sit down, doctor."

"I'm all right. Too hot in there, that's all."

A week later he and Lawrence were on their way, and the tight band around his head had already loosened. Cramped in his berth at night, he slept like a baby on the train. They stopped in Toronto to buy tackle and then started North, being dropped at their rented shack by a small river steamer. Chris stood on the bank and breathed deep of the crisp air.

"By gad, Ted," he said, "that's the first real lungful of air I've had in four years."

They were still there when war broke out in Europe. Chris, rowing out to meet the weekly boat with their supplies, brought the news back, and Ted upset the potatoes he was peeling for dinner.

"God, how I'd like to go."

Chris put down the paper and got ready to clean some fish.

"I imagine it won't last long," he said. "Damn fish anyhow. What was the idea in putting scales on them?"

They dismissed it at that. They were camping alone in a wooden shack far from civilization, sleeping on straw ticks and taking turns in the morning as to who got up and cooked the breakfast. They lived mostly in bathing suits and in canoes, and both men were brown and strong. Chris's big muscles bulged from long portages, and his hands were steady again. They would trudge along to this lake or that, hung with their rods, the coffee pot, a frying pan, salt and bread, and carrying the canoe. Sometimes they would hit a tree with a bump.

"Where the hell are you going?"

"How do I know, with this thing over my head. Come up here and try it."

They were relaxed and amiable, in the comfortable association of two men who like each other and like the same things. At night they built a smudge by the river bank and sat there talking or silent. Then they turned in and slept.

But that night when the war news came Chris did not go to bed. He sat alone for a long time on the bank while the fire burned low and then went out. The river in front and the pine woods behind seemed to cut him off from life. All color gone from the world and alone in this tremendous darkness like death; like death and awaiting resurrection. The body gone, and only the mind there, awaiting resurrection.

Death. War meant death. He stirred uneasily, seeing those men he had known and liked in Vienna now facing death; the bearded *Hofraths,* the eager young *Docents,* the sentry at the gate of the hospital, even the *Portier* with his bandage and his military mustache. All equal now in what they faced. And the people in the coffeehouses, on the streets and in the cafés, those gay *gemütlich* people, with their English dogs and spats, what were they doing and thinking now?

He was roused by the sound of a paddle, and to see the leaden sheet of the river breaking into small ripples. A canoe came out of the darkness, an Indian driving it rapidly and beaching it almost at his feet. He had brought a telegram, and Chris read it by the flare of a lighted match. It said: "Father shot and in critical condition. Can you come?" and it was signed "Beverly."

He went out that night with the Indian guide, leaving Ted

to break up the camp and taking with him only his suitcase. Hour after hour he sat cramped in the canoe, watching the darker shadows of the woods as they moved past with horrible slowness. He offered to paddle but the Indian gruffly refused, and at last he settled back, thinking of that ironic twist by which he had hated and fought Staunton Lewis and now was hastening to try to save him. He saw him in the hall, listening to the story of Jake's death and settling with Rachel the next morning. He saw him, after that interview with the press, slapping the paper down on the desk in the back office and demanding: "Did you say that?" And he saw him, still aloof but now small, a creature of no importance, standing by his wife's bed and seeing her hold out her hand, not to himself but to Chris. He had been punished then for those early sins against her. And now—

It was daylight when they reached the settlement and Chris sent off his wire to Beverly. He was weary and unshaven, but by taking a local at once he could catch the limited, and so he went as he stood. Already Canada was at war, the railroad bridges under guard, the faces of the people tense and brooding. The train seemed to crawl. When it stopped he could hardly sit in his seat. He felt as though he must get out and push it, hurry it along; not because Staunton Lewis might be dying, but because Beverly had called him and he was on the way.

CHAPTER XXX

LEWIS had been shot by a striker in one of his mills, and two days later Chris operated. Grant was ill, and Beverly had insisted that they wait for him. The wound was in the abdomen, and it was a case to try a man's very soul. The New York surgeon Jerry had sent for was opposed to an operation at all. "What's the use? He won't stand up under it."

Chris put the situation up to Beverly, white and quiet with deep rings under her eyes. She seemed thinner than when he had known her, but her gaze was as direct as ever.

"You understand," he said. "He may come out. He may not. In any case—"

"It's his only chance, isn't it?"

"I think so. Yes."

"Then do it, Chris."

But Lewis had more stamina than anyone had suspected. He had the will to live, too. For a week Chris hardly left him, day or night. He ate most of his meals in the hospital, even bathed and shaved there sometimes. The fight raged. Sometimes the man in the bed won, and death seemed to retire into a dark corner to wait for the next round. Then it would come closer again, lean over the bed, seem to spread its black shadow over man and bed and room. Chris could almost see it there, and he would try with all his will power to thrust it back.

"Where's the hypodermic?"

"It's ready, doctor."

Part of the time Lewis was conscious. Then Chris would occasionally find his eyes on him, ironic and slightly mocking, as though he said: "Why do it? You don't like me and I don't like you. I'm not afraid to die."

He was not afraid to die. Men and women may dread the thought of death but never the fact of it, and Staunton Lewis had never feared anyone or anything in all his life. Now he fought to live, but without terror and without drama. Chris, sitting beside the bed, knew that he would have preferred making the fight alone, was secretly ashamed of his helplessness before him; there were times indeed when the battle seemed to lie, not between life and death, but between the man in the bed and the man beside it. Even Beverly hardly counted. She was there in the room, but often Chris was only subconsciously aware of her, tense but quiet, watching those invisible struggles. Now and then however he would drop asleep in his chair for a few minutes, and then she was with him; close, within the touch of his hand.

He would rouse sometimes to find Jerry Ames in the room, tall and smiling, and his father-in-law fixing on him a look of concentrated venom. Indeed, one of the first indications of recovery was when Lewis ordered him out of the room. Not directly. He spoke to the nurse.

"Get my son-in-law out of the room and keep him out," he said distinctly. "And send in the orderly."

It was the first indication he had ever given of his dislike for Jerry and his distrust of him. He was smiling faintly when Jerry went out, and still smiling when he turned his head and looked at Chris. His lips were bloodless, his dapperness gone. He looked small and unimportant as he lay there, except for his eyes.

"Go on home, man," he said weakly. "Good God, I haven't adopted you."

"I'm going when I'm good and ready," said Chris. "Do you think I'm going to throw away a week's work?"

"I suppose that's what I am—a good job, eh?"

"That's all. But a damned good job, if I do say it," said Chris, grinning.

They understood each other after that. It was talk Lewis could comprehend. He was bored to tears by Jerry's hypocritical anxiety. "Let him go back to his women," he said one day. "What does he care what happens to me?"

One night, abruptly, he stared up at Chris with unwinking directness.

"What are you going to charge for all this?"

"All the tariff will stand. I need it," said Chris cheerfully.

"I'm a case, not an eleemosynary institution. You might remember that, young man."

On the first day he was able to sit up in bed he wrote Chris a check for ten thousand dollars. Chris folded it up and put it in his pocket.

"Well?"

"I'll send you a receipt."

"It's enough, isn't it?"

Chris grinned down at him. "If you think you're worth as much as that to the world, I'm not arguing. I'd figured on a thousand."

"You're an impudent young scamp," said Lewis. But later on the nurse coming in found him smiling grimly to himself.

It was about that time that Chris had his first real talk with Beverly since her marriage. She took him home from the hospital in the limousine. Both of them showed the wear and tear of the fight, and Chris leaned back in his corner and yawned.

"Sorry. I'm tired, Beverly."

She said nothing for a moment. Then:

"Of course you know how I feel, Chris. There aren't any words—"

"Don't thank me. I've done a job and been paid for it. That's my business."

"Is that all it was?"

"Nobody's motives are unmixed, my dear."

She stirred. "Don't be hard, Chris. I can't seem to get

near you. You shut me out when I try. Do you hate me so much, or is it just that I don't matter?"

"It's neither," he said stubbornly. "You chose your life and I had to make one for myself. I don't want to be hurt again. That's all."

"Did I do that, Chris? Did I choose my own life?"

"I don't know what else you can call it."

She glanced at him quickly, but his face was set. She looked away again.

"And you're happy, in this life of yours?" she asked impersonally.

"Happy? What is happiness, anyhow? I like my work, I'm ambitious, I suppose I'm getting somewhere. Even your father"—he hesitated, but she had reopened the old wound and he went on doggedly. "It hasn't hurt me, you know, to sign daily bulletins as to his condition. Good publicity, my dear. Good ethical publicity!"

"And that's all it was?"

"What else?"

The car had stopped at the house, and the chauffeur was getting out to open the car door. She flushed and put a hand in his.

"You are lying, Chris," she said softly.

He went into his empty house, angry at himself and at her. Katie was away at the seashore with Harriet Lee and he had the place to himself, but tired as he was he did not go to bed for some time. He paced the floor of the back office, smoking his pipe and thinking. When he went back to see that the maids had locked up he stood for a while at the kitchen door and looked out at the old ailanthus tree in the yard. It was slowly dying, and soon it would have to come out.

Well, that was life. It was an old tree, and the old passed on. Probably they did not mind. There came a time when all sap ran slowly, and the peace of age with all things behind it merged easily into the peace of death. The difficult thing was to be young.

Katie was gone for several weeks, but Chris did not miss her. Work drifted in. He made his calls, went to the hospital, played some golf, came back to quiet summer nights and his pipe. The papers showed the war a bigger thing than he had thought. It was going to last longer, too. He would sit there and be back again in Vienna, growing sentimental over sound German beer, and singing "Alt Heidelberg" at the Club. But it all seemed remote and unreal. He would go up to bed and read himself to sleep, and when he had to go out he could dress without anxiety.

He never admitted even to himself that Katie's absence was a relief. . . .

Katie herself was supremely contented that summer; contented to waken late, to rock long hours on the hotel veranda, to walk the boardwalk with Harriet and to stop in at auction sales.

"I'd like to bid on that."

"Better get a look at it first," Harriet would say cautiously.

In the end Katie would bid and carry back under her arm some useless bit of linen or china. Her room began to be cluttered with them. And once every day she and Harriet would put on bathing suits and lie in the sand. They would take a dip in the water and then lie for an hour or two, watching the other bathers.

"Good heavens, look at that one! If I had a figure like that I'd never go near the water."

"You have a lovely figure," Harriet would say, eying her enviously. Katie would bloom under this praise, stretch in the sand to see the curve of breast and hip under the damp clinging suit.

One day Barrett found them there. He was walking past, a youngish man in flannels, and his eyes traveled from Katie's hip to her breast, and from there to her face. Then he stopped.

"Well!" he said. "If this isn't a piece of luck. Here I am all alone, and I happen on beauty in repose, or expose! eh?"

He was the first man they had spoken to since their arrival, and in a moment he was sitting on the sand beside them. After that he met them there daily. It was all very proper, for there was Harriet, smiling and showing her big front teeth, and half-burying herself in the sand to hide her thin body. They would go into the water, and now and then Barrett would catch Katie and push her under a wave. She was conscious of a queer excitement when he touched her, but she would come out again to be very prim and rather short with him.

Barrett was not fooled. She was ambitious; she wanted no trouble. Certainly she did not care for him. But she had a sensual appeal which kept his interest, and she was not afraid to exploit it. Pretty soon they were on first-name terms.

"Look, Bob, there's a bit of shell in my foot."

He would hold and examine her small foot gravely.

"I don't see it."

"It hurts, anyhow."

"Shall I kiss it and make it well?"

Beyond that he had made little or no progress when he had to leave her there and go home. She was either virtuous or excessively prudent, and he was still puzzled about that when he stood on the train platform and waved to her—and Harriet—when they saw him off.

"The little devil," he said to himself. "The smart little devil!" And went rather complacently back to his growing practice.

It was some time during that interval that Chris went to see Ursula's baby, passing David and Letitia's house, now closed but still furnished, on the way.

"We took out a little. Not much," said Hiram. "Seemed a pity to tear it up, somehow."

Words at the time. They hardly registered with Chris, looking over the pattern of the lush summer fields, the wheat rolling like a golden sea in the sun and some flowers still in Letitia's neglected garden. It recalled many memories, but there was nothing that day to indicate that in due time it was to be sanctuary and even more.

"And the boy's a success?"

"Say listen—"

He stayed only over night. The boy was fine, a grave youngster who looked like Ursula but with Jerry's blond hair; and Amy was younger and happier than he had ever seen her. Chris sat for a long time that evening holding the child while she went about her work. It seemed a long time now since that last night before he left the hospital, when he had held the homesick baby in his arms and dreamed.

"You'll be having one of your own some of these days," Hiram said.

"Maybe. Maybe not."

They were adopting young Noel legally, and Chris left the next day knowing that all was well with him. He carried with him a picture of the boy taken by the local photographer, and on it Amy had written "Noel Martin Mortimer." When he got home he put it carefully in the drawer of the desk, but first, out of sheer pity that Ursula should have no part in it, he wrote her name on the back, and the date of the baby's birth. . . .

Katie came home late in August. She was sunburned and excited, glad to get back and almost too demonstrative.

"Darling!" she said. "How I've missed you! But Harriet was keen on staying and she couldn't stay alone. You didn't mind, did you?"

She had brought home her purchases, and she spent all that first day in setting them about. When Chris told her something of the Staunton Lewis case, however, she grew thoughtful and slightly hostile.

"I suppose you've been seeing *her* day after day."

"If you mean Mrs. Ames, I've seen her, naturally. She's been in great trouble."

"In great trouble about her father? Don't make me laugh, Chris. What does she care, or anybody else for that matter?"

"As it happens, she does," he said evenly.

He could not escape Katie, or evade her. She was there,

his wife, with her legitimate claim on him, on his time, his care, even his body. Katie had ripened in that summer sun, with Barrett beside her, eying her in her bathing suit, whispering little things when Harriet was not listening.

"I'm crazy about you, girl. You know that."

"Don't be silly. I'm not that sort."

"What sort? I just said—"

"Oh, stop it. Here's Harriet."

That night she drew Chris down on the living room sofa beside her and put her head on his shoulder.

"Have you missed me, Chris?"

"The house has been like a tomb, but I wasn't here much."

"You know what I mean. Oh Chris, I'm so crazy about you. You do love me, don't you?"

He knew that eventually she would get under his guard; not deliberately but with the instinct of all women to claim their men. That night he faced honestly the fact that he did not want her, then or ever. He wanted no woman, but only his life and its work. By the time she had gone through the complexities of her night toilet, bathing, brushing her hair, creaming her face, even daubing a little perfume behind her ears, he was apparently asleep.

She stood for some time in her elaborate nightgown, gazing at him with a small tight mouth. Then she put out the light and got into her own bed. She lay there for a long time, thinking and planning. . . . . .

That autumn was relatively unimportant. Already the domestic crisis following the start of the war had passed, and it began to be evident that Europe, in case of a long struggle, would have to look to America for supplies. In his offices Staunton Lewis sat over blueprints, planning plant expansion, watching the newspapers, even sending a man to London. The British were still pinning their faith to shrapnel. "Like spraying the Huns with a garden hose." The Germans were using high explosive shells. Sooner or later the Allies would need shells, and that meant more steel. On the strength of that he made his plans, even organized a new company and bought another plant. The war was going to last. Kitchener had said three years. If it lasted three years—

The Mayor was in an automobile accident that fall, and Chris set a broken leg. One day, while Chris was opening the cast, he looked up to find Barney's eyes on him. The nurse had gone for something and they were alone for the moment.

"Seen Beverly lately, doc?"

"No."

"Doesn't look very happy to me. Ames isn't any good. Never was."

"She wanted him."

"I'm not so damned sure she did. Did I ever tell you I warned her off you? Told her all you fellows were handholders."

Chris grinned as he bent over the cast.

"And do you think that now?"

"Ouch! Good God, no."

He did not seem able to escape them, that family on the hill. Once that winter Chris found Jerry Ames in the downtown office. He was looking older, the premature age of a man who has lived hard. He and Chris had exchanged the ordinary amenities during Lewis's illness, and Chris had not disliked him. But he had never quite forgiven him for his failure to reply to the letter about Ursula's death, and now he was coolly civil.

"Come in," he said. "Not sick, are you?"

"I'm all right. If you've got a few minutes."

"I've got a quarter of an hour," said Chris, looking at his watch. "I've a consultation after that."

Jerry, seated in the inner room and lighting a cigarette, was slow in coming to the point.

"It's about Ursula," he said at last. "About your letter, as a matter of fact. I didn't know what to do about it. How could I answer it? Suppose you'd moved on and it came back?"

"That's all right," said Chris evenly. "There wasn't anything to be done for her anyhow, poor girl."

"A man gets into a mess like that, and he can't get out."

"It's a mess for the girl, too."

There was a silence. Each man measured the other.

"About the boy. He's all right?"

"He's all right, but no thanks to you, Ames. He's got a good home. The people have adopted him."

"It would play hell with Beverly if she ever knew, doctor. And her father too. He's not too scrupulous about anything else, but a thing like that—"

"I've kept it to myself for a year and more. It's safe, I imagine," said Chris drily. "If that's all, Ames—"

"That's all." He got up. "Do these people need money? I suppose that's up to me."

"They need nothing. It's not up to you. The boy has been legally adopted. He's no longer yours."

"Well, that's something," said Jerry, and brightened. "I'm not a complete and utter skunk, you know. I want him cared for. If anything happens to me—"

"He's cared for all right. What's going to happen to you?"

"Nothing," Jerry said bitterly. "I wish to God it would. A fellow can die here of dry rot. I wanted to go to Europe in some capacity or other; but I've got a wife, and the old man simply called me a meddling fool."

CHAPTER XXXI

CHRIS was increasingly busy that winter. Grant was not well. He was going about, but he was thin and irritable. The hospital, watching him with a hundred pairs of sharp eyes, saw that he was slipping. One day there was an accident in the operating room, and while no death resulted it shook him badly. He gave up his evening calls, handing them to Chris; but the long hours alone with Janet got on his nerves. He would go down into his handsome offices and sit there alone at the desk, reliving his work, going over old case records. Strange to think that of all those years of work only these records remained, that a whole life could have been spent to leave so little.

He would wait until Janet was asleep before he went upstairs, going slowly, holding to the rail, stopping now and then for breath. He saved his breath, drawing it in carefully, letting it out slowly. Air was precious. He never seemed to get enough air.

"Worn out," he thought. "Worn out with the job. Too much work and not enough sleep for years on end. I'll catch up on sleep and then I'll be all right." But he knew better.

Chris knew it too. He did his night work for him, even some of his operations. Then one evening he got a frantic call from Janet Grant. Grant had collapsed on the stairs and was unconscious. When Chris got there he was dead. They had carried him up and laid him in his handsome bed, and he was still there, his face quiet, his long surgeon's hands lying idle on the silk spread. "We can't be gods. We're only men." Chris could hear him, saying that.

Grant's death still further disrupted the hospital, already suffering from the loss of some of the younger men. They would come in grinning to Burnett and say they were going over to get into the Big Push. Then in a day or two they would be gone, to England or to France, driving ambulances, joining sanitary corps, hunting trouble, still grinning, still happy-go-lucky and reckless.

"There's a *strafe* on for tonight."

"Let 'em *strafe*. What the hell do we care?"

Or:

"Salute, you ass. Salute. It's the general!"

"The general? Let's get a look at the son-of-a-gun. So that's a general!"

But sometimes it was different.

"Handle him carefully, fellows. He's pretty bad."

"All right, old man. We've got you."

The war was still raw and new. French soldiers sleeping in little churches, their heads on their round bread loaves as pillows; a truck behind the lines experimenting with wireless from the planes overhead; small towns with communication wires spread over their ruins; dead horses by the roads and peasants cutting them up for food; observation balloons with only a bar for the observer to sit on and a hand winch to pull them down; and enemy airplanes with black crosses flying low over massed troops at intersections, and little or nothing to drive them off.

Still new, this world war, with soldiers in Paris busses, inside, on the top, clinging to the steps, going gaily to the front. And with poison gas now, and against it only a piece of gauze and four tapes.

"Wet it! Wet it, man, and tie it over your face."

"I can't breathe. For God's sake get me out of this."

Still raw and new, the war. Not enough hospitals, almost no nurses and doctors. Englishwomen who had lived luxurious lives crossed the Channel, worked their way forward, and would find themselves at night in some railway station with wounded covering the floor, men who had not had their clothing off for weeks, men wailing, crying for water, dying. No dressings, even no lights. No morphia, no food, often no surgeon. They tore off their petticoats for bandages, found water and candles, tried to change old dressings, going out to be violently sick after the process. Sisters in heavy black habits moved about school houses, barns, even churches. Operations were often done without anesthetic, or not done at all. The wounded were carried back, put on trains and dumped hither and yon, and the advanced dressing posts changed from day to day.

"You'll have to get out of this, doctor."

"I can't leave these men, and I can't move them. I'll stay."

Moving the wounded to the cellar, if there was one, operating by candlelight, a candle set in the neck of a bottle; and shells falling, plaster falling. The candles burning out. "Light a match, somebody." And then perhaps a dead hit and silence. Not all soldiers; men, women and children injured as they fled before the oncoming hordes, caught between the two fires and running this way and that way like rabbits, like blind things.

War.

It was still a war on paper to America, a matter of maps and maybe pins to mark this line and that. One night at the medical society someone read a paper on the possible effects of the war on surgery, but it was purely academic. No one knew. Chris watched it with detached interest. Increasingly his work was his life. On the golf course, driving balls with surgical accuracy and co-ordination, he was only ostensibly playing. What he was doing was keeping in condition. He would come in with the other men, bathe and rub down his big body, aware that his hand was steadier for the exercise. He was drinking very little.

"Got a case to see," he would say. "Can't take a whisky breath with me."

His reputation was growing, not spectacularly but steadily. There were still days when the downtown office was empty and he began to worry about its cost. But there were others when he was busy. One day Barrett appeared there, to talk of a gall-bladder case and an operation. After a few minutes it was evident that he was a fee-splitter, and Chris refused to take the case.

"Better send in your bill for your own work, Barrett," he said, "and let me send in mine."

"Very noble, aren't you? Especially since you get the big end of the stick."

He did not get the case, and Barrett never sent him another.

At home Katie, having joined the Red Cross, was busy learning to knit because it was the thing to do, and because the most important women in the city were already doing it.

One day she met Beverly at a meeting, and Beverly, rather sorry for her among that group, immediately asked her to dinner.

"Very informally," she said. "Just you and your husband, and ourselves. If the doctor's busy tell him not to dress."

Katie went home walking on air, planning what to wear and telling Chris that with suppressed excitement. Chris however was tired. He received the news indifferently.

"I don't dine out, and you know it, Katie."

"If you don't do it I'll never forgive you."

"I'll try, but if anything comes up you'll have to go alone."

He was not comfortable about it, however. He did not want to go back into that house as a guest, taking a wife with him. It held too many memories. But Katie spent a happy week buying a new dress and on the morning of the day being manicured and marcelled. At noon Chris, still holding to his general work, was called on an obstetric case and she burst into tears.

"It's always like that," she wailed. "It doesn't matter to you what my life is. You could send Ted Lawrence, couldn't you? Why don't you?"

He was sorry for her, but he shook his head.

"I've brought their other babies," he said. "I can't let them down now. They're counting on me."

She stood by in the back office while he packed his obstetric bag, a disappointed and unhappy figure, her wave held tight to her head with a net. Beside his bulk she looked small and rather helpless, and Chris was moved to compassion. He stopped his work to put an arm around her.

"I'll probably get back in time. If I don't you can go and I'll come when I can."

"I won't move a step without you, Chris. Do you think it's easy for me to go there anyhow?"

"I don't see why not, my dear."

"Don't you? Well, I do."

He felt uncomfortable as he went out. After all she was trying to please him. She was running his house, watching his messages. And what did he give her? Odds and ends of time, while the best of him went to his work. True, there was a part of a man's life no woman ever reached, but—

He got to the house and climbed the stairs. The other children had been sent away, and the husband met him in the upper hall, a thin ineffectual man with faded blue eyes.

"She's frightened, doctor. I've never known her to be like this. She's been uneasy right along."

"She'll be all right, Henry. She's never had any trouble before."

"I tell her that. But she says she's had a premonition. Well, we're in your hands—and God's."

The baby arrived before seven that evening. It had been a long hard labor but normal enough. Nevertheless Chris was not entirely easy. The mother looked exhausted, and he spoke to the nurse.

"There's no history of hemorrhage, but I'd have some ice ready."

He ordered some ergot and then went down and called Katie, to find her in a state of nervous frenzy.

"I'll have to stay a while, Katie."

"Is the baby here?"

"Yes, but—"

"You come right home and get dressed or I'll never forgive you, Chris."

"Can't you go without me? They'll understand."

She was crying. Her voice was barely audible.

"I won't go alone. I've told you that."

She hung up the receiver and Chris was swearing as he climbed the stairs again. Somewhere the baby was crying, and Henry was sitting beside the bed, holding his wife's hand.

"It's all over, Mary, and it's a boy. A fine boy."

She seemed all right, but Chris still had a sense of apprehension. He stayed until a quarter to eight and then he left the house. Henry followed him down to the door.

"She looks queer, doctor."

"I'll be back in an hour or two. I'll be at the Staunton Lewises' if you need me."

He was miserably uncomfortable as he left. Henry's eyes followed him in mute anxiety, and at the corner he had a strong impulse to turn back. Then the thought of Katie, planning and waiting, sent him on again.

At the house he dressed hurriedly and in silence, with Katie restless in the lower hall, and they were only twenty minutes late. Katie, however, was profuse in her apologies.

"This thing of being married to a doctor!" she said. "No hours, no fun, no anything. I just got him here, and that's all."

She was very much at her ease, even when Staunton offered an arm to take her out to dinner. The excitement had brought color to her face and she looked pretty in her new gown and knew it. But to Chris, following heavily with Beverly and Jerry, she was not there. None of them was there, even Beverly. His mind, vaguely disturbed, was back in the upper room of a small house.

It was Katie's evening. Smiling and gay she dominated the table, but Staunton watched her from under his shaggy eyebrows, appraising her and saying little, as usual. What got into men to marry girls like that, he thought. Frivolous and silly girls, no help to them, just somebody to sleep in the same room, the same bed. Young Arden deserved something better. He knew his job. It was a pity after all that he and Beverly—

He smiled drily to himself over his wine glass. So he was worth a thousand dollars, according to this young whippersnapper! Well, he'd paid him ten. He was worth that to himself.

Katie was unaware of his silence, there in that big room with its high ceiling, its men serving, its glittering glass and shining silver. Some day she and Chris would have a place like it. She lost no detail of the service, or of Beverly's quiet dress and her pearls. "She's lovely," she thought, with a quick pang of jealousy. "She's not happy, but she's lovely."

She flirted a little with Jerry, sitting beside her and grinning cheerfully.

"And what do *you* do, while your husband's away all the time?"

"Me? I sit at home and wait for him to come back!"

"I don't believe it."

"No? What else is there to do?"

"Lots of things."

"Tell me about them."

All very harmless. Her dress a bit elaborate but her manners good and her smile engaging. Beverly let her glance flick over her and then across the table to Chris, silent and abstracted. What was their life, those two? Why had he married her? What could they have in common? She glanced at Jerry, gay and debonair. He was unfaithful to her; she knew that. But Chris was not like Jerry. He would be faithful to this girl across the table. He might not love her, but he would not let her down.

"Chris!" she thought. "Oh Chris, how could you?" She felt a little sick and dizzy for a moment.

It was toward the end of the meal that Chris was called to the telephone, to hear Henry's voice, almost a whisper.

"She's gone, doctor."

"Who's gone?"

"Mother. She's—*dead,* doctor."

He did not go back to the dining room at all. Before daybreak Katie roused to see him coming into their room and raised her head from the pillow.

"Well!" she said. "The idea of you running off and leaving me like that. I was never so ashamed in my life."

He stood over her bed, staring down at her with his face set and his eyes burning. As with Dick when Lily died he could have killed her, strangled her with his hands; taken that young throat of hers and torn the breath out of it. But he only made a sort of desperate gesture and turned away.

"Sorry," he said. "I killed a woman tonight."

She sat straight up in her bed.

"*Killed* a woman!"

"That's what I said," he told her, and went out.

When Olga went downstairs that morning she found him asleep in his office, with his head on his desk. She went away, shaking her head. That woman upstairs, lying in her bed until all hours while her man worked—

Later on she roused him with a cup of coffee, and he went upstairs and changed his clothes. He was different after that; some of his confidence had gone. He could hardly face Henry, red-eyed and shaken.

"I don't blame you, doctor. But mother set such a store by you."

"Don't, for God's sake, Henry!"

Luckily he was busy. The war boom began that year. Men and women, new to machines, were drawn into the mills, into factories, into plants of every sort by the high wages; and because they were new to machines, the machines took their toll of them. Plenty of money now also, more and more automobiles in use, more accidents on the streets and in the mills. The hospital was crowded. It was an epidemic again, but an epidemic of prosperity and its concurrent results.

"Ring for an ambulance, somebody."

"Here's a police wagon. Stand back. Stand back there."

All of the staff were overworked. The evening poker games in the interns' room were almost abandoned. Miss Nettie looked over the growing requisitions and sighed. The nurses were dropping on their feet. And Chris was only in his house for office hours, and then out again. Then one day Katie came home from a Red Cross meeting to find Dick standing in her living room, his hands in his pockets and his grin cynical as he surveyed her.

"Well, here's the jailbird."

"You needn't shout it. The servants—"

"The servants! High and mighty these days, aren't you?"

He looked well, however. He was bigger, broader in the shoulders. He was even tanned, having joined the sunburn squad at the prison before he was released. But his clothes were ill-fitting; and Katie surveyed him with distaste.

"You're not going to camp here on me, Dick," she said firmly.

"That's a welcome for you. Who said I was going to camp on you?" He looked around him. "Done pretty well by yourself, haven't you?" He lighted a cigarette and smiled. "I'd hardly know the old dump. God, when I think of mother's kitchen—"

"Don't you mention mother!"

"All right. Don't get excited."

"And I won't have you dragging me down. I've worked hard to get where I am, and I won't have it."

She had reverted to the old Katie then, fierce and defensive. She knew it herself, hearing her own voice, and wearily she took off her hat and ran her hand over her hair. "I won't let you do it, Dick," she said more quietly. "I won't go back to where I was."

He had no plans apparently. He borrowed some money from her, and when the doorbell rang and she heard Bob Barrett's voice in the front hall she smuggled him down the back stairs. But she was in a bad humor when Barrett came in, and later on when he attempted to kiss her she pushed him away pettishly.

"Oh, let me alone, can't you?" she said. "What do you think I am?"

When she had got rid of him she went downstairs, but there was no sign of Dick. The center drawer of Chris's desk was open, however, and she went over and surveyed it.

"Well anyhow," she thought, "he'd get nothing there."

She was mistaken, however, Dick had found something there. . . . . .

Two days later Jerry Ames was staring at him across his desk. Dick bore a faint resemblance to someone he had known. but he could not place him.

"I understand you have something to sell."

"So I have," said Dick with his impudent smile, and laid a photograph on the desk so that Jerry could see it. "That's for sale, Mr. Ames; and all that goes with it."

Jerry looked at it. No question now of what was happening to him. This fellow had known Ursula and knew her story and his connection with it. He merely opened the desk and got out his checkbook.

"I'll give you five hundred dollars."

"Better add another cipher to it, Ames."

"You'll take that and be damned to you."

He knew it was only the beginning of a long road, but he needed time to think, and when Dick came back ten days later he had done, for him, some pretty desperate thinking.

"Nothing doing," he said. "You'd better get out of here before I throw you out."

"It's like that, is it?"

"It's exactly like that."

"Well, it's your trouble, not mine."

"I'll take care of that. And get out before I kick you out."

He told Beverly that night, knowing that it was the end of their life together, but knowing too that she would keep his secret. After all it would be no blow to her. He had never won her, and she probably knew that he was not faithful. But he was badly frightened when the time came. He waited until she was alone in her room, and going in he found her at the window, looking down over the city and its lights. She turned, faintly surprised, when he came in. It was rare for him now to spend an evening in the house.

"Anything wrong, Jerry?"

"I'd like to talk to you. I'm—well, I'm in a bit of a jam, Beverly. Do you mind if I ring for a highball?"

"No. What sort of a jam?"

He waited however until the tray had come. His hands were twitching as he fixed the drink, but she saw that he was entirely sober. Then, after a sip or two, he sat forward and told her.

"I'm being blackmailed, Bev. Not much yet, but those things grow. There's only one thing to do, and that's to come clean and stop it. I'm no angel, but at least I'm a man."

She had been standing. Now she sat down, as though her knees would not hold her.

"It's a woman, of course."

"It was a woman, a girl. She's dead now."

"Then why—?"

"There was a child. That's why."

She sat very still after that. His voice went on steadily enough after the start, but she heard only a part of the story and none of his extenuations. She sat there, her hands folded in her lap, and saw Chris offering her up to some idol or other of professional ethics, and she was filled with cold anger.

When Jerry was through he sat back and eyed her. He felt distinctly better, almost cheerful.

"I'm not proud of it, but there it is," he said, and finished his highball.

"Yes, there it is," she said quietly. "And so you knew, and Chris Arden knew, that while you were marrying me this girl was having your child?"

"I've told you. She wanted the baby. God knows why."

"And now she's dead. Where is the child, Jerry?"

"Arden found a home for it. The people have adopted it."

She got up then.

"He took a great deal of trouble, didn't he, so that I could marry you!"

"Arden? He did the best he could. Give him credit for that."

It was the next afternoon that Chris found her alone in the downtown office, and realized that this was a new Beverly, one he had never seen before, icy, quiet and unsmiling. He knew what had happened before she spoke.

"I came," she said, "to try to discover why you have played God with me and wrecked my life."

"I never tried to play God with you, Beverly. If what I did was wrong—"

"And that last night when I called you up and told you I was frightened, you let me go, knowing what you did?"

"I thought you wanted to go, my dear."

When at last she had closed the door behind her and gone, he knew that she carried away with her a resentment which separated them even more completely than her marriage, or his.

He did not even see her again until America had entered the war.

Part V

CAPTAIN ARDEN

CHAPTER XXXII

CAPTAIN ARDEN of the Medical Corps was once again reorienting himself after a night's sleep. He opened his eyes, gazed for a second or two at his strange surroundings and then closed them again. The bare room bore no resemblance to reality as he had known it, and as he drowsed it disappeared from his consciousness. That comfortable state however did not last. There impinged on his latent senses the sharp odor of burning coffee, and finally a weight on his chest, certainly not there when he went to sleep, roused him sufficiently to open an eye and stare at it.

It was a pillow, and he reached out a long arm and carefully shied it over the partition into the cubicle next door. There was a yell, followed by a crash of tin cups, and Ted Lawrence's voice, raised to heaven.

"For God's sake! You just missed the coffee pot."

"I'll teach you to rouse your superior officer when he needs his sleep."

"Who says superior? And you'd sleep all day if I let you alone. Hurry up and bring in the canned milk."

Chris sat up in his army cot, and still yawning thrust out his legs in their pajamas. The bare floor was cold under his feet, and he drew them back again under the blankets. Sitting thus he looked more boyish than he had looked for the past few years. He looked rested, and the lines of his face had relaxed. Outside the cantonment was rousing, and in the next cubicle Ted had raised his voice in song to a Gilbert and Sullivan air:

"Oh, I'm the very model of a modern obste-tri-ci-an
So to this he-man's army I am sent as a phy-si-ci-an."

There was more to it, mostly unprintable, and Chris grinned. Then, sitting cross-legged on his cot, or as near cross-legged as his length of limb permitted, he surveyed his surroundings; the cot with its brown blankets, the bare uncarpeted room with its one window, its one table, its one chair. Under the table lay his bed roll, never yet unstrapped but containing his bed, his mess kit and all the requisites for active service. There was a radiator beneath the window, but the cantonment heating plant was still unfinished, and a small electric stove made a brave attempt to take the chill off the room. Chris had learned to point it under his cot at night, and its one red eye gleamed in the dark like a companionable thing, gazing at him in friendly fashion.

So this, as Ted said, was home, sweet, swee-et home.

Men were moving around him now in the jerry-built structure and he got up, drew on his heavy underwear and stopped to look out the window. It was raining again, the incessant cold winter rain which turned the new roads into rivers of mud so that they absorbed the cinders dropped on them like quicksand and bogged down the trucks heavy with lumber and other construction material. He reached out the door for his boots, neatly shined over night by his orderly, put them on absent-mindedly, and then remembered that his breeches had to go on first, and swearing loudly took them off again.

"Hell of a soldier I make," he muttered.

"What's that?" Ted inquired.

"None of your business. It's raining again."

"You're telling me! I had to sleep under a tarp last night. If those fellows don't fix this roof—"

"Well, keep it out of the coffee."

He had no time to bathe, but carrying his razor and towel he went to the bathroom at the end of the hall and shaved, taking his turn at one of the mirrors. The room was filled with men more or less unclothed, with the steam of running hot water in the cold air, the babble of talk. They were of all ages, all shapes, all types; the medical officers of the cantonment hospital, now hurrying to go on duty, to get to their wards and their work, and eventually some day to France.

Finished, Chris went back to Ted Lawrence and the coffee. The coffee in the mess across the road was weak and thin in spite of all protests. He carried in the can of milk and grinning cheerfully put it on the table.

"Feeling like a million dollars this morning," he said.

"Nice day, too," said Ted. "Everything's grand in this he-man's world. Look at the puddle I slept in."

"You're too fastidious. Lot of frogs would *like* that puddle."

They drank their strong hot coffee, standing at the table. It was a bit of luck, their being billeted together. There was between them the sturdy inarticulate friendship of two men, each of whom under stress might have died for the other, but would certainly have died rather than confess it.

"Time's up," said Ted. "Now to swim the Jordan."

Clad in army slickers, their caps likewise protected, they stepped outside into the rain and mud. All around them was the sound of hammering. A truck had bogged down and made a detour necessary, and a line of conscripts dejected and laden with their personal belongings slogged along under the drizzle, making for a roof, any roof. The two medical officers stopped to let them go by, and one face was vaguely familiar to Chris. He stared after the man, but he had not seen Dick for years and he was not certain. The line moved on, passing the truck in the mud, and the workmen on it began to jeer at them.

Suddenly Chris was angry, furiously and savagely angry. He stepped from behind the truck and confronted them.

"You sons of —," he shouted. "You're getting paid, aren't you? You're not fighting. You're not even getting ready to fight. If I hear another word I'll lay out the lot of you, and I hope to God I kill you!"

He looked enormous in his slicker. The jeers stopped, the men went sheepishly back to work. Chris, glancing along the line of conscripts, saw the one he had faintly recognized turn and put his thumb to his nose at the laborers. He was still shaken with fury as he went on. Queer things this war did to a man. It turned him primitive and even savage.

Ted Lawrence was grinning.

"Feel better now?" he inquired. "You're right, of course; but every man to his job."

"Then let them do their job," said Chris, still truculent.

They went on into the mess. Long bare wooden tables and benches, mess orderlies in soiled white coats hurrying about, the smell of bacon and of wet boots, the noise of dishes being thumped down, the babble of talk, the slamming of doors as men came in or went out, and the scuffling of boots on the bare floor, that was the mess hall. Around it lay the hospital, long wards scattered hither and yon, with connecting covered passageways. Some of the wards still were not ready, and there was a story that the Old Man, having looked things over, had banged into his headquarters and called Washington on the telephone.

"I've got a division here," he said, "and a hospital with nothing in it. I've tried every way I know to get the stuff. Now I'm ordering it myself."

"You can't do that, General. Sorry, but you know that."

"Can't hell! I'm ordering it, and you can deduct it from my pay!"

Whereupon he had hung up chuckling, and after that things began to come in.

Chris was busy, as were all the rest. He ate his breakfast, got up, reported and made his rounds. Now that he was at work his irritation had gone. He was contented with the contentment of a man who had left behind him for an indefinite time all the burdens and the small annoyances of a personal life. Here he had ceased to be a person. He was a small cog in a mighty machine, functioning efficiently but impersonally. And he felt younger. At night there were rags in the shedlike officers' barracks; pillow fights, the slamming about of wet sponges; or there would be poker for small stakes, with whisky bought from the kitty and sandwiches made by the orderlies.

"How many, Major?"

"I've got money in that pot. I'll take five."

"Back where I come from they kill men for less."

Somewhere overseas there was a war, and sometime they would be there. Incredible, of course. Whispers going about:

"Old Man's getting ready. Any day now."

"Well, if he's ready nothing else is."

No hint of long delays ahead. The camp seething with activity. Straw-stuffed dummies for bayonet drill hanging swaying in the wind. Young lieutenants, hardly more than boys, confronting men twice their age: "Come on, Bill. Give up those dice!" Night rides of the cavalry, guns on timbers rumbling along quiet country lanes, the thud of horses' hoofs, the good creak of saddle leather and the rattling of metal bit-chains. Here and there a practice trench. "Up and at 'em, boys. Let's go." A trial barrage, with officers on the hillside and a field telephone: "On the way, sir." Then the whistling of a shell and somewhere in some peaceful field a burst of smoke and dirt.

There were lectures at night, and twice a week a medical officer gave them lessons in conversational French. They sat on their hard chairs like school boys, grinning at him with his blackboard, and chanting in unison: *Vwa-see ler par-sa-von* or *Kel vil ess-ce?* There was one which never failed to get a laugh and a cheer: "Please give me your name and address," and translated on the blackboard into *Don-nay mwa votr nom ay a-dress, sil voo play.*

It seemed a long time to Chris since those days in Vienna and the German lessons. He had not wanted to be sitting here, a surgeon in a man's war, but he had tried to get into the line and failed.

"We need men like you, doctor, on the medical side. We've got enough cannon fodder"—that was the phrase then—"but we'll need surgeons. Not so dramatic, perhaps, but—"

"No intention of being dramatic, sir," Chris had said stiffly.

"That's the spirit, doctor." . . . . . .

He had not told Katie until after it was done. Then he had gone back to her and she had been sullen and suspicious.

"I suppose you never thought of me," she said. "What am I to do while you're gone, maybe for years?"

"I'm providing for you, Katie. That's the best I can do."

She was not reconciled. During the days before his commission she argued constantly.

"You've built up a big practice, and now you're leaving it for somebody to pick up. Why? Don't tell me you are going to save the country! There are plenty to do that. You're not even going to fight."

"I tried to get into the ranks. They don't want me."

"Sure you tried," she said hysterically. "You'd be willing to die to get away. For that's it, isn't it? You want to get away from me!"

She was frightened as well as angry, however. Whatever she felt for him, and Chris was no longer certain, he still represented security to her and even position. He would waken at night to find her crying in the next bed, and to try to soothe her as best he could.

"Katie dear, what is it? If it's about my going, I'll be safe enough. Too damned safe."

"You never think of anybody but yourself. Yourself and your work. That's all."

"It may last only a few months."

She was quiet enough when he left, however. After all, going to camp was not going to France; and he had left her the Lewis money, ten thousand dollars, in her name at the bank and taught her how to draw a check. It was a reckless thing to do, Katie being Katie, but he knew in his soul that she had been partially right, and that the money was the price he was paying for escape.

He made his calls on that last day with mixed emotions.

He went first to the Lee house, where the old colonel was gone and Harriet and Nancy were living alone. When America entered the war the colonel had stopped his drinking and made a plan of his own. He came to see Chris about it.

"I've been a National Guardsman all my life, doctor, and I was in the Spanish-American War. Now we're going to need men, and I intend to recruit a regiment of my own. I'd like to feel that I can count on you."

He had almost done it. He got together a skeleton personnel, held meetings, was sober and erect again. He looked ten years younger. Then one day he went to Washington. He stopped at the Shoreham, and he spent day after day waiting in the anteroom of the Secretary of War. It was a handsome room, high-ceiled and with chairs and a leather davenport or two against the wall. Always it was full of men coming and going. A secretary would come in, urbane and smiling: "He'll see you now, Mr. Haynes." Or some officer in uniform would rise with a clatter of spurs and stalk to the opened door. Then the day would end, the Secretary would go out through another door, and Colonel Lee would go back to the Shoreham to sit over his skeleton organization, which he locked up at night in his big bag against German spies.

When his turn finally came he was too tired to remember his prepared speech, and the Secretary, looking up, saw only an elderly man with pouches under his eyes and a sheaf of papers in his shaking hands. He listened, however; he had ten minutes. Then he shook his head.

"This isn't the Civil War, Colonel. We shall have to expand under the present structure, not depend on voluntary units."

"I've been a soldier all my life, sir, and I know the men I can get. Not country boys, to catch every disease going, but mill workers, men who have established immunities."

"Then keep them in their mills, Colonel. That's where we need them."

He walked back in the sun to the hotel and went into the

bar. When by some miracle he reached home the next day he had to be carried off the train, reeking of whisky; and the next night Harriet heard a shot and found him dead in his bed, his old-fashioned Smith and Wesson revolver in his hand.

They were alone now, Harriet and Nancy, looking lost in their black clothes, but they had seen Chris off with a smile.

"Good-by, doctor; and good luck."

It seemed strange that he should be going to the war, and the colonel dead. Like those old days in the hospital when some soul had passed and he had gone back to his bed and in the morning had almost forgotten it.

The war had changed everything, he thought, as he made his rounds that day. Here was Mrs. Betts, turning an exalted face toward him.

"I'm giving my son, doctor. His country needs him."

She had been unwilling to let him live, he thought, but now she was ready to see him die.

They were proud of him, those families of his, as he made his last rounds that day. He was deserting them, but they accepted desertion. "Good-by, doctor. We'll pray for you." Or: "Good-by, doctor. Bring us a German helmet!" It was the same thing. It meant the same thing.

He had of course had indefinite leave of absence from the hospital, but he found the farewells there particularly difficult. It amazed him, after the silent conflict between them of five or six years, to find Miss Clarke crying alone in the operating room.

"You'll have some peace now," he told her. "No more shouting and throwing things! And of course I'll come back. Don't you worry."

She kept on crying, however, and so he put an arm around her and held her until she was quiet. Amazing after all that time to find his arm around her and to see her weeping on his shoulder.

"I've admired you so, doctor."

"I've admired you too. Grand girl you are, my dear."

He had stood holding her and surveying the room. Here he had worked and learned and sweated. Here he had come nauseated and scared like a kid to do his first operation. And here, God willing, he would come back to work and learn and sweat again. Under his hand he could feel Miss Clarke's thin body, no longer young, and the stiff stays which supported it. They had been both friends and enemies for a long time, and yet they hardly knew each other. Outside of her operating room what was she, except a picture without a frame? And what was he to her? She knew him well and again she did not know him at all. He was to her a man in a white coat, masked and gloved, to be conciliated or contended with as the case might be. Yet now she was wiping her eyes with a piece of sterile gauze, and suddenly he knew that he would miss her, as he would miss all familiar things.

It was with Miss Nettie, however, that he had had the most difficult parting. She was really old now, a sort of superintendent emeritus. She had offered to retire, but the Board had kept her on. She was a part of the hospital's history and of its dignity. Her long sweeping skirts and her white pompadour were as much the hospital as its very walls and wards. They could find plenty of younger women, brisk and efficient, to do her work; but she was like a faded photograph, at which they might smile but which continued to embody their memories and even their youth.

Chris found her waiting for him on that last day of his, stiff and straight in her chair.

"Well, Chris, so you are leaving us!"

"Only for a time. They can't fight the entire world for long."

"Even a short time—" she began, and stopped. "Sit down, Chris, unless you are busy. I have nothing to do. I seldom do nowadays." She smiled faintly. "That is the tragedy of growing old, Chris. You don't leave the world. It leaves you. Never mind that," as he started to speak, "I want to talk to you. I suppose I want reassurance, and let's be honest for once. I may not see you again, and I have this thing on my soul."

"Of course you'll see me again."

She ignored that. "It's a delicate matter," she went on. "But if I forced your hand the night you left for Europe, Chris, I want you to know that I never dreamt of such a thing." He started to interrupt her, but she raised a thin hand. "Happy or not, I have carried that fear in my soul ever since."

"Then get it off your soul. Perhaps," he said carefully, "it might not have happened as it did, otherwise. But it would probably have happened in the end. Those things are written somewhere. In the stars, maybe."

"Then it is all right?"

"It is all right," he told her.

Long after that painful parting she sat again in her room; sat until twilight fell and the outlines of her familiar belongings grew blurred and dim. She had loved him like a son, although she had no right to wear a star, and she knew she would not see him again. She had only a few months to live, but she had not told him. Now he had gone, and whether he came back or not, she would not be there, in that room, waiting for him. It was the bitterest hour of her life when he stooped over her.

"Good-by, Chris, and God keep you safe."

She had stared at the door for a long time after he closed it.

Patients, the hospital, Katie. And then that last night, with everything done, his duffle piled in the front hall downstairs, his orders in the pocket of his uniform, Katie gone upstairs to sulk in bed, and Chris alone with his pipe in the back office, only his desk lamp lighted and his ghosts beginning to crowd around him. Mistakes in judgment, errors in this and that. Going to Grant, and Grant saying: "We can't be gods. We are only men." And then back inevitably to that last bitter talk with Beverly. The talk going on and on, and getting nowhere.

"Men aren't angels, Beverly. You knew him. You weren't marrying a boy. What was there to do?"

"Make him marry her. Why in the name of humanity let me do it?"

"It was her secret, not mine, my dear."

"What did that matter? I don't understand, Chris. I can live all the days of my life and never understand."

"If you cared enough to marry him, Beverly—"

"I didn't. I knew all along that I didn't."

"But you went ahead with it."

"Yes," she said drearily. "I went ahead with it."

He had never seen her since. She was twenty-seven now, at the height of her beauty, popular, an accomplished hostess. She and Jerry were a handsome pair. Once he saw a picture of them taken together at Palm Beach, and both were smiling into the camera. If it was acting it was good acting. And soon after war was declared he saw that Jerry had gone into aviation. It was like him to choose aviation.

Now in an hour or so he himself was going to the war. He did not care greatly whether he returned or not. He went up and kissed Katie good-by, sitting on the bed in her cluttered room and smiling at her.

"Be a good girl," he said, "and don't worry about me. I'll be all right."

He had a new distinction in his uniform, and suddenly Katie burst into tears and held out her arms.

"You're mine, Chris," she said. "Mine! Never forget that."

"I never have," he told her gravely.

Before he left he made his usual rounds of the house, and at the kitchen door he stopped and looked out into the yard. The ailanthus tree was gone now, and Katie had planted grass and shrubbery. But Henry's old shed still stood there, a mute memorial to the futility of human hopes.

CHAPTER XXXIII

AFTER the first break Katie was happy enough. She bought a small pin with a star on it, and put a card with a similar star in the window of the front office. She found that Chris's enlistment gave her a certain prestige, too; that and the Red Cross. She was meeting women she had never hoped to know, and going to houses she had never expected to see. The war had leveled all classes.

Dick had been a problem, at first. He found her bank book one day with that deposit of Chris's in it, and after that he was continually borrowing money from her. Then one day the draft caught him, and she breathed easier than for months.

Barrett was in and out of the house. She had a curious fascination for him. Again and again he swore to let her alone, only to come back, to sit in that upstairs living room, drink cocktails or highballs, and to make overtures to her which she resented and then to laugh at her.

"The eternal virgin!" he would say. "You don't look it, but that's what you are."

There were times when she almost yielded however, and it was this which brought him back. But she had too much at stake to risk what she had so hardly achieved.

"And what do you suppose Chris is doing all this time?" Barrett would say.

"Behaving himself. You might try it yourself."

"I don't believe it."

"Well, I do."

Luckily perhaps for her Barrett was busy. So many doctors had gone into the service that those who remained had all that they could do.

"Some of us have to stay," he told Katie. "You can't leave a city like this without medical assistance."

"You're making a lot of money out of it."

"Sure I'm making money. I'm working like a dog, too."

He gave up his city position about that time, and Jenkins drew a long breath of relief. He and the Mayor were old friends, and Jenkins on hearing the news put on his hat and went over to the Municipal Building.

"I'm not crying any, Chief," he said. "Nor anybody else, as I get it. Maybe I'm thick-skinned, but he's got the hide of a rhinoceros. He drew his pay and his breath, and that's about all."

Nevertheless that cool statement of Barrett's about Chris had roused Katie, and just before Christmas she turned up in the town near the camp. The first warning he had was when she called him from the local hotel, and at first he did not understand.

"But where are you?"

"I'm here, in town. I've got a room, but the place is jammed. Can't I come out to camp?"

"You couldn't stay here. There is a hostess house, but it's overflowing. Christmas, you know."

He had worked hard that day, but he drove into the town that night, to find her almost in tears in the small hotel bedroom.

"You go down and talk to that man at the desk, Chris," she said when she saw him. "They've got better rooms than this, and I know it."

He looked at her. She seemed strange to him, like someone from another life, and she was wearing an enormous corsage of violets tied with silver ribbon. She protected it with her hand when he kissed her, and he held her off and inspected her with a smile, although his lips felt stiff as he did so.

"Looking pretty fine, aren't you?"

"These?" She touched the flowers. "Bob Barrett gave them to me. He saw me off."

"Still hanging around, is he?"

"If you're going to be jealous, Chris—"

"Good God, jealous of Barrett!" But he was instantly ashamed of that. He leaned down over her. "Well, Merry Christmas anyhow, my dear," he said, and kissed her again.

He went down to the hotel office, glad to escape for a minute or two, to draw his breath and reorient himself. But he could not change the small single room, nor did he stay there that night or any night. He went in during the day, usually late in the afternoon, but after the first twenty-four hours it was usually to find the room crowded and an overflow into the hall; and Katie serving sandwiches and cocktails to all comers, mostly junior officers.

"This is my bit to win the war!" she would say.

"Go to it, Mrs. Arden. Down with the Hun."

They would drink, to her, to the war, to killing the Kaiser and marching to Berlin; and Katie, young and excited, would send for more ice, more glasses. In that crowd of exultant and slightly tipsy youth Chris felt old and out of place. He would take a drink or two, smoke a cigarette, and finally pick up his cap and edge out.

"Got to work," he would say. "You fellows only work from sun to sun, but my job's never finished."

On Christmas Eve he took Katie to the cantonment, where Ted Lawrence had got ready a supper and cooled a bottle of champagne. Katie stood in the door of Chris's room and surveyed it.

"What a sickening place," she said. "And it's cold."

"I rather like it."

He showed her his extemporized arrangements, the shelf where stood the condensed milk, the sugar, a pile of tin plates and cups. He even showed her how he warmed his bed at night. But to Katie it was cheerless and faintly ridiculous. She demanded a mirror to powder her nose, and none being at hand he took one from the bathroom at the end of the long bare hall and brought it in, to the fury of the major who was shaving by it.

"Hey! Bring that back."

"A soldier ought to know how to shave by sense of touch, old man."

"Hell, I'm not a soldier!"

She cheered over Ted and his wine, however, and after the party as they drove back she put her head on Chris's shoulder and ran her arm through his.

"You will stay tonight, Chris, won't you? It's Christmas Eve."

"I can't, my dear. I may have to operate in an hour or two. Anyhow, where would you put me?"

Then, the champagne having its effect, she lost some of the veneer of the past few years and reverted to the Katie of the early days. He was still in love with Beverly Ames, deny it or not. He had no pride, still caring for a woman who had thrown him over, and who was married to somebody else anyhow. He never had cared for her, Katie; sometimes he hated her. She was no fool. She could see that. Through it all he drove steadily, remorseful that so much of what she said was true, and filled with a sort of indignant compassion.

"I've been absolutely faithful, my dear."

"Faithful to what? To me? That's a laugh."

They parted at the hotel, Katie getting out without a word and declining his outstretched hand. He stood on the pavement watching her until she was out of sight. She looked angry and defiant and very lonely, and he had an impulse to follow her. After all, it was his fault more than hers. Everything else aside, he *had* married her. Now he had deserted her, and she knew it. Would she like a divorce, he wondered? She could marry again in that case and live her life as it should be lived. But he knew that she would not divorce him. Whether she cared for him or not she liked being his wife. He still represented security to her, security and place.

He got into his car again and drove back. The camp, covering its miles of once fertile farm land and now streets of low wooden barracks and a parade ground, was quiet after the evening. Here and there was a sentry, gloomily waiting to be relieved. There was a light in the commanding general's house, and a loose horse somewhere was pounding along over the hard frozen ground. And in the center of an open space still blazed the gigantic camp Christmas tree. He stopped his car and sat looking at it. His memories ranged over many trees. Over a Christmas at old Dave Mortimer's, and old Dave himself cursing at the ladder as he placed an angel on the top and then saying a prayer as he lighted the candles. Over the tree in the hospital chapel, and Beverly beside him; and the tree in the pension at Vienna. And that small tree long ago in the Walters' dining room, and Jake dying in the back office.

"I did a good job on that suit, doc."

Curious, how one remembered Christmas. Perhaps because other days might appeal to the head, but this one appealed to the heart. He shook his head, which felt heavy after the champagne, and drove on. He put away his car, and finding the medical officers' quarters still dark and empty, went across to the hospital. The effect of the champagne was gone by that time, and at two o'clock that morning he operated.

"It's all right, son. Just breathe it in. It won't hurt you."

He had entirely forgotten Katie. . . . .

Katie gave a big party at the hotel on Christmas afternoon, and at Chris's suggestion most of the medical corps were asked. A few brought their wives but most of them came alone, serious men abruptly dislocated from important work back home and now facing the drudgery and risk of war with no thought or hope of glory. They were not soldiers. Even in their uniforms, with the caduceus on the collar, they were not soldiers. They still saluted awkwardly and were faintly self-conscious in their breeches and tunics and boots; but they were men dedicated to service, and this showed in their eyes, their strong quiet faces.

They watched Katie with interest, Katie in a red dress, flushed and excited.

"Curious. Hardly Arden's sort, you'd think."

"Don't ask me why any man marries any particular woman. There isn't any answer."

They liked her, however. She was gay and young. The dingy hotel parlor seemed the brighter for her. They were loyal to their middle-aged wives, either absent or standing about with them, but it was good to hear laughter again.

"I'm drinking to you, Major."

"And I drink to your bright eyes."

When the last one had gone Katie stepped out of her high-heeled shoes and drew a long breath.

"Heavens, what a stodgy lot," she said.

Chris looked at her.

"I'd hardly call them stodgy," he said. "Some of the most brilliant men in the profession—"

"Oh, the profession!" she said lightly. "I'm fed up with the profession."

She went back a week later, leaving Chris a heavy hotel bill to pay, and blowing a kiss to him and a group of youngsters from the car window as the train started. Once out of sight however she settled back moodily in her chair. She had lost Chris again. She had lost him once to Beverly Ames, and again to his work. Now she was losing him to a war.

She cried a little, wiping away the tears surreptitiously. Then she sat up and ringing for the porter sent a telegram to Bob Barrett; and she found him waiting at the station on her arrival.

"Well, how's everything?"

"I've had a glorious time, Bob. But I'm glad to be back."

"Fall for any of those wooden soldiers?"

"Not in your sense of the word."

In the taxicab he put his arms around her and kissed her. Then he brought a small parcel from his pocket and held it just beyond her reach.

"Christmas gift," he told her. "What do I get for it?"

"I'll kiss you, if I like it."

"Damned if I know why I bother about you at all," he

grumbled, but he gave it to her and she opened it excitedly. It was a small gold-mesh bag, and she was enchanted.

"All right," he said. "Where's the kiss?"

It was a game and a one-sided one at that, as he knew. But he was persistent and vain. In the days that followed she let him make overt love to her, soothing her conscience with Chris's recent abdication; but there were other times when she fought him like a wildcat.

"Let go of me. I hate the very sight of you."

"You're a sweet little liar."

It could not go on forever, and when finally she drifted into real intimacy she could not have told how it happened. She did not love him. There were times when she actively disliked him. But he gave some point to her pointless days, was someone for whom to dress, to look her best. She took small gifts from him but nothing else.

"I don't want a bracelet. Not from you."

"Why not? You're a queer little thing, aren't you?"

It never occurred to him that this was the self-protection she gave her dignity, such as it was; or that in taking him as a lover she was secretly rebuilding her pride. . . . .

"If Chris doesn't want me someone else does," she said to herself fiercely.

In the city the mills were busy. Frantically, big furnaces turned out their molten steel, to be run through rolls, to be cooled and pressed, to be lathed and polished, and in the end to become some part of the great machinery of a great war; making something, which in its turn would become nothing. Freight trains crowded the sidings, vast trucks tore up the roads on their way to the ports. They rumbled at night through the city, long trains of them, so that they shook the houses and roused honest noncombatants asleep in their beds.

Steel would win the war. The old steel masters were now the hope of the world. Prejudice was forgotten, past sins forgiven; only let the light flames break through the lakes of molten slag in the furnaces, only let the pure metal be collected like butter out of a churn. The din night and day was terrific. Doors opened and threw out beams of hot white light in which half-naked men moved with a sort of angry frenzy. Rolls thundered, great cranes slid along their tracks, locomotives pushed and pulled, whistles blew; yet this chaos and apparent disorder were orderly. The pigmy men of the mills and their machines were fighting their own war, against other men and other machines far away. "Hurry up." "Speed up production." "He's hurt. Get a stretcher."

For this war too took its toll.

The Lewis concerns were coining money. Staunton Lewis did not know how much he was worth, nor did he greatly care. It had always been the game with him, not only the victory. One day he took a million dollars in bonds to Washington for the purpose of a contract, and his secretary left the brief case in a taxicab. He paid little or no attention to it, and the bonds were found. The story got about, and lesser men made it into a tradition. He had guts, the old man. It did not matter now that his political machine was still letting contracts at exorbitant prices. Steel was king, and he was the master of steel.

It was telling on him. Beverly rarely saw him now, and when she did he was abstracted and weary. She thought he looked ill, but he resented any suggestion that he rest.

"I'm all right," he would say. "What on earth has happened to dinner? Holmes!"

There were meals now when they sat through the elaborate service in almost complete silence. Once or twice she tried reading him the occasional letters from Jerry, still training in England and exceedingly cheerful, but he barely troubled to listen. He had never really liked Jerry. Now she thought that Jerry might be killed, and it still would not matter to him.

"Why in the name of heaven did he have to choose the air?"

"He likes it, father. He seems very happy."

"Well, every fool to his taste."

She herself was anxious. It was as though Jerry, having

ceased to be her husband, had become her child; a wayward, erratic but light-hearted child. Whenever she saw a plane in the air she was conscious of a constriction of the heart, as though Jerry sat up there alone. And she was careful not to think of Chris, as though such a thought would bring Jerry crashing down, touched by the finger of a revengeful God.

She did not even know that Chris's division had moved until one day Miss Andrews came to call on her; a determined Miss Andrews, facing the great adventure of the streets to do it; stopping uncertainly before venturing into the maelstrom of the traffic, but jerking away from the policeman who took her arm to help her.

"I'll thank you to keep your hands off me, young man."

And the policeman grinning.

"All right, lady. No offense!"

Beverly found her in the long drawing room, standing at a window and looking out.

"Who's that man out there, Beverly?"

"One of the gardeners. How nice of you to come. I'll ring for tea."

"He stared at me when I came in the gate."

"He's all right, really. We have to watch the place rather carefully since father was shot."

It was some time however before Miss Andrews was serene again. Then she told her news, watching Beverly carefully the while. She was no fool for all her vagaries, and she knew well enough that early love story of Chris and the girl in front of her.

"I suppose you know they've moved on? Chris Arden and all of them? My Mary has a cousin with them, and—"

"I'm sorry. I forget whether it's lemon or cream?"

"It's cream and two lumps," said Miss Andrews. "They sail in a day or two, and that will be the end of the lot of them." And when Beverly, still steady of hand, gave her her cup: "I miss Chris Arden. He's the only man I ever knew I'd give two straws for."

Beverly, holding herself rigid, was amazed to see two tears rolling down the other woman's face.

"I wouldn't worry. They'll come back, or most of them will."

"Not the decent ones. I know what will come back."

She took her leave soon after, with the look of a woman about to dive into a maelstrom, and Beverly watched her down the driveway. Then she turned back into the house, pale and shaken. Chris was going to war, and she could not let him go with that bitterness as his last memory of her. The bond between them was too enduring for that. It had nothing to do with their marriages, nothing really to do with romantic love. It was a bond, and it was there. She could not let him go out into the dark, alone, without knowing that. If they could sit together across a table and talk, just talk, get back for an hour or two to honesty so that there would be no bitterness to remember, it was all that she would ask.

Less than a week later they were doing just that, in a small hotel in downtown New York; Chris in his uniform and she herself across from him, saying to herself that he was sailing that night, and that after all she had nothing to say to him. Nothing to say to this strange man who was so determinedly impersonal, and who was smiling at her cheerfully across the table.

"Well, this is splendid. Let's have a real dinner, Beverly. I've eaten mess food for months."

"Chris, are you really sailing tonight?"

"Hush, my child. The waiter is almost certainly a spy, and not more than a hundred thousand people know about it."

He was hungry! She watched him eat, marveling after the fashion of women at the ability of all males to eat on the edge of tragedy. He ate and talked, lightly but pleasantly, but he was carefully impersonal, as though he had stretched out his arm and held her off. Then, with the coffee, he lapsed into silence. At last he moved and looked at her.

"And that, my darling," he said gravely, "will be that. I'm

coming back, of course, but it may be a long time. It can hurt nobody now for us to be honest. That's why you came, isn't it?"

"That's why I came, Chris. I've grown up now. I know—"

"You know that I have always cared for you," he said. "I've forgotten you sometimes; we all do that, Beverly. It's our salvation. But I have always loved you. I suppose I always will."

She was very quiet, looking at him with her direct gaze.

"No," she said slowly. "It can hurt nobody now for me to know that, or for you to know what you do. Just to be sure that somebody cares, Chris, that makes things easier; and harder too in a way. It wasn't necessary, all this. We might have—" She drew a long breath. "Chris, why did you never answer that letter of mine?"

He was instantly still as though all motion had frozen in him, but he kept his face impassive. So there had been a letter, and Lily—or Katie— But Katie was his wife now, and his voice was steady when he spoke.

"We are not looking back tonight, darling," he told her. "That water is over the dam, and let's forget it. We have a bit of time together and that's all I ask. Let's not spoil it."

A bit of time it was, for not long after that he looked at his watch and pushed back his chair. Then he leaned forward again and put a hand over hers.

"We may never do this again, my girl; but this was our hour. I'll carry it with me the rest of my life."

That was actually their farewell, although she smiled determinedly as he put her into a taxicab. "Send your men off with a smile." But he was not her man. She found herself violently weeping as the cab drove off, and after a time the driver slowed down and turning spoke to her.

"Hard luck, lady," he said. "But I expect he'll come back all right."

"I'm sorry," she gasped. "I'm all right now."

"Fine-looking soldier he makes. I could drive you to the

dock and maybe you'd see him again. You'd have to walk a ways, but I know the transport and where it is."

She could not go back to her lonely hotel room. Not yet, with Chris gathering up his stuff and getting ready to sail. So in the end she did just that, to retain forever in her mind a picture as small as the area under one street lamp, with herself on foot in the shadows, the background a paved yard and a ship, and under that lamp, weighed down with their rifles and blanket rolls and wearing their flat steel helmets, an endless line of men slogging along. They were silent, save for the shuffling of their feet on the stones. They moved out of darkness into the light, and then into darkness. The darkness swallowed them. It was as though they had had only that single moment of existence.

But there was no sign of Chris, and at last she turned and went back to the cab.

CHAPTER XXXIV

THIS is not a story of the war, but of one man who played his own small part in it and emerged perhaps more of a man and certainly a better surgeon. For Chris was always to divide his active life into two parts, before and after that summer of nineteen hundred and eighteen. With only a few weeks in France to its credit, the second battle of the Marne was launched and the division moved up.

He had been shifted about. He was a regimental surgeon now, and he knew what that meant. Along with the other medical officers he was to go forward with the troops, to provide first aid for them and to supervise the establishment of first-aid stations from which the wounded could be evacuated to the field hospitals a few kilometers behind the lines.

He was aware of a suppressed excitement when word came that they were moving up, and on the last night he wrote the letters which were to go in case things went wrong with him. He wrote four, to Katie first, then to Beverly and Miss Nettie, and lastly one to Hiram Mortimer about Ursula's boy.

"I know I have failed you in many ways," he wrote to Katie. "I have wanted you to be happy, but I probably could not have made any woman happy, my dear. Among other things I have been too selfishly engrossed in my work. The failure is mine, not yours; so in case you receive this I hope you will build yourself a new life, and be happy in it."

There was more to it, as though by very length he could atone for its failure to carry what he could neither feel nor write. But his letter to Beverly was just a line or two: "Don't grieve, my darling. I have never changed, and—strange how this war makes one think—there may be something after this mess we make of life. In that case I shall be there, busy perhaps, but still the same. Always the same, my dear."

Years later he came across those and tore them up. The impulse behind that letter to Beverly was gone and it sounded merely maudlin and sentimental. War was the supreme idiocy, and it turned men into fighting killing sentimentalists.

On the last night before the move Ted Lawrence made coffee and they sat talking until late. Ted was wildly excited. The orders had been read out by the C.O., sitting at a plain wooden table in a bare wooden hut. The hut was surrounded by noise, and the C.O. was almost obliged to shout his words. Cars were coming and going, motorcycles were apparently on the point of explosion, and by dawn the din had only increased. Great busses and camions were arriving, loading, moving off in a cloud of dust. Refugees were moving in as the troops moved out, driving their farm animals ahead of them and using carts piled high with their possessions. One woman was even shepherding a flock of geese. Now and then they stopped beside the road in small family groups, these waifs and strays, and cooked a meal of sorts. They seemed barely aware then of the road, which had become a roaring river which sooner or later they must breast again. And being French it mattered not at all to them that men should leave the line, relieve themselves in the open fields and then dart back again.

Against this moved the division, frantically attempting to clear the road, laughing and singing, shouting greetings to the peasants, growling over the delays. "How many kilometers now?" "God, I could kick a barrel faster than this." And then at last a rise over a hill and a small straggling village, with a few hospital trucks in sight, and Field Hospital No. 1 was located. It was in a schoolhouse, and Chris, making an inventory, felt discouraged at the amount to do and the small time in which to do it. Already the battle was raging fiercely along a wide front, and there were rumors and counter rumors. "Don't get out too much. We'll have to retire in a few hours."

The rest of the Sanitary Train came in. Ford ambulances appeared from nowhere. Tents were set up outside, some of them for gas cases where even the clothing might carry death;

portable stoves and field kitchens arrived. Later on trailed in the giant disinfectors, driven by a steam engine and providing a chamber for delousing. Ted had been appointed a sanitary inspector, and it was at this time that Chris came across him on a log in a field, balancing a long stalk of dried weed across a finger and his face a mask of dust and despair.

"Hello there. How's the javelin thrower?"

"My God, Chris, think of it. 'What did you do in the Great War, papa?' And I'll have to tell them I was a cootie inspector. A louse hound, by God." . . . .

Inside the schoolhouse, work was already under way, for some of the wounded had preceded them. They sat or lay in the courtyard, silent for the most part, while around them the dust flew and the roar of motor exhausts deafened them. Men were already moving among them, giving those who had not already received it the necessary anti-tetanus serum. Their faces were streaked with dust and sweat; the line seemed endless.

"Get another tray, and hurry!"

More syringes, more "T"'s marked by an iodine cross on the forehead; the line slowly lessening as the litter-beds went up or the ambulances were loaded and started back. There were not enough beds as yet. Men lay on their stretchers on the floor, or on the floor without stretchers. Morphia did not put them to sleep. Very often it started them to talking. They needed no audience; just words to keep up with their racing thoughts.

Chris was working at terrific speed. The operating room was small and boiling hot. The men were brought in, their wounds dressed, operations performed when haste was essential, splints applied from the butcher wagon, bandages put on.

"Feel better now, son?"

"Yes, but God, I'm tired, doc. Lemme lie here won't you?"

But they could not lie there. They had to be moved on, on and back, to make room for the others coming in. They came in hundreds, some only slightly hurt but some to whom the dusty road marked the last journey. All the medical personnel was going without food and without sleep. They grinned at each other when they met, at their reddened eyes, their stained and dirty coats. They ate when they could, or not at all. They seldom slept, except more or less on their feet. And in that chaos Chris labored for days, his surgeon's hands itching for the work he could not always do. Supplies began to give out, and one day a dresser opened a box of bandages and found them packed in newspapers of the date of the Spanish-American War. Chris swore, but he used them.

There was nothing now but the war. Life had contracted itself into that small hot room, with men being brought in and taken out. It was a thing of roaring guns, a pest of flies and heat, the smell of blood, and the filth of the trenches. The amenities of life were food at intervals on a mess plate and a cot on which to throw oneself for a few hours of sleep. One day Chris stepped out and looked at the village street, crowded and noisy. He had hardly seen it before; had never stopped and looked at it. It seemed incredible to see children there playing.

Then Peters in charge of the battalion aid station was killed by a piece of shell, and in the emergency Chris was moved forward. Close to the front now, the dressing station in a farmhouse already under fire and soon to be abandoned, guns roaring, shells exploding, and even then some of the ambulances being withdrawn. He had had no real sleep for days and his eyes were red with dust and fatigue when at last he reached it that night in complete darkness, and stepped through the curtain of gas blankets into a feeble candlelight.

He was exhausted when he got there, but there was no time to rest. There were hemorrhages to be stopped, quick field dressings to apply. He worked all that night and the next day, until at last he turned dizzy on his feet and found a corner to rest in. He had been on his feet for more than thirty-six hours.

The men continued to pour in, and as fast as possible to be moved back. Some ambulances still remained. The rest were carried in anything available, in cars, in wagons, in jolting trucks with the bottoms covered with straw. The wounded lay supine, bracing themselves when they could. The less badly gassed cases sat up, holding compresses to their burned eyes.

"All right there? Let's go."

The truck or whatever it might be would move off, lumbering through the night. Some of the men had not tasted hot food for more than a week.

There came a time when Chris and the others worked in gas masks in the heat, an added torture; and the number of wounded steadily increased. They covered the floor, cringing as shells exploded nearby but otherwise silent. They came in faster than they could be sent back, and supplies were exhausted before they could be replaced. And at last one night the dressings were almost completely used up and Chris, with no personnel to spare and ready to steal the stuff if he had to, went outside to look for a motorcycle with a sidecar. There was none to be found, but he did discover an orderly riding one horse and leading another.

Chris stepped out of the darkness and stopped him.

"Where are you taking that horse, fellow?"

The man grinned.

"To Black Jack Pershing," he said, and the voice sounded vaguely familiar. But Chris had no time to talk then. He reached up a long arm and grabbed a bridle.

"Tell Black Jack to take a little walk," he said pleasantly, and jerking the lead rein free was up and off into the dark.

He never forgot that night ride of his; the road congested with men, machine-gun outfits and camions, all moving forward, halting, going on again. In spite of all rules it was filled from bank to bank, like a sluggish river, and military police were helpless against the inevitable flow. At times he took to the fields, to be lost there in the darkness. At other times his only light was from the guns, like distant heat lightning. At last he reached the field hospital and loaded up some saddle-bags. Like old Dave, he thought grimly; old Dave riding Nellie on his country roads, his saddlebags thumping behind him. Only this was different. This was a war, a dirty, beastly, filthy war. The very fields smelled of it.

He returned at dawn to find that a shell had made a direct hit on the station; and that most of his personnel were either dead or wounded. He stood there in the gray light, sick and dazed. One of his dressers saw him and came on a run.

"We've got to get out, captain," he said. "It's all gone. Everything."

"There's still the barn," said Chris stolidly.

They moved there and the work went on. Now the war became a barn to him; a barn filled with wounded who came and went, with light from candles which swayed and dripped in the heat, and with odors which ranged from the ammonia of the old floor to that of blood, sweat and dirt. He had lost his razor. He could not remember when he had had a bath. And combined with the smells and dirt there was the incessant noise, the sound of men in pain, the vast thunderings of guns, the roar of constant grinding traffic.

"Wipe my face, somebody. It's hot as hell in here."

The war was a barn. It was tied to life by the crowded road behind it, and to death by the road ahead. But it was good to work and not to think. It was dangerous to think. One got queer ideas, about flag-waving at home and old Lewis making shells and other men sitting with their feet on desks or moving pins on maps. The man on the table in front of him was a pin. They were all pins. He worked on doggedly.

"Better get out of here, captain."

"We can hang on a bit longer."

They hung on. There was no past and no future, only this hour and perhaps only this minute. "Where's that splint? For God's sake, who took that splint?" "Gimme a sling, and hurry with it." "Use a skullcap here, Joe, I haven't time." "Listen, boy, there are men here hurt worse than you, and saying nothing about it." Sometimes a dive out through the gas blankets and into the night air; filling one's lungs with it, staring at the sky. "Looks as though they're coming over!" But no time to wait. Back again to the candles and the smells and the dirt, to work once more. "You can't bring him in until I get somebody out. Lay him out there somewhere."

The night came however when they were ordered out. Chris watched them go, and he was still watching when two exhausted stretcher bearers carried in a badly wounded man. They put the stretcher on the ground and sank down themselves, gasping for breath. Chris bent over the stretcher.

"Hello, son. Let's see what you've got here."

"I've got plenty," said a weak but familiar voice.

It was Dick.

Chris straightened. In the hot darkness he could see the bearers, now flat on the ground, and the pallid oval of Dick's face. He touched his forehead, thick with clammy sweat. Somewhere behind there was a car, but it was too small for the stretcher, and at the best it would be hours before he could get it through that road; and Dick had not much time, if any. He took one end of the stretcher and put the exhausted bearers at the other, and so struck back through the fields.

One foot in front of the other. The stretcher pulling his arms out of their sockets. A hole, and groan from Dick.

"Get out of step there!" And a voice from the dark.

"That you, doc?"

"You're all right, Dick. We'll get you back."

"Dirty trick you played me about that horse."

Once he stopped, to give Dick a hypodermic of morphia. Another time the wounded man asked for a cigarette, and got it. Then at last—toward morning that was—they took to the road and found an ambulance on its way forward, and managed to turn it.

Dick was still living when they reached the field hospital, and Chris got a cup of strong coffee and washed up. The place was a shambles, but he got a table and operated. Then, with the work over and Dick on his way back to the base, Chris dropped like a felled ox and lay there, not moving. . . .

A few years after the war the C. O. wrote a book and sent Chris a copy. He had marked a paragraph: "I wish here to mention, among many others, Captain Noel Arden. He did incredible work under impossible conditions, and was cheerful and tireless; an example to everybody. I particularly recall one night when, the advanced station being abandoned, he and two exhausted stretcher bearers carried a badly wounded man for several hours over rough terrain, in the end to save his life."

Chris sat back in his office chair and closed his eyes. Again he was wandering through the dark, holding to that stretcher and swearing when he stumbled; again Dick was groaning between intervals of unconsciousness; again the roar of the guns was in his ears, and he could not remember when he had eaten or slept.

War was the supreme idiocy. But perhaps too it was the supreme adventure.

CHAPTER XXXV

AND so the war was over. It was over for Dick Walters, lying in a veterans' hospital with a medal for bravery and an eye out for pretty nurses. "All right. Gimme a kiss and I'll go to sleep." It was over for Mrs. Betts, now wearing a gold star instead of a red one, and writing her desperate letters to the Graves' Registration Commission in Paris: "I am anxiously awaiting information as to my son and where he is buried." It was over for Ted Lawrence, now in Coblenz and teaching pretty German girls a song which began, "Sing oh sing of Lydia Pinkham, and her work for the hu-u-man race." It was over for Jerry Ames, now grounded and feeling like a fallen angel. It was over for Chris Arden, still working and learning in a great base hospital in France, plowing through seas of winter mud, his step a little heavier but otherwise unchanged. It was over for Katie, sick and tired now of Bob Barrett and wanting escape. It was over for Beverly. And it was over forever for Miss Nettie Simpson, with only a bronze tablet being prepared for the main corridor of the hospital to remind anyone of her long years of service there; and with Miss Clarke sitting behind her desk—when she did sit—and clearing out its drawers and throwing away the odds and ends of many years.

"Good heavens, she must have kept everything. I never saw such a place."

She found a small snapshot of Chris, taken in the courtyard in his intern days, and sat for some time looking at it. He had not changed much, she thought; with the exception of the deepening lines from the nostrils to the corners of his mouth, he still retained his boyish look. His unruly hair still fell over his face, to be brushed back impatiently. He was still likely to be violent on occasion. But something had gone out of his face since that picture was taken, the buoyancy and arrogance of youth. Miss Clarke sighed and put it away.

Almost the last thing Miss Nettie had done was to take Beverly into the training school as a temporary helper; for the flu had come by that time. It was mowing down the men in France like ripe grain, and in America it took a toll like the Black Death. People went around wearing gauze masks, on the streets, everywhere. The very waiters in the hotels wore masks. The hospital was jammed with cases and depleted as to staff, and in October Beverly had walked into Miss Nettie's room and asked to be taken on. Miss Nettie, hiding her swollen feet and legs under her desk, eyed her somberly.

"I am not afraid of work."

"What do you know about work? And what does your father say?"

"Does that matter, Miss Nettie? And I can learn. I must do something. To sit idle while people are dying—"

In the end Miss Nettie took her as an emergency worker, and that night she had a visit from Staunton Lewis. He had aged, but otherwise he had not changed.

"I won't have it," he shouted. "It's absurd. It's insane."

"Won't have what?" she asked calmly. "And don't talk like that to me, Staunton Lewis. I still run my part of the hospital, and if Beverly is bored and sick of what you call a home—'"

"I've given her a damned good home for a good many years."

"That's what you've called it," she said complacently. "And don't be a fool. Go on back to your money making, Staunton, and let your girl alone. I've known you longer than I care to think about, and I've seen you build yourself a monument here. But I don't like you, I never have liked you. And I've waited for thirty years to tell you that."

"You've lost your mind!"

"No," she said quietly, "but I've lost my life, Staunton. You can't hurt me now."

He gave her a long look, picked up his hat and stalked out. Even in defeat he was unflinching, indomitable. She had won, but she knew that he would never forgive her her victory. It did not matter, she thought. In a few weeks or a few months—

Two days later Beverly entered the hospital. She lay in her small room on her hard bed and listened to the sounds about her, to the procession of nurses to and from the bathroom across the hall, to the sound of the ambulance driving in, to the faraway wail of a crying child. In her closet were hanging her plain blue uniforms, her flat heeled shoes, and her laundry bag. The room itself contained the bed she lay in, a bureau, a table and two chairs. They were no longer new, but years ago she and her mother had gone to New York to buy them.

"They're so ugly, mother."

"We're not furnishing a house, my dear."

She did not sleep, but she felt more calm than she had felt for years. Here at last was sanctuary and work. Like Chris, she felt that the hospital was home as the big house had never been. But the hard bed bothered her, after her own luxurious one. "I'm soft," she thought. "Soft and spoiled." At last she got up and sitting at the table in her nightgown she wrote Jerry her daily letter, numbering it as usual on the corner so that he might know what he had missed, if any.

"Dear Jerry: Don't laugh when you get this! I am in my nightie in the nurses' dormitory at the hospital, where tomorrow I go to work. I know it sounds foolish, but they do need help, with this flu and everything. I am really quite excited about it, although I dare say I shall be scrubbing floors most of the time. They do such a lot of scrubbing here."

She was shivering when she had finished. With each letter she knew that she had failed him once more.

The next day she went to work, quietly and efficiently. In the emergency the hospital accepted her without comment. She scrubbed her first bathrooms cheerfully, walked incredible miles of hard floors in her flat shoes, carried heavy trays. At night, her hands were sore and her feet swollen. She would go to sleep, to be called at some hour or other to clean up an operating room, and for the first time she saw the tragedies of the mills. These were the things that Chris had seen and known, and when he had tried to help these people she had failed him. No wonder he had let her go.

She was scrubbing a bathroom floor when news of the Armistice came. She finished before she got up, but she had a sense of finality. For a time she had worked and lived. Now soon she would only live again.

Although the war was over the epidemic was not. She stayed on, growing to fuller stature as a woman. She looked much the same, except that her smile was less spontaneous; and she never mentioned Chris, although when the nurses talked of him she felt rather breathless, as though the air had been drawn out of the room.

One day she met Katie in a hall. Katie had been elected a member of the Women's Board that fall, as a tribute to Chris, and now she was going to a meeting. She stopped and held out her hand.

"Oh, it's you, Mrs. Ames! How are you liking the work?"

"Very much. Of course I have always worked here, in a sense. It's not entirely new to me."

There was no condescension in Beverly's voice, but Katie passed on with an angry flush. "She has and I haven't, I suppose that's it," she thought. "That was to put me in my place! She and the Simpson woman!"

Later on she went with the others to the usual tea in Miss Nettie's room. She went with a faint air of bravado, but no one appeared to notice it. Only Miss Nettie, her tea poured, sat back and watched her, carefully dressed, slightly rouged.

"She's painting her face now," thought Miss Nettie bitterly. She closed her eyes. In the babble of talk no one noticed. Tea, sandwiches, little cakes, roses on the desk, the rustle of well-dressed women, their quiet voices—and she had let Chris in for that marriage; forced his hand.

"I've just had a letter from Chris, Miss Simpson."

"Yes?"

How dare she talk about Chris, this upstart of a girl, climbing on Chris's bent shoulders, sitting here with these women who had devoted their lives to the hospital, spending Chris's money, being manicured and waved and made up while Chris— A wave of revolt and distaste swept over her.

It was the next day that Miss Nettie was found on the floor of her room. She was conscious, but she could not walk, and they put her to bed in her small adjacent bedroom to die. Not at once. That would have been too easy, and life had never been easy for Miss Nettie. But in due time and with Beverly beside her bed. Toward the end she roused from her stupor and looked at Beverly.

"Look after Chris," she said, very clearly. "He needs it."

She was asleep before Beverly could answer, and she never wakened again.

The flu ceased as suddenly as it had come, and Beverly went back to her empty life. Save for Miss Nettie's death the hospital became normal once more. Nurses and staff were drifting back, oddly inarticulate about what they had seen and done. The poker game in the interns' room was resumed, and upstairs in the X-ray room Scott was still talking the jargon of his trade, water-cooled tubes, aluminum filters, and general X-ray therapy.

"Pretty soon we'll do away with you surgeons," he would say boastfully. "Watch radium, watch us, and see."

Scott himself was going to need a surgeon, and soon. He was going to lose his right arm and knew it. He carried it in a sling now, but he refused to have the operation until Chris came back. In the interval he worked his assistants hard, watched his fish, and went home at night with forced cheerfulness to his wife.

"Go on out, honey, I want to take a bath."

He had never let her see that arm, naked and unclothed.

There were changes in the hospital, of course. A new thing called the Carrel-Dakin treatment, with pierced rubber tubes left in a wound and a gentle steady flow of solution from a glass container over the bed. A new paraffine cure for burned cases. Plastic surgery, brought over from the war. And perhaps everywhere a feeling of starting all over again, with the war and the flu both over.

"Go ahead, America. Get on. Move on and up." . . . . .

Chris came home in February. He started eagerly enough, but toward the end his spirits flagged. The crossing was stormy. Life lines were stretched along the decks of the transport, and men on their way to the galley for food clutched them wildly. But the wild sea suited Chris's mood. Pipe in mouth he paced the decks, knowing that each day brought him closer to the life he had escaped.

The medical officers on board were not universally cheerful. For months or years they had left their hard-earned practices, and a practice was not a business. It was easily lost, hard to regain.

"Might as well crawl in somewhere and pull up the daisies."

"It won't be as bad as that."

"Won't it? Wait and see."

Storm and wind, the long line of hungry men hanging to the life lines and clutching their tin plates, the eternal poker game in what had been the lounge, the roar of the fog horn off the Banks, the pitch and roll of the ship.

"God, she turned all the way over that time!"

Somewhere to the West home and the problems of living again.

On the last day Chris finished his packing and went on deck. Now at last he knew that the war was over. Quiet waters and winter sunshine; then at last the dock, with military police in charge and shouts and roars from the multitude being held back, their faces strained with looking.

"Mother, I see Joe!"

"Where? Where, Millie?"

"There! He's waving. Oh mother, look! And he's all right. He's all right."

Katie was there, in a new fur coat, a Katie somewhat plumper but very cheerful and gay until she learned that Chris could not be immediately demobilized.

"Why not?" she demanded, her face falling. "I'd counted on a week of theaters and shopping, Chris."

"It can't be done, my dear. But you can have your week. And I can get in to see you."

But once shut off together in the taxicab there was a marked constraint between them. They were strangers, meeting again after almost two years. It was as though all the years of intimate living had been wiped away and Chris, searching desperately for words to bridge the gulf, found himself talking inanities. When at last he reached out and took her hand she submitted, but her eyes were on the streets, the people, the shop windows. She was excited, he saw, but not with his return. When he released her she hardly knew it.

"It's a nuisance, your having to be demobilized," she said. "I was giving a dinner next week for you."

"Is that done?" he asked her, smiling. "'Mrs. Arden gave a dinner last night in honor of her husband, just home from the war.'"

"It isn't funny," she said stiffly. "I owe a lot of parties, and I have to pay them back some time."

The feeling of strangeness persisted in the hotel when they reached it, and it was not lessened when he found her smoking one cigarette after another.

"Got a little vice of your own now, have you?"

"Everybody does it these days."

He made no protest, but from that time on he was to watch her incessant smoking and to find in it one of the minor annoyances which drove him frantic; for Katie was an untidy smoker. She would flick her ashes onto the carpets, or forget them entirely until they dropped on her dresses. Her path would be marked by a trail of ash. "One thing," he would say, not unamiably. "You'll always be able to find your way back."

"Back from where?"

"From wherever you have been, my dear."

She was never certain what he meant.

The next few days did not bring them any closer. Chris tried, coming in from his camp when he could to take her out, admiring the clothes she bought, forcing himself to theaters and late suppers, trying to bridge the gulf between them, even trying man-fashion to catch and hold her wandering attention. It was useless. She was bored by the war, which she frankly regarded as well over and why worry? But she was proud of him in his uniform, aware that other women followed him with their eyes. One night however she suggested that he take the caduceus off his collar.

"Take it off? Why?"

"You needn't let everybody know you were only a doctor over there, do you?"

"I'm not ashamed of it."

After that he never mentioned the war to her. Indeed, he began to be alarmed as the days went on, to look out for some anchor to hold their marriage. Katie was slipping. She would lie in her hotel bed all morning reading romantic drivel, her clothes scattered over the room, the air close, and the bathroom littered with towels, with bath salts and face creams. He would come in from the soldierly neatness of his quarters to find her there, the bed sprinkled with ashes, and to remember Lily with a shiver of distaste. But when one day out of sheer desperation he suggested that she have a child she was as stubbornly resistant as ever.

"Don't be an idiot, Chris. If you think I'm going through *that*—"

"Why not think it over, Katie? After all we are not children, and I'd like to have a youngster running around the house."

She had a new argument now however, and she used it triumphantly.

"And raise him as cannon fodder for the next war! Nothing doing, Chris. That's that."

He gave it up then. When he was finally demobilized he went back home, but the feeling of strangeness still persisted. He had no sensation of home-coming. In some strange way the house—outside of his familiar offices—had ceased to be his and had become Katie's. It was filled with new furniture, and even Olga was gone and there were two new servants who seemed to regard him as a guest rather than a master.

"For God's sake, Katie! I feel as though I ought to tip them!"

Hardly the fictional return of a man home from a war, he thought, with a strange woman in a uniform asking where his bags were to go, and Katie herself busy over her projected dinner.

"I'm asking the Morrisons, Chris."

"Who on earth are the Morrisons?"

Late that night he went into the office and closed the door. He was confused and lonely. For a long time now he had never been alone, had been swept in some wild current from this place to that. Now he was in an eddy, still dizzy, still confused. Upstairs Katie was busy with lists at her small desk, her cigarette dripping ashes over her papers. The servants had gone to bed, and after a time he realized that the furnace needed attention, and going heavily down the stairs went through the familiar motions once more.

That was his home-coming, and as he undressed that night he realized that not the only graves left by the war were those which held its dead.

CHAPTER XXXVI

KATIE gave her party the next week. A strange butler came in, people he had never seen before straggled upstairs to the living room, drank cocktails, went down again to dinner.

"When I can get the offices out of the house I'll have some room," she told them.

"You've done wonders, Katie."

She was Katie to most of them. They ate his food, drank his champagne, played bridge, watched him covertly.

"How about the war, doctor? Tell us about it."

Tell them! With their eyes glassy with liquor and the women's dresses too low. Katie's dress too low, also.

"It's over. Let's forget it."

"Let's drink to its being over."

They were young and smart. Even Chris knew that. But he did not belong among them, as he had never belonged in the Lewis house a thousand years ago. He did his best, but it was not until they had gone and he was alone in the shabby back office that he felt at home again. He lighted a pipe and moved around it. There on the desk still lay his old books, his Gray's Anatomy, his Osler, his Materia Medica. He had left them there for sentimental reasons, but by his chair was a revolving bookcase holding others. In a corner was his medicine cabinet, in another his surgical chair. It was all familiar, all dear to him. This at least was home. Here he would live and here he would work; but a man should have something or somebody to work for.

He opened the drawer of the desk and rummaged about for little Noel's picture, but it was not there.

He had turned out the light and was about to go upstairs

when he heard voices, and saw Katie and Bob Barrett coming down. He had thrown an arm lightly around her shoulder, and both of them were smiling.

"Well, was it a good party?"

"You always have good parties."

Chris stood still, his empty pipe in his hand.

"Where's Chris?"

"Gone out, I suppose."

"All right. Then here's a kiss to sleep on."

It was apparently a light caress, lightly given and lightly received, but Chris froze as he stood. He waited until Katie had closed the front door and humming softly had gone upstairs. When he followed her she was emptying the ash trays, and she looked up, startled.

"I thought you were out."

"So I imagine. Does Barrett usually kiss you good night?"

"He was tight," she said, flushing. "Anyhow, what if he does? I suppose you've been faithful all this time! You needn't answer that. I wouldn't believe you if you did."

"It happens to be the truth. Are you telling me that you haven't?"

"How dare you ask me such a question?"

He did not know whether to believe her or not, but suddenly it seemed unimportant. Katie herself seemed unimportant, sullenly putting away cards and bottles and at last putting out the light and leaving him there. When finally he followed her it was to find her in her bed and pretending to be asleep.

He carried on, although those first few weeks of his return were disheartening enough. His private practice was scattered and there were days when no one came to either office, and he had not a call to make. If he thought of Beverly in those early days it was to put her away again, definitely and finally; the easier since his immediate problems were once more pressing. He found to his shock and surprise that Katie had not only spent his army pay, but all the reserve he had left for her in the bank; and before long he began to realize that she was also deeply in debt and was concealing it from him. The result was more serious than he had believed possible, for at first she denied owing any money at all.

"Let's get at the bills, Katie. I must know where I stand."

"Bills? What do you mean, bills?"

"Bills," he said patiently. "Statements of account. What you owe, in other words."

"I haven't any," she said, looking frightened. "I don't know what you mean, Chris. I have a few, of course, but they can wait. There's no hurry."

"I have to keep my credit good. This new car of yours, is it paid for?"

"Not entirely. I still owe something on it."

She brought him a few bills then, but it resulted in his going upstairs finally and conducting an intensive search. He found them everywhere, stuck away in hat boxes, some under her mattress, a few in her desk. The total appalled him, but she was over her fright then and furiously angry.

"How dare you go into my room and throw everything about?"

"Your room?"

"Well, it's been my room for two years. It isn't my fault that you choose to go away, is it? You didn't even fight. You only—"

"That's enough," he told her, white but still quiet. "It is your room from now on. I'll sleep in Dick's old room."

"And maybe you think that will break my heart!" she said. "Only don't expect me to come crawling back to you, Chris Arden. I'm through with that."

He moved his things that night, his clothes, even his uniform with the caduceus on the collar and about it still that faint odor of manure, dust and sweat which characterized all uniforms in France. Then and without so much as a good night he slammed the door on that back room and left her there. . . .

Looking back afterwards, Chris was never able to say just why and how he had found himself in this position or in that.

The strings which had moved him puppet-fashion were always invisible. But Katie that night deliberately destroyed any pride of achievement he might have had, and out of his later knowledge he wondered whether it was not something rather pitiful after all; an attempt to pull him down to her own level.

His anger was dead by morning, but his resolution remained. In a way he was relieved. She had done one desperate thing to him. She had cost him his faith in his work during the war. It seemed a small thing now, those hours of labor and dirt and danger. He tried to shut it out of his mind. But sometimes when, largely silent, they sat together across the candle-lit table, he would find himsef back again in France, working feverishly at the first aid station by the light of candles stuck in bottle necks, with men groaning on the floor and rats as big as cats lurking in the shadows.

Or he would look in at the hospital operating room, shining with cleanliness, and suddenly he would be back at the field hospital, with its dozen operating tables in a row, its day and night incessant labor, and its helmets and gas masks on every bed. He might bury it, but it was there; tired nurses on their feet for eighteen hours and then doing their own washing, the sterilizers running incessantly, the X-ray room in a low wooden shack, the guns booming steadily so that everything vibrated, and always the knowledge that in war men and supplies came first, and the wounded last.

The scar of Katie's contempt remained. When that spring he was coerced into reading a paper before the county medical society it was coldly impersonal. "Quite early in the war it was discovered that the old methods of moving wounded with only field attention had been a mistake. This method had resulted in all the scourges of old battlefields, gas and hospital gangrene, tetanus and—"

There they sat before him, old men and young, doctors who had come in from country practices to hear him, men who had tried to get to the war and failed. And this was not what they wanted. They wanted to be taken to France, to see it through his eyes, to be for an hour or so a part of the great drama. He could not do it.

"It was always necessary to go further than the wound itself, to search not only for the projectile but for what it had carried with it, the dirt and bits of cloth. In other words—"

Words, words! Boys going forward with roses stuck in their helmets and the muzzles of their guns, and then coming back—to him and others like him—or not coming back at all. Southern Negroes building railroads and singing spirituals as they worked. American youngsters in bad French coaxing French locomotives to take a walk with them. Colored porters from the South in white coats on the train of the high command, engineers building bridges and water supplies, little funk holes dug in the side of roads, East Side Jews dying bravely at the front, moonlit nights and air bombardments, beds emptied and refilled before they could be made up again; rats, mud, duckboards to sleep on, lice; all this, and his voice droning on:

"As a result, the percentage of mortality—"

They congratulated him after it was over, envying him his experience; brain surgery, abdominal surgery, the new thoracic surgery. Millions of young bodies in the laboratory of war, and out of them new knowledge, almost a new science. But he had disappointed them, and he went home that night with defeat in his heart.

He never spoke of the war after that.

"I didn't see it," he would say. "No one man saw it. Then you've got to remember that I was pretty busy. Always a lot of fellows needing something."

That was Chris's story of the war, and in a way it was the story of the war itself.

through his eyes to be just an independent [illegible] of the great drama. He couldn't do it.

It was always necessary to go further than the wound itself, to know not only for the properties but for what it had carried with it, the dirt and infected cloth. To get at words—

Words, words! Always going forward with masses of men [illegible] into the muzzles of their guns, and then coming back—to [illegible] [illegible] not coming back at all. [illegible] they wanted. American women were in at last [illegible] French [illegible] to [illegible] with them [illegible] from the North [illegible] the [illegible], the water supplies [illegible] due to the [illegible] at the front [illegible] before they could be [illegible] [illegible] [illegible]

[illegible] compensated him [illegible] was over, [illegible] [illegible] [illegible] [illegible] [illegible] [illegible] [illegible] [illegible] [illegible]

He never [illegible] the war after that.

"I didn't [illegible]," he would say. "[illegible] saw it. [illegible] remember [illegible] I was [illegible] [illegible]. Always a lot of fellows [illegible] something."

[illegible] story of the war, and [illegible] it was the story of the war itself.

Part VI

THE SURGEON

CHAPTER XXXVII

THE war was over for four million men. Rather less than half of them had been to France, but for all of them there had been a disorientation which made the return to normal life difficult. For months or years they had obeyed orders, had rarely had to think for themselves. Mostly they had been young, and if they had fought they had also played when the chance came. The war had been an escape from grim reality. Now once again they had to face it.

And so Jerry Ames came home, catapulted out of the blue skies where he had found himself and missing his wings like a dispossessed angel. No more for him the rising at dawn while the mist lay thick on the ground and the mechanics were shadows moving about along the field; no more the "All right, fellows. Let's go." No more the climbing into the plane, the roar of the propeller, the sweep and lift, and at last the good earth below him and the better skies above. No more that feeling that he and his ship were one, loafing above the poor devils beneath, then lifting on and up, on and up, eyes alert, every cloud a possible ambush but for all that freedom, the complete freedom of the air. Maybe a dogfight then, playing tag with the enemy.

"I know that dodge. Try this one."

Somewhere to go then, with a vengeance. He would laugh, there alone in his ship. What did he care? What the hell did he care? This was living, sport, adventure. "Get on his tail." "Smart fellow, that one." Letting go a burst of fire, missing, trying again. Once or twice a bit of luck, and then the slow easy return to the field, the landing, the men at the mess, plenty to eat and plenty to drink. Somebody playing a battered piano, and the crowd singing "Sweet Adeline." Somebody else missing. "Not back? He was due two hours ago." But the piano going on. No use to worry. What was done was done. "My Adeline, sweet Adeline."

Toward the end they were almost all replacements, but Jerry Ames' luck held.

"Thought you fellows got the railroad station."

"Sure we did."

"Then what were you dropping? Peanuts? Look at this photograph."

Then suddenly it was over, and on the ship coming home that spring Jerry took up a cigarette in a dark cabin and was unable to put it in his mouth. He tried several times and then struck a match and succeeded. But he was frightened.

"How much have you been drinking?" asked the ship's doctor.

"Like the rest. Plenty."

"Well, I could make a better nervous system than you've got out of a spool of thread and a few buttons, my lad. You'll have to lay off. Lay off for good. I'm telling you."

He did lay off for the remainder of the voyage and even for a short time thereafter. He was dead cold sober when Beverly met him in New York, but she was worried when she saw him. He looked thin and worn, and there were new tight lines in his face. He greeted her cheerfully, however, and after his usual fashion.

"Hello there. And how's the girl?"

He kissed her awkwardly. For a moment she could not speak. He was back again, incredibly boyish, incredibly debonair after all he had been through. She was filled with tenderness.

"I'm all right, Jerry. And I'm so glad, so—"

She choked, and he patted her on the shoulder.

"That's all right, Bev. That's great. For God's sake don't cry! I'm here. I'm fine and dandy. How about going somewhere tonight?"

That was more like him. He strutted about the pier, giving

orders, getting the taxi; but she saw how his hands shook and in the cab she took one and held it steady.

"Why go out tonight, Jerry? You need rest, don't you? I'd like—I'd like to take care of you if you'll let me. You look so tired."

"Tired? Me?" He grinned. "I've had the time of my life. How about a theater and some dancing later? Anything good in town?"

They went out, that night and the next, and others which followed. For a week or two he was careful. Then one evening he came into her hotel room, hardly articulate and barely able to stand.

"Sorry, old girl," he said thickly. "Met a few of the old crowd. Got to drink it up before prohib—prohibition comes." Then his knees slowly buckled under him and he went down like a stone.

She got him home as soon as he was demobilized. Holmes was at the door, and her father in the hall. Luckily it was one of Jerry's good days, and he passed Staunton's scrutiny fairly well. But that night he drank the better part of a quart of whisky, and he lay in a stupor for twenty-four hours. Toward the end she became frightened and sent for Chris, but Jerry was coming out of his coma then. It was not until they were downstairs again in the familiar morning room that they spoke, and then it was as old acquaintances and as though that night in New York had never been.

"He'll be all right, Beverly. This time anyhow. But of course he can't go on like this."

"He's been through a lot, Chris. He doesn't talk about it, but I can guess."

"Yes," he said absently. "But it's not easy to talk about, is it? How about you?" he said abruptly. "You look tired. If I send you something to pick you up, will you take it?"

"Of course, but I'm all right, really."

Doctor and patient, he thought as he went out to his car. All those months of remembering that last night before he sailed, and now by God he was sending her cod-liver oil! His mouth was tight as he drove through the gates. They had been closer when he could dream of her in France than now they could ever be face to face. Yet driving down the hill that day he knew that the bond between them was as strong as it had ever been. Stronger, for now they were man and woman, and the romance of the early days had developed into something much deeper; the controlled and carefully concealed but passionate love of two people who were innately decent.

He groaned inwardly. What did people do under such conditions? They went on, he supposed. Months passed, years passed, and in time probably the agony passed also. Love turned into friendship; two people sitting by a fireside, glad to be together when they could, but with all passion gone. Queer, that a man should look forward to those years when his essential manhood had ceased to trouble him.

Beverly, going slowly back to her vigil by Jerry's bed, was thinking much the same thing. She sat down quietly, watching the man on the bed. She did not blame him. She felt toward him as she might have felt toward a wayward son, and when at last he stirred and opened his eyes she leaned forward and put her hand on his forehead. That roused him, and he lay looking up at her out of sunken bloodshot eyes.

"I'm no good, Bev. I never will be. Why don't you leave me?"

"I'm not leaving you, Jerry. We're fighting this out together."

His face relaxed and he reached out and caught her hand.

He slept after that, a normal sleep. He was still holding her hand, and she was cramped and stiff before he wakened. But she did not move. This was her place, beside him, standing by. She would never leave him. Late that night however, in her own room again, she went to the window and looked down over the city lights. How often she had stood there, staring down at the ailanthus tree and beyond it to the lights from the blast furnaces. But now the tree was gone, and with the end of the war something like the peace of death had settled over the mills.

She and Chris. She and Jerry. Writing Chris and getting no answer. Marrying Jerry in the garden below and determinedly smiling into the camera. She turned back to her room, and in the mirror of her dressing table she saw her face, tired and white. She was beginning to look like her mother, she thought. Then still dressed in case Jerry needed her she threw herself face downward on her bed. This was to be her life. All there was to her life.

She was still lying there in the darkness when Jerry came into the room, a shaky and pallid Jerry, but with determination in his eyes. He came straight to her bed and stood looking down at her somberly.

"It's like that, is it, Bev?"

She turned, sat up. "I'm tired, Jerry. That's all."

"You weren't sleeping?"

"No."

"Then let's have this out." He sat down on the side of her bed, feeble but entirely sober. "I'm like this, Bev. You know it. I haven't any camouflage left. I'm stripped to the skin. Do you want to go on with it, or do you want to quit? Don't think about me; think about yourself. You're young. If you got rid of me you'd be better off, and you know it."

"I told you I was standing by, Jerry."

"I don't want that," he said roughly. "I don't want a nurse. I'm not so damned old myself, as far as that goes, and I've paid a price already for something that's over and done. I want a wife, not a sister of mercy."

"I've told you—"

"I'm not blaming you. Maybe I'm excusing myself, and God knows you've been tolerant enough. I suppose I don't want toleration; that's all."

"Jerry," she said steadily. "I want you to tell me one thing. Just one thing. Do you care for me at all? Really, I mean. I've never been sure. I'm not sure now."

"Certainly I care. I always have."

"You care but you've not been faithful, Jerry. I don't understand it. I suppose no woman ever does. Perhaps it is different with a man. I don't know."

"Different?" He shrugged his shoulders and got up. "Technically yes, my dear. A woman is still a good woman if she marries one man while she is in love with another. That's what you did, isn't it? While a man—" He did not finish, and a moment later she heard his door close and knew that he was gone.

But that coma had frightened him again. He fought hard during the ensuing months. For weeks he went to his office, trying not to look out at the sky, or to listen to the humming of an airplane overhead; gathering up the threads of his old life as well as he could. Then there would come a time when he was jerky and irritable, and when at the table he could not eat. Staunton Lewis would eye him.

"What do you live on anyhow? Air?"

"I'm not hungry."

A day or so and he would be gone again, and after two or three experiences of this sort Beverly one night sent for Chris and told him the story.

"I don't blame him, Chris. But he's killing himself."

"What can I do? What can anyone do, Beverly?"

"I think I know where he is. If you could get him and bring him home—"

Suddenly all her reserves were down, and she was sobbing wildly on his shoulder. "I can't bear it, Chris. I've reached my limit. And now to have to call on you!"

"Who else would you call on? You know you can count on me."

"I'm so tired, Chris."

"I know. I know, darling. Go to bed and try to sleep. I'll find him."

He let her go, and stood at the foot of the stairs while she obediently climbed them. He was filled with pity and anger, but when she turned to look down at him he was picking up his hat; a solid quiet man merely picking up his hat.

"Good night, Chris."

"Good night. And don't worry."

He brought Jerry home some time toward morning, a Jerry who confused him with the Military Police and got in several good blows before he was subdued. It was Chris who sat the rest of the night beside the bed where Jerry lay in a stupor. He sat there, his chin on his hand, waiting for his hypodermic to take effect and watching the man on the bed. It was a fine piece of irony, he thought, that the best he could do for Beverly now was to give her a few hours of release; and to try to save for her a man already burned out at thirty-five, and whom she had never loved. . . .

That was only the first of several such episodes. Sometimes Jerry was missing only for a day. Again he would be lost for a week, and Chris in such leisure as he had would comb the city for him. He was a pathological case by now, a psychopathic drinker. Chris knew it, Beverly knew it, even in time Staunton Lewis realized it. It was only one addition to his rapidly mounting troubles, however. He had over-expanded during the war, and with its abrupt termination he found some of his great enterprise dangerously near the rocks. Late at night Beverly, waiting for Jerry to come home, would see the light under his study door and know that he was there. In the morning his waste basket would be filled with scratch paper covered with his small neat figures.

He had built an empire, and now it was crumbling about him.

He lasted, however, through that first year after the Armistice and well into the second. Then one morning his valet tapped at his door and found it empty. He went into the bathroom, but Lewis was not there and so he notified Beverly. It was not until the house had been searched that she remembered her mother's closed room, and it was there that she found him.

Apparently he had been standing beside the bed, because when his heart gave out he had fallen across it.

She did not call for help. She saw at once that he was dead, had been dead for hours, and so for a little while she left him there undisturbed on Annie's bed. It was as though those two, so long separated in life, were now united again. Probably he had come there often, slipping in at night when the house was quiet and standing beside that bed, perhaps even wandering about the room as he had while her mother still lay there; picking up the tortoise shell mirror on the dressing table and staring at it. Remembering.

"Where'd that come from?"

"You bought it for me in Naples. Don't you remember?"

Beverly stood by the bed, looking down at him. Strange, she thought, that he had allowed death to unmask him. In his own queer fashion he must always have loved her mother, even built his success in order to be important to her. It had been his compensation for his smallness of stature, his early poverty. Then he had lost her.

Beverly leaned over and put a hand on his arm.

"I think she knows now, father," she said quietly. "Perhaps she always did know."

She was still there when Holmes found her; and at her order they kept him there, laid out neatly in Annie's bed. Later on they put him in the mausoleum, close beside Annie again, and on the casket Beverly had engraved only his name and a line from the Stevenson he had kept by his bed. "Here he lies where he longed to be." Because he had had his pride and his bitter reticences, she had it covered with a pall of flowers. It was as though for once they two, father and daughter, shared a secret.

She was still very calm when his will was read. It had been made during the great days of his empire, and what with bequests, the endowment for the laboratory and a vastly larger sum to build a new and modern hospital on the site of his house and grounds, she learned that there would be little left. It did not matter greatly to her. Money never had been important to her. But when a day or two later she tried to dismiss Holmes and he refused to go she wept heartbrokenly for the first time since her father's death.

"I'm staying, Miss Beverly," Holmes said stolidly. "They'd have liked to know that, both of them; that I'm looking after you."

All those years of living, and now only Holmes was left to her!

Jerry remained sober during all of that trying time. He had had his own losses since the war, and the collapse of the Lewis fortune was serious for him. But he had never come back to her. He was quite definitely living his own life now. He would come in, bathe and dress and go out again. She would hear his car going out the driveway and wait for it to come back. Sometimes it came, sometimes not.

She would go to bed then, but not to sleep. She would lie in the dark trying to make her plans. Eventually this house would be gone and they must go somewhere else. But where? She made her small practical plans, not daring to think beyond them; as though by furnishing a house she could furnish a future.

CHAPTER XXXVIII

IT WAS good to be back at the hospital again. Quite definitely now it was Chris's spiritual home. True, he slept and sometimes ate at the house; but outside of his office hours it had ceased to be important to him. At midnight or later he would go back, occasionally to find the place lighted and some of Katie's friends still there, but often to find it dark save for the light in the hall. He would go upstairs then to Dick's old room, undress, read for a while, perhaps drop to sleep with his lamp still burning. But of personal life he had little or none. He was an efficient working machine, more efficient than he had ever been, but that was all.

Work was coming in again, after that early discouragement. He had a nurse in the downtown office now, a practical young woman with no nonsense about her, and everything was grist that came to his mill. If he had misgivings at times, he could draw a deep breath of thankfulness when a crisis was safely passed. But his responsibilities lay heavy on him. Sometimes he failed—"Not gods, but men"—and carried away with him a bitter feeling of failure. But on the whole he was entirely self-confident. When sometimes he found a victim of inexpert surgery he was filled with profound indignation.

"It's outrageous," he told Ted Lawrence. "Any fellow these days with a knife and a pair of rubber gloves thinks he can go into an abdomen."

"And I suppose," said Ted, "that you're so damned good that you never make any mistakes."

"Am I as smug as that?" Chris demanded, flushing.

"Pretty complacent sometimes," Ted said cheerfully. "You'll get over it."

Chris thought over that later. Where was the line between smugness and sureness in surgery? He watched himself thereafter, and was annoyed to find that after the completion of a good job he was looking about the operating room for tacit approval. He had seen other men do it and been mildly contemptuous. Now he was doing it himself.

He stopped it. Thereafter he finished a case and asked for the next briefly and curtly. It cost him some of his popularity. There had been something engaging in that half-boyish demand of his for approval. For that one minute when he straightened and glanced about he and the group around the table had been one, united by his success.

The nurses resented the change in him.

"Pretty high and mighty, isn't he?"

"Well, the war did queer things to a lot of people."

At home Katie ran his house efficiently, although she raged over his irregular meals, and realized that if she gave him little of herself, he gave her even less. Even their hours rarely coincided. Long before she was awake he was up and on his way to the hospital, and often he came in after she had gone to bed, closing the front door quietly and smelling again that persistent odor of mold in the hall which told him that he was in his own house again.

He was gradually giving up his general practice, but one night in the fall of that year he delivered Mrs. Gus Strobel—nee Miss Sophia Barker—of a fine boy, and together he and Gus carried the baby down into the darkened shop and held him in the meat scales.

"Eight and a half pounds without your hand, Gus!"

When he looked there were tears in Gus's mild blue eyes.

"So," he said brokenly. "I have a son. I was a lonely man, doctor, until I married her. Now all is different. And she has borne me a son. God is very good, doctor."

But Chris was rather uncertain about any God at all those days. He counted only on his skill and on his own competent hands. When he went to the hospital the operating room would be ready. He would put on cap and gown, tie on his mask, draw on his gloves and dip his hands. The case would be ready, sheets now with windows cut in them, alcohol, ether and iodine at hand, the house surgeon to help him and a nurse now at the instruments. He would bend over the table, examining, dissecting; when there were students, explaining.

"This is a case of duodenal ulcer. As you know, the duodenum—"

He could talk and work at the same time. The students watched, envious of his certainty, his deftness, and he would be comfortably aware of that envy.

"This looks like an ovarian cyst with torsion. We'll find out." And he would grin at them, sure of himself and his diagnosis, daring the case to be otherwise. Arrogant at times, but uneasy at others, that was Chris Arden in that first year or two after the war. If he wondered sometimes whether what he had saved was worth saving he held the thought in abeyance. This was his job. The rest was up to Gus Strobel's God, or luck, or Providence, or whatever one cared to call it.

It was in the autumn of 1921 that he finally decided to give up his general work entirely. The night hours were bad for his surgery. He would go into the operating room tired, his hands not too steady, and so one day he handed over his general practice, lock, stock and barrel, to Ted Lawrence.

"You won't keep them all," he said. "But some of them will stick." He grinned. "You're an ingratiating young devil, Ted. They'll like you."

"I'm a demon with the women," said Ted modestly.

Together they ran down the list. Chris had unlocked his file, and now he threw out on his desk the records, one by one. He was throwing his past overboard, and he knew it. Cold and detached as were his case histories, through each one ran some part of his life blood. Here he had fought and won; here he had lost. When he came to the Henry Jamieson file he sat gazing at it with a revival of that old agony of his. Henry's voice over the telephone: "She's dead, doctor." And Katie in the Lewis dining room, talking volubly, flirting with Jerry.

He crumpled it up and threw it into the basket. Ted watched him.

"All washed up, that one?"

"All washed up."

In the end Ted gathered up the records.

"I don't need to tell you what I feel about this, Chris."

Chris was carefully filling his pipe.

"Take care of them, Ted. That's all. Most of them are friends of mine. I'll miss them, I suppose. Surgery's a detached sort of thing; now you see them and now you don't. It's a plumber's job."

"Even the lowly plumber has his uses."

He saw Ted out that night with mixed feelings, a Ted who carried that past of his in a brief case under his arm. There was nothing there to show those battles of his with death lurking in the corners, or those days when the fight was over and he would enter some house miraculously brightened after long strain.

"She's better, doctor. I think she's passed the crisis."

Going up the stairs then with a lighter step, into some room, beside some bed. Looking down, smiling.

"Decided to get well, have you?"

That transfer to Ted Lawrence had its comic side, however. Two days after it had occurred Ted marched solemnly into the office and held out a document which looked suspiciously like a case record.

"I'm giving this one back," he said, very softly.

"Back? What are you talking about?"

"About a dinner suit," said Ted, still gently. "A dinner suit. You know what I mean. A thing you wear—"

"I know all that. What about a dinner suit?"

"Well, it isn't a swimming suit. I just thought I'd tell you. And when it comes to hauling your cases out of the river—well, I'm a doctor, not a diver. Old Josh went crazy last night and tossed his grandson into the river. I got him ashore finally, but it took a lot of steam. If I'd had paddle wheels—"

But by that time Chris was roaring with laughter.

"In your dinner clothes?" he gasped when he could speak.

"In my dinner clothes. I lost a top hat, and when I got to my party they stood me on the kitchen floor to drip and fished for minnows in my pockets. If you think that's funny—"

Josh was in jail by that time, on his way to the asylum, but Ted left the record there and not so many years afterwards Chris was to find it in an old trunk, along with Lena the doll. To find it and sit holding it, with its mixture of tragedy touched with comedy that only medical men can know. . . .

He had burned his bridges now. He retained his offices in the house, but only out of sentiment and for emergencies. His work as consultant was done in the downtown office. He had not only a nurse there now; he had added a secretary. She sat at a desk in the waiting room, handling the telephone, watching his appointments; a spinsterish young woman who brought her lunches in a box and who kept his books and sent out his bills. Chris teased her unmercifully.

"Out all night again, I suppose?"

"Certainly not, doctor."

"Well, why not? That's what I want to know."

The nurse would help him into his long white belted coat, he would run his eye over the appointment list, and look at her severely.

"You'll have to do better than this, Miss Evans. Our expenses are going on, as you may have noticed."

"I'll do better tomorrow, doctor," she would say demurely.

He could be himself there, in that office of his.

But the list was seldom empty now. He was becoming an important local figure, and his reputation was beginning to spread. Doctors out in the country began to send him cases, and now and then he went himself to some remote spot when the patient could not be moved. He would take Ted with him and Miss Evans, the nurse, and work with what he had at hand.

"The kitchen table, Miss Evans, and get somebody to hold the lamp."

A hot fire in a stove to boil the instruments, the odor of the anesthetic, the uncertain lamp light, Miss Evans unwrapping her sterile towels and dressings, Ted giving the ether and the local man gazing at Chris's masked and ghostly figure. Then gloves and the first red line and to work, to the tune of the hissing teakettle and perhaps the cackling of chickens in the yard outside, or at nights to the twittering of a sleepy bird.

"Like the war, Ted!"

"Why bring that up?"

He would go back to the city, tired but jubilant. Often he slept, in car or train, but sometimes he sat tired and relaxed. Now and then he thought of old Dave Mortimer. This had been his work. In a sense he felt that he had been carrying on for him. Life was a queer thing, a damned queer thing. He could see old Dave at such times, hear him: "Those fellows in the Civil War had the right idea. They packed an amputation in sawdust and let maggots clean it up." Now a group of men were talking of sterile maggots, and even experimenting with them. Queer, damned queer, all of it.

Sometimes the cases came to him from the outlying districts; a stretcher flat on the floor of the baggage car, and some weary country doctor sitting on a box beside it. One day Chris stood on the platform and saw a gray-faced man getting out.

"My son, doctor," he said, "and my wife is praying, for you and for him."

It was touch and go, that case, but Chris fought it doggedly. The picture of that unseen woman was behind everything he did, and in the end he—or she—won. He felt exhausted after it, but triumphant.

"Well, I guess we've turned the trick!"

"Yes, with the help of God."

He went himself to the train when they started back, father and son. He felt that he wanted to give the boy back to his mother again. Yet on the way he wondered if he had not given that particular case more than he had to give, and to think about

David's belief in prayer. Was there after all something he had denied, and that old David had been able to summon when he needed it? He did not know, but always after that he had a phrase for it. He called it working better than he knew how.

Quite definitely now his patients were cases. He did his best by them, sent a bill in due time and then forgot them. Before him passed a kaleidoscope of the world's misery, but it touched him more and more lightly. He was armored against it. He worried over his cases, of course; and at such times Katie kept out of his way. He showed a fidgety annoyance with her.

"Why don't you take some time and darn some socks for me?"

"If you'd get a car you wouldn't wear out a pair a day."

He did get a car about that time. Now he drove himself through the gates and into the hospital courtyard, his new shining car among the others. It seemed a long time since he had watched Bergman and Grant and the others with envious eyes, doing the same thing. But save for this semidetachment he himself had not greatly changed. He still kicked chairs when they got in his way, still fought inanimate things, such as collars and dress ties.

"Hell and damnation," he would shout, and tear the collar off his neck, or throw the tie on the floor. Katie, hearing sounds of these distant battles would tighten her mouth and keep out of his way. But he was usually indulgent and often apologetic with her.

"Sorry for the noise, my dear; but if you will give parties and make me dress for them—"

For Katie was now carefully building a life of her own. He did not blame her. He had less and less to offer her; but as a result he seldom saw her alone. He had a shrewd idea that if there had been anything between Bob Barrett and her it was over, for she was flying high these days, cultivating the smart young married crowd; but he sometimes found Barrett at the house. Not alone, however. He would open the front door to find a crowd there, the inevitable clinking upstairs of highball and cocktail glasses and ice, and the loud sound of voices. When he appeared, as he sometimes did, the noise would gradually die.

"Hello, doctor. I didn't know you were in."

They never really accepted him, although now and then a girl would make overtures to him, using what was then a new line.

"Where have you been all my life?"

"I'm a plain working man, you see."

"Not plain, I'll tell the world!"

He would grin down at her.

"That goes two ways."

"Good gracious, is that a compliment? And from *you?*"

She would drift away like the others. It was not his game. He could not play it, this light give and take, this casual love-making and increasing tippling after the war.

To the passing eye he still might have been some young business man, going briskly about his business. There was nothing in his face or carriage to suggest that he dealt in life and death instead of stocks and bonds. He belonged to clubs now, although he had little time for them. When he could steal an hour or two he played golf, and sometimes after his late rounds at the hospital he joined the poker game downstairs. He was a member of the College of Surgeons too, going to their meetings, listening intently to the Mayos, to Crile, to Cushman, to all the big men. The war had seen the final end of the isolation theory in surgery. Now men moved about, attending clinics, exchanging ideas and experiences.

Once or twice too he went to a convention of the American Medical Association. Watching some of the older men there he found them philosophical rather than eager, as though, having failed to rationalize the human race as to care of the body, they had finally recognized its supreme idiocy and lost hope. Yet he knew that most of them were still practical idealists, dedicated to what was at once a profession, an art, a science and a career of service, often without hope of reward.

Watching them reading their careful papers, often written in the long hours of the night while other men slept; realizing the breadth and depth of their experience, he felt that they were giving more than they had to give, as though the daily drain on their own vitality was slowly exhausting it. Most of them carried in their faces their own record of sleepless nights, of constant strain and of their failures. As against this fatigue the younger men were eager, optimistic, filled with energy, but some day they too—

What other profession labored so constantly to put itself out of business, he thought? Or paid so high a price? And this was the road he himself was to travel. Shaving in front of his hotel-room mirror he could see the deepening lines in his own face.

"It's the hell of a life," he would think, and feel a secret envy of the business men he knew, leaving their work behind them by the mere closing of an office door. . . .

It was the next year that he took off Scott's arm at the shoulder. He had tried to save it, but the time had come when there was nothing more to be done. He sat by the bed until the anesthetic wore off, and Scott's first words were characteristic.

"Suppose I won't have to wear that damned sling any more, Chris?"

"No. No sling, Scott."

He almost never saw Beverly Ames. After those first months she had ceased sending for him when Jerry disappeared. It was not fair to him, busy as he was; and she knew too that it was not fair to any of them. Their lives were fixed, settled for all time, and the only safe thing was to leave them so.

When she told him so Chris had agreed, unhappily but gravely.

"We have made our own lives, Chris. We have to live them."

"You can't carry this alone."

"I have Holmes."

"Yes," he said. "You have Holmes, and you have me if you need me. Always, if you need me, my dear. Never forget that."

She had not forgotten, but she did not send for him. She had deserved this. Now she would carry it alone.

He did see her, of course, and when he did the chance meetings had all the impact of a physical blow. But he was armored now. The thing would pass and he would go on about his work, his success, his career. He was sleeping badly, however. He began to lose flesh and to be sharply irritable, and some time in that third year after his return from France Ted Lawrence, doing well by then in internal medicine, went to Katie about him.

"He can't go on like this," he said. "How long is it since he's had a vacation? Why don't you talk to him?"

"Talk to him!" she said. "Try it yourself. He wouldn't listen to me, anyhow."

"He'll break, as sure as God made little fishes."

But she was unconvinced. Chris was strong, and if he chose to put his work before anything else— She shrugged, and Ted inspected her, her short hair, her cigarette, her feet in their high-heeled pumps.

"If he breaks where are you? I don't suppose you let him save much," he added, brutally.

"He won't break," she said comfortably. "He likes to be busy. If things fall off for a day or two he starts to banging everything around. If you think life with him is easy you'd better think again."

Ted lighted a cigarette, and watched her flicking her ashes onto the floor. Then he carefully brought an ash tray and placed it between them.

"See here, Katie," he said. "Chris isn't happy. He isn't even comfortable. You know why probably better than I can guess. But he's a decent chap. Why don't you make him happy? Why don't you make an effort to hold him? He's the faithful sort, if you give him a chance."

She laughed shortly. "Faithful! I don't believe it. What about the war? What about the hours he's shut in his office with all sorts of women? They fall for him, you know. He's the sort to attract them. All women fall in love with their doctors more or less, don't they? You ought to know!"

"That sounds like Bob Barrett," Ted said grimly. "It's a lie, like most of his talk. Chris is a one-woman man. Don't make a mistake about that."

"Then you can be darned sure I'm not the woman," said Katie calmly, and flicked her ashes onto the floor again.

He was thoughtful when he left. He had defended Katie so far as he could, but he began to wonder if the alienation between her and Chris had not gone further than he thought. He wondered, getting into his car to make his rounds that afternoon. Was Chris still in love with Beverly Ames? And in that case, what? For Jerry's story was common property by that time. They were a local scandal, those disappearances and returns of his, although Beverly still carried her head high and smiled her faint rather wistful smile. Only recently he had been picked up on the street and brought to the hospital by the police and had been later found by a nurse on a fire escape, about to soar into the air on invisible wings.

"All right. Let's go," he had been saying when she caught him.

"Better come back, Mr. Ames. It's cold out here."

He had looked at her blankly, but she was pretty and young, and he smiled.

"If you say so, my dear."

"I do say so."

They had put him in a room with barred windows after that. The hospital, moving on its business past the door, could see Beverly there beside the bed. Sometimes she read to him. Sometimes she merely sat there quietly while he slept, like a woman beside her dead. But those who knew her knew that she would never leave him. The war had left him to her, as definitely as though he had been maimed, and she would look after him as best she could.

"Shall I read, Jerry? Or would you rather sleep?"

"I'll try to sleep."

He would hold out his hand and she would take it. Then he would doze off and she would sit, cramped and trying not to think, until he roused again.

She had plenty to think of, however. The postwar depression was still on, and the settlement of her father's estate had left her with huge debts and an uncertain income. The mills had closed down, and she would have to sell the big house if she could, and take a smaller one. But she told Jerry none of this, sitting there beside his bed and holding to his hand, and feeling more alone than she had ever thought possible. Now and then Chris passed along the corridor. She could hear him coming, the heavy firm walk, the lighter steps of a resident, the sound of their voices. But he never went into the room.

It was some time after that episode of the hospital fire escape that Chris heard through some medical underground that Jerry Ames had been committed to an institution in a distant city. He called Beverly at once, but she was out of town and he knew then that it was true. He hung up the receiver with a sense of defeat. She had built without him with a vengeance, he thought; and went about his work half heartedly for days.

CHAPTER XXXIX

ACTUALLY Jerry had committed himself. He had come through another bout—this time at home—to discover once again that in the dark he was no longer co-ordinate. The next day he called Beverly in and told her.

"I've got no choice," he said, "and I can't make it myself. That's the fact. Besides"—he smiled at her ironically—"some day I might let go of a fire escape, and that would be a mistake."

She could hardly believe that he meant it, but he did. She helped him to pack, and at his request she went with him. After that she settled herself at a small hotel in the near-by town, and prepared to wait. He had entered under an assumed name, and under that name she had registered.

It was a long waiting. Sandy was dead and so now she took her long walks into the country alone; swinging along, a still girlish figure in tweeds, glad of movement, glad to be tired at night so she could sleep. Once a week she was allowed to visit Jerry, but the visits were constrained and none too happy. He was nervous and irritable at first.

"For God's sake don't look sorry for me. I'm all right."

"You don't really mind it?"

"Mind it! I mind it like hell! But I've said I'll do it and I will."

She looked at him, at his haggard twitching face and shaking hands. He had had no liquor since he entered, and she wondered if that was safe. She was anxious. If he got desperate— She saw his eyes on her, and his ironic grin.

"Don't worry, my dear. I'll not cut my throat. They take precious care I don't have the chance."

As time went on however he began to improve. The prolonged baths, the enforced exercise, had their effect. He even began to eat again, and tried to flirt a bit with the pretty nurse who had him in charge.

"How about a little hand-holding? Very soothing, I understand."

"I'll think it over."

"Nothing to that. Ought to be spontaneous. Two hands with but a single thought. That sort of thing."

He was popular, and in time even contented. Now no longer did he have to make his own decisions, fight his own battles. In a way he had gone back to his boyhood and the institution mothered him. "Better put on your sweater. It's cold today." He began to play, bridge on rainy days, tennis on better ones. Beverly, coming regularly on visiting days, began to feel that he did not want her there; that she reminded him of an outside world he wanted to forget for the time. Yet he was proud of her, of her beauty, her air of breeding.

"Come in, Sims. I want you to meet my wife."

But he was never sorry when the time came for her to leave. He would kiss her lightly and watch her go.

"Well, cheerio, my dear. I'm going for my walk now."

Even there he was doing things and going places.

She felt relieved during those months, almost happy. She was still hopeful when he came home. And for two months he remained sober, going to the office and facing for the first time the financial chaos of the Lewis businesses. He would sit back in her father's study, and once again the wastebasket would be filled with scratch-paper, covered with figures.

"Of all the damn-fool things to do, to build and endow a hospital!" he would say angrily. "And on this property. It ought to be yours. If we have to get out—"

"We will have to, Jerry. We couldn't keep it up anyhow, could we?"

When the Board sent in the belated blueprints for the new hospital buildings he threw them into the fire, and it was all she could do to save them. He was not drinking, however. He went for two months without drinking. Then one night he did not come home, and Holmes could not find him at any of his usual haunts.

He was gone for three days. In her despair she sent for Chris, and Chris searched without result, making the rounds of hospitals and the morgue as long ago Henry Walters had done for Dick. One morning the mechanics at the new air field saw a debonair but unsteady figure get out of a taxicab and waver across to where a small open plane was warming up.

They knew him. He had helped to build the field. He grinned at them.

"All ready, I see, Manning," he said to the boss mechanic, and climbed in.

Manning was uncertain. He stood by in his stained overalls, but off his legs Jerry was apparently sober and sure of himself. He grinned again over the side of the open cockpit.

"All right, let's go," he called, and Manning stepped forward.

The plane rushed across the field and lifted; and once more Jerry felt the sweep and the rise, with the good earth below him and the better skies above. At first he loafed along. Then as the sun came up he began to scan the air for possible ambush. This was living, this was sport, adventure. He reached forward and opened up the throttle of the engine. Now he was flying wide open. He was getting all the ship had. Out of sheer joy he rocked his wings, saluting some invisible foe. Suddenly he hit a down draft. A bump, by God! Well, he'd show them! He brought up with a smack, still grinning, and then fought his way up again. Plenty of lift to this ship. Plenty of everything. God, it was good to be up there. Let the Huns come!

He ducked deeper into the cockpit, away from the fury of the wind, and pulled up the nose of the plane. It slid up and up. The sky above him was a brass bowl, and he was flying the rim of that bowl. He had no helmet, and the wind tore at his blond hair, gleaming in the sun. Up and up to the rim of the world.

Now he was free. Those poor devils far below in the

trenches, what could they know of this freedom? Down in the mud and dirt, with the guns booming and the rats crawling about them. For sheer joy in this new freedom he put the ship into a roll. Ah, this was flying, flying indeed; for now he had no ship. He was in the air, and small clouds like angels—

He never knew that he had fallen . . . .

For weeks Beverly lay in her bed, a thin white figure with enormous eyes and hands which seemed to have lost their clutch on life. Chris, sitting beside her, was frightened at times. She seemed to be slipping away from the sheer burden of living. He would stay there in the darkened room, knowing that his being there gave her support, but groping for words of comfort which she seemed hardly to hear.

"I did it, Chris. If I had cared more—"

"You did all any woman could do."

"I can see him all the time. I can shut my eyes and see him."

"Try not to see him, my dear. That can't hurt him now."

"But he loved to live, Chris. He loved life. He didn't want to go."

"Listen, dear. Either he is asleep, and God knows we all want to sleep, or he is busy and happy somewhere else. It's one thing or the other, darling."

He never touched her, save now and then to stroke those lifeless hands of hers. Sometimes she seemed not to know that he was there. When he moved to go however she would look up at him.

"Can't you stay a little longer? I don't want to be alone."

He would sit down again, aware of his work, of waiting cases, of office hours, of the thousand and one things which were the agenda of his day. But he would stay as long as he dared.

"Are you there, Chris?"

"I'm here. Try to sleep, won't you?"

One day however he told her that she ought to rouse herself, even to see people, and she obeyed like a child. After that she would sit up in her bed in her flower-bedecked room and see her visitors: the decorous women who had been her mother's friends, the younger ones who had been her own.

"Bev darling, is there anything I can do?"

"I'll be all right. I just need time."

There was a gulf between them, the gulf of her own tragic life and their contented complacence. They talked of their babies, their houses, their clothes; and while she listened she could hear the empty house around her, filled only with her ghosts. They would be quiet, those ghosts, until she was alone again. Then they would come in through the door and stand around her.

On the first day she left her bed she made her pitiful journey through the closed door into Jerry's room. It was as he had left it, his clothes—his innumerable clothes—hanging in his closets, his collars and shirts in the drawers. They were gay and handsome, those possessions of his. What did it matter now that he had not loved her? She had meant something to him. And toward the end he had tried. Poor Jerry. Poor dead Jerry.

In an upper drawer she found those bronze wings of his which he had worn like a flag through the war. They were in a small satin-lined box and she stood with it in her hand, staring down at them. Why try to measure him by other men's standards? He had been as gay and irresponsible as the birds outside, and she had tried to hold him down.

"I never meant to, Jerry," she said softly. "Maybe you know that now."

It was some time after that day that she asked Chris about Jerry's child.

"I am alone now," she said, "and if I could have this boy—"

"That's morbid," he told her sternly. "The boy is fine and well cared for. Loved, too. Let him alone, my dear."

That was the last day he came. She was well now, he told her, and didn't need a doctor.

"Besides," he said, smiling down at her, "it is getting to be a habit. And all habits are bad."

She let him go without a protest, but for a moment she held his big hand between her two thin ones.

"I'll miss you, Chris. You know that."

"Yes, I know that."

When he left he stooped and kissed her lightly on the forehead. "That's for being a brave girl," he told her, and went rather dizzily out into the sunshine.

CHAPTER XL

THE city had changed. If the war and the postwar deflation had reduced and even lost some fortunes, it had made many new ones. The result was a new social order which discarded the old and set up its own standards, particularly of pleasure. The days were too short for its spending, its gaiety and extravagance, and so it extended them into the night.

In this new and rather mixed realm Katie was highly popular. No hour was too late for her to dance, no extravagance too much if it suited her mood. She made and kept her place by sheer vitality, and Chris watching her sometimes marveled at her endurance. The telephone rang constantly. She kept a page-calendar and a pencil on her untidy bedside table, and scrawled on it this appointment and that until it was full.

Chris saw little of her in those early days of the jazz age. She spent hours in beauty parlors, and other hours in arranging parties and what not. In the evenings she would saunter downstairs, short skirts over legs she was trying now to reduce, short hair carefully cut and waved, breasts flattened to conform to the new boyish figure, and glance in at him in the office.

"Don't expect me until you see me," she would say, and wave him a casual good-by.

As times improved the pace, if possible, increased. There were days when he never saw her at all, save for his morning visit to her in bed in that back room before he went out. He still punctiliously saw her then, however, standing tall above her bed and looking down at her with noncommittal eyes.

"Busy all day, I suppose."

"Rushed to death."

She looked badly in the morning, before she made up her

face for the day. Much of her early prettiness had gone, and she had the faded look of Lily when he first knew her. She was tired, he saw, and more as doctor than as husband he remonstrated with her now and then.

"You'd better rest up a day or two, my dear. You look tired."

"Meaning I look like the devil," she would say, and snatch at her hand mirror.

By noon and especially by evening she would be herself again, gay and sparkling at some gathering or other, dancing in her high heels, showing more of herself than she sometimes knew in her abbreviated and décolleté dresses. She drank very little but she smoked incessantly, and one night Chris, smelling something burning, went into her room to find her asleep and a deep hole burned in her mattress.

Nevertheless she was making her way socially. The new society asked only to be amused, to go places and do things, and she was always ready to do either. But she was ambitious to go still further. One day, a year after Jerry's death, she came to tell him that Janet Grant was putting her house on the market, and suggested that they buy it.

"It's cheap," she said, "and you ought to put up some sort of front, Chris. Nothing succeeds like success."

"Nothing succeeds like good hard work. And I've got the downtown office. It's all I can carry."

She persisted, and one day he found himself and Katie in the house, with Janet showing them around and Grant's ghost at his elbow.

"It's well built," Janet was saying in her flat voice. "We put a lot of money in it. More than we should, I suppose. Here is the drawing room."

Katie was enchanted. Before they left she was planning the rooms, seeing herself coming down the wide staircase, giving dinners, giving parties. She sailed gaily through the house, leaving a trail of cigarette ashes behind her but looking younger and happier than she had for a long time. It held no ghost for

Katie, that house. But in the car going home that day Chris flatly refused to buy it. "I can't afford it," he said. "And besides, it killed Grant, that house. He worked himself to death to keep it up."

"That's idiotic, Chris. Anyhow, it won't cost you so much as it did him. And I'll save in other ways. You needn't smile. I *can* save."

He held out for three months, with Katie alternately sulking and cajoling. Then one day out of sheer desperation he went to the bank, drew out his entire balance, and signed the necessary papers.

"Very good investment you've made, doctor," said the agent when it was all completed. "Doctor Grant was very proud of that house."

"Well, I'm not," said Chris morosely. "I'm being a damn fool, and I know it."

He was sure of it within the next few weeks. By the time they had moved in and Katie had done it over, he was obliged to borrow money. For weeks and months decorators were busy. He seemed never to move without coming on a plumber, busy over some mysterious job of his own, or a painter. Katie, lying in her bed, would be almost completely obscured by blueprints, by samples of silk and chintz, by drawings of this and that.

It was only by main force that he kept her out of Grant's old offices and installed there the shabby but substantial furniture from the old house.

"But I can't bear it," said Katie, almost in tears. "It spoils everything."

"I have to draw the line somewhere, my dear. We've spent too much already. Besides, I like my things. I've had them for a long time."

She surrendered finally, but she managed to install their new carpets and curtains, and one day he came home to find a man busy doing over his old desk. He stood looking grimly down at it, remembering the grime which once had covered it, seeing Lily flicking at it with a feather duster, recalling Annie Lewis sitting across it and looking at him with her handsome haggard face, seeing Beverly standing beyond it:

"Your work will always come first, won't it? Before me. Before everything else."

"No, by God. But it's got its place."

The workman looked up.

"Pretty good desk, doctor. Just needs a little going over."

"Yes," he said, absently. "It's seen a lot of history, that desk."

"Antique, is it?"

"You might call it that."

He was working feverishly now. Sometimes he did half a dozen operations in a morning, emerging from the operating room exhausted. Now and then he would fall asleep in his chair, or beside some bed. Once he even dozed in the car while he was driving himself, and narrowly escaped an accident. He needed money constantly, although he was earning considerable amounts; and that next spring he raised his prices in a desperate attempt to get even with the game.

He sat for some time with the bills before him, shut in the inner room of his downtown suite while his secretary waited outside to mail them. He hesitated about letting them go. All very well to say that he had spent the best years of his life learning to do the work he was charging for; all very well to know that he served the poor slavishly for nothing, and had limited his increased charges to those able to pay them. Deep down in his heart Chris knew that day that he was making others pay his price for peace, and that an ambitious and self-indulgent woman might give him that peace.

Nevertheless he sent them out, driving home afterwards to that house of Grant's where by some subtle metonymy he sometimes felt that he was Grant himself; looking about him, trying to orient himself, wakening in the mornings to look for his old familiar surroundings and not finding them, shaving in Grant's elaborate bathroom to see the lines deeper from his nose to the corners of his mouth, and then going doggedly about his work, the old round of office hours, calls, laboratory, hospital. But some of the spirit had gone out of him.

Scott spoke to him one day about it, a Scott with one arm but two clear-seeing eyes.

"What's wrong, Chris?"

"Wrong? Nothing that I know of. Of course a specialty is the devil. Fellow loses touch with his people. I used to know them and they knew me. Now they know about me. That's different."

"Like a watchmaker, eh? Take them apart to see why they don't tick, put them together and send them out again! Well, that's the job, isn't it?"

"I miss the other, that's all."

He was almost stunned one day about that time to hear that Beverly had taken over his old house. If she was never out of his mind she was seldom consciously in it. He was too busy, too tired. Now Katie told him, watching his face.

"Your old love has taken the house, Chris. Did you know it?"

"What house?"

"Our house."

"I hadn't heard. No."

So she was there, alone in that house they had hoped to share. Life had done that to her and to him. It was Beverly now who would go up and down the familiar stairs, Beverly who would listen to the creakings of the old floors, Beverly who would sleep there. Not a thought; a picture. Katie, watching him, was rather disappointed.

"I wish her joy of it," she said. "If ever I was glad to get out of a place—"

She was not malicious, however, and her old jealousy of Beverly had died with her increasing indifference to Chris. For a few weeks after Jerry's death she had been watchful, even uneasy. Then nothing happening she had gone back to this new and enthralling life of hers and dismissed the whole matter from her mind. Chris could not dismiss this news about Beverly, and after a month of indecision he went to the house, ringing the bell where just above he had once proudly stood by while the small brass plate was going up, stepping into the hall when Holmes opened the door and once more seeing Lily there, and Henry, and an odd little slattern of a girl called Katie. He drew a long breath. Strange to feel more at home here than in Grant's house. Strange to feel that after a long absence he was coming home.

There was nothing of this in his face as he gave Holmes his hat and stood gazing about him.

"Changed it quite a lot, haven't you, Holmes?"

"Well, there's the paint and paper, sir. And of course the furniture—"

The old offices were still there, but the double doors had become an arch between them. The rooms themselves were gay with chintz, and Beverly's grand piano sat in the back room where his desk had been. The washstand had gone, there were old mirrors over the mantels, a few of the smaller pictures from the big house hung on the walls, and here and there were flowers. But they were the same rooms, for all that. On the marble mantel in the back office was the scar he had left from a forgotten cigarette. He was standing eying it when Beverly came in, holding out her hand, determinedly smiling; as though this were not incredible, as though this could be happening at all.

"Well, Chris," she said, "and what do you think of your house?"

"Why did you do it? Why did you come here, Beverly?"

She hesitated. Then she looked at him with her direct gaze.

"Haven't I a right to something, Chris?" And then, seeing his face: "I had to leave the other house, you know. They were getting ready to build."

She sat down, but Chris did not sit. He lighted a cigarette and took a turn or two about the room. Here by the register

Caesar had lain on cold nights, or had waited for the sound of his key in the door. Then he had been killed, and Chris had followed the car and beaten up the man who did it. The man had sat on the floor and stared at him. "Where'd you pack that wallop?" he had said. Caesar.

"I have a dog buried in the yard," he said abruptly. "I'd be glad to think—"

'I shall not disturb him, Chris."

"There was a tree there then. It's gone now. Anyhow that's where he's buried."

"I remember the tree. The tree of heaven, Chris."

Suddenly he threw away his cigarette and faced her.

"Why didn't you tell me, Beverly? After all, to come here—it's no escape. If you want to get clear away from everything—"

"Perhaps I don't want to. After all, Chris, haven't I a right at least to my memories? They hurt nobody. Even Jerry."

It was dangerous. Too dangerous. He brought himself up with a jerk, and his next words were carefully casual.

"Of course you have, my dear. So have I. And now—how are you?"

"Quite all right, or as right as I can be. I am not like you, Chris. I make no contribution to the world. Why shouldn't I be right?"

He stayed for a while after that, but the talk was careful surface talk. Was he busy? And didn't he need a holiday? When had he taken a real rest? And how did it feel to be growing famous? He answered, but the constraint was there, heavy between them, like a wall. Here in that room they had met for the first time, here they had quarreled and separated, each to go his different way. Now they were not children playing with romance, but a man and a woman, their lives fixed. It was not until he rose to go that he surprised an odd look in her eyes, as though she wanted to break through his defense and did not dare to.

"It is queer, seeing you here like this," she said.

"Perhaps I shouldn't have come."

She was on guard again instantly. "Why not," she asked. "Surely I may see my old friends. I need them."

She was smiling, and when at last Holmes let him out he went away with a feeling of finality and loss. She was living in his house, but she had taken herself out of his life as carefully and as painlessly as she could. Driving away he knew that the last page of that book of the past had been closed. But alone in that back room Beverly was standing in front of the old marble mantel, staring blankly at the brown scar on it. After a long time Holmes heard her going up to her room, and the quiet closing of her door.

CHAPTER XLI

IT was that year that Chris undertook the education of Ursula's boy, now a tall handsome lad of twelve. Things had not gone too well with Hiram following the war, and Chris spent a week end with him and Amy. Young Noel took to Chris at once.

"I've got a puppy in the barn."

"Fine. Let's go and see it."

It was in the barn that Noel, sitting on the floor with the puppy in his lap, looked up at Chris and said shyly:

"You're a doctor, aren't you?"

"I'm a surgeon. That's a sort of doctor."

"I'd like to be one, like my grandfather."

Chris leaned down and picking up a rather grubby hand, examined it carefully.

"Look like good hands," he said. "Maybe you'll make a surgeon some day, and when I get old you can help me. How about it?"

The boy flushed with pleasure, and Chris himself felt happier on his way home after the visit; he had someone to watch now, someone to train and care for, and eventually to carry on for him. After that he wrote to Noel regularly, and that fall he spoke to Katie about having the boy there that winter and sending him to a good school. Hiram and Amy were worried about his education. Katie however was not interested.

"Don't be ridiculous," she said. "If they chose to adopt the boy, that's their business."

"We have plenty of room here. He could spend the winters in town and go to school. He's old enough to look after himself. Just food and shelter—and we have more than we need of both."

"I think you're crazy, Chris Arden," she said flatly. "If you think I'm going to take on anybody's illegitimate child, you can think again."

He tried further, arguing patiently; but she only grew shrill and resentful, and at last he left her on the verge of tears. It was the first of many such scenes, for Chris found that he wanted the boy badly, wanted some young life to whistle and play about the house, something to come back to after the day's work. Not that the house was quiet, even now. There were times when he felt that he was running a hotel. He would come home at night to find the rugs turned and people dancing, and even once or twice to turn on the lights in his office to find some amorous couple snugly settled there. Sometimes they did not even know him, for Katie's tastes were young and catholic.

"Say, what's the idea?"

"Unfortunately I belong here, and I need this room."

"Jeez! It's the doctor!"

New words in common use, new bad and casual manners, new drinks, new dances. He did not belong among any of them. Nor, he came to see, would young Noel belong there either.

"I would like to have the boy here," he wrote to Hiram, "and to see that he got his winter schooling at least. Then you and Amy could have him during vacations and the summer. But for a number of reasons this is not feasible, and so I make an alternative proposition which I hope you will consider."

The alternative proposition was that they accept an annual sum from him until times were better, and find a good preparatory school not too far from them. "As you know, almost all I have and am is due to your mother's legacy, and I should like to feel that young Noel will carry on as she enabled me to do."

He sat for a long time over the letter however before he sent it. The idea of youth in his house died hard; and young Noel, if he studied medicine, would start in where he left off.

Medicine was moving on, working hand in hand with science. Even his own case records now were a combination of X-ray plates, laboratory reports, electrocardiograms. Outside of accident men were living longer. Preventive medicine was taking the place of drugs, and over in the Lewis laboratory Dickinson was working hard on cancer. Down in the basement were his carefully tended mice, his guinea pigs, chickens and rabbits. Above were his laboratories, his microscopes, centrifuges, sterilizers, his long rows of tubes, his glass retorts, his staff of enthusiastic assistants.

He had a god of sorts now; a sandy-haired young scientist at the Rockefeller Institute.

"He's on the right track," he would say. "He'll get it some day."

And when years later Doctor Murphy made his announcement of the control of cancer in mice by placenta extract, Dickinson was as proud as though he had done it himself.

"Always said he'd do it," he would say. "He'll do it in people too. Watch him!"

It was indeed a new world, of group clinics, of painless childbirth, of arrested tuberculosis, even of arrested age; the Steinach operation on elderly men, and Barrett now besieged by middle-aged women asking him to attempt painless rejuvenation under the X-ray. Going in hopefully to lie down on his table, to receive the treatment; hearing as they lay there the pressing of a switch and the low humming of the machine, and then going home, slightly nauseated perhaps, to watch in their mirrors for a change, for youth again.

A strange world of all sorts when young Noel came into it, if he did.

By early spring of the following year Chris had been in practice fourteen years, and he had gone far in that time. It was a long cry back to the early days with the sample men leaving their laxatives and baby foods. Now when they came they brought the hypnotics and sedatives required by the jazz period; and the baby foods and laxatives had gone into the magazines and were soon to take to the air. Chris too had changed. He was a conservative now in surgery, as opposed to his early more reckless days; a man to be counted on. If he had lost his close touch with his patients, if they had ceased to interest him as human beings, at least he gave them the best he had. Now and then he was obliged to undo the work of other men and occasionally his gorge rose at some butchery or other. He was perhaps too outspoken at such times for general popularity in his profession, but he was now recognized as a sound man.

And by summer of that year he knew that he was a tired man and a defeated one.

He carried on as best he could. The house was cool and with Katie gone on a round of house parties, was quiet. He was not busy, but cases came and went. At night sometimes he and Ted would get into the car and drive aimlessly about, talking or being still, content man-fashion once more to be together. But Ted felt tension under Chris's frequent silences, and began once more to worry about him.

"How long since you've had a vacation?"

"I don't know. Not since the war."

"If you call that a vacation!"

But Chris was stubborn. He did not mention Katie's bills or the cost of the new house, but Ted required no telling. In the end he gave up the attempt to get him away. Only once in those hot months did Chris mention Katie at all, and then only by indirection.

"The trouble with all of us," he said, apropos of something or other, "is that we can't divide our lives like other men, so much work and so much play. We can't even divide our minds. It's a rotten break for the people who have to live with us."

"It's a damned good break for the other people!" said Ted truculently.

Chris was worried about money that summer. As usual, collections were bad during those months, and the expenses of the house and the downtown offices continued. He began to be irritable in the operating room. The heat was terrific there, and under his long wrinkled linen coat and his mask he would be covered with hot sweat. Sometimes he felt as though a tight band were fastened around his head, and one day he threw a dull pair of scissors scross the room.

"Good God!" he shouted. "I don't ask much, but I do ask for proper instruments."

He was becoming taciturn too. He would walk doggedly along the halls, an uneasy intern beside him, saying little or nothing. Then, his rounds over, he would go out and into his car, step savagely on the gas and get away, to make his few calls and then to go back to the empty house which still somehow belonged to Grant—and of course to Katie—and to sit for long hours at his desk. More than once he fell asleep there, to waken perhaps on toward morning and to go heavily up to his bed.

Now and then he had a letter from Katie: "Dear Chris, This is a lovely house and I am having a wonderful time. Not much sleep but plenty of everything else. Dozens of servants, and a perfectly sweet beach. But I've lost a lot of money at bridge, so I'd better have some."

He answered them meticulously, sending the money, saying nothing of the heat or his own fatigue; sitting sometimes for a long time before he could think of anything to say at all. And Katie, receiving these replies of his, looked first for the check and then read the letter. "My poor old Chris," she would say, to some idle man at hand. "When I think of him in the heat—."

"That's what you get for marrying a doctor."

"He likes it. He won't even take a vacation."

"Well, that's all right by me. How about a little seawater? Or don't you want to get wet?"

She was very happy that summer, living luxuriously, lying for hours like a contented kitten on this beach or that, playing bridge, dancing, not eating. It was the mode to be slim, and even under her new one-piece bathing suit she wore a bandage to flatten her breasts. In the mornings she rolled on the floor to reduce her hips, and she was always hungry. But she was happy. At the end of her visit she would pack her innumerable scanty garments in suitcases, leave extravagant largess for the servants, get into her car and move on.

"Good-by, I've had a lovely time."

"Good-by, come back next year."

One day there was an accident at one of the houses. One of the men took a cramp in the water and was drowned. They recovered the body, but all day the house party sat about, shocked and decorously grieving. That night Katie got up resolutely and turned on the radio.

"We can't help poor Harry by acting like this," she said. "Let's pull down the shades and dance."

They did dance, relieved, the tension broken. After all Harry was gone, but they were still there.

"Good girl, Katie. I was about to locate a good sharp razor and cut my throat."

"Let go of Katie, old man, I'm cutting in." Brave Katie, practical sensible Katie. Why grieve over what is done and gone?

"Have a drink, somebody?"

"Scotch for me."

"Pretty good liquor. Comes right in from the boats. They land it up the river." "Yes, we have no bananas, we have no bananas today." A voice singing. The radio blatting, the bare shoulders and backs of the women, the crumpled collars of the men, and somewhere Harry, young and dead and already forgotten.

CHAPTER XLII

KATIE came home in the early fall, beautifully tanned and filled with enthusiasm for the summer and with plans for the winter. Chris, listening patiently, wondered at the breadth of the gulf between them. For days he heard of nothing but luxury, of easy living and hard playing; and one day he came home to find a butler installed, and to listen to Katie's vociferous explanations.

"He's as cheap as a parlor maid, Chris. And anyhow, with your success and everything—"

"What success? I'm spending more than I earn. If that's success—"

"You'd earn more if you charged more. Everybody says that."

"Everybody?"

She flushed. "Don't patronize me like that," she said. "You know what I mean. And if you are going to be superior—"

He listened to her. She was learning fast. Even her vocabulary was changing. And she was very pretty, now that she was slimmer; prettier than she had ever been. Strange that she held no attraction for him. Watching her as she moved about he wondered at the curious urge which drew some men and women together without their own volition, so that they would commit any indiscretion, almost any crime, to achieve union; and at that other repulsion, current or whatever it might be, which could separate two people so that they might live together in the same house and be as far apart as the poles.

As the days went on he wondered if the situation as it was was fair to her. There was nothing vicious about her. He never suspected her of actual unfaithfulness. Her high spirits flagged when he was about. Sometimes he even thought she was afraid of him.

He was still pondering that when one day she came into the office on some errand or other. She was planning a big party for the early winter, and he suggested that she ask some of the hospital staff and their wives.

"Doctors?" she had said blankly.

"It is still considered an honorable profession."

"I know all that. But they won't mix with this crowd, Chris."

"Why not? And they are my friends. After all, I suppose I am giving this party too."

"Good heavens, Chris, if you are going to step in and spoil things— A party isn't just a party. You have to get people together who know each other."

It was an old difference between them. Katie, never forgiving the hospital and refusing to entertain its staff, and Chris, whose friends and supporters were there. In the end he won, however, and Katie went off to prepare her revised lists. Not however before she had fired a broadside at him.

"I've had to make my own life and my own friends," she told him. "I've never meant anything to you. I used to care, care terribly; but you never did. You've never cared for anything but your work and yourself. Don't blame me, Chris. Blame yourself for once."

She gave her party that fall, and Ted Lawrence, wandering in late, found her gay and triumphant in the midst of it.

"Got about everybody in town here, haven't you?" he shouted above the noise of the orchestra.

"Everybody who is anybody!"

"Good for you. Where's Chris?"

"Why bring that up!" she said. "Where is Chris at any party?"

"Beat it, eh?"

Chris however had not beat it. Ted found him soon after

that shut in his back office, his empty pipe in his mouth and his eyes gazing at nothing. He started when the door opened.

"Come in, Ted. I've run away from that infernal din. It drives me crazy."

"Why not go up to bed?" said Ted prosaically. "Most of this crowd won't know whether you're here or not."

"I can't. I have a call or two to make later."

Ted examined him critically. Chris was pale and the hands which held his pipe were unsteady.

"You can damn well go to bed or break up. That's about where you are."

"Nonsense. I'm all right."

But he was not all right. He was dizzy when he got to his feet, and had to put out a hand to steady himself.

"I've no business touching champagne," he said, and grinned. Ted pushed him back into his chair.

"Listen to me," he said. "You're on the verge of a break-up, my lad. What you need is a doctor! Take a bromide and go to sleep. I'll make your calls tonight. Give me the list."

Chris shook his head.

"I want to get out into the air. Anywhere but here."

Ted left him there finally, and Chris sat alone at his desk. Through the closed door he could hear the sound of the jazz band, of voices raised above the din, of loud laughter. This was the life, they seemed to say; the one life one was sure of. Eat and drink and dance. You'll be a long time dead. He stirred uneasily. The beat of the music and of dancing was in his ears, in his brain. One worked to the limit, day and night, so that this might happen. So that people one had never seen before and would never see again might play at your expense, get drunk, flirt, grow amorous in dark corners. What was that thing in the oath he had taken? Old Hippocrates and his oath: "With purity and with holiness I will practice my art." Purity and holiness!

A girl opened the door of the office, smiling back at the man behind her, but when she saw Chris she closed it again quickly. He got up then, still steadying himself by the desk, his face gray above his evening clothes, his eyes hot and scornful. A moment later he was in the wide hall, shouldering his way through the crowd. Outside he stood for a moment looking up at the sky and drawing in great breaths of the clean night air. The chauffeur was on duty in the driveway, and Chris turned abruptly and went back to the garage where Katie's new limousine stood beside his own car. The dizziness had passed by that time, but the hot contempt for himself still blazed in his eyes. He backed his car out, turned and drove away. The driveway was lined with cars, and he was obliged to go carefully. At the gate he turned and looked back at the house, blazing with lights, but even there the music followed him, and he stepped suddenly on the gas and shot along the darkened streets.

Once away from the din however he moved more slowly. His eyes were burning in his head, his mouth hard as he set about that strange hegira that night, gathering together his memories and his past. He drove deliberately now, passing this district or that, seeing familiar houses and collecting those old cases of his like beads on a rosary. Here he had failed, here he had succeeded. Before the Jamieson house he came to a full stop. He met Henry now and then, a thin and discouraged man who looked away quickly when he saw him. Some of that old pain came back as he sat there. Not gods, but men. Perhaps Grant had been right; but now Grant was gone, and Katie was giving a party in his house.

He reached the mill district at last. The furnaces were going again, and the blasts were close at hand; a dull roaring, blue and yellow flames, the figures of men moving about like pigmies, and then darkness and the figures gone, blotted out as by some monstrous death. Here too the houses were familiar, more beads to that rosary of his. In one of them he had found the dead woman one night, and her drunken husband on the bed with his throat cut.

The district had changed since the early days. There were

playgrounds for children here and there. District nurses visited the sick. The water supply was carefully watched, and now in hot weather the fire department turned on the hydrants and children splashed in the water. Perhaps after all the world was growing better. He didn't know.

He moved on to the river. There was Joshua's old shanty boat, moored to the wharf. Joshua in his white robe waiting for the coming of his Lord, and the crowd jeering. Katie jeering. Now Joshua was in an asylum somewhere and Katie was giving a party and the boat was dark. Or was it dark? Wasn't there a light in it?

He got out of his car and walked down over the cobblestones to the gangplank. There was a light inside and a voice speaking, a familiar voice, aged and supplicating. "Lord, remember me when Thou comest into Thy kingdom," it said. It was Joshua again.

Chris went on board and ducked down into the low cabin. There was a candle burning there, but the room was cold and filled with the dank smell of the river; and old Joshua, clad in his white robe, was lying on the bunk. How he had got there Chris did not know, but that he was dying he saw at a glance.

He stooped down and caught the failing pulse under his fingers, and Joshua opened his eyes and looked up at him, his faded eyes filled with joy and wonder.

"I was waiting," he said quite simply. "I knew that You would come, Lord."

He closed his eyes again, and Chris realized with a shock that he was dead.

For a long time Chris sat by the bunk, with the candle burning low and Joshua beside him. His anger was gone. What did life matter as compared with the great adventure of death? His anger was gone, and his resentment. Let Katie live. Let her live and be happy. Perhaps there was a pattern somewhere, and she was a part of it.

It was two o'clock in the morning when he reached the hospital, but the staff was accustomed to his eccentric hours.

He notified the authorities by telephone of Joshua's death, and then went upstairs, making his rounds much as if the hour were usual, going into quiet rooms, speaking to the nurses, leaving this order and that. Rows of flower vases outside the private rooms, here and there a red light over a door, the desk and some weary woman in uniform sitting over her records and rising at his approach, far away a child crying—what did those people at the house know or care of this other night life, of darkness instead of blazing light, of a crying child against the blare of jazz, and where pain and not pleasure was king?

If they knew perhaps they would care, but they did not know.

Before he left he went in to see Bessie Smith, shot in a drunken brawl and now slowly dying. There had been a time when he could have fought for her; when he might have held back the shadows to their corners by sheer will power, given her something perhaps which was more than relief. But he had lost that power now. When she roused and looked at him she knew it as well as he did.

"All over but the shouting, doctor," she said weakly.

"We're not through fighting yet, Bessie."

She was dull with morphia, and he thought she slept again, but she opened her eyes once more.

"That girl," she said. "Years ago. You came to me to find her. Do you remember?"

"Yes, I remember, Bessie."

"And—she's all right?"

"She's all right now, Bessie," he said steadily, and sat by her until she slept.

He was very tired as he turned toward home. It was still dark, and the streets were quiet save for the occasional slow hoof-beats of a horse drawing a milk wagon. Just outside of his driveway he ran over a cat, and drew up to see if it was dead. He had not killed it, however. It lay in the gutter, spitting and crying, and at last he picked it up and wrapping it in a rug, placed it carefully in the back of the car. At the house the music had gone, but the phonograph had replaced it, and the party if smaller seemed even noisier than ever. He slipped in by a side entrance, carrying his burden, and got to his office without being seen. . . .

Long after sunrise Katie, opening the door, found him there with his head on his desk. There was a can of ether beside him, and on the floor, on a stained automobile rug, lay the body of a dead cat. The sight exasperated her.

"So that's what you've been doing!" she said indignantly. "I put you on the map socially in this town, and then you run out on me. As for that cat—"

He roused and yawned.

"Is that so important, my dear? Being on the social map?"

"It's brought you a lot of work."

"I had an idea that I got the work because I was a fair-to-middling surgeon," he said, and seemed drowsily to remember having said something like that before, a long time ago.

The cat had scratched him, and a day or two later he developed a mild infection in a finger of his right hand. It amounted to little, but it brought home to him the value of that right hand of his. On it he had built his life, such as it was, and his work. If anything went wrong with it he was through. The beat and throb in it were like the beating and throbbing of his heart.

"You fuss a lot over that finger," Katie said.

"It's a bread-and-butter finger. Don't forget that."

He went back to work when it was healed. He had learned philosophy by that time. He could do his best and no more. When he lost a case he accepted the fact without his earlier shock and worry. Over the operating table, masked and gowned, he was coolly efficient, and as his reputation grew his revenues poured into the hospital, helping it to carry on. Burnett took him into the office one day and showed him some figures, and even Chris was surprised.

He was working on his nerves, and one day he told Dawson, the new hospital psychiatrist, that life was the cheapest thing in the world, and that he was sick of trying to save a lot of people who didn't deserve saving. Dawson eyed him sharply.

"What makes you say that?"

Chris grinned.

"It's true, isn't it? Not all of them, of course, but a good many. I fight like hell to send them back to their guzzling and their wenching, or whatever they call living; but I don't fool myself. I haven't added anything to the world."

"You're traveling on your nerves, Arden. How long do you expect to keep it up?"

"As long as I can earn money by it."

Dawson saw that something was wrong, but when he suggested that Chris come in and talk to him he merely laughed.

"And have you probing into my mental insides? No, thanks. I'm keeping my own secrets."

"Probably that's what's wrong with you."

Chris went on, still grinning.

CHAPTER XLIII

IT was not until the early spring of 1925 that he finally met catastrophe. To the eye he was much the same. He still retained his strong body, his heavy dark hair. He was, for all that bitter new philosophy of his, still gentle of hand and compassionate in his work.

"Just hold still. I'll be as easy as I can."

Now and then he went to some distant town or out into the country. If the case was urgent he took a plane, tucking in his instruments, climbing in himself. Once the plane had to make a forced landing at night in a field; he wakened the farmer, borrowed a car and went on, to operate and save his patient. It was all in the day's work. His reputation continued to grow, although it was still a local matter. He never joined the small group of nationally known surgeons, but within his orbit he was a definitely shining star.

He had very little personal life. Now and then he saw Bob Barrett at the house again, and wondered about Katie. It was ironic to think that she might possibly care for Barrett, now at forty developing a small neat paunch, and to realize that if she did care she had no intention of changing a life which she found satisfactory in most respects. It might be so, however. Once at that time after a serious difference over her extravagance he asked her if she wouldn't be happier with someone else, and she looked at him quickly, as though she were startled.

"Someone else? What do you mean by that?"

"I just asked, that's all. I'm not much to live with. If you'd be happier free—"

She moved uneasily.

"When I want to be free I'll come and tell you," she said and went away, leaving behind her the scent of expensive perfume and—of course—the bills piled high on Chris's desk.

He sat in his office chair for some time after she had gone. What was she, he wondered, behind that masked face and small tight mouth? Had he ever known her? What went on, day after day, in that head of hers, with its carefully marcelled hair? She was not even Katie. She was a strange young woman with plucked eyebrows and a face skillfully made up to hide the ravages of late hours.

What was she? She was generous enough to her friends, as the bills before him testified. On occasion she went to church, because the best people did so. She gave perfect dinners and fasted for a day or two afterwards to keep down her weight. She made him physically comfortable, after her own fashion. But where was she in all this? What did she lack, that he could study her in this manner, under a sort of mental microscope? Tenderness, perhaps; the deep compassion that women should have.

Some time later he heard the butler closing the front door and the purr of her limousine as it drove away. He roused then and began to read the bills: "To James Carter, caterer, four quarts of Maryland terrapin, thirty-six dollars."

He held it up and looked at it. He had overheard her telling someone that their cook did the terrapin. Why say it if it wasn't so? He put it down and ran rapidly through the others; clothes, house bills, a jeweler's account, a new radio. It was all there in front of him, the absurd travesty of their life together; and it was for this that he was selling his professional soul. . . .

Up on the hill the hospital was rising to completion. It covered all the acres of the old Lewis property, an imposing structure which seemed to dominate the city, and now and then Chris saw Beverly there. She seemed a small lost figure, still valiant but rather silent. Once he found her there, standing among the bricks and mortar with a garden flower in her hand.

He saw tears in her eyes; but she turned away and he passed on awkwardly.

One day the new buildings were ready. If the staff felt a vague disloyalty in abandoning the old structure they said little about it. Time moved on. There were new ideas in hospitalization, some of them learned from the war. If Miss Clarke, efficiently preparing for the moving, went back to those shabby rooms of Miss Simpson's and wept over her packing, who was she to stand in the way of progress?

"Twenty years," she thought. "Twenty years I've been here." And going to the mirror over the mantel tried to see in it the girl who had come there so long ago to be interviewed in that very room. She could hear Miss Nettie's voice:

"The work is hard and exacting, Miss Clarke. We can afford no mistakes."

Well, she had made her mistakes, but on the whole she had done well. She had every reason to be satisfied. She put her head down on the mantel and cried the hard burning tears of empty middle age.

Scott too was moving, watching his files, his plates; his empty sleeve slipping out of his pocket, doing the work of two hands with one. Once he came across his old glass aquaria and stood looking at them. He had no time for fish now, but he remembered Chris Arden looking at them one day; and that he had shown Chris a small burn on his finger, and had said that his wife had wanted another child. They had never had the child, of course. He had sacrificed his manhood to his work, but the work had saved many lives. There was a law of compensation somewhere, he supposed, and now with his new equipment— He brightened and went whistling about his preparations for the move.

The break was not easy for any of those who had built their lives around the old structure. This hospital had been theirs. The new one would be Staunton Lewis's. It was as though he had reached out from that mausoleum where he lay to make a final arrogant gesture. "Take this," he seemed to say.

"I give it to you. I, Staunton Lewis. Forget the old things and go on to the new. Forget the Christmas mornings in the chapel, and the old horse-drawn ambulance; forget Bergman and Nettie Simpson and old Joe and all the others. It is no good to remember; but always you will remember me."

On the night before the formal opening of the new hospital there was an informal meeting of those who had served the old one. Most of them were elderly, stooped with service. They sat around the familiar rooms, now worn like themselves with years of service, and were conscious of a sense of disloyalty. Tomorrow and for all the tomorrows they would be abandoned, these rooms. They would stand stark and empty. Then some day the wreckers would come and destroy them. Piece by piece they would wrench them apart, and with them would go a part of their lives which they could never relive.

They made little speeches, these older men, or tried to. "When I first came here forty years ago—" Their voices would thicken, their throats contract. They would mumble something further and sit down; for the passing of the hospital marked the passing of their youth, the passing even of their maturity. Now only age lay ahead, and they were too old for new things.

Chris, listening, was moved and resentful. What right had Staunton Lewis to reach out after he was gone to uproot these men, too late for transplanting? Why not let them alone for their remaining years? The buildings were old but adequate. They could have been replaced one by one, an easy transition, but he had chosen the grandiose gesture. Chris moved impatiently in his chair.

Late that night he found himself alone in the operating room. He switched on the lights and gazed about him. It was clean and in order, but already some of the equipment was gone, and it looked empty and deserted. The sight depressed him. In a way it had been the focal point of his life. Other men had homes, wives, children. He had had only this.

For fourteen years this had been the theater and he one of the actors. Now the curtain had fallen on it. That play was over, and tomorrow a new one would begin.

He was morosely unwilling to go home. Instead and still alone, he made his way through the hospital. The wards were sleeping, but in the children's ward a child was crying, and he went in, surprising a harassed night nurse.

"He's all right, doctor. But he's homesick. He's just come in."

"Let me have him," he said. "I'll look after him. It's time for your supper, isn't it?"

"I can't do that, doctor!"

"Run along," he told her, and picking up the boy he sat down in one of the low chairs. The child stopped crying, and Chris held him closely.

"It's all right, son," he said. "Go to sleep. It's all right."

The small body relaxed in his arms, and he sat there in the semidarkness, his long legs stretched out in front of him, the child sleeping with its head on his shoulder. So he should have sat, he thought, in some warm darkness of his own, holding his own child. But there was comfort in the contact of the small body, and after a time he too relaxed. It was as though they had each something to give the other, man and child; and that that something was escape from loneliness. He tightened his hold unconsciously.

When the nurse returned she found them both asleep, and took her story to the night supervisor.

"I don't know what to do," she said helplessly. "He made me go, and now—"

"Let him sleep. I expect he needs it."

Some time later she went back into the ward, but Chris had gone and the child lay quiet in his bed.

The new hospital was formally opened the next day. No patients had yet been moved, and the wards stood open and empty in their spotless newness, the private rooms gay with chintz and flowers. By Lewis's will the old house was the nucleus, the core around which the great buildings had been erected, and it was in the main hall there that Miss Nettie's plaque had been installed.

People stopped and looked at it.

"Look here, Bess. Who's this?"

"I haven't an idea. Come on."

The staff was there, such nurses as could be spared, the city fathers, even much of the city itself. News photographers were lining up people in what had been the drawing room, taking their pictures by flashlight. "Steady, please." A glare, a cloud of smoke and it was done. In the midst of the crowd Chris encountered Barney O'Neill and found him grinning.

"Got to hand it to the old man after all, haven't you?" he said. "He was little poison ivy to you once. Remember?"

"I guess I was pretty much poison ivy to all of you later."

"I'll tell the world you were!" He chuckled. "And that after Beverly getting you that job!" he said. "Sitting on my desk and coaxing it out of me! She was a great little girl. She still is a great little girl."

The crowd separated them then, and Chris moved on. People pointed him out, "That's Doctor Arden." His big figure towered above most of them, and he knew that he was conspicuous. They crowded around him, paying tribute, looking up at him, worshipping his success.

"Is *that* Doctor Arden? But how young he looks!"

"He's the coming man, my dear. Look at his hands. I say you can always tell a surgeon's hands."

Always afterward he remembered that voice, whispering behind him, and the half-amused pride with which he had heard it. His hands. The hands of a surgeon. He moved on; saw Katie, gay and laughing and surrounded by a small court, mostly men. She waved to him as he passed. He saw Beverly, looking tired but smiling. And here and there, quaint in old-fashioned hats and ancient cutaway coats, the men and women who for so long had carried the hospital through its years of struggle.

Their work was done now, and so they stood unnoticed in corners, tired with good works, no longer important and facing an empty future where they were no longer needed. It was ironic, Chris thought, that Staunton Lewis should even in death have dealt them this final blow. The Socialists were wrong. Something would go out of the world when men and women need no longer give of their efforts and their money to help others, and a beneficent state would do it for them.

It was late and most of the crowd had gone when at last Chris made his way upstairs to the Annie Lewis suite. Here, in this upper room with the bronze plate on the door, Annie Lewis had died. Now it was the Annie Lewis Memorial Suite, the bed indeed changed but the other furnishings as he remembered them; and Staunton Lewis's room next door, that room where once he had retired to his solitary nights, was now permanently attached to it as a sitting room.

"With such few changes as may be necessary, it is my desire that these two rooms be left as they now are, and that they be used as one, to be known as the Annie Lewis Memorial Suite."

Strange buried remorse in that, perhaps, some attempt at restitution; the door to be left open now, and the two rooms to be used as one. What had he felt, writing that—as he had written it—with his own small clerkly hand?

Chris moved over to the window and stood there. Far away was the river, sparkling in the sunlight. It was the river which had divided his life, he thought, as clearly as it divided its two banks. Its pollution had destroyed a part of him, as it had killed its other victims. It was changed now, harnessed, purified, but still it flowed on, an inevitable force, like the blood of a man, like life itself.

He was startled to find Beverly beside him.

"I followed you, Chris. Do you mind very much? This thing we've wished on you, I mean?"

"Mind? You've done a fine job, my dear. Why should I?"

"I don't know. I've wondered, that's all." She turned

and surveyed the room. "It seems odd, doesn't it," she said, "not to see mother's bed here? And to see father's room—"

"With the door open," he finished rather grimly. "Well, that's the way of life, isn't it? We close our doors, and then it's too late. Sorry, Beverly. I've had a hard day. I needn't have said that."

She did not answer him directly. She stood beside him, looking down over the city, and he saw that she looked thin and weary.

"So now it's done, and what am I to do, Chris?" she said. "This is over. It has been something to do, but what comes next? I am such a useless woman. There isn't any place in the world for useless women, is there?"

"Never useless, my darling," he said unsteadily. "Just to know that you are you, and somewhere near—"

"Don't, Chris."

"Why not?" he said roughly. "Isn't it at least time to speak the truth? I'm sick of camouflage. I've reached my limit."

"Please! You have your own life. You have your work—"

"My work," he said. "Yes, I've got my work, and by God that's all I have got. I'm a man like other men, and— Sorry, Beverly dear, I shouldn't have said that. And don't look like that. I'm all right. Don't worry about me."

Someone opened the door then, and glanced in.

"This was her room. Look, even her toilet things are still there."

"It's hardly decent, is it?"

It was Katie, showing a visitor around. She gave Chris a quick suspicious glance and closed the door.

An hour or so later he found her in the lower hall, flushed with anger, and tapping a high-heeled pump on the floor.

"Well, of all things!" she said shrilly. "Was this any time to hide away with Beverly Ames?"

"We were not hiding. That's absurd."

"No? Then what were you doing shut up with her in that room?"

He controlled his anger.

"If it were true would it really matter to you, Katie, one way or the other?" he asked quietly.

"I'm not going to be laughed at behind my back. That's flat."

"And that's all?"

"That's enough, isn't it?"

She was still angry when they got into her car and she put her foot on the gas. They shot down the driveway through the traffic and into the street, Katie blind to caution, blind to a policeman's signal, and finally and forever blind to Miss Andrews, desperately launching herself across the street at that signal.

Chris saw it coming and braced himself, for Katie did the only thing left to her to do. She twisted the wheel violently, there was a crash and the sound of breaking glass as they struck a street lamp, he saw Miss Andrews safe in the street and a white-faced Katie beside him, and then he felt a sharp pain in his right arm and saw blood pouring down from his sleeve.

He sat there dizzily, clutching at his arm.

"Chris, are you hurt?"

"Only my arm," he said. "Get my coat off. I've got to stop this bleeding."

With the aid of the policeman he did stop it, using his own handkerchief for a tourniquet. He even managed to walk back up the driveway again, the officer steadying him.

"You'll be all right, sir. Just lean on me."

"Damn it all, man, don't hold me. My legs aren't hurt."

"Well, you've had a shock, and you've lost a lot of blood. Knocked your head too. Just take it easy."

All perfectly reasonable. Calm and reasonable. Walk along. One step after another. What's a cut in the arm? Don't make a fool of yourself. Now the steps. By God, I can't make the steps. I'm like a scared kid. I can't make the steps.

"Sorry, officer, I'm afraid—"

They were the last words he spoke for several hours.

CHAPTER XLIV

HE became conscious again late that night, to find himself in a strange room and with a nurse sitting beside the bed. He did not move. He lay there, trying to orient himself. He knew the room, even in the half-light, but at first he could not place it. Then he recognized it. It was Annie Lewis's room. He stirred, and the nurse rustled to her feet.

"Are you comfortable, doctor?"

"I don't know. My head aches. What happened?"

"You've had a little accident. You're all right. If you'll try to sleep."

"My wife, is she all right?"

"Absolutely. She's just gone."

He said nothing. He looked down and saw his right arm, bandaged and lying on a pillow. She followed his eyes.

"What about this? What have I done to it?"

"Nothing much. A cut. It's been attended to. You'll be up and around in a day or so."

He hardly heard her. He knew hospital talk too well to take what she said at its face value. He knew the fixed professional smile of the nurse, too. He focussed his attention on the arm. It felt dead, dead and heavy. He tried to flex his fingers, but there was no response. Perhaps it was the bandage. But as he told himself that he felt a cold shiver of sheer horror. It was not the bandage. His mind was clear now, his keen professional mind. He knew what had happened to him; he had cut the musculo-spiral nerve, and only Providence could save him from a useless arm. In that case he was through. Almost before he began he was through.

"Get somebody in here," he said. "I want to know what's

happened. Go on," he said sharply, when she hesitated. "I don't care what time it is. I've got to know."

It was Ted Lawrence who came in, from a chair in the hall; a Ted suspiciously cheerful, standing by the bed and grinning down at him.

"Now will you take a vacation?" he demanded.

"What have I done to myself, Ted?"

"Got a cut and eleven stitches. That's all. And a nice neat job it is."

"I think you're a liar," he said. But he was faintly relieved. That cheerful face of Ted's—Good God, he couldn't smile like that if the trouble was serious.

"That's the truth, is it?"

"That's what they tell me."

He lay back and closed his eyes. The relief was almost more than he could bear.

"Where's Katie?"

"I took her home and gave her something to make her sleep. She's all cut up over this; no joking, Chris. Blaming herself all over the place, poor girl."

Some time later that night they gave Chris morphia. It stopped the pain, but it did not stop his mind from racing. It flung itself in wide and wider circles. It took in his whole life, his errors, his driving ambitions, his ceaseless work. And then it contracted, until his world became a pillow with his right arm on it, and a numbness which might yet be the final catastrophe.

He did not know the truth until the next day. Then something like a delegation filed in and examined him; but he did not need to be told what they found. It lay there on the pillow beside him. He lifted the arm himself and saw the characteristic wrist drop.

"A nerve suture!" he said bitterly. "And then how long, if ever? You fellows know what it means. What's the use of talking? I'm through."

They quoted cases to him, results, and he listened faintly

smiling. They were good fellows. They meant well. They stood over his bed, cheerful and hopeful, talking their jargon, making small jokes for his benefit. But he knew that when they went out it was to meet soberly elsewhere, their smiles gone, their acting over.

He was operated on a few days later. He had lost a good bit of blood, they said, and there was no hurry. But he was impatient, furious at the delay.

"I can't lie here," he said. "Get it over, or by the Lord Harry I'll go in and do it myself!"

So they operated, going in carefully, dissecting out the nerve ends and uniting them. After that he was again in his bed for a time, trying by sheer will power to force strength and motion into that right hand of his, and failing. It lay on its pillow in its cockup splint, still inert and unresponsive, and he would swear at it with despair in his heart.

"I'm through," he thought, day and night. "I'm through! I'm through."

He hardly saw Katie, sitting with unaccustomed patience by his bed; a Katie with swollen eyes which she tried to hide with powder. A Katie determinedly cheerful, coming in smiling, lugging in her boxes of flowers, bringing fruit, fresh eggs, small jars of broth. But a diffident Katie for all that, not coming too close, never offering to touch him. Standing a little way from the bed and playing up breathlessly.

"Been a good boy and eaten your spinach?"

He would try to answer her in kind.

"Absolutely. I'll soon have to be hoed and weeded."

When the nurse left the room however she had little to say. Her old chatter was gone. Caught off guard she looked frightened, but if he noticed it at all it was to think that her fear was for herself rather than for him. Lily's fear all over again, for her security. She would stay for an hour or two, then she would get up.

"I'd better go, Chris. I'll see you tomorrow."

"Right-o. Get out and get some air. I'm pretty poor company."

Once he wakened from a doze, however, to find her furtively wiping her eyes. He was astonished. He even made a move to put out that helpless right hand of his toward her.

"What is it, Katie?"

"You *will* be able to use it again, won't you?"

He looked at her. Did she care that she had destroyed him? Or was she merely anxious for her own safety, her own future?

"You mustn't blame yourself too much, my dear. We both contributed to what happened."

He smiled wryly.

"We'll get along somehow, you know," he added. "I can still practice medicine, if that's it. We may have to cut down, of course."

She got up.

"I suppose I deserve that," she said, and went quickly out of the room.

She was still Katie. Gradually her visits grew shorter, little by little she took up her old life again. She came in one day wearing a corsage of gardenias, and he guessed who had sent them. He was not greatly concerned. She would have to go down with him in the general wreckage, or ultimately she would leave him; and lying there in his bed it did not seem greatly to matter which she chose. He had no illusions. He was crippled, certainly for a long time and probably forever. All well enough to talk of another operation, another attempt to find and unite the nerve ends. Repair at best would be a matter of six months. It might be a year; it might be never.

He was sorry for Katie, even then. Lying there during the long days and endless nights, he knew that his failure to love her had lain behind all the other failures. She had given him her youth, her vitality and at one time at least her love; but he had not wanted any of them. Perhaps it was only fair that in the end she had destroyed him. For destroyed he was, in spite of all reassurances. Men did not drop out of his highly competitive world for a year and then come back easily. Too many others were waiting to take their places, and a surgeon's reputation was like a woman's—a word could destroy it.

Not once in that time did he see Beverly, but Ted came across her one night standing outside the gates and looking at the building. He came on her suddenly, and she made a swift movement to turn away. But he was too quick for her.

"Out for a walk, Mrs. Ames?"

"Yes. I often walk this way. It's habit, I suppose. After all—"

"Home's home, of course. Mind if I walk a bit with you? I've been sitting with Chris Arden, and my legs need stretching."

There was a pause as he fell into step beside her. Then she said, rather breathlessly: "How is he? How is he going to be, doctor?"

"Nobody knows. It's a matter of time at the best. At the worst—"

"I suppose there's nothing anyone can do."

"They'll have to operate again probably," Ted said carefully. "Just now he's pretty bleak. He'd put all his eggs in one basket, and it looks as though they were smashed."

She stopped and caught his arm.

"I can't bear it," she said suddenly. "I can't bear it. He had worked so hard, and he never did anyone any harm. He didn't deserve it."

Ted looked down at her. There had been times when he had hated her for Chris's past, but no one could hate her now, clutching at his arm for support, white-faced and shaken.

"No," he said gravely. "No, he didn't deserve it. He hasn't deserved a lot of the knocks he's had, Mrs. Ames. But then most of us don't. He was off to a bad start from the beginning. His wife's all right. No use blaming her for it. It could have happened to anybody. But of course—"

To his amazement she stopped dead and stared at him.

"*She* did it?" she asked. "She was driving the car?"

"That's what happened."

"My poor Chris," she said, as if she had forgotten that Ted was there. "My poor Chris. And I did this to you!"

She was silent on the way down the hill. Ted talked on comfortably, as though she had not spoken. Probably this second operation would do the job. Chris had been working too hard anyhow. Maybe the rest would be good for him. He'd needed a vacation for years, but they spent a good bit and he had had to earn it. It wasn't like owning a mill or a factory. A professional man was his own plant. "Get an attack of tonsillitis and the works close down!" But he did not think she was listening, and he was not surprised when at her door she stopped and spoke abruptly.

"You are very close to him, doctor. Tell me what I ought to do. I haven't even dared to see him. Yet we—"

He nodded.

"You are old friends. I know about it, Mrs. Ames."

"Then you know that I've ruined him," she said with bitter honesty. "I hadn't the courage to marry him, and I haven't had the courage since to let him go. Now I don't know what to do. Maybe if I go away for good it will help. I don't even know that."

"I rather think," he said, still carefully, "that he may like to know that you are somewhere around. Even if you don't see him—"

"I'm not sure of that. Not now."

"Listen, Mrs. Ames. I can't speak for him, of course. He's made his life and he has to live it. He's damned unhappy just now, and he needs his friends. It's no time to leave. A little later maybe."

She nodded without speaking, and he left her there, on that doorstep where she had first seen Chris. She let herself in with a latch key, and went into the back room and stood there alone. In the dark it had ceased to be her room and became the old office again. There was the desk, there on the mantel was

Chris's pipe and his tin of tobacco, and in the corner stood his instrument closet. She was holding Sandy, and Chris was young and competent in his white coat and saying: "We'll get it out; or at least we'll have a darned good try."

Competent. And now he was through. Katie had found them together and had gone out raging and destroyed him. Was there never to be an end to it? One made a mistake, and it went on echoing down the years, beating on the ears until it drove one frantic.

For the first time since Chris's accident she cried that night, there in the office. Cried the heartbroken tears of a woman deeply and passionately in love and facing utter wreckage and defeat. Early the next morning Holmes found her asleep there in a big chair, her face swollen with tears, and shook his head over her, as Olga had once shaken her head over Chris in that same room. Then he turned and tiptoed out, and not until he heard her go up to her room did he let the parlor maid go in for the early dusting.

Ted never told Chris of that meeting. For this was a new Chris, a strangely quiet man after that second operation, spending long hours pacing the floor of his room at the hospital, eating little, sleeping badly, and patiently unapproachable. Submitting to faradic currents and massage and diathermy, submitting to Katie's visits and her new and vocative sense of grievance, submitting to interns' jokes and the more sober visits of the staff. But spending long hours alone when he merely walked up and down the room, trying to plan, trying to think.

A day came when Ted, entering the room, found Chris at the window staring out, and when he turned abruptly to announce that he was through.

"I've had enough," he said. "I may get better or I may not. But by God I'm going to get off somewhere and work this thing out for myself."

"And that," said Ted cheerfully, "is the first rational thing you've said for weeks. What you need is a good funk hole for a while. Now where's the hole?"

"I used to have an old uncle in the country, a doctor. His house is still there, and it's empty."

"Made for you," said Ted promptly. "Then when you come back—"

"I may not come back."

"Tut-tut. Two or three tuts, in fact. You'll be at work again in a year. Maybe less."

Katie, listening to him later on, grew pale when he told her.

"The country?" she said blankly. "What will we do with the house?"

"I'm not asking you to go, my dear. You would loathe it, and I'm no company these days for man or beast. You know that. Later on, of course—"

She eyed him shrewdly.

"You'll be glad to get rid of me, won't you? I'm just something around your neck. Like father and mother, and even Dick. I'm just nothing. That's it, isn't it?"

"Not at all," he said patiently. "We can't go on as we have, that's all. The house will have to go. I don't know when I'll be earning again. And it's a long time since you were poor, Katie. You've forgotten how."

He tried to talk to her about it, sitting there in Annie Lewis's chair by the window and looking out rather than at her. If his arm did not improve in time he could perhaps do a little general practice in the country, at least enough to support them with care; and if they sold the house they could pay their bills and there would be something for her until things improved. Not much, but it would have to do. There was no use in his staying here. He had been a surgeon. That was over, probably forever. In any event it would be a long pull, and in the meantime he would have to live somewhere.

"But not with me!"

"I've told you," he said, with that new and rather terrible patience of his. "I know very little about you these days, Katie; but I know enough to realize that you can't change your manner of living overnight. And I want to say this, too.

I've said it before. If you would like to be free, my dear—"

She sat staring at him with curiously desperate eyes. Free? What would she do, with Bob Barrett running after another woman now, and her youth going, almost gone? Suddenly she was crying, crying uncontrollably; as a child cries, openly and unashamed. He got up and tried to quiet her, using his left hand awkwardly to touch her.

"Don't, Katie. Don't cry. I thought you might want it. Why stick to me? What can I give you? Not even a living."

"I did this to you, Chris. You can't go to that place alone."

"You don't know what you are talking about, my dear."

"I didn't see that woman in the street. You know that, Chris."

"Yes, I know that."

She had wanted exculpation and so he gave it to her. But even as he held her awkwardly, soothing her, he knew that for all her apparent regret she would be happier without him. She had cared for him, and he had let her go, to fill her life with inessentials. There had been good stuff in her, but he had never given her a chance. He had been strong and arrogant, and he had despised her and let her go.

"Don't cry, dear. It will be all right."

"I must look terrible, Chris."

"You can never look terrible, Katie."

Soon she was powdering her nose, wiping away the streaks of mascara from her cheeks. She was the eternal adolescent, he thought. She would never grow up. Somehow she and her kind must always be cared for; and there would always be men to do it. He had a feeling of helplessness after she had gone, as though he had ceased to be master of his own fate. . . .

Time went on. Nurses and doctors came and went, all cheerful, all optimistic. "Give it time, man." Or: "Now please eat something. The dietician made this specially for you." But his room was a quiet eddy, into which willy-nilly he had been washed. The work of the hospital went on around it. Ambulances came and went. Now and then he could hear through the door the shuffling of feet and the sound of wheels as some case or other was taken to the operating room. The elevator doors would open, then close again, and upstairs in the new room which he himself had helped to equip he knew that work was going on.

At first it drove him frantic. Then he succumbed to an almost complete inertia. There were times when Katie found his door locked, and after knocking once or twice went away again. And other times when in sheer helpless rage he fumed against the other men, the nurses, life itself. The very sling which carried his splint became the badge of his uselessness.

"Get this damned thing off me," he would say furiously. But without the splint and the sling his arm hung, heavy and lifeless, with the hand dropping inertly. He had to put it on again, a sort of crowning ignominy.

One day Scott came in, his empty sleeve stuck as usual in his pocket. He was cheerful and as neat as ever, but Chris had a picture of himself like that, carefully dressing with one hand, even learning to tie his tie, to lace his shoes; and found his lips trembling, although his voice was under control.

"How do you do it, Scott?"

"Do what?"

"Get along? Manage. You know what I mean."

But Scott was entirely matter-of-fact.

"It was hard at first. Later I got used to it. I hardly miss it now. Of course my wife helps."

Chris closed his eyes. Katie, trying to fix his tie or fasten his shoes! One day after that, however, he got a pencil and paper and began practicing his signature with his left hand. The pencil was awkward in his fingers but he tried it over and over, his mouth set, his eyes determined. Other men had learned. He could. He would. But the result was heart-breaking. He threw the pencil out of the window and grinned up at the nurse.

"Go on out," he said. "I'm going to blubber like a kid."

CHAPTER XLV

HE saw Beverly just once during that time. His door was open, and she was passing along the hall. He saw her and called to her.

"Come in," he said. "Come and cheer the cripple!"

There was mockery in his voice, and in his face when he held out his left hand; as though now and finally he meant to break the thread between them.

"You see where I am! The best rooms are not too good for me!"

"I'm glad you're comfortable. And they tell me you'll be all right, Chris."

"All right, in the best of all possible worlds," he said. "They lie, but they mean well."

"But there's a chance, isn't there?"

"Of course. There's a chance I'll be president some day too; but I think it's unlikely."

She was wretched, uncomfortabe under his eyes and the lash in his voice, as if he dared her to pity him. She went rather pale.

"I'm so terribly sorry, Chris," she said. "That's inadequate, I know, but there really isn't much to say, is there?"

"Why be sorry?" he said lightly. "I've needed a rest for a long time. Now I've got it. And I'm learning to use my left hand. Would you like to see me sign my name with it? It's worth watching."

She ignored that, as she ignored the jeering tones in his voice. He was badly hurt, and now he was hurting her; like a small boy, like a man whose pride had been destroyed.

"You say you've needed a rest. Why not take it?"

"What am I doing? Want a thing long enough and hard

enough, my dear, and you get it! That's true, isn't it? Then there's another saying. Maybe you've heard it; about pride going before a fall. I've thought up quite a few lately."

"Chris, if you are going to let this make you bitter—"

He dropped his jibing voice.

"I'm not bitter, Beverly," he said, more gently. "I've been filled with resentment. That's natural; and maybe I'm scared. But I'll make a fight of it. Don't worry about that."

She stayed a little longer. He was more like himself after that, more friendly. He even talked of his plans, such as they were. But when she got up to go, drawing on her long gloves, picking up her bag and taking a final glance around that familiar room, she felt that at last she had lost him; that the Chris she had known was gone.

"Shall I come again, Chris?"

"Why not? Come and brighten the day for me. Any day."

He held out his left hand, smiling down into her eyes; but the jeering note had come back into his voice, and she knew that she would not go back; that having her see him as he was was only another blow to his pride.

A week later he left the hospital. The chauffeur had been dismissed, and so Katie took him away, driving their car carefully, his bag in the back of it, his arm in its sling. The house —Grant's house—was unusually quiet and in order. Upstairs his bed was ready for him, neatly turned down, and the table beside it set out with whatever he might need. Whatever her faults, Katie was making such amends as she could.

"Is there anything I can do, Chris? Can I help you to undress?"

But he did not want her help. He wanted to be alone, and he waited impatiently until she had quietly and efficiently unpacked his bag and put his things away. Then with some difficulty he got into his pajamas. He was still weak, but he did not go to bed. Instead he took to pacing back and forward, his feet making no sound on the carpet, his big shoulders slouched forward, his head bent. Now at last he was alone and free to think, to face the facts and to chart his course.

There would be some money coming in. There was a good bit outstanding on his books, but with the fatalism of his profession he knew that a part of it would never be paid. And there would be bills, Katie's bills of all sorts: dressmakers, food, caterers, even bootleggers. He paced back and forward, glad at least to be at grips with facts again, planning, even stopping to write down figures now and then with his clumsy left hand. So much in the bank, so much to come in, so much to go out.

He was astounded to find how much he owed, and that night he told Katie the house would have to go as soon as possible. She looked shocked.

"We can't sacrifice it, Chris. Look at all the money we've put into it."

"We'll have to get some of it out again, if we can."

"But you talk as though you were never going to be well again. I don't believe it."

"I have to go on that theory until I know, Katie."

She fought hard for the house. They could close it, and if Chris still wanted to go to the country for a rest she had a lot of house parties which would fill in the summer. Then in the fall they could make some plans. He listened patiently.

"It's not a matter of the summer, Katie. It's a matter of a year, or two years; God knows how many years. I can't carry the house, under any conditions. It was all I could do before. Now it's out of the question."

She turned and went out of the room. Later on that night on his way to bed he stopped outside her door. He had not meant to make her unhappy, and it was with a feeling of guilt that he opened it and went in. But Katie was not unhappy. Sitting up in her bed she was busy with a list and the evening paper, and she looked up at him with a smile.

"I've found a lot of apartments," she said. "Plenty of people are living that way now, and liking it. It's rather smart, and when you think that heat is included in the rent—"

When she looked up he had gone.

Certainly he was very difficult during that period. For a few days he stayed indoors, gaining in strength, learning painfully to care for himself, to dress his big body, to shave with his left hand. Katie, moving about, would hear him swearing softly in the bathroom, and take care to keep out of his way. One day he came across his golf clubs in a closet, and she saw him standing there looking at them. Then he quietly closed the door.

"He ought to get away soon," she told Ted Lawrence. "I'm worried about him, Ted. And if he wants that awful Mortimer place— You might talk to him about it."

"Why not do it yourself, Katie?"

She shook her head.

"No influence," she said. "I've lost all I had, if I ever had any."

That day, sitting soberly in what she had called her morning room, she told Ted flatly and without extenuation the story of her marriage.

"He didn't want me, of course," she finished. "He never has wanted me. I was a fool. I thought he might care if I gave him time enough. But he never did. Then lately, when I thought he might be better without me, I did this to him. I can't leave him now. I never can leave him, Ted."

Ted looked at her. Did she honestly feel that she could not leave Chris? With that story behind her he could suspect her of anything. He looked at her, her expensive dress, her long earrings, the amber holder with a band of rubies that she now used for her cigarette. She looked brittle and rather hard, but there were tired lines under her eyes, and a droop to her mouth.

"How about now, Katie? Do you still care for him?"

She flushed under her rouge.

"It was a mistake, Ted. After all I was very young. And how many people really care a lot after a dozen years? Maybe I don't care, but I'm sorry for him. Desperately sorry. He wanted children, and I didn't." She shivered. "I was afraid. And of course he has always wanted somebody else. You know that, don't you? I just got in the way, and stayed there."

"If there is anything I can do—" he said awkwardly.

"Not unless you can turn the clock back!" she said, with a touch of her old gallantry. But she was still Katie. "What's ahead of me, Ted?" she said. "I'm still young. He may stay in the country, and if I'm to be buried in that hole I'll go crazy. And I can't leave him now. We're tied together like two cats by their tails."

She was crying out of sheer self-pity when he left her. . . .

It was late spring when Chris finally fared forth into the world of living men again. Little by little he was becoming accustomed to his condition, could drive his own car, could sign his name with greater ease. But he knew he was through. He had built his reputation as a surgeon, but even if general practice had offered itself, it required two hands. As a matter of fact, it did not offer itself. The medical colleges were grinding out new doctors year after year, and most of them gravitated to the cities. His market, such as it might have been, was glutted. And he was tired, too tired to make the effort at once, if at all.

He spent the following days burning his bridges. He closed and gave up the downtown office, and submitted his resignation to the hospital, doing it at a staff meeting and standing rather white but very calm.

"In view of my present disability, and in fairness to the younger men who are coming along—"

He was surprised and moved when they did not accept it. They gave him a sabbatical year instead, and more if he needed it; and told him that he would be back among them long before that. Afterwards too they were very cheerful.

"Go away and play for a while," they said. "You've earned it." Or: "What's all this about not coming back? You ought to know better. Give it time, man. Give it time."

It was when the house was being dismantled that he found that case record of old Joshua's, and came across Lena and held her up, her short skirts dingy with dust, her flaxen braids dark and untidy. Vienna, with all his hopes, and now those same hopes like the doll, finished, useless, to be thrown out with the other rubbish.

By June he was ready to go. Katie was busy with her new apartment, taking such furniture as she needed and selling the rest. Now and then he came home to find people there and once more the clink of glasses and the sound of loud voices. On the day the carpets were lifted he found a dozen or so people there, dancing on the bare floors.

"Come on in and dance, doctor."

"It's not fair to a pretty girl to hold her with one arm."

He was relieved, however, that Katie was taking it so well.

When the day came for his departure he stood with her in the hall. Piled about them was the salvage of their common life, and his bags lay at his feet as they had that night a dozen years before when she had come in, frightened and obstinate, and he had taken her and married her. Now he looked down at her, a little older, a little heavier, and not a little sulky. Then he bent down and kissed her.

"Try to understand what I'm doing, Katie," he said. "It has nothing to do with you or me. But I want some time. I've taken it on the chin, I suppose, and I've got to readjust somehow. I'll do that better by myself. At first anyhow. After that I'll ask you to come if you care to."

"Who will look after you?"

"I think Hiram Mortimer has found a woman to do that."

"I see," she said sullenly. "A woman. Any woman but me!"

That was their farewell.

Part VII
THE PATTERN

CHAPTER XLVI

CHRIS lay in Letitia's room in the Mortimer house. His right arm was on a pillow. When he turned in the night he moved the pillow also, and placed his arm on it. Folded over the foot of the bed was Letitia's star-of-Bethlehem quilt, beside him was a table with an oil lamp, a few books and his pipe and tobacco; and across the room was the old maple bureau, with his brushes on it and the splint he wore during the day.

The bed was wide, but there was a hollow on old David's side, and wherever Chris started at night, in the morning he would find himself in that hollow. He was there now. From outside came the early morning sounds of the country, cocks crowing, the deliberate movement of horse-drawn vehicles, someone at a distance letting down bars for cows and calling softly to them: "So, boss. So, boss. Come along. Get along, there." Soon Mrs. Miller would come from her cottage nearby, and he would hear her rattling the big coal stove in the kitchen where Letitia had fed her big sons, and the odor of coffee and frying ham would ascend the steep staircase and it would be time to get up.

To get up, for what?

He pulled up the sleeve of his pajama coat and looked at his arm. It seemed to him that the muscles already looked atrophied, and lying there he began to massage them awkwardly and patiently. The men in town had not wanted him to leave his treatments, but after months of them he had lost faith in them. Either the nerve resumed its function or it did not. Best to start right now, to accept that it would not. Then if it did, in six months or a year—

Then what? Go back to Katie, and the old grind again? Was it worth it? he thought, lying there. Here was peace and growing things, and before long a small straight figure would come across the fields from Hiram's house and whistle under his windows.

"Are you awake, Uncle Chris?"

"Sure. Come on up."

Young Noel would stand by to give him a hand while he dressed, or to watch him shave with one hand.

"There's some soap in your ear."

"Thanks, old man."

It was Noel who bandaged the cockup splint now, doing it with a frown of concentration.

"That too tight, Uncle Chris?"

"No. Just right. You'll be a surgeon yet, you know. That's it, turn the bandage as you go. Now what did I do with that safety pin?"

It was a regular morning task, discovering where Chris had left the safety pin.

He turned in his bed, taking the pillow with him. The house once again was much as he remembered it. The Mortimer daughters-in-law had brought back some of the old furnishings, had carried over their blankets and pillows, their carefully hemmed table linen; making him as comfortable as they could. But, after he was installed they saw that he wanted to be alone, and went away again. Solid middle-aged women, they went back to their farmhouses, tactfully leaving him to himself.

"Just call on us if you need anything, Chris."

"Need anything? I'm supplied for a lifetime."

He had smiled, but there was that helpless arm of his to speak for him, and they went back across their fields knowing that they had faced stark tragedy, and that tragedy was a lonely thing. Back in their comfortable farmhouses they thought of him often, and now and then there would come some mute reminder of those thoughts, a basket of eggs, a fresh baking of bread or a pat of butter from their cool springhouses, wrapped in grape leaves and still damp. They seldom came themselves. Only Noel, after he came home for his vacation, came regularly.

"Are you sure he wants you, Noel?" Amy would ask.

"Wants me? Say, how could he get that splint on without me?"

For the first few days, save to eat and sleep, Chris had scarcely left the front porch. He sat there in David's big old chair, staring across the road at the waving wheat or the fluttering ribbons of the cornfields. He was possessed entirely by fatigue, a mental and physical collapse so great that even memory was dulled. It might have been another man in a long-ago past who had walked day and night out of the operating room to confront those faces where fear and hope were so tragically intermixed and to listen to their voices:

"Is she all right, doctor?"

"All right so far."

But their eyes still on him, watching his expression, his very movements. Was he telling the truth? Or was there something hidden? No feeling of a bit of God in him then. A man, and only a man, the philosophy which carried him through his work sometimes failing him when the news was bad.

"Come downstairs, will you? We'd better talk this over."

The elevator and silence; a room and a closed door, and then turning to confront some face or other. "It's not easy to tell you this, but it's got to be done. We found—"

His voice going on uttering platitudes, the familiar odors of the hospital, people walking by on the hard floor outside, and hope slowly draining out of the eyes that looked at him. Not this man, that one. Another man. A man who could do that and then go home to dinner or out to play golf; but not this man, alone in David's chair and gazing across the fields without seeing them.

One day—that was before Noel arrived from school—he looked down and saw a small dog sitting beside him. After that the dog came daily. He took to keeping part of his dinner for him, and to watching for him. The dog would eat with dignity and then sit beside him, thinking the long quiet thoughts of his kind and asking nothing.

"Queer little devil," Chris thought. "All dogs are queer. Of all the beasts the only ones to forsake their kind and take up with us. Only God knows why."

It was the dog which first broke through that apathy of his, for one day he took him for a walk. After that it was a settled matter, Chris striding on, the dog pursuing its own interests but coming back to his heels. It was companionship with no demands, and slowly he began to improve. Then Noel came back from school, shy at first, sitting on the porch and making friends through the dog.

"What's his name?"

"I don't know. I would call him Caesar—I had a dog named Caesar once—but he's rather small for such a name. What do you think?"

Noel considered.

"The Warrens call him Jessie," he said.

"Jessie? But he's a gentleman dog!"

"I know, but one of the kids liked the name. She—she didn't know the difference."

Sitting there in his blue overalls and looking up at him with Ursula's eyes under that blond thatch that was Jerry's; anxious like the puppy to be friendly and uncertain how to go about it; very tactful about the arm, too—that was Noel in those first days. Chris wondered later if the boy had not saved his reason, if not his life; for there were times at the beginning, especially at night when he lay in bed with the oil lamp burning beside him, when he played with the idea of giving up the fight for good. His arm helpless on its pillow, the throb of insects and tree toads outside the open window, and the end quick and easy, so that one slept and never wakened—unless of course one did waken somewhere else, as David had believed.

He would put away the thought, however. He did not

believe that suicide was essentially cowardly. It took a certain amount of courage to face the unknown. But life was still strong if pointless, and after Noel came home it ceased to be pointless.

Nevertheless, while he could get through the days, the nights still were bad, with Noel gone back to Hiram and Amy and even Jessie deserting him for a familiar corner in the hay of the Warrens' barn. Mrs. Miller would hang out her dish cloths and go back to her family, and Chris would sit alone in that office of David's, smoking his pipe until his tongue burned but unwilling to go up to bed. One evening in a closet he came across David's familiar black bag and opened it. It was as it had been left, the forceps in their towel, some dusty bandages, the worn leather case for his drugs. He reached down further, and his hand closed on something else. It was the horseshoe.

He took it out and placed it on the mantel, and after that he often looked at it. It was a symbol of something. He did not know what, unless it was of courage. Not of luck. He no longer believed in luck.

He lay there in Letitia's bed, casting back over all this. Down below he could hear Mrs. Miller moving about heavily, and knew that it was the beginning of another day. And then at last he heard Noel's whistle. It was a whistle he had taught him. "All policemen have flat feet," were the unsung words behind it, and Noel was thrilled with it. Chris whistled back and got carefully out of his bed. This was his life, the life he had chosen. Don't think. Don't remember. Don't even hope. Live this day as it comes, and every day; and be thankful for a boy with clean eyes, for a puppy, for the good smell of coffee and bacon in the air, and for the sunlight on fields ripening for harvest. . . .

He was not altogether cut off from his old life. Now and then there was a letter from Ted. The free gratis business was great, but everybody else was away. "You're not missing anything." One day he wrote that he had joined a private clinic. "All the works," he said. "Our motto is, 'If one of us can't soak you, another will.'" They had taken a large suite of rooms in the new medical building, but there was still a vacant room or two, and when Chris came back—

There were letters from Katie, too. Cheerful letters from here and there, for she was making the usual summer round.

"I haven't written for a while; there is so much going on. Everybody seems gay and prosperous these days, which reminds me that I'll need a little extra money, Chris. The tips at these places are devastating. And do let me know how your arm is. Everybody asks and I don't know what to say."

He sent her money, writing his checks with his left hand and swearing furiously over his clumsiness; but letters were too much for him. Now and then he sent her a night letter, dictating it over the telephone. She was moving so rapidly that he never knew whether she got them or not.

Nevertheless he had improved somewhat during those first few weeks. There was no visible change in his arm. He still wore his splint, or when he tired of it the sling which supported it; but his walk became sturdier, there was even some of the old eagerness in the forward thrust of his shoulders. And he was using his left hand with greater efficiency. He had learned to fill his pipe and to light it, to tie his necktie and even with great care to fasten his shoes. One day he took a hoe and going out into Letitia's garden viciously attacked the weeds there. Some of the flowers went too in that assault of his; he sweated profusely, his back ached, the sun beat down on him mercilessly. At the end he felt better, as though once more he had attacked and beaten something, and that night he slept and did not dream.

After that it was a daily chore, and sometimes Noel helped him.

"You don't dig them out. You kill them!"

"That's because I have a buried desire to murder any number of people."

Noel looked puzzled, but Chris was reading psychiatry

now, puzzling over the problem of whether a man's life was the result of forces he could not control; or whether he himself determined it. He had thought always of the human body. Now he began to wonder if there was something else, and if so, what it was. "Religion calls it God, philosophy calls it the absolute, biology calls it life, psychology calls it mind." And if that were all, what became of old David's God? Where could a man turn when his own strength was exhausted?

"Do you believe in God, Noel?"

"Sure. Don't you?"

As simple as that to Noel, hoeing wildly, his fair hair moist and his face red with effort. As simple as that. You got into trouble and asked God to help you; and He bent down from His great white throne and did so.

It was some time after the boy's return before he mentioned Chris's infirmity, and then he did so delicately.

"I don't suppose Mrs. Miller is much good with that bandage."

"She's rotten," said Chris, with an eye on the house.

"If you like I could come over and help, in the mornings. I'd like to. I might as well practice, if I'm going to be a doctor some day."

"Then come along."

And so it was fixed. After that the hand came out into the open between them.

"How is it today?"

"Just the same."

"Funny, isn't it? It looks all right."

"It's asleep. You look the same when you're asleep, don't you?"

He could talk to the boy about his arm. To Noel there were no connotations of tragedy.

"I suppose it will get well sometime."

"Maybe. Maybe not. The thing to do is to be a sport about it, old chap."

He was not much of a talker, young Noel. Years with

Hiram had made him laconic. But on one subject he was loquacious enough. This was the study of medicine, and Chris, delving deep into his memory, found himself back in the early days at medical college, at the hospital, starting out on his own. There was a certain release in it; the boy perhaps gravely whittling on the step—he was making airplanes at that time—and Chris going back, going back.

"You didn't get much sleep in those days, did you?"

"I was young and strong."

"You're not so old now. At least you don't look old."

Or: "It's hard work, son. Don't forget that. Hard work and trouble. You know they used to have what they called trouble shooters in the war. Well, that's what a doctor is. Nobody wants him when things are going fine."

The boy was good for him. His world was expanding again, he thought with a faint grin. It included a boy and a dog now. It was still very small, so small he could reach out and touch it. Nevertheless he was better. The tight band around his head had relaxed, and it no longer exhausted him to work in the garden.

"Next year we'll put in some vegetables," said Noel, mature and practical. "That's a real job, if you want one."

"Now that's an idea!"

But his heart sank. Next year! And the year after that, and so on to the end of life. Chris found himself staring blankly into the future. Next year, and the next, and the next. Katie playing through her days, Beverly God knew where, and he himself— One thing however happened that summer. He definitely abandoned any idea of suicide. He was seeing the thing through. And after reading some of the new psychiatric journals he ceased sitting in David's office in the dark. That way lay not escape but madness, like those men and women who sat in some dark corner of certain institutions, covered with blankets to shut out the life they could not bear, and seeking in this fashion the safety of the long-ago mother womb.

Noel helped him there too. He was normal and healthy.

He would wander over, his feet bare, his overalls faded and patched, to look at Chris seriously from under his heavy thatch of hair.

"Looks as if the fish are rising in the creek, if you feel like trying it."

"I'll try anything once, son."

They would go together, the man and the boy. Chris, looking down at the indomitable young figure, would feel himself strangely stirred. Why hadn't he had a boy like this? Why indeed hadn't he had this boy? And once more he would be back in Vienna, and Katie was staring at him incredulously.

"She left it to *you?*"

"So Miss Nettie says."

"It's ridiculous. Why would she leave you a baby?"

And then becoming angry, refusing to take the child. "Not in my house! You don't expect to hand me a baby like that, do you?"

Young Noel would install him somewhere and then wander off; and Chris would cast with his left hand, jerking the fish out onto the grass. Sometimes he was unable to release the hook himself, and Noel would find him sitting quietly on a bank, a small dead trout beside him and the face he turned toward him smiling but bleak.

"Couldn't make the grade, son."

"Sorry. Have you been waiting long?"

"Only a minute or two."

Noel would find the fish very dead indeed, and know that he had been sitting there, silent and alone, for a long time.

It came as a blow when the summer was over and the boy had to go back to school again. Chris, seeing him young and forlorn on the station platform, felt a sharp contraction of the heart. He wanted almost fiercely to catch him to him, to hold him close for one minute. Instead he shook hands gravely, saving the boy's dignity and his own self-control.

"Good-by, old pal," he said. "It won't be long until you're back again. Then we'll have some high old times."

"Three months," said Noel in a flat voice. "And maybe you won't be here then."

"I'll be here, don't worry."

Amy was frankly crying as the train moved out, and Hiram was trying to comfort her. Surely the boy had love enough, if Ursula could look down from some heavenly mountaintop and see him. But in the hard light of the autumn day Chris saw that both of them looked old, old and tired. Whatever the boy was to be they would not live to see it, and they knew it. He felt a wave of pity for them, that this young life had come to them too late. When they got into Hiram's rattling Ford he put his arm around Amy.

"He's a fine boy, my dear. You and Hiram have done a good job."

"And some day," said Amy drearily, "we'll be going on, Chris, and he will be left behind."

"Not alone, Amy. Not while I live. That's a promise. . . ."

He missed the boy even more than he had believed possible. Sometimes Hiram came over in the evening and sat with him, a quiet contented man with huge hands and no particular gift of speech.

"Guess we let the old man do all the talking when we were kids," he would say. "He was a great one for talking."

But like the dog he had the gift of silent companionship, and one night Chris told him his story, told it without mitigation; his marriage, his failure with Katie, Beverly. Hiram listened through to the end without comment. Then he said:

"Most men have something like that in their lives. Another woman, I mean. Take father, now. The old man only went off the rails once in his life, but it nearly killed him. He didn't think we boys knew about it, but we did; and I guess mother did too."

She had been a city woman, he went on. She had looked queer among the rest, all dressed up and perfumed. Hiram was only a boy, but he could smell that stuff still. Funny, how a smell brings things back, isn't it? Anyhow she wasn't well and had come to the country for a rest, and of course in time David had been called to see her.

"Mind you," said Hiram, "she was a good woman, and you know the old man! He wasn't old then, of course, and he was a fine-looking chap. You're something like him yourself. She was different, and he fell for her. But he lived through it, and I guess he was glad afterwards that he stuck to mother."

There was more to the story, and after Hiram had gone Chris wondered how much he suspected; for it appeared that Hiram had found his father in that very office one night fiddling with his revolver, and had taken it from him and got a licking for his trouble.

"But that was the end of it," he said, grinning. "Somebody had a baby that night, and the woman left the next day. He was all right after that. Sometimes I'd come in and see him here at his desk, just sitting and thinking; but I reckon it doesn't hurt a man to have something like that to think about."

Curious, Chris had thought after he had gone. Perhaps all men must have some world of their own to escape into, the unpossessed woman, the unfulfilled ambition. Perhaps it was men who were the incurable romantics, following their dreams to the ends of the world and even into the sky, or living ordinary workaday lives and escaping into books, into movies, into whatever offered vicarious romance. And he remembered Letitia, who had known about that affair, and had known he would return to her.

"He needed me, Chris. And I made him a good wife."

He lay awake for a long time that night. He was thinking of David and Letitia, lying side by side in that bed long ago, and David dreaming of another woman. All that living and suffering, and now the two of them again asleep side by side, not caring any more; or perhaps remembering in some land of the blessed, and smiling together over such long-forgotten things.

CHAPTER XLVII

HE missed Noel even more than he had expected. The days were growing shorter now and one night there was a frost, and Letitia's autumn flowers turned brown and drooped on their sapless stalks. The evenings became intolerably long and Chris, lighting his fire in David's study after Mrs. Miller had gone, would read as long as he could, and then sit for long hours staring into his fire. Now and then he would rub his arm, working gently. There was very little atrophy but it still hung, without its splint, a dead and heavy thing. He would put every ounce in him into the will to move his fingers, but they gave him no response.

It was about that time that he began to take a drink at night in order to get to sleep. He had brought a bottle of Scotch with him, and after lying awake for hours he would get up, pour some into a glass, add a little plain water and drink it. It would send a comfortable glow over him, then after a time it would act as a depressant. The blood would go out of his head, he would stop thinking and sleep.

When that bottle was exhausted he got another from the village bootlegger. It was pure escape. He held it in his hand and looked at it, remembering the early days of his practice, and Henry Walters. Now it was he who was seeking release and forgetfulness.

He was not proud of it. He took to staying up late at night, hoping to be weary enough to sleep without it. And it was on such a night that he heard a car outside and the clicking of high heels on the porch. It was Katie.

She came in, rosy with health and the frosty air, blithe and cheerful.

"Well!" she said. "Of all the places to find! I've been

all over the county. And what a place when you do find it!"

He stood there, staring down at her, trying to smile, trying to welcome her.

"You look as if you've had a good summer."

"I can't wait to tell you about it. Can you bring in my bags, Chris? Or is there somebody here to do it?"

"I'm alone, as it happens; but I can do it."

He went out into the dark, glad for a moment of readjustment. When he came back Katie had made a quick survey of her surroundings and was waiting for him in the hall.

"Of all the places to live, Chris! How can you bear it?"

"It's better in daylight. It's pretty fine in summer, too. I've become quite a gardener. And next year I'll be growing my own vegetables."

"Next year? Then your arm—"

"I can't see any change yet. Of course it's early. I told you it would be a long time."

She was an incongruous but attractive figure standing there in her smart clothes, her high-heeled pumps. Amazing how young she looked, he thought. A trifle pathetic too in those surroundings. There was a place for her somewhere. She had something to give, her vitality, her gaiety, even her cheerful inconsequence. But she did not belong there, nor to him.

He gave her a cigarette, and letting her ashes float she moved about, looking at this or that and gradually extending her investigations to the rest of the lower floor. When she came back her face was expressive.

"I don't see how you stand it. And to talk about staying on here — How can you, Chris? How can you?"

"Let's talk about that tomorrow," he told her. "That is, if you are staying?"

"Staying? Of course I'm staying. There's nobody in town yet, and anyhow I feel guilty as hell, leaving you all this time. Chris, is the arm just the same?"

"Yes. That may not mean anything, my dear."

Her face fell however, and he put a hand on her shoulder.

"Don't worry, Katie," he said. "You must be tired, and you'd better go to bed. I'll put your car in the barn and then I'll show you."

When he came back she was standing at his desk, holding under the lamp a snapshot of Noel which he had autographed in his boyish hand. "To Uncle Chris, from Noel Martin Mortimer," she read aloud, and looked up at him.

"That's Ursula Martin's boy," he told her. "Fine-looking lad, isn't he? The Hiram Mortimers adopted him. He's like their own son."

"He's like Jerry Ames, too," she said shrewdly. "Is that the story, Chris?"

"That's the story," he agreed quietly.

Suddenly she laughed. "Jerry's child," she said. "So you took him and hid him away so she would never learn about it. That's it, isn't it?"

"She knows. She has known for a long time."

"Who told her?"

"Ames told her, himself."

She put the picture down and turned away.

"All right," she said tonelessly. "I guess I am tired. I'll go up to bed now."

He wondered as he led the way to the stairs. Did he really mean anything to her, so that this discovery had hurt her? Or was it merely her vanity which was hurt? Glancing at her he saw that her mouth was shut tight, and knew that she was bitterly resentful.

"I think you might have told me, Chris."

"Why? It wasn't my secret. And don't say anything to the Mortimers, Katie. They know."

"I have no intention of seeing the Mortimers at all."

He let it go at that, conscious of a vague relief that in that case apparently she did not mean to stay, and ashamed of that relief. Both of them were silent as he led the way upstairs.

"I'm in here," he told her, and showed her that room of David and Letitia's with its broad bed. "You can sleep here or—there are other rooms, but I'm afraid they're not ready for visitors."

She took one look at the bed however and turned away.

"Not for me," she said practically. "We'd only keep each other awake, and I'd like to sleep in the morning. I've had the devil of a day. I suppose I can have my breakfast in bed."

"I dare say Mrs. Miller can manage. It will be a novelty to her, I imagine."

It took two heavy slugs of Scotch to send him to sleep that night, and the next morning he saw as he shaved that his eyes were congested. He would have to watch himself, he thought. It was easy, that escape of his.

Katie stayed for a week. Chris, watching her, knew that she had intended to stay longer. She had unpacked all her bags, set out the innumerable trifles which were important to her. There were little pink and blue pillows on her bed, and silver-framed photographs wherever she could place them, signed with a sprawl. "Ever thine, Mae," and "Lots of love, old dear, Bill." They were of people he did not know. On the table by her bed was a small jeweled clock, incongruous under the oil lamp; the closet was filled with her elaborate clothes, the old bureau drawers with the silk and chiffon undergarments which Mrs. Miller eyed with mute disapproval. In the mornings he would hear that hard-working woman carrying up a tray, and sometimes a word or two of conversation.

"I don't know as there's enough water for your bath, Mrs. Arden. I'm washing today."

"Well, so am I! The washing can wait."

There was constant conflict between them, over such small matters as the food, the service, even Katie's bed. He could hear the bickering going on.

"I don't see why you can't get that silk bedspread on properly."

"Maybe I'm not used to them." Or:

"If this is the food you've been giving Doctor Arden, no wonder he looks thin."

And Mrs. Miller's significant reply.

"Maybe he's got other things than his meals to worry him."

Katie tried, he knew. They both tried, she and Chris. But the life was too much for her. Once she left her lamp too high, and went back to her room to find the walls and ceiling coated with black, and her dresses and pillows ruined. She cried over that. And she had come from luxury to her hard bed, her inadequate mirror, the tin tub in the bathroom. There was not even a place to connect her electric curling iron or, as the nights grew cold, for her heating pad. Nevertheless she tried. Sitting at the table she would make talk, of this house or that; and one day out of a clear sky she said she had seen Beverly that summer.

Chris felt his face stiffen.

"Where was that?"

"Bar Harbor. She wasn't going out much. Just taking walks and things like that."

She dismissed Beverly then, as after that first night she had apparently put her out of her mind. But she could not dismiss this burial alive which was Chris's life now. She kept on trying for a while. One afternoon Amy and the other Mortimer women paid a formal call, and Katie watched them from a window as they came across the fields; substantial women in dark clothes, lifting their long skirts against the dust of the path.

"Here comes the missionary society."

"They've been pretty good to me, Katie."

"Probably laying up treasure in heaven!"

Nevertheless she did her best that day to be friendly, and it was not entirely her fault that she failed. They sat there in Letitia's stiff parlor, staring at her short hair, her careful make-up and her painted fingernails, and found little or nothing to say to her. When Mrs. Miller brought in tea they held their unaccustomed cups in work-hardened fingers and tried to pretend that afternoon tea was a normal thing in their everyday lives. But they left with evident relief, and Katie collapsed into a chair and lighted a cigarette.

"Well," she said flippantly. "That's one examination I didn't pass!"

She did not give up at once, however. For a day or two longer she endured the solitude, the long rather silent evenings, the walks which were a part of Chris's day; hobbling along in her inadequate shoes and trying to see beauty where Chris saw it, instead of the death which is autumn in the country. But she saw no beauty and no interest.

"They call that the hanging oak, Katie, because a woman from the village once hanged herself on it."

"From the village? I don't blame her."

Afterwards he was to give her credit for her persistence; but one day she came home in her stocking feet, carrying her shoes, and that night she told him she was going.

"I'm not made for this sort of thing," she said. "I like lights and pavements and people, Chris. And you don't really want me here, do you?"

"I want you if you want to stay."

She grew a trifle shrewish then, eying him over her cigarette.

"You won't take any of the responsibility, will you? It's up to me. If I go I desert you. That's what everyone will say, isn't it?"

"Does it matter so much what they say?"

"Not to you, I suppose. It never did. It does to me."

He moved in his deep chair.

"Does this mean that you are going for good, Katie? Because if it does I want to ask you something first."

"What?"

"I want to know first if you are leaving me."

"I don't know," she said half-hysterically. "How can I

know? I won't stay here. That's flat. If you— What is the question?"

He put down his pipe and getting up took a turn or two about the room. He stopped in front of her and stood looking intently down at her.

"The question was this," he said at last. "Why did you destroy that letter of mine, years ago? The one from Beverly Lewis?"

She looked terrified. The color drained out of her face.

"What letter? I don't know what you are talking about!"

"Then it doesn't matter," he said quietly. "When do you want to go? Tomorrow?"

She was still frightened, he knew, when she went up to bed, and she left the next morning. He knew that the departure was final, that she was taking herself out of his life for good, and he tried to feel some regret when he kissed her. In a sense he did, at that. She was the last tie he had to his former life— [illegible] somewhere in storage an old desk and the few things with which he had started practice, and so he held her for a moment before he let her go. She had destroyed him, doubly destroyed him; but she was Katie, and once she had loved him.

"Good-by, my dear; and be happy."

She looked at him.

"Happy!" she said. "With my life knocked to pieces! I suppose I just don't understand you, Chris. Maybe I never did."

She went away on that, not looking back, leaving him alone in that dying garden, with his useless hand tucked in his pocket, with the wind ruffling his hair, and with a strange tormented look in the eyes which followed her until she was out of sight.

Now at last he was alone, stripped bare of everything, even his pride. That night for the first and only time since he had been appointed to the hospital staff, he drank himself into a stupor. Then and only then he managed to sleep. . . .

Katie got her divorce in Reno that fall. She wrote Chris asking for it, and he drew against his rapidly depleting bank balance to finance it. He sent the check and then went for a long walk through the bare farm lands. Long ago he had known that no man could travel two roads at once, yet he had tried it and failed. And long ago also he had walked through an autumn day like this, watching the leaves scurrying before his feet and thinking that Nature went about her business prosaically, and without emotional nonsense, that only mankind cluttered up its life with pity, romance, grief and passion. He was young then, or he would have added remorse to the list. He had let Katie go her headstrong way, too busy and too self-engrossed to check her. There had been good stuff in her, and he had let her go.

The dog marched soberly beside him. The excitements of the summer were over, and he was more adult. Also like Caesar long ago he fell in with his master's mood. He too was free now to range far and wide, but the time for ranging was over. He walked sedately at Chris's side.

Fourteen years. For fourteen years Chris had loved one woman, and for most of that time he had been married to another one. The human heart was a strange thing, he thought. It could go through the gestures of love with one woman and yet hold the image of another. It craved freedom and yet dreaded to be alone; and now that he had the freedom he had craved for so long, it meant nothing to him. To be free was to be lonely.

He found a letter from Ted when he went home. It was a long one, and he waited until evening and then read it by the firelight.

"I hope you will not blame Katie too much, old man. I have talked to her, and your temporary disability has nothing to do with it. What I gather is that she merely wants to be happy and that—sorry!—she hasn't been entirely for several years.

"She takes her own share of the blame and more. She

says, and I believe her, that the accident was the finishing touch, and that she can't even look at you without hating herself. That apparently is the reason she left you there.

"The papers have been very decent about it; merely an announcement, and as you know the charge was purely technical."

So Katie had divorced him because she was sorry for him! That was her case for the defense. He remembered her in that room, moving about uneasily, talking of the summer and its parties, longing for the city, with its lights and gaiety. And yet she had tried; walking home in her stocking feet, giving tea to the Mortimer women, watching him at intervals with furtive eyes like a scared child; lying about that letter, too, looking frightened and lying. She had been afraid of him then. Perhaps she had always been afraid of him.

He leaned over and put Ted' letter in the fire. That was that, and one phase of his life w over. . . .

Oddly enough another phase beg that same night.

He was ready for bed and abou o take the final drink which would allow him to escape whei e heard the banging of an old car coming up his neglected driv vay, and went down to the door. One of the village men was th re, a worried little man, to say that his baby had the croup and would he look at the child.

"My wife's scared, doctor. I don't like to bother you, but if you'd come and take a look—"

"I'm not practicing; but I'll come, of course."

He went upstairs to throw on some clothes, and on his table sat that bottle of his. He stood for a moment surveying it. Then he went deliberately to the window and upended it. When he went downstairs again there was a rather grim smile on his face.

"All right," he said. "Let's go."

He picked up his bag with his left hand and went out into the cold darkness.

He spent most of that night by the child's bed in a small

village house, content to be there, to hear the long crowing intake of air grow less stertorous, and to change into normal breathing until finally the baby slept. When at last he emerged into the dusk of a wintry dawn his face showed fatigue but there was a new set to his shoulders. Once more—small as it was—he had made a fight and won it. He buried the empty bottle that day in Letitia's garden, along with several of its fellows. That was over, thank God. He was still needed, could still be useful.

For the first time since the accident he felt fully a man again.

It was the beginning of a new life for him. The news went around the countryside that he was available, and little by little after that the country people began to come in. He had no hours, there was no sign on that door of David's. They came afoot, in ancient buggies, in mud-spattered cars.

"I know you're here to rest, doctor, but if you'd look at this wrist—"

Some things of course were beyond him, but the simpler ailments of the village and its outlying district were within his limitations. He could use a stethoscope. He even managed, awkwardly enough, to take blood pressure. Sometimes when he needed an extra hand Mrs. Miller came in.

"Hold this, will you? I can manage the rest."

At first he made no charge. Then finding that this hurt their pride he let them pay him, old David's prices; a dollar for an office call, two dollars for a visit. At the end of that first month he found he had taken in twenty dollars, and was instantly back to those first days of practice in the city, and his statement to Beverly that he had made the same amount.

"We're getting rich," he said to Mrs. Miller one day. "How about some chicken tonight? Working men need plenty of good food."

He had commenced to eat again.

Noel, coming home that year for Christmas, found him cheerful and more talkative. His right arm still hung, useless for all practical purposes, but he was increasingly adept with the left. It was the boy now who helped him in the office, interested and filled with importance.

"Now watch this, Noel. Catch the end, will you? Righto. Hold it tight. That's the way."

The bandage would go on, snug and sleek with the boy's help, and like the bandage Chris felt his hold on life tightening. He had Noel for a while at least, and he had these country people depending on him, holding out hands gnarled with years of labor so that he might take a pulse or examine an injury, looking at him with eyes weary with the long fight for survival against the land. He began to realize that it was cruel, not kind, the land. Men fought it for sustenance against storm and hail and drought, but in the end it won and they went back to it, some small part only of it conquered at last, and that a grave.

He added another Christmas to his list that winter, with Hiram and Noel cutting down a tree in the wood lot, and Chris joining them to carry it home; the horses brisk with the cold air, the tree on the sledge scraping along a snowy lane, and the two men and a boy trudging along beside it.

"Get along there, Nellie. What's wrong with you?"

There was always a mare called Nellie on David's old farm.

That night they trimmed the tree, and at last Hiram mounted the ladder and placed an ancient and dilapidated angel on the top. When at last he came down he looked around him sheepishly. "The old man always said a prayer about now," he said. "We might just be quiet for a minute anyhow."

Chris missed Noel when he went back to school, but he was afraid by that time, afraid to care too much for anything. Also he was more and more busy. The country people came in increasing numbers. Frequently now at night a car or a buggy would stop under his window, and he would find himself jolting along through the darkness. Then a turn into a side lane, a lamp in a doorway and a waiting figure.

"Here's the doctor, mother. How is she?"

"Just the same, Jim."

He had little or nothing to work with. Off in the cities science was waiting: laboratories, fluoroscopes, electrocardiographs, the entire progress of medicine at call. Here he had nothing but that bag of old David's, and a few drugs. There were times when he was half frantic at his helplessness.

"If we could get him to a hospital—"

"It's been a bad year, doctor. I wish we could."

It made him desperate. Even the poor in the city could be cared for. The very rich and the very poor were the best cared for in sickness; but these people were proud. They would accept no charity.

"Why not put that in the baby's bank?" he would say when they offered him money. They would stiffen.

"We pay our way, doctor."

Something hard and tight in his chest began to soften during that winter, his smile was more spontaneous, his voice more gentle. Here again were the intimate contacts of his early days in practice. It did not matter that he was still earning less than it cost him to live. What mattered was that he had found a place for himself, small as it was.

He was lonely that winter, lonely as he had never been before in his life. Noel's departure left him with long hours empty even of sound, for Mrs. Miller went home after his early supper. Snow came again in January, clogging the roads, banking up against his windows and cutting off most of his outlying cases. He cut a path to the woodhouse and one to Mrs. Miller's cottage, but with one arm it was slow heavy work. He would put a foot against the shovel, push it under the snow and loosen it. Then a little at a time he could lift it out of the way. His back ached at night with weariness, his hand showed blisters; but he kept doggedly on.

Just as he had finished the snow melted, leaving his work for nothing. The roads turned into seas of mud, the paths became small streams of running water. Mrs. Miller, plowing along through the slush, caught a cold which turned into pneumonia, and he had a long fight for her life.

He lived alone then, doing such cooking as he could, attempting man-fashion to keep the house tidy and failing lamentably. He would move about, swearing furiously to himself at his helplessness and at the diabolic ingenuity with which inanimate things got in his way, fell over, disappeared. But his old violence was gone. When things got in his path he no longer kicked them out of it.

His rages had been a part of the zest for living. Now that zest was gone. But he had not lost his courage. He would lie in his bed at night and remember Grant—"Not gods, but men"—and somehow be able to face the sun and a new day. Now too he faced death, not as in the city, where he signed a certificate, sent in his bill and closed a record. Here he saw it as it was, the unhealable wound. He saw the empty beds, the empty chairs, and over where David and Letitia lay the new fresh mound.

Death was once more a personal enemy, to be faced and fought.

CHAPTER XLVIII

IT was on a day when Mrs. Miller was still sick and things had gone very badly indeed that he opened the front door to find the village taxi driving away and Beverly on the porch, looking at him much as she had looked the first time he had seen her.

"I'm here, Chris," she said simply. "What are you going to do with me?"

He stood still, gazing at her as if he could not look away. It was a moment before he could speak. Then:

"Do with you, my darling?" he said. "I'm going to love you all my life, and I'm going to send you back by the next train."

He opened the door and she came in. She did not look about her, like Katie; she looked only at him, and suddenly there in the hall she put her arms around him and laid her head quietly on his shoulder.

"My poor Chris," she said. "Don't send me away. I couldn't bear it. Isn't it time I stayed, Chris? Isn't it time, darling?"

He held her there against his shabby coat, held her as though he could never let her go again. Then he groaned and released her. She was very pale, and suddenly she sat down on one of Letitia's old hall chairs as though she could not stand. She tried to smile, however.

"It wasn't easy to do this, Chris."

"Just sit there, darling. Sit there and let me look at you. I've wanted to see you, God knows; but now that you're here—"

She had no eyes for the house, untidy as it was. The house did not matter so long as he was in it. Nothing mattered but that he was there in front of her, with that look of terrible patience in his face and his right hand tucked out of the way in the pocket of his coat.

"What am I to do with you?" he said. "You can't stay. I'm alone here, Beverly."

"Does that matter, if you need me? Or don't you need me, Chris? Maybe it's too late, I don't know." She slid off her fur coat and her hat and ran her hand across her forehead, as though to steady herself. "It's time to be honest, isn't it? All these years and all the talk, and no real honesty between us! I don't know what is true now."

"You can take it from me, my dear," he said quietly, "that what was true once is still true. But things are changed. I don't want compassion. I don't even—" He hesitated. "I am building myself a life of sorts here, and you must try to get my point of view. I can work this out alone. I can even support myself in a small way. But you—"

"I don't fit into the picture. Is that it?"

"Listen, my darling," he said, almost violently. "I'm managing. I'm finding myself, if there is such a thing. I grope a bit; that's natural. But I can't support a wife, and no woman in the world is going to support me. Not even you, my dear."

"You're sacrificing me to your pride, Chris. Is that fair?"

"I seem to recall that you did something of the sort to me once."

They might have been enemies for that moment, confronting each other in the dingy hall, with the winter sunlight revealing its dust and general desolation and picking out the lights in her hair. Her pretty hair. The hair he had always loved and remembered. Even then he wanted to touch it.

"I suppose that ends it," she said drearily.

"Not at all." He smiled again. "You're coming in to a fire, and I am getting you a cup of tea. I'm not much on cooking, but I'm hell on tea."

She followed him into the back office and watched him while he built up the fire. He was amazingly adroit with his left hand, drawing up a chair for her, picking up wood, even sweeping the untidy hearth.

"I'm not usually as bad as this," he explained, "but my housekeeper has been sick. I've learned a lot, believe me! I'm the champion one-handed dishwasher of the world. I'm not so good with a broom, but then—"

She said nothing. She lay back in that big chair of David's as though she were exhausted, watching him and feeling his deliberate cheerful aloofness like a curtain drawn between them. She felt that she could not go on, that she had reached the end of a road which had after all led her nowhere. She sat quite still while he went out to the kitchen. She could hear him shaking the stove there and fumbling with the kettle. Then he came back, his big figure bulking large in the low doorway.

"Sorry," he said. "I'm a careless sort of brute, and you've had a long trip. If you can endure the sight of the upstairs—it's worse than this—you'd better go and wash up."

He let her go alone, watching her from below with inscrutable eyes, her slim body, her curious air of breeding, her high-held head. Every atom of him groaned for her, to hold her and keep her; but not there, not in that house through the long winter days, not in his life as it was and would be. When she stopped at the top of the stairs and looked down he was smiling up at her.

"My room is straight ahead," he said, "and I'll try to run down a clean towel somewhere."

She stood inside his door, looking about her. There was the wide bed, with the star-of-Bethlehem quilt spread awkwardly over it. On the old maple chest of drawers were his small necessities, the few things a man requires, his brushes, an extra stud or two, a discarded tie. Beside the bed was a table with an oil lamp and a book, and on the floor was a pair of muddy boots. She put her hand to her throat. So this was his life now, this cold bleak room stripped to the bare requirements of living. It was here that he lay and slept, or lay and thought. What did he think as he lay there, alone in the darkness?

She went over and put her hand on a pillow, touching it lightly and gently, her eyes filled with tears. Then she went back to the mirror and stared at herself, as she had seen her mother stare, appraising herself before her toilet table, looking for the lines life had written into her face. She looked like her mother, she thought. She was not young. She was in her early thirties now. A woman, not a girl; and it was the girl that he had loved, not her.

His voice roused her.

"Clean towel in the bathroom," he called, "and tea below when you're ready."

"I'm coming."

She ran a comb automatically through her hair, bathed her eyes with cold water and went down the stairs again. Her hat was in the hall, and she carried it with her into the room.

"You'd better look up a train for me, Chris."

"Tea first. And do you mind cutting the bread? I'm awkward with a knife. Funny, when you think of it. I used to be damned good with one."

He had drawn a small table to the fire and put a clean cloth on it. The tea pot was there, the cups and saucers, a loaf of fresh bread and a pat of butter.

"Pretty quick work, if I do say it," he said cheerfully. "But a pretty slim tea. Next year I'll be better organized, of course. Noel says I'm to keep chickens and have a vegetable garden."

"Noel? Who is Noel?"

He was shocked into silence for a moment. He poured out a cup of tea and placed it in front of her.

"I'd forgotten, Beverly. I'm sorry. Noel is Ursula Martin's child, and a fine boy he is. The Hiram Mortimers adopted him long ago. He's like their own son now, and I wish to God he was mine."

"Don't be sorry. Why shouldn't I know? I have often

wondered, Chris. And it doesn't hurt any more. Don't think that."

For a moment the ghost of Jerry was between them, gay and debonair Jerry, taking life as he found it and finding it good. He had wanted to live. Even at the end he had meant to live. Never had he meant to die, that bright morning up among the clouds. Chris was talking quickly now, driving away Jerry, talking of a man, a boy and a dog through the summer days, trudging the fields, fishing, and digging among Letitia's flowers. She felt faintly jealous.

"I suppose," she said, "that no mere woman could break into that triumvirate."

"We got along. The going was poor sometimes, but we managed."

"And the woman? Has she got to go along by herself? That's rather worse than poor, Chris."

He lighted a cigarette and gave her one before he answered. He was standing in front of the fire, looking down at her as though he was filling his eyes with her before he let her go forever. When she looked up however his face was quiet.

"Why alone? You're young and very lovely, Beverly. It isn't too late to make a life for yourself."

"I don't want it without you, Chris."

"You don't know what you are talking about. You don't belong here. I do, or I will in time. And one thing's certain, Beverly. I can't support you, and the last vestige of pride I've got would be lost if I let you support me. When things get better, if they do—"

She rose abruptly.

"Then I suppose I can come back, on your terms? Is that it? No, Chris, I've tried. I've done something I never thought I could do, and you're still too much for me. If I go now I go for good."

"My darling," he said gently. "I am not altogether the egotistic fool you think I am. I know this life. I saw an aunt of mine going through it, and I know. And I saw someone else try it and fail. I can—"

She made an impatient gesture.

"Must you always play God with me and with my life? If that is love—"

"It is love, Beverly. Some day you'll see it yourself. I've loved you always. I've never changed. Perhaps if I cared less for you—"

"You'd make me happier! That's silly, Chris, and it's sentimental. It isn't like you. It's romantic nonsense."

He gave her a twisted smile.

"But I am romantic," he said. "Incurably romantic, until I look at this."

It was the first time she had seen his hand since the accident. Now he drew it out of his coat pocket and looked at it, still with the same twisted smile. "You see?" he said. "It doesn't belong to me. I can't give it orders any more. But I'm tied to it. I can't even cut it off."

"Don't, Chris. It's dreadful to hear you. It's your own hand, your dear hand. It's a part of you, and who knows? Some day—"

He was putting it carefully and slowly back into his pocket, and his smile was more normal.

"If only a fellow could cut his fingernails!" he said. "I'll take to biting mine soon. And don't look like that, my darling. I was only pointing a moral. I didn't mean to hurt you."

She stayed until train time, but never once did either of them again touch that debatable ground. Only when at last he had brought his car around and came in to get her did he touch her at all. Then he crushed her to him with almost a groan.

"Good-by, my girl," he said. "Always my own girl, whatever happens. . . ."

It was that picture that she carried away with her that day, going back to her empty house and her quiet life, sitting at her piano, buying flowers and putting them around, even going out a little now and then when she became afraid to be alone. She would put on her fragile evening dresses, go to this house or that, talk, even smile; but the vitality had gone out of her. When she was alone she could see Chris, alone too in that untidy house of his; could see him in the cold bedroom upstairs at night alone with his lamp and his bitter thoughts.

She could have helped, but he had not wanted her. His arrogant pride was too great. She could not fight it.

She was not very well after that. Sometimes she had a pain, a small nagging pain. It came and went, and at first she hardly noticed it. At last however came a night of acute agony. She could not even call Martha at first, and so she and the pain were alone together, shut in, walled off, so that there was nothing in all the world but that pain. Later she got help, and when it was over and certain tests had been made Ted Lawrence told her one day that she ought to have an operation.

"Better get it done before long," he said. "You don't want any emergency stuff."

She managed to smile at him from her bed.

"Is it my mother's trouble?"

"Cancer? Good God, no."

"That's the truth, is it, Ted?"

"I'm a fair liar, but I never lie about things like that, my dear."

They were friends by that time, and she saw that he meant what he said. It was before he left that she asked if she couldn't wait until Chris Arden came back.

"What for?" he demanded forthrightly.

"To operate. I'd like him to do it."

"Nonsense! Suppose he doesn't come back?"

"Then it wouldn't matter so frightfully one way or the other, would it?"

He looked down at her, exasperated. He was more than half in love with her himself, but he managed to grin.

"You're talking like a child. He wouldn't do it, for one thing."

"He would, for me."

Leaving her that day, however, Ted was far from cheerful. She was badly run down. Her slimness was rather more than slenderness now, and he suspected too that she had lost the will to live. He debated whether to write to Chris about her or not, and finally decided against it. Why add that to his other troubles? What could he do?

It was during Beverly's convalescence that she saw in the paper that Katie was going to marry Bob Barrett, and wondered if Chris knew it, or if it would hurt him. But Chris knew it already and was not hurt.

"They'll get along," he thought without resentment. "They're both ambitious, and she'll help him. He's making money, too. She'll like that."

For Barrett had definitely joined the racketeers in medicine by that time, playing the game for all it was worth; wearing a belted smock in his office, serving tea or something stronger, charging enormous fees for those more or less secret treatments of his. He had added plastic surgery now, rejuvenating old faces. He was no charlatan. All over the world reputable men were doing the same thing. But he was charging all the tariff would bear, and more.

"I don't see how I can pay it, doctor."

"I didn't think you wanted it sent to your husband."

"No. Please don't. You see I never told him. I'll manage somehow."

He would smile softly to himself. He saw nothing pitiable in the attempt of aging women to hold their men. Often it was a furtive matter, and he capitalized on that secrecy.

Chris knew all this, but he knew too that Katie would probably be contented in her marriage. It rather puzzled him that after so long a time together he felt it so little. But he was busy now, and he had not much time to remember. Work was coming in steadily. When the case was beyond his capacity he would send to some town for help or, as happened once or twice, bundle it up in the car beside him and take it to the nearest hospital, half a day's drive away.

It looked as though his life was fixed for all time. There were even moments now when he felt a return of that old power of his, when he fought back death or even pain as though they were personal devils, and sometimes won and sometimes lost. Physically too he was well, and he was occasionally aware of a sense of life and warmth in his right arm, although it was still useless. Even the arm, he thought, had ceased to matter vitally. If it came, well and good. If it did not he had his place and his work.

Outside of that, however, he had very little. He was not even physically comfortable. Mrs. Miller had not yet been able to come back, and he managed with a village woman who gave him such time as she could. The place was neat enough, but he would go home at night to find the fires burned out and as often as not the lamps not filled. More than once he went to bed without a light, and lay in the cold darkness, unable to read and unwilling to think.

One day there emerged a bit of the bread he had cast on the waters years ago, and as is promised in such cases it was returned to him many-fold. . . .

He was at his desk that morning when he heard the front door open, and was aware of someone in the hall. He looked up to see a tall vaguely familiar figure in a too-blue suit and with a cigarette dangling from an impudent lower lip. The figure saw him at that moment and gave a semimilitary salute.

"Hello, cap," he said. "How's the good old horse thief?"

It was Dick Walters, a Dick as insouciant as ever, with a cheerful grin and a suitcase in his hand.

"Dick! What on earth are you doing here?"

"Well, that's a long story," said Dick, coming in and settling himself comfortably on the edge of the desk. "I was back home and I heard of your little trouble, so I thought I'd come and look over the ground."

Chris grinned.

"Well, how does it look, now you're here?"

"Bad to fair. Nothing doing with the arm yet?"

"Not yet."

"Rotten luck." He got off the desk. "Well, I'll go up and park this bag somewhere. Then I'll take a look around and see what's what."

"Look here," Chris said, "let me get this straight. Is this a visit you're making me?"

"You can call it that if you want. No wages anyhow."

Cigarette still dangling he picked up his suitcase, walked into the hall and climbed the stairs, leaving Chris staring after him. In ten minutes he was down again, sauntering into the office as if he owned it.

"Not a bad dump," he said. "I picked out a good bed, anyhow. Now what's in the house to cook?"

Neither then nor later, when he went back into the limbo from which he had come, did Chris ever know just what that emergence of Dick's meant. He never mentioned the war, save once to boast that he was drawing partial disability compensation. "And believe me, boy, I earned it." He never expressed any gratitude to Chris for the night he had saved him. But after his own fashion he paid back every jot and tittle of that debt, from the first evening when Chris, coming in from a call found him over the stove, his eternal cigarette in his mouth, and holding off the irate day woman who had come in to get the supper.

"It's all right, grandma," he was saying. "I'm a cook. I used to cook when I was in the pen. Don't you worry about his stomach. I'll fill it."

He literally drove her out and Chris had some difficulty in pacifying her.

"But if he's been in the penitentiary, doctor—"

"That's just his little joke. He's a relative of mine, by marriage."

There commenced then with Dick a new era in Chris's life. Dick had no repressions, no delicacies. What he thought of Katie was bluntly told, once and for all. But the healthiest thing was his attitude toward Chris's infirmity.

"Let's see it, doc. Don't be a fool. Maybe I can rub some sense into it."

Chris let him examine it, and he did so through a haze of smoke.

"Humph!" he said. "Looks like something you found under a stone! Well, let's get at it."

He massaged it daily after that, with singularly skillful hands and infinite patience. He would sit, his cigarette dangling, and work over it, talking to it as one might to a child.

"Come on, now get some sense into you. Quit playing possum. Get a move on you. How's that, doc?"

From the first that hand and arm were his job, although he took over the entire establishment. He was not an unmixed blessing. He was noisy in the house, whistling and singing. Like Katie, his cigarette ashes were everywhere. There were days too when he simply let the dishes pile up. Then he would look into the kitchen and grunt.

"God," he would say. "Just like mother's! I'd better get busy."

He fed Chris well, he cleaned the car and drove it on occasion, and he was even useful in the office, for he had no squeamishness. Chris, coming home one day, found a youngster in tears and Dick armed with David's old dental forceps laughing at him.

"It's all right now, my lad. Just spit it out in papa's hand."

He saw Chris grinning at him, but was in no whit abashed.

"Cripes, doc," he said. "I'll bet I could deliver a baby."

It was soon after that that Chris realized that there was a faint tingling in that dead arm of his, and found his knees weak as water under him. He said nothing to Dick about it, but Dick was shrewd. He increased his efforts. He would pick up a finger and hold it.

"Come on, baby. Just a flutter now. Wiggle a bit. Try it, doc."

Then one night in response to this urging a finger did move, and Dick let out a whoop and did a dance over the room.

"We've got it, doc! We've got it beat. A couple of months and you'll be fighting me with it."

Chris could not speak. He sat in his chair looking at the hand. Now he willed the finger to move again, and it did. When he looked up at Dick he found him noisily blowing his nose.

"I'm the stuff, doc. Who said your uncle couldn't do it?" He bent down and gave Chris a terrific wallop on the back. "And now how about a shot of liquor to celebrate? Where's the whisky?"

It was over that temperate celebration that he leaned back suddenly in his chair and laughed.

"Remember the night you took a horse from me in the dark, doc?"

"It was you, was it?"

"Yep. Well, I'd just stole that horse from another fellow. Me and a chap I knew were going back to get some liquor."

"Did you get it?"

"Hell, no," said Dick with deep disgust, and took another drink.

Before he went upstairs that night Chris put an arm around Dick's shoulders, much to his embarrassment.

"You've been damned good to me, you know, Dick."

"Don't go soft on me, doc. I've had the hell of a good time."

He banged out of the door, leaving on one of those mysterious night excursions of his, sometimes taking the car to go incredible distances to dance or, as Chris suspected, to go no distance at all with one of the village girls. And Chris, alone in the house, lighted the lamp in his room that night and stood looking at his hand and arm. There was motion there, not much but some. It would come back, that hand of his. He had an odd feeling that perhaps after all Noel's pragmatic God had bent from His great white throne and made a gesture toward him.

He still had a long way to go, but at least he had a direction now. The time came when he could bend his fingers, but there was as yet no grip to them. It was shortly afterwards that he wrote to Ted, in that clumsy left-handed writing of his:

"You'll be glad to learn that there are some evidences of union. The hand's still pretty useless, but it's coming back. If it goes on as it has—" He sat there at the desk, looking at the paper, and from it around old David's office. He had made a place here. He could stay on, grow old himself among these new friends who were his patients. And there was Noel. His pen moved on. "If it goes on as it has I shall have to decide what to do. Whether to remain here or go back to the city. I have a good bit of work now and it will grow, of course. But young Noel is the problem. If he studies medicine he will probably want the city. He'd be safer here in some ways, but have I the right to hold him?"

He sat at the desk, rereading that, the lamplight shining down on his dark hair, on his quiet face. What was he doing? Playing God with Beverly again, and now with Noel? He was through with that. People must live their own lives, make their own decisions. He crumpled up the letter and began again. "You'll be glad to hear that there are some evidences of union—"

His only reply was a telegram, indicating that Ted was having a streak of patriotism, and saying merely "Three cheers for the red, white and blue."

Dick was still there when Noel came home for the Easter holidays. Chris left the meeting at the station to Hiram and Amy, but all morning he watched across the fields for the boy's young figure, and Dick watched him.

"Think a lot of that kid, don't you?"

"Wait until you see him."

There must have been some strange thoughts in Dick's mind as he waited, going about washing his arrears of dishes, a barred gingham apron around his waist, a cigarette stuck to his lip, and his eyes now and then wandering out the window to the pale green of the winter wheat fields. Noel was one of his little experiments which had failed! But the house was in order and a fire burning in Chris's study when at last a young figure leaped the gate and marched sturdily up the path.

Dick whistled softly to himself. Jerry Ames all over, he thought. Yet the boy's face was soberer than Ames' had ever been, and the eyes more direct. He listened to the door as it opened and shut.

"Anybody home?"

"Home and waiting, son," Chris called, and Dick recognized the new depth in his voice and its carefully repressed eagerness. "God, he's been lonely, the poor beggar," he thought.

He gave them an hour and then appeared with a plate of sandwiches. He found Chris lying back in his deep chair, and the boy sturdily planted in front of the fire. Chris stirred when he entered.

"This is Mr. Walters, Noel," he said. "He'll tell you that he won the war. But he won't tell you what he's done for me."

Dick looked embarrassed, but he grinned as Noel gravely shook his hand and thanked him.

"What's he been telling you?" he demanded. "I wanted free board for a while, and I got it. That's all."

They became great friends, the boy and the man. Chris, wandering into the kitchen after a patient had gone, would find them washing dishes together, or perhaps Dick turning out pancakes with the air of an artist.

"Look at that. That's a natural, that is."

Dick was full of memories. "When I was in the pen—" he would say. Or it would be the war, and Dick would be drawing pictures of his own daredevil courage. "So I slid forward on my belly until I heard them talking. Then I gave a whoop and landed on them."

Very possibly it was true. Certainly somewhere, perhaps in his suitcase upstairs, there was that medal to prove that he had done his bit and more. Nevertheless his cheerful amorality, his purely pagan philosophy, began to worry Chris. Noel was at the imitative stage, and behind him too was the heritage of Jerry Ames. Already in those few days he had accepted Dick's flippant speech. Perhaps, Chris thought, he was a little jealous, too. The boy was all he had now, and with Dick's coming there had been a subtle change in their relationship.

"Want to see a case with me, Noel?"

"I told Dick I'd go fishing."

But Dick was playing fair. One day he found Noel regarding him with bright curious eyes.

"Did you save his life? He says so."

"That was my job, son."

"But he says you carried him for hours, and then operated."

"I couldn't very well leave him where he was. It was pretty messy."

Chris was rather quiet that week, and Dick watched him with amused and understanding eyes. Then one morning, coming down to breakfast, he was astounded to find Dick's suitcase in the hall, that gentlemen in his bright-blue suit in the dining room eating, and a rejuvenated Mrs. Miller bustling about the kitchen.

"What's all this, Dick? You're not leaving?"

"I always migrate in the spring, doc," he said, airily. "Time for my flight, that's all."

"There's nothing wrong, is there?"

"Wrong? I've been living high, wide and handsome all winter. What d'you mean, wrong?"

Chris tried to persuade him to stay, but he only grew restive. It was when Chris suggested that he ought to settle down somewhere and marry that his eyes became somber.

"Nothing doing, doc," he said. "I liked a girl once, but somebody got ahead of me. Get 'em and forget 'em—that's my motto now."

"Where is she now?"

"She's dead," said Dick viciously. Then his voice softened. "Say good-by to the kid for me, doc. He's a good kid. I'm not the man to help raise him." He eyed Chris with his sardonic grin. "It's a far, far better thing I do, doc!" he said, and throwing back his head roared with laughter. The next minute he was shouting to the kitchen.

"Hey there," he called. "Where are those eggs? You don't have to lay 'em. Just cook 'em."

Chris drove him to the station that morning, divided between relief and a sense of loss.

"I'll miss you, Dick. You know that."

"Well, I suppose a fellow would miss a bad tooth."

They stood on the bare platform, empty save for a few milk cans, constrained with the fear of grown men for sentimentality, and aware that here they had reached the forks of the short road they had traveled together. Both of them knew that it was not likely they would meet again; and Chris, looking down at Dick's thin figure in its fantastic clothing, could find nothing to say. Dick however was whistling lightheartedly, his eyes on the track.

"Funny," he said. "Trains always excite me. I like to be going places."

"If you're ever in trouble you'll let me know, won't you?"

"If I'm ever out of it I'll tell you. That'll be news!"

Noel reached the platform as the train drew in. He was breathless and puzzled, but Dick merely waved him a cheerful good-by.

"Be a good boy and wash behind your ears, kid," he yelled. Then he swung his suitcase to the platform and mounted it himself.

"If either of you ever needs me I'll come on the run," he shouted. "Run! Hell, I'll fly."

The next moment he was waving the conductor out of the way and demanding his private car; and that was Chris's final picture of Dick, his impudent grin, the bewildered man in uniform and the train moving off along its single track. A few years later, watching a moving picture, he saw a familiar face, still jaunty and swaggering, among the extras. For a moment it looked at him, unabashed, the old devil-may-care Dick; then it vanished, not to reappear. Chris wrote at once in care of the studio, but there was no answer.

CHAPTER XLIX

IN the early fall of that year Chris had a visit from Ted Lawrence. He came unannounced, to find Chris busy in the office and a line of vehicles of various sorts outside. He was sitting complacently on the porch when Chris came out, and he gave him a long look before Chris saw him.

"Great Scott! Ted!"

"What a memory you have for names," said Ted admiringly. "You old scoundrel! It looks as though business is good, anyhow."

Chris grinned.

"The daily round, the simple task," he quoted. "And where did you come from?"

"All over the state, my lad. I've been lost, if that interests you, and I've been in a ditch twice and arrested once while hunting you. Damned if I think it's worth it. So this is the works?"

"This is the works. Come on in and park your bag. By the Lord Harry, I didn't think I'd ever be so glad to see that ugly face of yours again."

"People have traveled miles to see this face, my boy. Is this your office, or do you live here too?"

"I'm a business man. I have to live over the shop."

They were happy to be together again, even boisterous for those first few moments. However, Ted was eying Chris appraisingly. He looked better, although he was still carrying his right hand and arm as though they were useless. What alarmed him was the look of quiet resignation in his face. It was still the face of a defeated man, accepting his defeat with gallantry, but defeated nevertheless. He was cheerful enough, showing off his small domain, boasting about his chickens, exhibiting pridefully what remained of Letitia's resurrected garden. Ted, stooping to pick a small chrysanthemum for his buttonhole, straightened to find him staring out to where the harvested fields stretched empty and bleak, and saw that his fingers were clenched tight on the bowl of his pipe. He relaxed instantly, however.

"Pretty country," he said.

"Plenty of it, anyhow. What's it like in winter?"

"Not so bad. Hard to get around sometimes, that's all. I can understand now why old Dave Mortimer stuck to a horse. I may have to get one myself."

Ted let that go, and it was not until they were back in Chris's office, with that horseshoe of David's on the mantel, that he reverted to it.

"Let's get this straight," he said. "Do you mean to stay on here, Chris?"

"I don't know. There's some regeneration, but it will be a long time yet. Too long, Ted. A man can't drop out for a couple of years and hope to get back where he was. You know that. Besides—"

"What?"

"I have a life here, such as it is, and it's not a bad life. I like these people, and they like me. And I have no assurance that I'll ever hold a knife again. I've got a hand, but it's clumsy as the devil. No grip to it at all."

"Let's see it."

Chris held it out, slowly opening and closing the fingers. "You see how it is," he said. "It's coming back, but God only knows how soon or how far. I can't count on it yet, or on anything, for that matter."

Ted examined both hand and arm carefully. The wrist-drop had gone and the fingers were fairly mobile; but the hand certainly lacked strength and grasp. Still holding it he looked at Chris's face, quiet but bearing the deep lines of long tragedy.

"It's just a hand, Ted. That's all."

"It's a pretty good hand now. Better than I had expected. You'll be operating again before you know it, man!"

"That's as it may be. In the interval I'm here. That's all."

They made rounds together that afternoon in Chris's muddy car, jolting over back roads, turning into this lane or that. Once or twice Chris took Ted in to see a case or to help him with something, and ever after Ted Lawrence was to remember those farmhouses, scattered and remote, the trees around them draped in autumn coloring, and Chris with that familiar forward thrust of the shoulders, stooping to enter some low doorway.

Chris was right. He had made himself a life out of wreckage; not the life he had wanted, but at least a useful one. Sitting waiting in the car he wondered if after all it might not be better for him to stay where he was, to grow old with the land, as these people were doing, and then at last to become a part of it. To go back now and begin all over again—

That night, however, with the early darkness and the lamplight, he began to find the silence and remoteness depressing, and to understand what the long winters must be to the man quietly smoking across the hearth from him. Mrs. Miller had gone home, and the talk had been desultory; professional talk, the hospital, the usual bits of medical gossip. They were still young, but their world had changed since they had gone into practice. Now they talked of Loeb and Landsteiner and Theobald Smith; of Dochez and pneumonia, of Murphy and Minot and anemia, of Banting and insulin. A new language too, of vitamins and hormones, of serums and filtrates and viruses; and of men working for years under endowment, patiently laboring to add to the term of human life.

"And they talk of State medicine!" said Ted. "Can you see the politicians paying for that? Millions of dollars and a handful of votes? It's the end of the profession, Chris. I'm telling you. Good God, don't we treat the poor now? Where's initiative? Where's the human element? Look at Barrett when he got the city job."

He flushed, remembering Katie. But Chris's face in the

firelight was impassive. It was after that, coming out of a silence, that he asked abruptly about Beverly.

"Have you seen her?" he said.

"Once or twice."

"And—how is she?"

"How do you expect her to be? She's lonely and pretty hopeless. And she's not particularly well. That stiff-necked pride of yours—"

"Did she tell you that she came here?"

"She did, and damn you for the obstinate fool you are, Chris. She came and you turned her out. I suppose it didn't occur to you that you would hurt her! She has her own pride. Aren't you ever going to learn anything about women?"

"Do you think I'll let any woman support me?"

"Exactly. So you are noble and heroic. You get the martyr's crown. You're fine. You've done the decent thing—by yourself. And she goes away feeling tawdry and cheap, like something you put in a dust can. By heaven, if I had had your chance—"

Chris flushed.

"She knows better than that."

"How do you know she does?"

"I couldn't sacrifice her, Ted."

"Who's talking about sacrifice? She wanted to do it."

When Chris spoke again it was after a long silence.

"You see," he said painfully. "I knew what it would be. She didn't. I'd seen Katie try it and fail."

"Oh, damn Katie!" said Ted.

He left the next morning. He had slept that night in one of the upper rooms, a lamp and a book beside him; but he did not read. The silence of the countryside beat on his eardrums, and nearby he could hear Chris moving about, the deliberate heavy movements of a man for whom time had ceased to have any vital importance.

Ted lay for a long time staring into the darkness after he had put out his lamp. Now at last he understood why Chris had sent Beverly away and chosen to go his way alone. He could not condemn her to that life. He had already seen Katie try it and fail. And he—Ted—had a shrewd idea of what that life must have appeared as seen through Katie's eyes.

"The poor devil," he thought. "Mad about her for years, and then sending her away."

He resolved that night to say nothing of Beverly's condition until the time came.

When he left the next morning it was on a more cheerful note, with the house bright with morning sunlight and the odor of coffee and bacon emanating from the kitchen. Early as it was Chris was already busy in the office, and Ted ate his breakfast alone. When Chris came in it was with more of his old manner.

"How'd you sleep?"

"Well enough. Your silence is pretty noisy."

Chris laughed.

"I don't notice it now. At first it drove me frantic."

Neither of them referred to the night before, but with Ted's bag in the car and the engine running Chris seemed loath to let him go.

"Sure you know the road?"

"I got here, didn't I?"

Chris stood with his foot on the running board, the wind ruffling his hair, and stared down the road ahead. Once, a hundred years ago, life had been a barn in a French countryside, with a road that led back to life and another one that led ahead to death. Now it was a low white house, but the road was the same. It led forward and it led back. But perhaps now there was no road back.

He leaned over and put a hand on Ted's shoulder.

"Good-by, old man. I hate to see you go."

"Then get in and come along. If you let this beat you now—"

"I'm needed here. Or somebody is."

"Don't be a fool, Chris. You're a surgeon, not a general

practitioner. There are a thousand young men who'd be glad to come here, and most of them have forgotten more about modern medicine than you ever knew."

Chris shook his head.

"Not yet, Ted. Perhaps some time."

At the bend of the road Ted looked back. Chris was still standing in the road, a tall wind-blown figure in shabby tweeds, gazing after him. . . .

The winter came early that year, and Ted's visit had vaguely unsettled Chris. He worked hard, pushing his car as far as it would go through the early snowfalls, then trudging on foot the rest of the way. When he cut a path now with a snow shovel he would use his right hand also, although it was still awkward. The long evenings were bad. In vain he read, the papers, the medical magazines, the surgical journals. New things were on the way, new techniques, new anesthetics; but the journals daunted him. His confidence, the essential quality of the surgeon, had gone. The mere thought of once again standing by a table and picking up a knife sent him into a hot sweat. He wondered now, sitting there alone, at his own temerity in the past. Ted was right, he thought. He was a beaten man.

It was about that time that he was shocked one night to find that he had fallen into the habit of all lonely men and had commenced talking aloud to himself. After that he was watchful, and he never did it again.

He could see a change already in his arm. He would flex it and extend it, watching his big muscles filling out, beginning to bulge. His hand too was definitely better. One night he tried to write with it and failed utterly. He persisted however, and his co-ordination improved. He began to form letters, large and sprawling, but legible, burning the paper later for fear Mrs. Miller would find it in the morning. He was more hopeful now, even more active. He could shave and dress better. But there was still a long way to go, and there were times when he threw his pencil on the floor and raged up and down the room.

He kept Beverly rigidly out of his thoughts as much as he could. However, strong as was his conscious and intelligent mind, buried beneath it somewhere was the blind force which activates and dominates all men: the will to go on, to persist and to fulfill its purposes. He could cut her out of his thoughts but not out of his dreams. And now recurred that old and long-forgotten one, of a girl with a dog on a doorstep, looking up at him with a wide and direct gaze.

It was after such a dream, in his chair by the fire, that he got up and made his first attempt at a letter to her. Slowly he wrote: "I have been such a clumsy fool, my darling, wanting both you and life on my own terms. Now I know that I want you on any terms, and that life without you is not possible. If you can forgive that last and utter stupidity of mine—"

He sat back and looked at it. It was the sprawling hand of a schoolboy, uncertain and stumbling. He tore it up and put it in the fire. There was only one thing to do, and that was to see her. She was entitled to that, at least; to know why he had sent her away, and that he was still wholeheartedly hers. Now too he might go to her with something to offer. Not much as yet, but a hope. More than a hope.

He looked over the small black book in which he kept the record of his calls. He could spare a day or two. He would wire her that he was coming. Then, if all went well, they could talk and plan together; whether he was to stay where he was, or whether he would go back to the city and start again. Not much for her in either case, he thought wryly, but that was the way it was.

But he did not go. Amy had not been well that winter and Chris had been watching her heart. Now on his way to send that telegram the telephone rang, and Hiram Mortimer spoke over the wire.

"Can you come over, Chris? Amy's pretty bad. I found her on the kitchen floor and—I think she's dying."

He found her still on the floor, with Hiram on his knees beside her and her face gray, although she was now conscious. Later he and Hiram carried her up the steep farmhouse staircase and laid her on her bed. She did not speak until Hiram had left the room on some errand or other. Then she whispered.

"It's the end, Chris."

"Nonsense! We'll have you around in no time."

"Don't send for Noel. Not yet."

He agreed, and she lapsed into her semicoma again. Toward morning Chris, sitting by the bed, reached into his pocket for something and discovered there the telegram to Beverly. He took it out and read it. Then he went to the fireplace and dropped it into the flames.

That was finished. He could not leave Amy now.

She lived for two months after that. Noel came home for the Christmas holidays. She was cheerful when he was about, talking with those blue lips of hers, even trying to eat for his benefit. Chris, watching that heroic acting of hers, was moved beyond words.

"I'm not going back to school."

"I want you to go, Noel. See who I have to look after me!"

"And leave you sick? Not me."

"If you're going to be a doctor you'll need to go."

When she had won and he came in, tall and tragic, to say good-by, she held him in her arms as though she could not let him go.

"My boy," she said. "My own boy. Don't worry. I'll be all right by the spring. And be a good boy, Noel dear. Always be a good boy."

"I don't want to go, mother."

"I want you to go. Please."

So he went, resentful and suspicious. Chris and Hiram took him to the train, and as they stood together watching it pull out Hiram's eyes were tired and bleak.

"If Amy goes," he said heavily, "I'll not be long behind her, Chris. And what's to become of him?"

"We'll not let Amy go, Hi. Not yet, anyhow. And you can trust the boy to me. You know that."

They had to let Amy go, however. Chris fought hard for her, calling for help from wherever he could get it, spending days and nights by her bed. Then one morning he was at the station again, meeting a pale boy whose eyes were red with weeping, and who needed Chris's steadying hand to get him to the car.

"You sent me away, and now she's gone!"

"She wanted it, Noel. And she is all right, son. No pain any more. Just sleeping. Can't you think of it like that?"

His heart ached for the boy. He longed to put an arm around him, but he knew that he was holding on to his control with difficulty. Instead he talked quietly: that death was either sleep—and sleep was a splendid thing, especially after pain—or it was something quite different; a new life, active and busy. An open door, not a closed one.

Noel listened, his young face set.

"Which do you believe?" he said.

Chris hesitated. What did he believe, here in the fullness of his life, with that hand of his now strong on the steering wheel, perhaps lacking only confidence to send him back to work again, and with an ordered universe about him? For a long time now he had lived with growth, growth of the soil, growth of human individuals dependent on the soil. There was a pattern somewhere, even if he did not understand it. What did he believe?

"I don't know, son," he said slowly. "I think there must be a God, and that if there is He will take care of her."

Two days later they laid Amy beside David and Letitia, his wife; and Chris, standing by the grave, realized how inevitably that big family of theirs would join them, until at last they were all united once more, either in the quiet earth or in some far kingdom of the soul. There was a pattern, after all.

Five days later Noel took sick, suddenly and violently, and Chris knew that he was facing a ruptured appendix. There was no time to get help from a distance, and no help at all nearby. He went out into the narrow hall outside the bedroom and stood there, opening and closing that right hand of his. Then, his mouth tight and his face set, he turned to Hiram.

"I'll have to do it, Hi," he said. "There's no time to get anybody here, even if I could find someone. Get the girls to boil some water and put a blanket on the kitchen table. I'll be back as soon as I can."

An hour later he stood beside Noel as he lay on the table. He had given him the ether, and Hiram was keeping him under. In Amy's shining dishpan at his side lay his few instruments, now boiled and sterile. The boy was breathing easily, relaxed at last; and the room was silent, save for that breathing. Chris stood for a minute looking down at the valiant young body, so dear to him and now in his hands to save if he could, and for the first time since his boyhood he muttered a prayer.

"Oh God, give me strength and skill," he thought.

Then he reached out his still awkward right hand and picked up a scalpel.

CHAPTER L

IN THE early spring of the following year Chris was preparing to go back and start his life again. He had no illusions. For two years he had been a country doctor, with all that that implied; and in that two years his city practice had been scattered to the four winds of heaven, and much of his reputation had been forgotten.

He was still a young man, as such things go. The body which had lain long ago in the sagging bed at the Walters house had filled out to full maturity, and there was a quiet strength in him now, as of one who had passed through deep valleys and no longer walked alone.

He was free now. As Ted had said there had been no difficulty getting a young man for the work, and he was out now making the evening rounds in Chris's old car; a serious young man with a friendly smile. His people would be all right with him. Chris, remembering that early office of his, had watched him unpacking with mixed feelings. He had brought a microscope, a small centrifuge, all the equipment of a modest laboratory; and now that electricity was coming to the village he even talked of turning Letitia's old preserve closet into an X-ray room.

"Liable to get most anything in these country places," he had explained cheerfully.

"Yes," said Chris, and went out feeling as extinct as the dodo.

His people would be all right, but he felt as though he were deserting them. All day they had been driving in, bringing him their gratitude, their friendship, and even such small tribute as their means allowed, knitted socks, a sweater, even a basket of eggs!

"They're fresh, doctor. There's no nourishment in city eggs. They're packed."

It had been like going to the war again. In a way he was going to a war again. Only before there had been a place for him and now he did not know.

His few possessions were already packed; and somewhere among them was that small brass plate of his early days. It was sixteen years since he had first put it up and consulted Beverly about it.

"It may be a trifle modest, you know."

"It looks like a very nice sign."

Sixteen years. Not a lifetime. Not a long time as such things go even in the life of a man; but long enough to have left his youth behind him, and easy hope and quick desire. Alone that night in David's office he paced the floor, his empty pipe clutched in his teeth. He was leaving in the morning. For what? For where?

He stopped and glanced about him. On the mantelpiece beside David's horseshoe still stood a recent snapshot of Noel. He went over and picking it up took it to the lamp and studied it. Strange that this should now be his boy, his son; this tall lad with Jerry's hair and his long-fingered sensitive hands.

"I'm going to be a surgeon like you," he had said, after that operation of his.

"You'll have to be a lot of things first."

"Sure. That's all right with me."

Grieving over Amy, grieving again over Hiram, who had followed her so soon, and yet with the adaptability of youth adopting Chris as both father and mother and already writing his cheerful letters from his school:

"They call me 'doc' here, because I say I am going to be a doctor. Please write and say I can play football next fall. I feel fine only all my pants are too short for me. And thanks for the money. I sure needed it."

Strange, this life. Strange that long ago he had sat in the old back office talking to a girl in trouble, a brave girl who meant to bear her child; and that later on it had been that child who had brought back his confidence in himself. Now, stranger still, the child was his, to love and care for. He meant to make a good job of that; a damned good job.

He had gone to the cemetery that day and now lighting his pipe he wandered out into Letitia's garden. It was still bare, but even in the twilight the forsythia gleamed yellow with bloom, and beyond it lay the fields, fallow and rich with potential growth. Once he had hated those fields. Now he knew that they had given him something. They died and lived again, and even so a man might do. Even in their death and resurrection there was a pattern, the orderly pattern of the universe. . . .

Save that he was going back, he had no plans. Tonight for the last time he would sleep under Letitia's star-of-Bethlehem quilt, while the new man lay in that room which Katie had filled with her pillows, her dresses, her silk bedspread and her photographs. "Ever thine, Mae." Katie was going strong now, her name often in the papers. "Mrs. Robert Barrett entertained yesterday at luncheon and bridge. Among those present—" She was heavier again, according to her published photographs, as though she had relaxed somewhat in this new and easier life.

Now it seemed incredible that he had ever been married to her. He could hardly remember her as his wife. When he thought of her at all, it was as the sulky child of sixteen years ago, glaring up at him from a hospital bed.

"How about it, Katie? Want a doctor in the house?"

"I never want to see a doctor again."

His mind drifted to Beverly, if indeed it ever left her. She had gone South that winter, but now she was back. Back in his house again, with the scar on the marble mantel and with the spring grass sprouting over Caesar's grave. Once long ago she had written him a letter and Katie had destroyed it in that house. He could tell her that now. It was indeed almost all he had to offer her, that explanation, and a vague and uncertain future, together and on her own terms if she said the word.

There was a new buoyancy in his walk as he turned back toward the house again, and the old eager forward thrust of his shoulders. He looked vital again, strong and dominant; but the light from the open door on his face showed its old arrogance gone and a new understanding. As though like the fields a man might die and live again and grow in the so doing.

He was very cheerful when he re-entered the house. He whistled over his final preparations, slipping the horseshoe into a suitcase for luck and because it had been David's, putting Noel's picture in his wallet, strapping his bags with two good hands, and then straightening for a final survey. Outside in the barn his old car stood ready, oiled, greased, even washed; and tomorrow he would start back for the battle. It was like the war. It was like the time he had commandeered the horse, and brought it back, by God! Bandages and dressings in his saddlebags, like old David, and then riding back to a hell enclosed with gas blankets and lighted by candles. It was like—

He was still whistling when the wall telephone rang and he heard the village operator's voice.

"Wait a moment, doctor. It's long-distance."

He held the 'phone, surprised but not apprehensive. As he stood there he was inspecting various untidy memoranda he had scribbled on the ancient wallpaper, and was thinking that the new man would never do that. He seemed a tidy soul, Chris thought grinning. Then the connection was made and he recognized Ted Lawrence's voice.

"Chris?"

"Yes. What's wrong?"

"It's Beverly. I thought I'd better tell you. They're operating on her tonight. It's ulcer, and it looks like perforation."

He went on. Chris stood rigid, listening. Now and then he said "Yes," or "All right, I'm here." But he was not aware that he was speaking. Beverly was ill, very ill; and he was not with her. She was facing that alone. She had nobody. In a way she never had had anybody.

That was his buried mind, however. His surface mind, the mind of a surgeon, was canvassing the situation, measuring her chances; was still cold and alert. When he had finally hung up the receiver he went out into the hall. He still looked entirely calm, although his eyes were curiously blank.

His hat was in the hall and he must have put it on, for later he discovered that he was wearing it. Also he remembered dimly getting into the car and shooting out onto the main road, although he remembered nothing else of that ride later on. Apparently he had ceased thinking. Ahead of him was the road, white before his headlights, and nothing mattered but that road. There was no world to right or left of it, but only somewhere an end. Now and then he rattled over a bridge or slowed down for a curve. Sometimes a barn loomed up beside him, and once a cow rose out of a ditch. They came and were left behind, parts of a shadow land without real existence. Once he crossed a railroad track only a foot or two ahead of an express and never knew it. He left a sweating engineer in a locomotive cab, leaning out and looking back.

"Drunk or crazy, the God-damned fool!" he said, and wiped his face with a greasy handkerchief.

He did the usual things, but largely by sheer automatism; stopped for gas and water, and once to telephone. Beverly was still in the operating room, but that was all he learned. He got into the car again and rattled and banged along. After that telephone call his mind had commenced to function once more, his surgeon's mind which spared him no possibility and no horror. Driving like the madman he probably was he could see her there in the operating room; that new room with its glassed gallery and its modern equipment; and Beverly there on the table with the masked white figures about her, and then at last the thin red line—God, they couldn't do that to her. Not to Beverly. Not to his girl; always and forever his girl. . . .

At four in the morning he turned in at the gates and stopped the car before the doors. He was almost unrecognizable, covered with grease and dust and now hatless. The night clerk stared at him.

"Mrs. Ames," Chris demanded. "Where is she?"

"She's in the Lewis suite. I'm sorry, doctor. I didn't know you."

He did not answer. He moved on, up the familiar staircase and into the familiar corridor, passing nurses on the way without seeing them and bringing up at last in front of a closed door. He had his hand on the knob when Ted Lawrence saw him and caught him by the arm. Even Ted did not know him at once.

"See here, you can't go in there." Then he looked again. "For God's sake, Chris, how did you get here?"

"How is she?"

"She's over it. As for the rest—she's all right so far. It's a little soon."

"Who did it?"

Ted told him. It was a good job, he thought, but it had taken time. There might be a transfusion soon, but they had a donor ready. Not essential, perhaps, but she had been run down and it would do no harm. Chris listened. Just so had he talked when a situation was desperate, soothingly and hopefully. It was the old familiar patter of the hospital, and he brushed Ted aside roughly.

"I'm going in," he said. "I've heard that talk before."

"Go in, if you want to kill her. She can't stand a shock, man. You ought to know that."

He hesitated and then turned away. He had no right in that room. Everybody else, but not him. Now at last he had joined the ranks of those who wait. It was his eyes which looked their unmasked questions as the door opened and closed again. Doctors and nurses came and went. There was a battle going on inside, and he was on the sidelines, an onlooker, useless. Useless, by God.

He stayed there, however. Sometimes he sat there outside the door, sometimes he paced up and down. Toward morning the transfusion took place, and he found himself wiping his clammy hands with an incredibly dirty handkerchief and remembering something about a similar handkerchief a thousand years ago. Just at dawn a nurse told him that she had rallied, and looked bewildered when he muttered something about a great white throne.

After that they got him away for a while, long enough to wash and to drink a cup of coffee. He went back at once however, watching the door again, searching the faces of nurses and doctors as they came and went.

"Still all right?"

"Better. Much more than holding her own, Chris."

It was then that he walked down the corridor to where a basket of flowers had annoyed him as he walked the floor, and with cold deliberation kicked it almost the length of the hall. A new nurse saw it and told the night supervisor.

"I never saw anything like it," she said. "He's a wild man. He's crazy. To kick those flowers just because they got in his way—!"

The night supervisor was smiling.

"Don't worry," she said. "He's all right. Probably"—she added gently—"more all right than he has been for a long time. . . ."

Inside her room Beverly lay in her bed. Shadows came and went. She would see them, then they were blotted out and she was alone with herself. Sometimes she felt as though she were in feathers, falling through feathers. That was pleasant. If it were dying then why be afraid of dying? But they would not let her sink. People kept coming and going, holding on to her. Standing by the bed holding on to her.

A long time ago they had brought in a table and she had looked at Ted Lawrence, and he had bent down to her.

"If anything happens tell Chris it is all right. I understand. And tell him I have never changed."

"Nothing's going to happen, my dear."

"But you will tell him?"

"Of course. You'll be telling him yourself pretty soon."

Then they had lifted her onto the table and rolled her out of the room. Ted walked beside her, holding her hand, and at the elevator he stooped and spoke to her.

"He's on the way," he told her. "When you wake up he'll be here."

So as she lay in her bed she watched the shadows, but Chris was not among them; and after a time she was not herself at all but her mother, watching the door into the next room.

"It's open," she whispered.

A nurse stooped down.

"Open? What's open, Mrs. Ames?"

"The door into the other room."

The nurse went to her blue record sheet, which had a notation on the left margin which said it was reserved for binding and no writing there, and put down the two words: "Slightly delirious." Then she brought in the house surgeon, who had been trying to snatch a few minutes sleep on a couch in Staunton's room, and he stood by the bed and took Beverly's pulse again, that being all he could think of at the moment.

"Feeling all right?"

He was not her father. He was a tall thin young man with ruffed sandy hair and a small mustache. She smiled faintly up at him.

"All right," she said, and dropped back among her shadows.

In due time the sun rose and came in through the windows, and she roused again. A long time ago she could stand here and see the tree of heaven, far below. But that was long ago; now it was dead, and it did not matter anyhow.

They gave her a second blood transfusion that morning, for her continuing weakness alarmed them. It was still touch and go. And some time or other they let Chris in, but she did not see him. He stood beside the bed looking down at her, his face almost as white as her own; but the hands which picked up the blue record sheet were steady. After that he stayed by the bed, and once again he felt as though he was holding death back by sheer will power; as though he could hold her there within reach of his arms, his strength and vitality against her weakness and defeat.

And something happened. At noon, himself drained, exhausted, the pulse under his fingers was stronger. She opened her eyes and looked at him.

"Don't speak, darling. I'm here," he said.

She nodded and held out her hand. It was enough. He was there, and now she would get well for him; well and strong, so that they could stay together. Some day all this would be over, and she would make a home for him and bear his children. Her hold on his hand tightened and, the nurse's back being turned for the moment, he stooped and kissed her, very gently, on her forehead and on her trusting eyes. . . .

An hour or two later the house surgeon, shaved and immaculate again, stuck his head inside the door and finding her awake, spoke to Chris.

"Sorry as the dickens, doctor, but there's a case in the operating room they'd like you to see."

Chris sat quite still. He was back. They had taken him back. He was one of them once more. He looked down at his right hand, strong again, ready for work, ready for anything that came. He could hold a knife with it, he could hold Beverly, he could hold his world again. He got up with a new lift to his shoulders.

"Coming," he said, and the head withdrew.

But Chris stood for a minute looking down at Beverly in her bed.

"I'll be back, you know, darling," he said. "Always I'll be coming back to you, my girl."

"I know," she said, and watched him as he left the room.

That would be their life from now on, and she knew it. She was utterly content, however, watching the eager forward thrust of his shoulders as he went out. In a minute, in five minutes, he would have forgotten her. He would be bending over a case, intent and absorbed, all surgeon again, all doctor. Always he would be that. But he aways would come back to her. He would go out and forget her, but even then he would know that at the end of the day she would be somewhere, waiting for him.

Outside the operating room Chris was getting into his long wrinkled coat, his cap, his mask. Standing there he could distinguish the familiar odors of hot linen, of anesthetic and drugs, and hear the muffled sound of voices over the table. When he opened the door a wall of hot air confronted him, and once more it seemed to him as he entered that it was like a stage setting, with the movement suddenly stopped, frozen, and all the faces turned toward him, smiling and welcoming.

It was over in a second. The action on the stage commenced again, the movement accelerated. The table was there, the patient on it, and around it the group of masked and ghost-like figures.

"Come here and see what you think, Chris."

They moved aside for him, and now he was there once more, where he belonged. Instantly he was absorbed, intent. The past was wiped away, even the present. All that existed for him at that moment was the case before him.